D0202208

03/21
$ 2.00

THE POWER

The sorcerer's eyes began to glow as he probed the two captured leaders. In amazement, he could see the Essence growing within them. "Apparently no one in their world has been exposed to the Essence before," he said to the first assistant. "Thus they have no immunity to wielding it."

"Which do you think will affect them more, the powers or the increased lifespan?"

"The latter," the sorcerer said. "A lifetime of a thousand years will terrify them! But I wonder...

"Will they ever want to return to their own world?"

Worlds of Fantasy from Avon Books

THE BLIND ARCHER
by John Gregory Betancourt

BLOOD OF THE COLYN MUIR
by Paul Edwin Zimmer & Jon DeCles

THE CRYSTAL SWORD
by Adrienne Martine-Barnes

THE DRAGON WAITING
by John M. Ford

FIRESHAPER'S DOOM
by Tom Deitz

THE FIRE SWORD
by Adrienne Martine-Barnes

HEAVEN CENT
by Piers Anthony

NIGHTREAVER
by Michael D. Weaver

THE RAINBOW SWORD
by Adrienne Martine-Barnes

THE SHADOW OF HIS WINGS
by Bruce Fergusson

Avon Books are available at special quantity discounts for bulk purchases for sales promotions, premiums, fund raising or educational use. Special books, or book excerpts, can also be created to fit specific needs.

For details write or telephone the office of the Director of Special Markets, Avon Books, Dept. FP, 105 Madison Avenue, New York, New York 10016, 212-481-5653.

THE CRYSTAL WARRIORS

**William R. Forstchen
and Greg Morrison**

AVON BOOKS ◆ NEW YORK

THE CRYSTAL WARRIORS is an original publication of Avon Books. This work has never before appeared in book form. This work is a novel. Any similarity to actual persons or events is purely coincidental.

AVON BOOKS
A division of
The Hearst Corporation
105 Madison Avenue
New York, New York 10016

Copyright © 1988 by William R. Forstchen and Greg Morrison
Cover illustration by Joe DeVito
Published by arrangement with the authors
Library of Congress Catalog Card Number: 88-91948
ISBN: 0-380-75272-7

All rights reserved, which includes the right to reproduce this book or portions thereof in any form whatsoever except as provided by the U.S. Copyright Law. For information address Dominick Abel Literary Agency, Inc., 498 West End Avenue, 12C, New York, New York 10024.

First Avon Books Printing: December 1988

AVON TRADEMARK REG. U.S. PAT. OFF. AND IN OTHER COUNTRIES, MARCA REGISTRADA, HECHO EN U.S.A.

Printed in the U.S.A.

K–R 10 9 8 7 6 5 4 3 2 1

We dedicate this book
to the three women who gave us
the support and assistance we needed:
Our wives, Mer and Patti,
and our editor and friend, Chris Miller.
Thank you.

Acknowledgments

Ben Nelson, Steve Bohn, and Bonnie Lidle

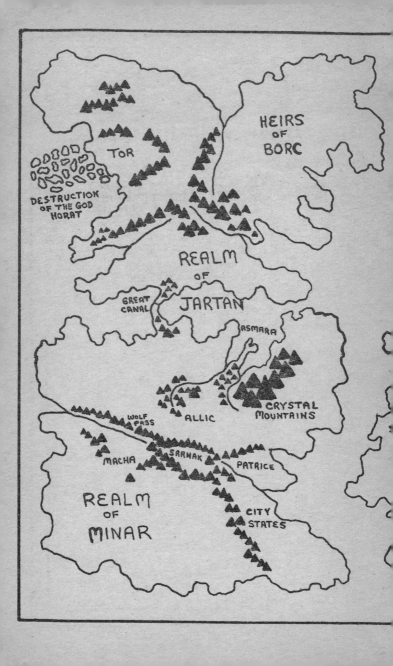

Prologue

The twin moons of Haven shimmered on the horizon, casting their double-lined shadows on the valley below. Mornan could not help but turn her attention away from supervising the preparation of the pentagram to appreciate this final moment of tranquility.

There was a stirring behind her—Danuth, the second in command. She knew that in his mind there would be no admiration, no deeper understanding for the beauty she was admiring; anything that could so easily be destroyed was beyond his caring.

"Too much light," Danuth whispered. "It favors them and their power."

"Precisely," Mornan hissed in reply. "Do you think our master is completely without cunning? Tonight of any night, when the twin moons are full and command the sky, is a time when those fools will think themselves safest, and not watch so closely."

Mornan settled back for a moment, wishing to enjoy the contemplation, but Danuth was insistent—she could almost feel the anxiety in the old sorcerer's voice.

"It is time to conjure the demons. We have no time to waste."

Mornan turned and smiled softly. "Frightened?"

"Allic is the son of a god—of course I'm frightened. You

1

trust Sarnak too much, I dare say. If Allic realizes who conjured a pack of demons on his border, he'll not leave off until we are dead, or worse. 'Cross not a demigod, for they are without a sense of humor,' or have you forgotten?"

"'If you wish much, you must risk much,' or have you forgotten *that*, my dear Danuth? Come, come, my old friend," Mornan said mockingly, "aren't you tired of casting the same old tricks to amuse some bored princeling? Even if he is Accursed, Sarnak offers us power. Think of it—a fiefdom for each of us, after we have unleashed the demons upon Allic's domain. They'll never guess we did it. Why do you think the Torm border was selected for our attack? Allic will blame the Torm sorcerers, and thus fuel the tension between him and his neighbors."

"My masters."

Mornan turned. It was one of Danuth's apprentices; he must have finished the pentagram. Mornan looked at him and smiled sadly. Poor boy, he thought that being asked along on this mission was a high honor. Yes, he would learn to conjure demons tonight—but little did he know that if the demons proved intractable, he would be given to them as a sacrifice.

Mornan walked over to the pentagram, examined the lines cut into the turf, and nodded with approval.

"Danuth, we're ready."

Mumbling in some arcane language, Danuth wandered over to one of the points.

"You, boy, over there," Mornan directed. "Be sure to stand within the marks of protection, and leave them not unless I tell you."

Even as she spoke, Mornan looked at Danuth, who gave a silent nod.

From out of the shadows the other two sorcerers appeared, their long robes waving in the breeze. Stepping forward they took their places around the pentagram, making it whole.

Mornan reached into her robes and brought forth the precious crystal given to her by Sarnak. Its power would help protect them from the chaos about to be unleashed. Focusing her thoughts through the crystal, Mornan projected her will to the others.

"Open your minds to find demons in the worlds too long denied us by the gods. Guide your minds through the myriad portals, and when you find our goal call to the rest of us and together we shall draw the quarry out. I can shield us from Allic's power of sensing for only so long. If you are not ready for this, tell me now!"

The only response was the gentle crying of the wind.

"Begin!"

The hilltop glowed with a pulsing, unworldly light as the four sorcerers and their apprentice projected their minds through the crystal and then outward, searching for the openings into universes concealed from all but the most powerful.

War between the gods had been unknown on Haven for three thousand years. The sacred peace was about to end at last.

Chapter 1

"Kochanski, what does radar show?"

"Their Zeros are holding back, Captain."

"All right, gunners, stay sharp. They'll jump us on the other side of this flak."

Captain Mark Phillips felt a nudge on his shoulder, and looking over, he saw Younger, his copilot, pointing forward and up to where the first cotton ball bursts of flak were opening up. They were a little high but Mark knew that the Japanese would soon get the range.

"Two minutes to drop." It was Ed Watson, his bombardier, cold and steady, as if the half-hour running fight with the Zeros were nothing more than a sideshow to provide them with some excitement before the bomb drop. Mark could see him down in the nose, hunched over the bombsight, guiding them in for their first visit to the Japanese-held steelworks.

The flak was dropping lower, coming into range. There was a mild buffet, then another. The B-29 surged and tossed as it knifed through the turbulence. Another burst straight ahead, and the *Dragon Fire* bucked up as it plunged through the rolling black clouds.

4

"Hold her steady, hold her steady, Mark. One minute."

Icy sweat soaked down Mark's back and his arms grew numb with the tension of holding the lumbering B-29 on course. Another minute, just another minute till bomb release, and they could get the hell out of here to face an eight-hundred-mile flight back to safety. Back to Nationalist Chinese territory with a running fight all the way against the flak belts and fighters, but at least they'd have the tons of death out of their belly.

"Steady, steady...We're lining right up the chute. Steady..."

A blinding flash cut off Ed's words. With a howling, splintering roar, the entire port side of the plane caved in around Mark as flying shards of glass and steel swept through the cabin.

Screams filled the air as the *Dragon Fire* rolled onto its starboard side.

He was numbed by the howl of the wind; still not sure if he was hurt. He gave a quick glance over to Charlie Younger and all he could see was the wide-eyed terror.

Everyone was shouting, screaming, filling the intercom with a cacophony of noise that could not be separated into the individual cries of fear as the bomber started to slide into a deadly rolling dive.

Mark fought the controls, trying to pull her out. The wheel wouldn't budge. The cracked windscreen was filled with the Manchurian landscape rushing toward them.

He looked again to Younger who was motionless, his hands off the wheel.

"Pull, you bastard."

He wanted to reach out and smash him, to pummel him out of his terror, but he was locked to the wheel in a desperate struggle.

"Damn you, *pull*. Bring her up!"

Younger looked at him, and as if Mark's rage took hold, he snapped out of his catatonic fear and returned to the struggle.

Jesus, they were red-lining her; the wings were going to rip off. *Not now, dear God,* Mark begged, *not now.*

He could feel the first response coming into the craft: she was coming out of the dive, edging back up. He pulled his left hand off the wheel and slammed the throttles down, cutting back their speed.

Sighs of relief filled the intercom. As everyone started

talking, Mark snarled, "All right, you guys, shut up!"

The voices dropped off.

"Anyone hurt?"

"Yeah, José took it bad in the arm and shoulder. The whole radio compartment was blown out by the hit," replied Giorgini.

"Will he make it?"

"Hard to tell."

"Mark, it's Goldberg."

Mark looked over his shoulder to the flight engineer, Sam Goldberg.

"Go on."

"We're losing oil pressure on number three. I'm shutting her down."

"All right, take care of it."

It was hard to hear anything—the hull was ripped wide open and the air screamed past with a high, piercing shriek that was maddening. He looked out his shattered portside window. The wing was a sieve; rolling black smoke poured from the inboard engine.

Mark looked back at Goldberg again.

"Fuel?"

"I'll have it for you in a minute, but it doesn't look good."

Ed! What about the bomb drop? Mark leaned over and saw with relief that his friend was uninjured.

"Say, Ed, you all right down there?"

Ed looked up at him and Mark could see that he had been as terrified as the rest of them.

"Any hope of lining back up on target?" Mark asked.

"We're already passed it."

"Dump that load and let's get the hell out of here."

The *Dragon Fire* surged up as the bombs dropped free to land in the hills beyond the city.

Mark could see the other bombers in a cloud of flak, already several miles away. They were clear of the target area and were already turning in a broad sweeping arc. *Dragon Fire* had lost the protection of the herd, and with a crippled craft there would be no hope of regaining the shield of fire that a formation could place around itself. The wolves would soon be closing in.

"Look out for company—we'll soon be getting lots of it. Kraut, you still with us?"

"I'm okay, Mark."

Thank god the navigator was all right.

"Listen, Kraut, I'll be following the squadron back on a heading of two seventeen, but if Goldberg says we don't have the juice, I want you to line up our choices and get them back to me."

"Captain, this is Walker."

"How are things back in the tail?"

"Not good, Captain. Three bandits approaching at seven o'clock low."

"I've got them on my screen!" Kochanski shouted.

"Giorgini, lock them into central fire control."

"Locked in."

"Here they come. . . . "

The *Dragon Fire* shook as her guns, guided by the B-29's central fire system, swung into action, setting out an arc of tracers to greet the first Zero as it rolled in low for a sweeping pass. The camouflaged plane shot past, soaring upward in a steep climb that would position him for a dive.

"Mark, it's Goldberg."

"Go on, give me the word."

"Losing fuel at over thirty gallons a minute from portside fuel tanks. Our radius of action is four hundred and ten miles at the present heading."

"Can't we switch off starboard fuel and use up portside first?"

"Already done that."

"Watch it," Walker shouted. "Two more boring in."

The *Dragon Fire*'s guns fired deep staccato bursts, which were counterpointed by the enemy's 20mm shells.

Suddenly Ray Welsh, the left side gunner, gave a wild shout of triumph. "We've flamed one, we've flamed one! Look at that bastard burn!"

"Shut up, Welsh, let's keep some discipline!"

"Mark, this is Kraut. It's not good."

"Go on."

"There's no way we'll make it back to base. Our only hope of safety is to head for Soviet territory."

Russia would mean internment. The Reds were still at peace with Japan, and it could take months before they would be cycled back into the fighting. But there were the unofficial orders, as well. The B-29s were the best the U.S. had. Russia might be their ally, but the longer the Russians had to wait before getting their hands on a model, the better high command would feel. Russia was out.

"Here comes that one from above!"

Mark braced himself for the impact. The *Dragon Fire* shuddered as the enemy's guns stitched yet more holes in the damaged wing. Trying to knock off the Zero's aim, Mark desperately rolled the plane, but he could see they were taking more damage. The enemy shot past, followed by twin arcs of tracers from the bottom guns.

"She's not going to hold up much longer," Younger shouted. "Number four is starting to lose pressure."

Mark could almost smell Younger's panic. How had he ever got stuck with this clown, anyway? His old copilot Tom Seay had been with him in Europe along with Kochanski and Walker, and together the four had made a good team. But a bout of amoebic dysentery got Tom pulled from this eight-hour run. Younger's old commander, John Foss, had ditched him at the first chance, and now Mark could see why. The guy was a coward—he couldn't hack the pressure.

"Russia's out, Kraut. You wanta eat borsch for the rest of the war?"

"Thought you'd say that," Goldberg cut in. "My old man never did have anything good to say for them cossacks, anyhow. Listen, Mark, our fuel loss is increasing. I can give you three hundred miles max, more like two fifty."

"Where does that put us, Kraut?"

"Puts us over to a heading of, just a minute . . . puts us onto two sixty-five. If we can make two hundred seventy-five miles, we'll enter guerrilla country, along the China–Mongolia border. We might have a chance there. Rough terrain though—we'll have to bail out."

"Mark, we can't jump." It was Kochanski, the radar operator.

"Why not?"

"It's José."

"How's he doing?"

"Not too good: he's unconscious. I've stopped the blood loss; his arm looks pretty bad. He's in no shape to jump."

Shit! He'd have to order the crew out and then pull the heroic act. If he jumped from a plane leaving a crew member to certain death, he could never live with himself. Once they cleared Japanese space, he'd order the men out and be forced to try to land the plane. Damn it!

"Look, Mark, we might be able to bring her in," Kraut said, trying to sound optimistic. "'It's rough country but there are some long, narrow valleys with open fields. Wonderful terrain for guerrillas. Some of them are probably old warlords still fighting for themselves against everyone else, but it's our only chance."

"I'm on two sixty-five," Mark replied, unsuccessfully trying to sound relaxed and self-assured. "Keep me posted on our fuel."

The Zeros rolled in for one more pass, and with ammunition depleted, finally turned off. Within minutes the *Dragon Fire* was alone. Number four held on at reduced power and Mark's right leg was soon numb and trembling, as he kept the rudder over to counter the imbalance of the engines.

Every ten minutes or so Goldberg and Kraut updated him and it was soon obvious that they were gradually losing the race. They just might make it out of Jap territory, but the odds were stacking up against them.

"How far to disputed territory?"

"As near as I can figure, another twenty miles."

"Right. Now listen closely. We're down to fifteen hundred feet. I see a ridge line up ahead, looks to be five hundred below us, but it's an open valley beyond. We'll fly straight down that valley and once we cross that twenty-mile mark, I want all of you out."

Suddenly number four engine seized up and cut completely. For a frozen moment of horror Mark looked back at Goldberg who shook his head like a doctor giving up on an injured patient.

The *Dragon Fire* started to drop out from underneath them, the ridge line ahead filling the cracked windscreen. There was no time now, nor enough altitude, for a jump. With the fury of despair Mark hauled back on the wheel, watching the airspeed indicator drop to the stall line. It was as if he had two choices of death—hit the ridge head-on or stall the plane and then have it drop straight in.

"Forget the jump. Brace yourselves, we're going in!"

The ridge passed by not a dozen feet below them. The stall indicator alarm kicked on and the plane started to shudder, and then they were past, dropping into a long, sloping valley.

"Prepare for emergency landing. Wheels up! Ready!"

They drifted down the long open slope and the *Dragon Fire* settled—the props hit the rock-hard ground, metal shrieking as the blades bent back into the wings.

The plane touched, skipped lightly, then came down hard. A shudder ran through the craft as her bottom ripped open.

The impact slammed Mark forward into the instrument panel and his world plunged into darkness.

Captain Ikawa Yoshio of the Imperial Japanese Army was exhausted to the point of numbness. His aching body cried out for him to give up, to fall upon the ground and surrender. *Not yet,* he thought almost sadly. Through aching eyes he watched as Sergeant Saito weaved his way down the slope and came to attention, snapping a weary salute.

"Captain."

"Yes, Sergeant."

"The plane is just on the other side of this ridge, but I think the Chinese are already moving in."

"Thank you, Saito. Corporal Kantaro, take four men and try to slow our pursuers, but do not sacrifice yourself. That is an order. Just give us enough time to reach the plane."

"Yes, Captain."

Following the sergeant, Ikawa crept up to the brow of the hill and looked over. Yes, the giant was there. Intact. He had heard about the new bomber but this was indeed the first time he had actually looked at one, and he admired its sleek, sweeping lines.

"Captain, look over there!"

He looked where the sergeant was pointing. From out of the hills on the other side of the narrow valley, several hundred men dressed in dark uniforms were slowly advancing. He looked down at the plane again. Yes, the Americans had seen them, as well.

"And there, Captain, look," Saito said softly, "one of the Americans is going over to them. See, there along the trail, he's waving a white shirt."

"The fools. They'll soon find out."

For several minutes the captain watched the drama unfold. Behind him he could hear the high-pitched staccato of a machine gun. His corporal was slowing the Chinese bandits advancing from the other direction. For six days Ikawa's men had been running. Once they had numbered over a hundred, a garrison outpost, but that was before a running retreat that had left a trail of dead over forty miles. Now, with his back to the high mountains, the game was nearly up. Less than a score of his men were left, all knowing that death would overtake them before the day was out. And then came these Americans, landing right in a nest of the bandits who had been trying to cut off their retreat.

Ikawa half suspected what would happen. He should leave them and push on; they could serve him by momentarily slowing the pursuit. But a perverse curiosity compelled him to watch.

The Chinese column swept down around the lone American waving the signal of surrender. The swarming host stopped for a moment. The other Americans were gathered around their fallen plane, waiting, watching.

Suddenly there was a glint of steel. The American carrying the flag turned and started to run but was overborne by half a dozen men. They forced him to his knees, and a moment later a shower of scarlet washed over his severed head.

The captain looked at the sergeant, who smiled sadly.

"Now they know," the sergeant whispered.

The bandits let out a shout and advanced towards the plane. The Americans started to run, straight up the hill to where Ikawa was waiting.

"Captain, shall I open up?"

"No—order the men to hold their fire. I think this can be useful."

At that moment the Japanese machine gun on the hill behind them fired a sustained burst. The captain looked back to the opposite hill a hundred yards away and watched as the corporal and his four men picked up the weapon, then ran back down the hill to rejoin them.

Ikawa watched the enemy sweeping forward, driving the Americans before them. Behind him the enemy was closing in as well. A high, solitary mountain soared up on his right —an impenetrable barrier. He looked closer. Yes, there was a possible way out of this trap, which the bandits had laid long before the Americans had fallen from the sky. There was a narrow defile heading straight into the mountain fastness. Without hesitation Ikawa formed his plan.

"Sergeant, I want you and four other men to stay with me. Lieutenant Mokaoto, move the rest of my command towards that defile."

Saluting, the lieutenant barked some quick commands and the rest of the unit started out. "Sergeant Saito, let's get ready to greet our new visitors. Fire only on my command."

The sergeant cradled his machine pistol and waited with the rest, either to shoot the Americans or those behind them. In his mind the two were nearly the same.

Ikawa could hear them now—their heavy gasping as they came running straight up the slope towards his concealed position. A quarter mile away the Chinese were already closing around the plane. Some of the men were shooting at the Americans and laughing. Bullets hummed through the air, some of them striking the ground around the Americans, driving the fugitives forward. Several Americans were armed with light carbines and two held Thompson submachine guns. They turned occasionally to trade shots with their tormentors, but with no effect. They could have been moving faster, but their progress was slowed by a wounded man who was half-carried, half-dragged by two of his comrades.

"Get ready, Sergeant, they're almost on us. If they make a move with their weapons, open up."

"Yes, Captain."

Ikawa took a deep breath, trying to remember the correct words. He stood up and barked a command.

"Halt!"

Mark snapped out of his exhausted stupor.

"Jesus, a Jap," someone screamed behind him.

The Japanese officer extended his hands, to show he was weaponless.

"Don't shoot," the Japanese officer shouted. "My men have you covered."

He had to decide, he had to decide *now*. Mark looked over his shoulder. Giorgini was already swinging his carbine around.

"Giorgini, freeze! Don't move a goddamn inch!"

"But, Captain . . ."

Mark turned back to face Giorgini and started to raise his own .45.

"Giorgini, if you move, I'll blow your goddamn head off."

He stared at his men for a moment. They were silent— the only sound was the snapping of the bullets overhead. Gazing beyond his men he saw the swarm of Chinese bandits advancing up the slope.

Mark looked back at the Japanese officer.

"Captain, you're trapped. I offer you quarter," Ikawa shouted. "Those men behind you are the soldiers of a renegade warlord. He doesn't care if you're American, Japanese, Nationalist, or Communist. Any outsiders meet death at his hand. You saw what they did to your man."

"Goddamn it, they killed Ed," Goldberg cried.

"You've no time, Captain. Surrender and I will give you quarter. If you do not, my men will finish you or leave you to them." The Japanese officer pointed back down the hill to the advancing horde.

Mark followed his gaze. There was no hope; he had to take the chance.

"Drop your weapons," Mark cried.

"But, Captain!"

"Drop them now!"

He heard the carbines, Thompsons, and .45s hitting the ground.

"Good," Ikawa grunted. "Follow Sergeant Saito, he'll show you the way. Now move!"

Mark looked again at the Japanese officer, and hesitated.

"Move your men out. Or do you want the bandits to finish you the way they did your comrade?" Ikawa asked softly.

Ed, damn them, they killed Ed. He looked back at the advancing host, while the air reverberated with the *snap-crack* of passing bullets.

"All right, move it," Mark commanded. "Follow their sergeant. Let's go!"

The Americans fell in behind Sergeant Saito, but Mark stayed behind. Several Japanese soldiers sprinted to pick up the American weapons, then rejoined the retreat.

Mark fell in at the back of the column, running alongside the Japanese captain.

The Chinese gave a shout of triumph as their comrades crested the opposite hill. Within seconds a light machine gun opened up on the fugitives, stitching a line of tracers up the slope. A Japanese soldier in front of Mark crumpled with a loud grunt as a bullet ricocheted off a rock and struck his helmet a glancing blow.

"Nishida!"

One of the Japanese privates was bent over his stunned comrade, trying to help him up. Mark looked over to his captor. Ikawa yelled at the soldier who had stopped, then ran back to help the private pick up his comrade. Together they started off towards the narrow defile that offered their only hope.

Mark felt as if his lungs were about to burst. Every breath was an agony of fire. Fifty yards, thirty yards—the machine-gun bullets whined around them. Another Japanese went down, his head smashed like an overripe melon, and the radio on his back a shattered ruin. Overhead there was a sharp *crack-whine*: The Japanese in the defile were opening up with cover fire.

He stumbled into the protection of the rocky path where

the rest of the men, Japanese and American, were bent in exhaustion. The officer and private finally came in, dragging their dazed comrade and dropping him behind the protection of the rocks.

The captain shouted some quick orders in Japanese. His men stood, loaded their weapons, and laid down a pattern of fire that slowed the Chinese column. Kochanski came up behind Mark.

"Damn it, Captain," Kochanski whispered to Mark, "there's less than twenty of them. Once we get out of this scrape they'll finish us off or hand us over for interrogation. Let's jump them while we have a chance."

As if sensing their conversation, the Japanese officer turned away from the firing line and came up to Mark.

"Don't even think about it. You're in trouble just as bad as we are."

Mark eyed his captor closely. He was taller than Mark had expected. His deep-set eyes seemed to look straight into Mark. The officer had a casual, almost relaxed stance, strangely different from the accepted image of an Imperial Army officer.

"Where did you learn such good English?" Mark asked. "When I first heard you I thought you were one of us."

"I studied at MIT before the war. My name is Ikawa Yoshio—Captain Ikawa to you."

"What the hell is going on here?"

"The Chinese are a renegade band left over from the old civil wars. They cut off my garrison six days ago. I had to pull out, and was trying to withdraw to our lines, but they flanked me this morning. We were being pushed into a pocket when you so conveniently arrived to divert them, giving us the time to gain this defile."

"Why didn't you just kill us or leave us to them?"

Ikawa looked at Mark for a moment. These Americans were the enemy, the same as the Chinese. Maybe because he was the hunted, and these Americans were the hunted as well...He just couldn't answer that one. Perhaps it was simply that he had lived with them for several years, and in spite of the war he felt an empathy with them.

He started to turn away.

"Why?"

Ikawa looked back at the American. "Captain, you are my prisoner," he said coldly. "If we get out of here, and I truly doubt that, I shall turn you over to army intelligence for whatever information they can get out of you. But for now we are in this together. If your men make any move, I shall execute all of you at once. If you give me your word that there shall be no action against me, I shall treat you honorably."

Mark nodded his agreement.

Ikawa went back to the firing line. His lieutenant, Okada Mokaoto, came up to his side.

"Captain, if I might speak."

"Yes, Lieutenant."

"Kill them now. They are the enemy as well."

"We might need them. I have less than twenty men; we may need these Americans to carry our wounded, or even to fight, if we are to survive."

"Captain, don't let it be said that you are soft towards the enemy."

Ikawa scowled at his lieutenant. "Mokaoto, I don't care if your father is a general," he hissed softly so that no one else could hear. "I am your superior; it is not for you to question my commands."

Mokaoto glared defiantly. Ikawa could well imagine what would be reported, but he didn't care—he had just about had it with this man who had connections because he was the spoiled son of a general.

"Captain." Sergeant Saito was peering out towards the enemy line, which had stopped several hundred yards away. "Captain, they're bringing up that captured 37mm cannon."

The gun had been lost when the garrison was overrun. He knew the enemy had it, but didn't realize they had manhandled it all this way in the pursuit.

"Mokaoto, have you scouted up that trail yet?" Ikawa pointed up the narrow defile that weaved up into the heart of the mountain.

"No."

"As I thought." Ikawa's voice was icy. "Mokaoto, take Sergeant Nobuaki and four men. You are to stay here and delay their advance."

Mokaoto looked at him with hate-filled eyes. The orders were an invitation to die for the emperor, but he had to obey.

Mokaoto looked at his men. "Nobuaki, Denzo, Kurosawa, Teruzo, and Takeo."

Ikawa looked at Mokaoto and said nothing. He knew Mokaoto picked Takeo as revenge. Takeo was the go master of the company, and Ikawa had actually broken the barriers between officer and private during the lonely months of garrison duty to indulge in his favorite game. Takeo had been like a younger brother, but there was nothing to be done about it now.

"The rest of us move out," Ikawa shouted, and started to scramble up the narrow gorge. They had barely gone fifty yards when the first shell screamed in and detonated at the opening to the pass.

Within minutes the shelling had stopped and a loud shout echoed up from the valley below. They were advancing again. The enemy elevated his range and shells were soon impacting along the walls of the gorge, driving the fugitives onward. After half an hour of steady climbing the party came out onto a small plateau where Ikawa called a brief halt. Far below they could see a serpentine column weaving into the gorge. Ikawa stepped out onto the edge of the plateau and looked up to the towering mountain. His vision could trace the line of the trail as it climbed the slope, and with a cold shudder he realized that the path did not go over the mountain. It simply led into a small canyon surrounded by cliffs. He called Mark over to his side.

"Do you see where our trail leads?"

Mark studied the terrain for several minutes. "Once we get to the top of this gorge, we're trapped."

"Precisely."

Mark looked at Ikawa as if trying to gauge his reaction to impending death. There was no sign of emotion and Ikawa could only hope that his own fear was not revealed, for he now knew how a condemned prisoner must feel who could measure almost to the minute how much longer he would be alive.

Chapter 2

Haven

Mornan was furious. She could sense that Danuth had given up completely and was just playing along. The bloody incompetent—she would call him to account later. The others had found nothing.

"Open up your search," she hissed. "Go farther out. Centra, you're supposed to be good with symbolic matching —do a broader scan for large-winged forms. And feed your sensory returns to us all.

"Danuth, you damned fool, go to the outer edge of the Void and see if there are any demons feeding at the focal points."

Masters! The thought whispered through them. It was the apprentice. *I've found the image of a large winged beast*— and his mind flashed an image of a dragonlike creature—*and I read a score or more lifeforms nearby.*

The boy wasn't supposed to be trying—he might misread the shadowy images from other realms—but Mornan could not chastise him now. If he had found something, she would use it. Groaning with effort, Mornan tried to sustain her barrier to prevent Allic's detection of them, but the power created by their spell was leaking through in several places. An alert watcher could pick them up at any time.

"Quickly, Danuth, work with whatever the boy has found. Try to lure them near the portal."

"But I've found four small demons at the Void's edge in another plane."

"Pass them over to Centra. Open up that portal the boy has found and see what it is."

She felt a shudder run through the shielding. Something was probing them.

"Danuth, we've been scanned. Get that portal open and bring them through as quickly as you can!"

China

While the long shadows of evening were reaching across the land, the exhausted, bedraggled party inched its way into the canyon. Their retreat was counterpointed by the echoing crack of rifle fire. Mokaoto's rear guard was still in action.

Ikawa and Mark drove their men onward. Every minute was precious if they were to reach the canyon in time to fortify their position.

As the sun lit the far horizon with a blazing crimson, the trail suddenly opened into a smooth stone-paved path that cut straight into the mountainside. The overhanging cliffs caught the evening glow, so that the mountain seemed to be washed in the color of blood.

The men gathered around their two leaders, seeking orders and some small comfort in their final moments.

Below, the sound of small arms fire grew louder, and suddenly from around a bend in the gorge a Japanese soldier came into view.

"Denzo!" someone shouted.

A sergeant appeared next, and with labored breath they came up the slope, shouting that the enemy was not far behind.

A flurry of activity greeted this announcement. Kraut and Kochanski called for help in moving several boulders across the trail to provide some cover. Mark came alongside and put his shoulder against the stone. He looked up for a moment and saw that Ikawa was still looking into the dark passage.

Calling for Welsh and Goldberg to help with the barrier, Mark went over to Ikawa.

"You're not thinking of going in there, are you?" Mark asked.

"We have to check it out. The position might be better in there. I feel as though we've been drawn to this place, and there will be protection in there."

"That's crazy—it's a dead end. At least out here we can die in the open."

"Are you so eager to die?"

"I thought you bastards were the ones who wanted to be killed for your emperor."

"Only when necessary, Captain, only when necessary. Are you coming?"

Ikawa drew his pistol and started into the dark passage. Mark, seeing that the others were watching, realized that in spite of his misgivings he had to go along, or appear a coward. There was something strange about this place—a feeling that reminded him of the air before a storm.

Pushing aside his concern he started in. Soon they were wrapped in darkness, the only light the thin sliver of sky and the blood-red evening left behind.

"Notice this is paved. The stonework is superb. Whoever built this did so with loving attention."

Mark was silent. He didn't give a damn about the stonework—he just wanted to check this claustrophobic nightmare and get back out.

"There must be something back here. They wouldn't have built this passage into the mountain for nothing. Look, the path turns." Ikawa rushed ahead, then disappeared to the right.

Mark hurried after him, and came up short as he turned the corner, and bumped into Ikawa.

They followed the path for another twenty yards, until it opened into a small courtyard fifty yards across. Sheer cliffs rose hundreds of feet on all sides. Overhead, the crimson-streaked sky gave off a soft glow that reflected down onto a small, pentagon-shaped temple.

"Wondrous, absolutely wondrous," Ikawa whispered, stepping forward as if onto sacred ground.

From back down the pathway came the echo of gunfire. Mark, awakening from the awe of such a sight, rushed past Ikawa to the doorway of the temple.

The heavy oak door glided back noiselessly. There was an eerie, unearthly feel to the place; Mark felt as if he was treading through some remote past. The evening light streamed in behind him and he quickly surveyed the single large room that was covered in a layer of dust. The windows were narrow slits in the stone walls that formed the structure. It was better than a pillbox!

Turning, he started out of the temple, brushing past Ikawa who stood enraptured in the doorway.

Sprinting across the courtyard into the tunnel, Mark raced down the narrow pathway back out towards the light. The sound of gunfire rolled up louder, and reaching the edge of the path, he crouched down low and came up alongside his men.

"Jesus, Captain," Walker shouted, "there're hundreds of them coming up. They're swarming out on either side of the path."

"What about the other Japs—they get back?"

"Yeah, that bastard lieutenant made it," Giorgini growled, "but one of the scum bit it."

"We're going into the tunnel. There's a hell of a fort back in there. We can hold 'em off for days."

"And then what?" Younger cried. "We're dead anyhow!"

"Shut up and get moving," Mark said softly, but with a definite chill in his voice. Crouching low, he started back into the passage.

Suddenly the Japanese lieutenant was before him, shouting wildly and pointing a pistol straight at Mark.

This is it, Mark thought. He could see the finger on the trigger getting set to squeeze.

"Mokaoto!" It was Ikawa.

The lieutenant looked up.

"The American is right. We move in here."

Mokaoto didn't lower his gun.

"Mokaoto, move! The rest of you follow me!"

Mokaoto looked back at his soldiers, evidently sensing the quiet contempt from his men for his losing the argument.

He spit on the ground in front of Mark, and turning away, called for the rest to follow him. Within seconds the Chinese could see the pullback, and they started to rush forward.

Pushing and jostling, the Americans and Japanese ran down the narrow corridor, turned the corner, and raced for the temple. Bursting into the building, the Japanese soldiers fanned out, covering the window slits. Mark and Ikawa put their shoulders to the temple door and swung it shut. There was a heavy wooden beam resting to one side.

"Shigeru, Uraga, help lift this," Ikawa called.

Shigeru, the sumo wrestler of the company, and Uraga, the muscular farmer, came over to their commander and along with Mark they lifted the bar into place.

Mark watched as the Japanese secured the temple and saw his men standing in one corner. He could well imagine what was going to happen shortly.

Nerving himself he approached Ikawa.

"We want our weapons back," he said evenly.

The Japanese officer turned and looked at him.

"You know as well as I do that the Chinese will be on us in minutes. Chances are we'll die. I want my men to die fighting."

"Out of the question," Ikawa snapped, and turned away. Mark grabbed him by the shoulder.

"Either we fight by your side or my men will rush yours and you'll have to kill us—but at least we'll take one or two of you with us."

Ikawa stopped and looked at Mark. The American captain was now as dusty and sweaty as the rest, but he stood straight and hid his fatigue. He was tall and well built, with short brown hair and steel-blue eyes. Typical American, Ikawa thought. Still, the man had determination and guts—confronting him like this when a wave of his hand would suffice to have them all killed. Courage was always admired, even in an enemy. But should he take the chance?

"We can fight by your side," Mark argued. "At least to make those bastards out there pay for this place."

"You give your pledge that your men will fight under my command?"

"Yes."

"That when we escape here, you'll give your weapons back?"

"Do you really believe we'll get out of this?" Mark asked quietly.

A sad smile crossed Ikawa's features. "You have Bushido, Captain. . . ."

"Phillips, Mark Phillips," and he extended his hand.

"Captain Ikawa Yoshio." He shook the American's hand; then as if embarrassed by the ritual, he released it and turned away.

"Sergeant Saito." Ikawa explained to the old soldier what was to be done.

There was an angry murmur from a couple of his men, but a cold look from Ikawa suppressed it, at least for the moment, and he could see where several of them actually seemed glad to have the additional firepower brought in on their side.

The Americans settled in around several of the window slits. Soon the only sound in the temple was the nervous breathing and softly muttered comments of soldiers waiting for a fight.

"Here they come," Walker shouted, and he opened up with one of the Thompsons.

The Chinese came around the corner four abreast. The Japanese machine gun stitched into them, halting their rush. With wild shouts the Chinese fell back. From down the corridor, more shouts echoed into the courtyard. The men listened silently, tensely; then heard a burst of gunshots, and the sound of the argument drifted away.

"Captain."

Ikawa turned to face Nobuaki. "Yes, Sergeant."

"I could hear what they were saying."

Sergeant Nobuaki was an old China hand, serving in the army since 1933. Of them all, he knew the language of this region the best.

"Go on."

"They're frightened of this place. One of them said that it was death to come here. I think they turned on one of their officers and shot him."

Ikawa could feel the fear coming up in some of his own men.

"Peasant superstition, but it serves our purpose. Maybe they'll pull back and we can still get out of this."

He knew the Americans couldn't understand what he was saying, and it was just as well. As long as they were desperate they were allies, but the moment survival seemed possible the old animosities would be back.

Mark stepped up to Ikawa's side. "Why did they pull back?"

"We're too strong in here."

"They're afraid of something. You could hear them arguing, and they sounded frightened to me."

"Let's explore this place," Ikawa said, changing the topic. "Do you have a light?"

Mark fumbled in his pockets and pulled out an old, battered Zippo. Striking a light, he held it aloft.

"There, along the wall: torches."

Soon the five-sided room was filled with a soft glow. Ikawa posted guards at the window slits and the rest of the men settled down in exhaustion.

Kochanski joined Mark and Ikawa as they quietly surveyed the room.

"Looks T'ang period to me. This place is a hell of a find."

"How do you know that?" Ikawa asked in surprise.

"Studied it in college," Kochanski said. "I was a history major at Yale before the war."

Ikawa smiled. "Yes, I was there once. I was at MIT studying engineering."

"Yeah, I would have graduated by now, but then you folks started this little mess."

Ikawa shook his head.

"Let's not argue. I did not start it, nor did you. We simply are following our orders. I would rather have finished my schooling, as well!"

"Okay, Kochanski," Mark interrupted, "enough of the homecoming routine. Check the rest of this place out. See if you can find a back door or tunnel, that's our main concern. And stop worrying about the history."

Mark had been staring out the narrow window when he heard a moan. It was José Laurel—conscious but obviously in great pain.

"How you doing, buddy?"

"Arm hurts like a bitch, Captain." His voice was weak and slightly slurred.

Mark leaned over and gently pulled back José's flight jacket. It was soaked in blood. He looked up at Goldberg, who had been caring for his friend.

"It's badly broken," he whispered, moving Mark over to one side. "That flak burst nearly tore it off. If we don't get help soon, he'll die."

"Have you shot him up?"

"I've used the medic pack aboard *Dragon Fire*. There's some more morphine in the survival gear."

"Use it."

Mark looked up at Ikawa.

"Captain Ikawa, do you have a medic with your men?"

"Private Koki was a medical assistant. As soon as he's done with my wounded man, he'll take care of yours. Do you have any medical supplies?"

Mark shot a quick glance back to Goldberg. What they had was limited.

"Captain Phillips, if you don't share your supplies, I will not share my medic."

"All right, have him go through the equipment with Lieutenant Goldberg."

"Captain Phillips, we're in this together. I propose that we pool what we have, and share accordingly."

"Captain, all those Japs have are their weapons and ammo," Giorgini shouted. "Let the bastards starve."

"When I want your advice, Giorgini," Mark snarled, "I'll ask for it."

Mark looked at his men and could see that they agreed with Giorgini. He turned back to face Ikawa.

"Captain Phillips, my men would undoubtedly agree with your sergeant," Ikawa whispered softly. "I have an officer who would shoot me this minute if he thought he could get away with it." Ikawa made a subtle gesture toward Lieutenant Mokaoto.

Ikawa turned away from Mark for a moment and looked over his men. "Where's Kurosawa?"

"Dead, Captain," Takeo replied. "He was hit by a shell."

"I see. Captain Phillips," Ikawa continued, "I have fifteen men under me, you nine. We have a light Nambu machine gun; the rest rifles. Our ammunition is enough for the moment. You have several carbines, two Thompsons, and the rest .45s. What else do you have in your survival gear?"

Mark looked back over at his men. There was no sense in lying or holding back now.

"A first aid kit, signal flares—the usual survival pack gear—and rations for my crew to last three days."

"Or all of us for a day and a half."

"Yes."

"Good, then it is settled."

"I guess so."

A few moments later, Ikawa saw Kochanski come out from the back of the chamber. He stopped for a moment in the middle of the floor and scuffed at the dust with his feet. After a quick examination he backed away from the middle of the room and came up to where Ikawa and Mark were standing together.

"No way out, but there's a spring in the back of the temple—all the water we need.

"This place is weird," Kochanski continued. "It looks like it hasn't been touched in centuries, yet the building seems well maintained. There're even those fresh torches. It's obviously a temple, but for what? Just look at the carvings!"

Ikawa looked to where Kochanski was pointing. Tortuous carvings of interlocking dragons and demons covered the wall.

"And there's a pentagram inlaid into the floor. Strange, I thought the pentagram was a western symbol of the occult."

Kochanski walked back to the center of the room and several of the men followed him. With his foot he brushed aside the dust and pointed out the design. Kraut came over and examined the inlaid work, then went over to the altar that dominated one side of the temple.

"Holy Christ, this altar has bloodstains all over it!"

Kraut's words sent a faint prickling up the back of Ikawa's neck. It was as if a hidden door was slowly opening to reveal a coiling, insidious terror from beyond.

"Something moving outside," Walker said, still guarding the window slit with Smithie, the waist gunner, at his side.

"Open up on it," Mark told him.

Walker squeezed off a short burst. There was a sharp cry, then a rising babble of voices.

Mark and Ikawa went to the nearest slit and looked out. In the shadows of the pathway something large was moving.

"Goldberg, get me the flare pistol."

Goldberg loaded a charge in and tossed it over to Mark. He aimed it through the slit and fired. The round slammed down the narrow path, exploding with a brilliant flash.

"My God, they brought up the 37mm!" Mark exclaimed. "How the hell did they do that?"

In the white magnesium light Ikawa could see the cannon positioned in the pathway, its front armor skirting protecting the crew which was feverishly at work.

The Japanese machine gun opened up again, bullets bouncing off the gun's armor.

"The bastards must have manhandled it all the way up the trail," Giorgini cried. "We're trapped!"

"All right, everybody get ready. They'll blow the door. Once that's gone, they'll charge."

Even as Mark barked the commands, the cannon spat a thundering flash.

The doorway exploded.

"Hold your fire," Ikawa yelled. "Wait for the rush!"

Another round barked out, and then another. Over the ringing in their ears from the explosion came a roar as the Chinese, screaming with fury, braced themselves for the attack.

Ikawa came over to Mark's side. In spite of his fear of approaching death, there was a terror that was far worse, and growing stronger with each passing second. It was like an electric charge running through his body, triggering some primordial dread. Something was horribly wrong with this room.

"I'm getting out of here!" Ikawa shouted above the roar of battle.

"You're crazy!" Mark cried. "You'll get cut down the moment you step out the door."

"I don't care. It's worse in here. There's an evil here—it's a nightmare." His words were edged with hysteria.

Another shot barked out and the remains of the door crashed in with a thundering boom.

The bugles brayed triumphantly. The Chinese were preparing to charge. But Ikawa and the others did not hear them. A louder, howling roar suddenly drowned out all other sound, all other thoughts, all sense of place and time—and the room was suffused with a white, pulsing glow.

Ikawa drew his sword, and with a cry, rushed for the door. Kochanski was in front of him looking back towards the altar and pentagram, his mouth wide open, screaming, his eyes wild with terror. So riveted was that gaze that in spite of his own fear, Ikawa stopped and looked back into the room, now awash in a ball of pure crystalline light that shimmered and grew, lapping over them with a strange pressure they could actually feel.

Ikawa screamed. The 37mm gun barked one more time. The shell howled past him, merging with the ball of light and the nightmare image from beyond. Ikawa screamed even as he fell towards the light, drawn in by a hurricane roar that sounded as if the universe were being ripped asunder.

Chapter 3

The center of the pentagram swirled in a maelstrom of arcing flames. Flickers of lightning crackled over her head, and Mornan looked to Danuth. The other two sorcerers were useless, their powers nearly spent. Mornan felt a ripple of fear, knowing that just Danuth and she might not have sufficient control over whomever it was that Danuth and the apprentice were bringing through.

A bolt of lightning slashed out from the center, booming with a deafening roar that caused Mornan to stagger. There was tremendous power here, she thought. What had Danuth and that damn fool apprentice locked on to? There was another surge of power, and then the first portal worked by the exhausted sorcerers opened wide.

For a brief flicker of time she could see into the realm beyond. She saw the winged demons and started to form her words of command, but there was something wrong—

The other portal was opening too soon! The two should never have opened together. Danuth had fouled up and let the power they were generating get out of control!

Fascinated, she gazed through the opening. This was a place she had never seen before, and to her amazement she saw that this was a realm of men, not demons. Something had gone wrong.

What was this? She screamed with rage as the demons

27

escaped the sorcerers, fleeing through the other portal to the land of men. She turned to Danuth but before she could even voice her anger, it ended.

A 37mm shell, fired by the Chinese, burst through the mysterious portal and exploded. Mornan was cut in half without ever knowing how or why.

Mark felt as though he had been sucked into the heart of a tornado that was the pathway to death. He was falling, tumbling through an endless corridor in which time seemed to have no meaning. Memories of Dante came to him and he remembered how some of the condemned souls—was it for adultery?—were forced to tumble forever in the middle of a maelstrom. Seized by panic, he wondered if this was Hell. And the despair of such a thought caused him to cry out.

Even as he screamed he hit the ground. A body landed on top of him and he heard Goldberg swearing.

So Goldberg was down here as well. Opening his eyes, Mark dared to look around. In front of him was a swirling cloud of light, and he saw bodies hurled out of it like riders tossed off a merry-go-round gone berserk.

He rolled away from the cloud and came up against something warm and sticky—the shattered body of a woman. Mark recoiled and stood up. Other forms were standing up around him: his men and the Japanese. Ikawa was already standing to one side, surrounded by some of his soldiers.

The whirlwind was starting to lose power; its light was growing dim. It pulled in on itself, and with a faint hissing pop, disappeared.

"*Has nalarn, Kulmica!*"

Mark turned. A shrouded figure stood in the shadows that surrounded them, its arm raised like the hand of death.

"What the hell is this?" Goldberg whispered to Mark.

"*Has nalarn, Kulmica Sarnak. Juikal!*"

A lightning bolt snaked from the shadowy figure's hand and slammed into a Japanese soldier. He disintegrated into a vaporized mist.

"You bastard!" Walker screamed. Leveling his Thompson, he fired a quick burst. The bullets stitched into Danuth, knocking him off his feet.

Danuth tried to get up and point in Walker's direction. There was another bolt, but it went high, arching over Walker's head.

A fusillade snapped out from the Japanese and American

guns. Within seconds Danuth was torn apart, his body bleeding from a score of wounds.

"Jesus, Captain," Goldberg asked, "what the hell was that?"

Mark shook his head. He struggled for control, trying to decide what his next action should be. Were they dead? Was this Hell or a nightmare that he would awake from, screaming? Hell or not, they had just offed some of the residents, and he was certain that someone would be around to check up on the mess.

He could hear his men, some crying, others shouting, their voices trembling with panic. The years of training took over like an instinct, restoring his control.

"Damn it, let's have some discipline here. Everybody shut the fuck up."

Even as he barked out his command he heard Ikawa's voice rise up in a sharp volley of Japanese, and Mark knew that his counterpart was echoing his own actions.

Torn from his dreams by an inner sense of warning, Allic, Lord of Landra, sat up in his bed and turned his thoughts outward, probing for the source of the disturbance. He could feel an imbalance, as though the proper order of things had suddenly been shifted.

Kicking the cover aside, Allic rose, pulled on a long burgundy-colored robe, and pushed open the door to his meditation suite.

With his approach, a gentle wash of blue light welled from a fist-sized crystal mounted on a pedestal of gold.

Reaching out with his right hand, Allic touched the crystal of farseeing. Instantly the chamber was bathed in a brilliant glow that caused him to close his eyes. He knew where to direct his thoughts, and turning to the south wall of the room, he bent the flow of energy and directed it outward. Opening his eyes again, Allic watched as the power of the crystal was directed into an intense beam which revealed a map inlaid with gems and gold. The map was highlighted in stark, glowing colors as the power of Allic combined with his crystal to direct the map for a search.

Emblazoned on the wall was a representation of the realm under his control. Such was its power that only Allic's father, the god Jartan, could have created it.

The minutes passed. In the distance he could hear his guards changing their watch.

Slowly his attention was pulled toward one point on the southern border of his realm.

What was this? Now that he started to focus, the hazy sense of an outside power was confirmed. Someone was tampering with the Essence. It had to be an outsider, since none of his own sorcerers would be there.

Could it be Prince Macha's people? Whoever they were, they were trying to block his probing, and so he knew their actions were hostile.

He bent all his will to the task. Soon he was drenched in sweat; his entire body ached with the effort as he battled through the barrier of wills. He could feel them breaking, their shielding crumbling.

Suddenly there was a presence, a presence which he had never experienced before. At that same moment he broke through, and for one brief second there was a flash of an image; then nothing.

Exhausted, he stepped back from the crystal, and the room went dark. Concentrating on his communications crystal, he turned his thoughts to the castle command center.

"Who's on duty?" Allic asked.

"It is I, Ulnarn, commander of the third watch."

"Awaken Pina, tell him he has a little journey ahead of him, and bring him here at once."

"Acknowledged, my lord."

If there was anyone he could trust with this, it would be Pina. A quick flight with his triad and Pina would find out who these sorcerers and intruders were, and if necessary kill them without further ado.

Far from where Mornan and her sorcerers had opened the portal was a land of mountains, the princedom that Sarnak had made for himself in the desolation that followed the Great War 3000 years ago. Towering battlements and massive fortresses covered every entrance and blocked every exit.

Each mountainside was terraced with small farms and vineyards, and the river valleys were dotted with small villages and farmlands. Only in the desolate higher mountains of the interior were there factories and mines spewing refuse into inaccessible valleys and pits.

In the center of the land, high above a river valley stood a mighty walled city that glowed in the moonlight of the Twin Sisters.

Sarnak the Accursed, so named for his unproven part in the betrayal and death of one of the Creators, sat on his throne in his darkened chamber. He had watched Mornan's efforts and her death through a crystal—the mate of the one she had used.

For most of the night he had been watching, and with Mornan's death he had to fight for self-control. But finally even his iron control weakened and his rage began to show, causing his aura to grow brighter.

Now Sarnak pushed his crystal aside and looked around the room. He was tall and lean, with dark hair and black eyes that were large and mesmerizing, and few there were who dared to face that gaze in the moments of his wrath.

"Who selected those incompetents with Mornan?" he asked, death in his voice.

"Wika made the initial assignment." Ralnath, Sarnak's chief sorcerer tried to conceal the fear in his voice.

"And who approved Wika to coordinate this mission in the first place?"

Silence.

"I want an answer," Sarnak said softly.

"I did, my lord."

Sarnak turned away with a snort of disgust. Everyone in the room did his best not to draw attention to himself as Sarnak moved to his master crystal, activating it with a wave.

Quickly Sarnak merged it with those observation crystals set high in his border mountains that overlooked Allic's realm. The room again became dark as his aura slowly died, his frustration giving way to the cold analytical force that was the heart of his power.

"Allic is projecting his power in a field of interference so I can't see very much," he said to Ralnath, who had come to stand by his side. "But I sense an alien presence, perhaps men from another plane. They're definitely not the demons we had planned for."

He looked coldly at Ralnath. "Which of our forces can get in there and find out what they are before Allic arrives?"

The head scribe, standing in the far corner, consulted his master file and nervously walked over.

"At this moment," the scribe said, "we've almost emptied that part of the border to prevent any possible suspicion of our involvement. But there is a force of twelve demons under Chaka that can be there within two turnings."

"Send them in immediately. I want at least one prisoner

for interrogation; the rest are to be destroyed before Allic can get his hands on them."

"At once, my lord."

Sarnak turned and swept them with his gaze.

"All of you leave me except Ralnath."

Ralnath could sense the relief of the others as they fled the room, leaving him to his fate. He could remember more than once hurrying from the room as well, and returning later to remove what was left of a man or woman who had failed. He braced himself.

"I want Wika relieved of his post and crystals. Have him chained to the gallows against possible execution. I'll decide his fate later." Sarnak paused, staring at Ralnath.

"You know that my first move in this campaign has ended in a fiasco because you approved that idiot's selection of sorcerers?"

Ralnath nodded. "My lord, each had done well in the trials, according to Wika's reports."

"I want you to check the validity of those trials, and if there is any falsification you will personally remove the heads of Wika's wife and children and tie them to his chains. I can't help but suspect that he gave the task to Mornan as a reward for more than just her behavior on the testing field."

Ralnath breathed an inner sigh of relief. The blame was to fall on Wika and not on him.

"Ralnath, I understand your mistress has just given you twin sons."

He froze for a moment, then nodded, not trusting himself to speak.

"Never fail me again, Ralnath. Now get out of my sight."

"Gather round to me." Mark made a quick count.

"Who's missing?"

"It's José, Captain," Kochanski called. "He's unconscious." And he pointed to the ground where José was already covered with somebody's flight jacket. The pale moonlight made his face look deathly. Mark looked up, and gasped. There were *two* moons—very bright and set about twenty degrees apart.

The men followed his gaze, and began shouting again.

"Shut up, all of you!"

The only thing that kept Mark from blind panic was the responsibility that by now was part of his nature. He had to get his people doing something—anything—to divert them from their fear.

The orders rattled off.

"Goldberg, see to José and try to make him comfortable. Kraut, set up a defensive perimeter. I don't know where the hell we are, but we'd best be prepared."

"Could be Mars," Kochanski ventured.

Several of the men started to talk again. In the distance he could hear the same with the Japanese. Hell, there were still the Japs to deal with.

"What do you mean, Mars?"

"Ever read any Burroughs? Twin moons, Carter, Martian princess, and all that?"

"Later, Kochanski, later. Just do what I've told you for now."

Mark looked towards Ikawa and saw that he already had his men lined up and was speaking to them in a low voice.

Several of them broke away and fanned out into the darkness.

Mark turned back to his men.

"Kochanski, Smith, Welsh," his voice lowered to a whisper. "Watch the Japs, especially Ikawa and that other officer, you know the bastard." He started to move but turned back. "And for god's sake, if they open up, knock out that machine gun first or we're all dead."

The men nodded, their faces shining softly in the light.

"On my command, and my command *only*, you're to take them out. Now that the Chinese are gone..." His voice trailed off. Gone. Gone to where? He forced himself to refocus his attention.

"Just keep a watch on them.

"Captain Ikawa." Mark turned away from his men and prepared for the possible showdown with their captors.

"Private Yoshida, control yourself!"

Any other officer would have slapped Yoshida for the nearly hysterical display, but Ikawa could well understand it. He could barely control his own fear.

"We are not dead, Yoshida! We are still alive." Ikawa forced a laugh, and gave Shigeru, the sumo wrestler, a sharp punch in the stomach.

Shigeru grunted.

"See: If old Shigeru here can still feel pain, then you know we are still in the realm of the living."

He patted Shigeru on the shoulder and turned away. They had relaxed just a little and he took advantage of it.

"Sergeant Nobuaki, pick five men and form a defensive perimeter. Sergeant Saito, come over here with me for a moment."

He stepped back from his men so they couldn't hear.

"Saito, take the rest of the men and deploy to face the Americans. Be ready to kill them if they make any move. Do you understand?"

"Yes, Captain."

Ikawa hesitated for a second. His words would be dangerous in the Empire—but they were far from the Empire now.

"Sergeant, you are to answer only to me. If Lieutenant Mokaoto attempts to order you in any way regarding the Americans, you are to refer him to me."

He could see the astonishment in Saito's eyes. Etiquette and discipline had just been broken, but he knew that Saito could be trusted. Ikawa turned and walked over to Mokaoto.

"Who was killed by that blast of light?"

"Superior Private Teruzo, Captain."

"We have everyone else?"

"Yes, and the Americans as well."

"Yes, the Americans as well." Ikawa looked past Mokaoto to the twin moons on the horizon.

"Captain Ikawa."

He looked up and saw Phillips approaching him, his hands extended out to either side showing that his weapon was holstered.

"Don't trust him, Captain," Mokaoto hissed.

Ikawa ignored him and walked over to meet the American.

At a cautious distance of several feet they both came to a stop.

"Any idea of where the hell we are?" Phillips finally asked.

Ikawa looked away from Mark. They stood upon a low cresting hill and Ikawa could see the broad, treeless valley beyond. The twin moons cast a double shadow pattern of light and dark. The air was warm, dry, with a faint scent of the prairie carried by the gentle night breeze.

Now that it was quiet he could hear the night noises. Some were familiar, but some different—insects, birds, then a deeper rumbling growl that sounded like a tiger but was not.

The moons alone forced him to admit a terrifying reality; the feel of this place, the savannahlike vegetation, only helped to confirm that somehow, someway, they had traveled far from the conflict that had nearly killed them only minutes before.

He looked back to Phillips and saw the same sense of wonder and fear.

"Are we dead, is that it?" Mark asked.

"Captain Phillips, your guess is as good as mine."

"But it's a safe bet we're no longer in China," Mark replied, and his tone carried all the implications of that.

"Yes, we are no longer in China, Captain Phillips. And I could state that again you are my prisoner."

"Bullshit. I have half a dozen people behind me, all of them with weapons pointed straight at your head. Go ahead and give the command, you Jap bastard, and you'll be the first to die."

Ikawa started to laugh while looking straight into his eyes.

"We are cut from the same mold, Captain Phillips. The moment one of your men fires, my people will cut you down, for I've given the same order. So here we stand."

Ikawa looked away from Mark towards the moons and then back.

"But we are not your prisoners," Mark replied.

Ikawa stepped closer and Mark did not back away. Each looked into the eyes of his enemy, a man he would have killed without hesitation only hours before. But under these circumstances . . .

"We have to make a choice, Captain Ikawa. We can have it out here and now. Chances are you and I will both die, and in the end maybe, only a couple of yours or mine will live. I don't see any sense to that."

"No," Ikawa said with a soft chuckle. "Even back in our war, I never did see any sense in that."

"Then it is agreed that for the moment at least our agreement formed when fighting the Chinese still stands?"

"Agreed."

"With the additional understanding that we are no longer your prisoners, here or anywhere else."

Ikawa hesitated for a moment. But he knew that the balance had been changed forever; the old rules simply no longer applied.

"It is agreed," Ikawa said softly.

There was a gentle exhale from Mark, and Ikawa realized

that Mark would have given the order to open fire if that point had not be agreed to.

Again the thought came to him. "You have Bushido, Captain Phillips."

Mark nodded slightly at the compliment. "Now we have two alternatives," he said, "the first being that we can split up and go our separate ways."

"Is that what you want?"

Mark smiled. "Is that what you want?"

"Don't play a game with me, Captain Phillips. The advantage to separating is obvious: We remove the chance of a confrontation and the fear of a stab in the dark. Tell me, Captain Phillips, would you stab me in the back?"

"You Japs are noted for that. I lost an uncle on Bataan, Captain Ikawa."

Ikawa avoided the possible confrontation and turned his gaze to a movement behind Mark.

"Say, Mark." Kochanski was approaching out of the shadows.

There was a low call in Japanese; Ikawa gave Mark a quick look of appraisal, then called back to his own men.

"Captain Phillips, tell your man to approach cautiously. One of my men almost shot him, thinking he was making a move on me."

"You hear that, Kochanski?"

Kochanski came up to the two officers. "No hostility intended, Captain," and he gave a slight bow to Ikawa.

Ikawa found himself liking this young American sergeant, who understood their courtesy and used it.

"Go ahead, Sergeant," Ikawa replied.

"Mark, I've taken a little look around this place."

"Go on, Kochanski."

"Well, sir, over there where we got thrown out of that whirlwind I found the outline of a pentagram on the ground, just like the one in the temple."

"You think there's some connection?"

"Can't think of any other theory, Captain. We got drawn into the pentagram in the temple and got thrown out here. Wherever *here* is," and Kochanski looked up at the moons.

"I also found six bodies. One of them is Japanese, Captain Ikawa."

Ikawa nodded. Teruzo had been a good man, lighthearted and devoted to his parents.

"What about the other bodies?" Ikawa asked.

"Never seen them before. Three men, one of them the guy we shot up. Then there's a boy and a woman.

"Blown all to hell," Kochanski continued, "like from an artillery round. Same with the others. All cut up by shell frags . . ."

"Go on, Kochanski, what are you thinking?"

"This is like something out of the Wizard of Oz gone berserk—I mean, with that tornado thing that brought us here. It seems like we got sucked from one world to another—maybe through the force of those dead sorcerers playing around with occult-type stuff. They obviously got more than they bargained for, and the shell from the Chinese wiped them out, except for that last guy."

"This leads us to our second alternative then, Captain Phillips," Ikawa said. "We must assume that whomever they were, they have friends."

Mark hesitated for only a moment. "Bring your men over here, Captain Ikawa. Kochanski, bring our guys over too."

A couple of minutes later the men were gathered into two lines facing each other.

Ikawa turned to face his command and said something, while Mark spoke to his men.

"Captain Ikawa and I have agreed to an armistice, a truce. Only God knows where we are. But we're going to get back sooner or later, that I promise you."

He paused. The last statement sounded so hollow, but he had to promise something.

"We're going to work in alliance with the Japanese. We have to, in order to survive. You saw what that one guy did to the Jap. If the people around here can do that, our only hope is to double our strength by fighting together rather than against each other. I'm *ordering* all of you to honor this agreement."

He stared at them, searching out each man and holding him with his gaze. Just one hotheaded action could screw the whole deal.

"If anybody makes so much as a move against the Japs without my direct and personal order, I'll shoot him."

There was a snort of derision from the ranks and he thought he heard the word "traitor" mumbled. He could guess who said it.

"Captain Ikawa!"

"Yes?" And Ikawa came to his side.

Mark unholstered his .45 and walked over to Giorgini.

"Did you say something, Giorgini?"

Giorgini smiled sarcastically. "No, Captain."

With one sweeping movement Mark cocked the .45 and put the barrel to Giorgini's forehead.

"Captain Ikawa."

"Yes."

"This bastard thinks I'm a traitor for making our alliance. Give the word and I'll blow his fucking brains all over the ground."

Mark prayed that he had judged Ikawa correctly. He knew the Japanese were watching and hoped that through this act he could convince them, while at the same time show his own men how serious their situation was.

"Go on, Captain Ikawa, decide."

Giorgini was trembling, and Mark prayed that he wouldn't start to beg, for he would lose face for all of them if he did.

Ikawa sensed it as well and acted quickly.

Coming up to Mark's side he pushed the automatic away, and spoke to Giorgini in a loud voice so that all could hear.

"Many of my men feel the same about me, Sergeant, but our war is gone—somewhere on the other side of that," and he waved towards the smoldering pentagram. "I want you to live to help us survive."

He turned away from Giorgini, and walking back to his own men, explained what had transpired. There was a murmur from the Japanese ranks.

"All right, men, get ready to move out in ten minutes," Mark ordered. "There was a hell of a lot of action here and maybe the friends of those stiffs over there will come by to check up on it. We've hung around here too long as it is."

Mark left his men and went over to where Ikawa was standing on the crest of the hill. Beyond them the broad open valley was bathed in silvery light.

"We better get a move on, Captain."

"Yes, you're right. But to where?"

Mark was silent.

"I remember a movie I saw in your country. What one of the characters said seems appropriate for this situation."

"What was that?"

Ikawa smiled, looked over to Mark, and extended his hand. "It is an alliance then, until we return home?"

"Yes, until home," Mark replied, and grasped Ikawa's hand firmly.

"You know, Captain Phillips, somehow I don't think we're in Kansas anymore."

Mark gaped at him for a moment and then a smile crossed his face.

Chapter 4

They had walked for several hours, crossing a terrain of gently rising hills covered in waist-high grass and occasional groves of small windbent trees. The twin moons, low on the horizon, were still shining brightly over the plains, and ahead on the horizon there was the faint glimmer of the coming sunrise.

Kochanski found himself wondering what color and type of sun he would see. He was now firmly convinced that at the very least they were light-years, if not galaxies, away from home. The star fields were different, and even with the brightness of the twin moons, he could see glowing star clusters arcing across the heavens, spanning the sky like beads on a necklace—most of them far brighter than the Milky Way.

Kochanski no longer shared his thoughts with the others. His comments only frightened them, and after the first hour he learned to walk in silence and helped with the carrying of José, who drifted in and out of consciousness.

Someone nudged him from behind: Giorgini.

"Do you see something over there?" Giorgini asked, pointing behind them.

"Where?"

"There, low on the horizon."

He followed where Giorgini was pointing and saw what appeared to be a darker blackness moving across the far ho-

40

rizon. He didn't want to say anything yet—the others would simply say it was his crazed imagination.

"Naw, you're seeing things." But he kept his eye on it—something was there. It seemed to be headed towards the place they had come from. Moving low, it disappeared, came back up, then disappeared again as though it was hugging the valleys to avoid detection.

Kochanski moved forward to Mark's side.

"Say, Captain," he whispered. "Giorgini and I think we've seen something moving in the sky behind us."

Mark looked off where Kochanski pointed but now there was nothing.

"What was it?"

"Couldn't tell. It seemed to be flying and was like a dark cloud moving across the sky low to the horizon."

Mark thought for a moment. The bogey could be their exhausted imaginations, but after that character with the lightning bolts he wasn't taking any chances.

He scanned the terrain in front. A quarter mile ahead there was a small grove of trees, their forms silhouetted by the twin moonlight. If something was looking for them, it would be as good a place as any to make a stand.

"Captain Ikawa, there might be something behind us."

Kochanski explained what he had seen and the Japanese captain's reaction was instantaneous.

"Quick march," Ikawa cried, and he directed his men towards the grove.

Several minutes later there was a flash on the horizon behind them; then another. A rumbling boom like thunder washed over them.

"Bet they're back where we first came' through," Kochanski ventured, and Mark grunted agreement.

They pushed faster, and some of the Japanese sprinted ahead to secure the grove for the rest of the group.

"Something's coming," Lieutenant Younger shouted from the rear of the column. The cloud was visible again, and moving towards them.

The party broke into a run—the four men carrying José lagging somewhat behind.

"Holy shit, it's coming in quick!" Giorgini screamed. Turning, he cocked his carbine, ready for a fight.

"Fire on my command," Mark cried, and falling in with the four stretcher-bearers he turned with Giorgini to provide cover.

The cloud turned, cut to one side, and then came sweeping in directly over their heads.

Like a bursting balloon the darkness ripped asunder. A dozen flying creatures appeared, screaming with rage. They were the medieval image of demons: reddish in hue, eyes of fire, with blood-red talons extended to grasp their prey, and wings that swept out above them.

The stretcher-bearers ran past Mark and Giorgini, gaining the edge of the grove, just as the demons soared down upon them with cries that stung their ears.

"Fire!" Mark yelled, took aim, and shot. Shrieking, a demon burst into flames and tumbled to the ground, igniting the tall grass.

There was a wild cry of anguish and Mark turned to see Lieutenant Mokaoto fall to the ground, several demons on top of him.

Horrified, Mark watched as one of the nightmarish forms dug its talons into Mokaoto's legs. Mark lifted his pistol to fire—

"Captain, look out!"

Mark was knocked off his feet. Rolling, he found himself staring into eyes of raging hatred, talons raised to slash.

There was a wild cry and a shimmer of reflected light as a sword hissed across his field of vision. The demon fell away, bursting into flames.

A rough hand grabbed Mark by the shoulder, pulling him back up. It was Ikawa, his samurai sword dripping a liquid that smoldered and stank.

Giorgini and Walker came in on Mark's side and together with the Japanese captain they pulled Mark towards the protection of the grove.

"Mokaoto!"

The Japanese soldiers screamed as two demons gathered around the struggling lieutenant, and with wings flapping, lifted him into the air.

Goldberg took careful aim, and his shots slammed into one of the monsters. It tumbled from the sky, but the other demon soared, bearing Mokaoto into the darkness. Above the *crack* of the rifles and jeers of the demons, the men could clearly hear Mokaoto's screams, which grew fainter as the doomed lieutenant was carried away.

"They're coming in again!" Goldberg cried, slamming off several rounds. The Japanese machine gun opened with a high staccato shudder, catching one of the demons and cutting him in half.

"Something else coming in!" Kochanski shouted, and pointed towards the sunrise. The dot of movement soon resolved into three men flying in formation.

"Jesus Christ!" Mark yelled in astonishment. "Captain Ikawa, hold your fire on those men, there's something about them. If they're a threat, let them make the first move."

Maybe it was the way they were flying around like Superman that made him hesitate. Hell, he was almost past the point of astonishment anymore. Batman and Captain America could show up right now and he wouldn't think twice.

"Can you beat that shit?" Kraut cried in amazement. "In formation, no less."

The demons, seeing the formation, turned as one and pulled back. They attempted to reform into the ball of darkness, but it was already too late as the three flyers closed in, cutting off their retreat. The air crackled as bolts of light slashed into the demons. One tumbled from the sky, wings torn, and the rest scattered. The triad followed two, bringing them down in explosions of fire, while the rest escaped.

The triad came back towards the astounded soldiers, circled the grove, then alighted thirty yards away.

The three human forms stood their ground as if waiting for something.

"Think they want a parley?" Ikawa asked.

Mark looked at him. "With power like that we damn well better hope so. You with me?"

Ikawa nodded. They started out, avoiding the spreading circles of flame caused by the fallen demons. Ikawa stopped briefly to examine the ground where Mokaoto had been taken, then rejoined Mark as they approached their three deliverers.

"What do you think of them?" Mark whispered.

"One thing is for certain; they weren't friends of those things we just fought."

"That doesn't mean that they'll be any friendlier to us. They might be friends of the ones back at the pentagram and blame us for what happened."

Even as they spoke one of the three lifted back into the air and flew over to one of the demons who had been knocked out of the sky by a light blast. A pale shimmer of light spread from the man, and the demon shrieked as the pulsing blue aura closed around it, so that it could no longer move.

As the two captains approached the new arrivals, the single flyer returned and joined his comrades. Mark and Ikawa stopped about a dozen feet away from the flyers.

Their clothing was white, or light blue; it was hard to tell in the predawn light. Their garments were plain: a collared tunic held by a broad leather belt with glowing crystals in it, trousers, and calf-high boots of black leather. They also wore wristbands set with a brightly shining crystal on each arm. Each man seemed to be covered by an aura of light, and they glowed in the fading starlight. The three men were motionless, slender, almost fragile looking, but Mark would never have said so to their faces. Mark took another step and held out his hands, palms downward.

"Be careful not to point at them," Ikawa warned, stepping forward as though he didn't want these strangers to think him inferior to the American.

"Do you speak English?" Mark asked.

They were silent.

"Damn it, you Americans always think that everyone else should speak English," Ikawa muttered.

"Well, what else do you expect me to ask?"

"Let's not argue in front of them," Ikawa replied, and smiling, he gave a bow reserved for a possible superior.

The flyer on the left nodded in Ikawa's direction and then whispered to the one in the center.

Mark correctly guessed that the one in the center must be the leader and he advanced another step towards him. Feeling foolish, he imitated Ikawa's bow, realizing that the courtesy had most likely made a positive impression.

"Ilya na, mui vaneria na?"

Mark locked eye contact with the one in the center who had just spoken and smiled, shaking his head.

"Ilya na, masa du nara, Sarnak tu Allic tu Patrice."

Again Mark shook his head, then threw in the typical American gesture of shrugging his shoulders and cautiously raising his hands.

"Naga!" the one to the right shouted and stepped to the center, raising his hand in Mark's direction.

"Toman bishu," the one in the center yelled. Stepping in front of his protector, he forced his arm back down. He stepped towards Mark and cautiously raised his hand.

"Mark, step back," Ikawa warned.

"I think it's all right. Look, Captain Ikawa, we've got to make friends somewhere; I prefer these to those demons we just faced."

Before Ikawa could protest, Mark stepped closer, keeping his hands down.

The man before him was light skinned, not quite Caucasian but neither was he Negroid or Oriental. It was as though the three had been blended together. His eyes were penetrating, with an intensity of power that Mark felt was somewhat superior to his own. But he forced himself to hold the gaze and the stranger smiled and held up his hand.

He's going to strike me, Mark thought. He waited for the blow but there was only a light touch to his forehead.

"My name is Pina, second commander of my lord Allic. This is his fief you tread upon, stranger."

He thought this Pina was speaking English and for a moment he wanted to laugh at Ikawa's comment about English, but then he realized that the language was strangely different.

"I can sense your confusion, stranger, by the power of the crystal." He pointed to a softly glowing crystal centered on his belt. "I have given you the power to understand our speech."

"How?" Mark asked incredulously.

"Let us not waste time with such talk now. There is much to do, and first I must decide about you and your companions."

"Decide what?"

"Is it not obvious? You are strangers here, interlopers on my lord's fiefdom. Is that not enough to decide? Now tell your comrade that I wish to touch him so that he might speak as well, and that I mean him no harm."

Mark turned to do as he was asked.

Pina could sense more caution, more wariness, but also an iron control in the second outlander as he reached out, giving him the power of understanding.

Pina could feel a slight draining of his strength and resolved that for the moment he would not waste the power of his crystal on the others.

These were not Sarnak's demons, at least. He had seen them fighting Sarnak's servants, and their performance was credible. But they were obviously not of the world of Haven. Such warriors as these must be from another portal, perhaps caught by accident in what he suspected was an attempt to bring forces from another dimension.

Well, it looked like the attempt had turned against whomever had tried it. Now he had to decide quickly what to do with the results.

"Where are you from?" Pina asked Mark.

"Pennsylvania."

"What is this Pennsvana?"

"America."

"Never heard of this America."

And it was with that single statement that Mark felt a deep sense of despair. It stated to him perhaps more than anything else just how far away they must now be. In a world at war, there was hardly anyone alive from Eskimo to New Guinea native who had not heard of America. With the realization came a sudden premonition that he most likely would never see home again.

Pina looked appraisingly at the two of them.

"I have decided," he intoned. "You are outlanders, caught in the web of another. You seem to be warriors and that is good. I shall inform my lord and you shall pledge vassalage unto my master."

"Vassalage? What the hell is this?" Mark replied. "Listen, buddy, I'm an American, even if I am in some other godforsaken corner of the universe, and I'm no serf to anyone."

Pina stepped back.

"Mark, shut up," Ikawa said. He stepped forward and spoke quickly.

"The nation of America is very proud; there, every man is his own lord with no vassalage. He means no insult to you, I swear it."

Ikawa turned on Mark. "Listen, we need an alliance if we are to survive. You and I made an alliance and some of your men and mine called it treason. But we did it. It's the same thing here. I am in pledge of vassalage to my Emperor, yet I live with Bushido, with pride."

Mark, feeling calmer, nodded; and Ikawa approached Pina.

"I can pledge alliance to you as well but my first pledge is to my Emperor, and not I nor any of my men is an oathbreaker."

Pina nodded. These men might be useful. They had pride. He could blast them with a wave of his hand, but he knew that his lord could always use warriors.

However, there was something strange about these men; they did not feel like mere mortals. It was almost as if . . .

Pina's eyes began to glow, probing deeply into the two leaders. In amazement he could see the Essence growing within them. These men did not have the cellular restrictions bred by the Creators into nearly all of the humans on this planet. He was looking at potential sorcerers! This was like a gift from the gods.

He stepped back, whispered to his companions who gave him a shocked look, and with a sense of urgency touched his communications crystal.

A moment later, he announced, "My master Allic has decided that you may be of more value than was first thought. He is willing to make terms in return for allegiance. It is now important that your men understand also, so bring them to me and I will teach them our tongue."

The map still shimmered with a soft glow. It had been a long night and Allic settled into a high-backed chair, stretching his legs with a groan.

"Well, Varma, what do you think?"

"A game within a game, my lord. Was it Sarnak or Macha who planned us harm, and why the outlanders at this time? Is their arrival a plot within a plot?"

Varma the jester sat by Allic's feet, for the moment comfortable in his role as soundingboard and confidant. There was no formality when the two of them were alone, no need to play the idiot jester entertaining with jokes upon himself and his deformity.

"The Essence flowing in them is pure, unalloyed," Allic said quietly. "Obviously, they come from a world where the Essence does not exist, they aren't even aware of what is now happening within their own bodies. With the proper training these men could be powerful."

Varma knew that only one person in a million was born with the power to control the Essence. To have so many potential sorcerers arrive on their very doorstep was unprecedented. Varma examined Allic closely, and sensed that yet again he was looking at the opportunities, and not the possible perils.

"Remember, my lord," Varma said cautiously, "they could be a threat. Who knows what type of power they might be able to control?"

"Yes, therefore we must make our enemies their enemies."

"Could you one day be such an enemy to them?" Varma paused for a moment and pressed ahead with his real concern. "Could this be a ploy by Sarnak to get them accepted by us? Is there a chance they are not really from another world but are merely sorcerers hidden by Sarnak, unregistered with any guild and trained by the Accursed to deceive us? Ask Borc's descendants what Sarnak the Accursed is capable of.

"Even if they *are* from another world—kill them now, my lord, before they grow strong. Too often the victim does not see his undoing when it is still helpless in the cradle."

"My, we are bloodthirsty tonight. As usual, Varma, you see plots everywhere."

"No one watches the fool watching them, and so I often see what is hidden in men's hearts."

Allic was silent as he pondered Varma's suggestion. These men could one day rise in power to be rivals. But they could be allies as well. If Pina's report was accurate, they would be a tremendous boost to his power. But was the gain worth the risk?

"Fetch me a brandy. A large tumbler, Varma."

"Drink so early, my lord?" Varma asked with a note of concern.

"Don't mother me, Varma."

"My lord, it's only that you know how you get at times. . . ."

"Damn it, just get me the brandy!"

Varma scurried to the sideboard where he filled a large snifter. Returning, he placed the glass in Allic's hand.

Allic had barely sipped it when he heard a high-pitched shrieking. It was soon matched by a similar tone, and then another, so that within seconds he was overwhelmed in cacophony.

"The alarms," Varma screamed. "A Presence is coming!"

There was a stirring of wind, though they were in a sealed room. The wind became a roaring thunder, a cyclonic fury that twisted and turned upon itself, spitting fire and thunder.

"It is a god!" Varma shouted as the winds bowled him to the floor.

A pillar of fire filled the far side of the room. Allic was motionless, silent, waiting.

"Varma!" It was a deep thundering voice from the pillar

of flame. "Varma, you are in a Holy Presence. Begone from My sight."

With a cry Varma pushed open the door and was gone.

Still motionless, Allic waited.

"Well, how do you like my entrance?" the booming voice asked.

"Little heavy-handed, isn't it, Jartan?"

There was a rolling peal of laughter and then the pillar of fire collapsed inward, taking a form of light that looked somehow human as it shimmered and shifted.

"You know, father, some people might think that this pillar of fire stuff is a bit much."

"I like it. Impresses the hell out of everyone, except for jaded family members like you," Jartan replied. "It looks to me that you're hitting the bottle a little early this morning."

Allic waved the comment aside.

"I think I should talk to Varma about your drinking. He should look out for you."

"Now you do sound like my father. Besides, don't do it to Varma—he'd die of an apoplectic fit if you approached him. Jartan, I'm surprised to see you here so early. I'd have thought that you'd be in human form right now entertaining one of your female companions."

The vision lifted its head and laughed.

"The son of your mother, to be sure. She never was impressed by my powers—that is why I loved her as I did. But let's be on to business: I felt the disturbance and I can tell you, so did nearly everyone else on this continent with the Power. These are the first humans to have arrived here in some time from the realm of another god. I sense as well that their Essence of magic could be developed on this plane of our existence."

"I surmised as much myself. Pina reports that already, though they are not yet aware of it, their bodies are absorbing and merging with the Essence."

"Then you must assume, my son, that others will be looking to use them as well."

"Sarnak, of course. His demons attacked and carried one of them away."

"That's not good. I wasn't aware of that."

"And you a god," Allic chided with a smile.

"You know as well as I do that there are limits to my powers."

"There are times when I wish you were all-powerful. It could make these games a little easier."

Jartan chuckled. "Now, if you're willing to accept my advice, I'd think it would be wise for you to go out and meet these men."

"Why? They should come to me—they are pledging vassalage. Should not the servant come to the master?"

"I am a god, but I come to you out of my love and concern. For those who rule there should be no fear of what the forms require. Such things are beyond them, and they prove themselves by not doing what is usual or expected. Go to them now, my son. Their power is growing by the minute. If you come to them when they still think themselves weak, you will gain respect and gratitude in their eyes. With that gratitude you can win their friendship and alliance."

Allic considered this. "You're right. I'll go."

"I knew you'd see it my way."

"Talk about conceit," Allic laughed. And Jartan laughed with him.

The form started to grow again, the waves of light expanding outward.

"Please, don't trigger any alarms when you leave. It scares my people half to death."

"Oh, all right." The pillar of fire held for a moment. "Something to warn you about before I go. I can imagine there'll be a great deal of interest in the outlanders from my darling niece."

"Oh yes," Allic said with a sigh of despair. "Patrice."

"Precisely. She'll see the value of these men as well. Her game will be completely different from the one you are playing with Sarnak. And Patrice is not the only one. You are lucky that they arrived in your realm, but you can expect that others will want to use them also. Best move quickly, my son; your all-so-friendly neighbors are probably plotting their next move. Act now before you regret it."

"Father, can't you just this once give me a little more help, at least against her?"

"Not this time, son. I have other concerns right now that would wither if I were not there to direct them. Besides, you are a match for Patrice. It just means you have to work a little harder."

Allic bowed his head. "And this strange attempt to open a portal inside my realm—do you have any idea who might have done that?"

"I can't imagine Macha working such a scheme, even though this incident did take place near his territory. Could be Sarnak, since it was his demons that showed up afterwards. Could be Patrice as well. That's for you to figure out. I have other business to worry about at the moment."

"Some help," Allic mumbled, shaking his head and giving his father a rueful smile.

"I'd best be going," Jartan replied, ignoring his son's last comment.

There was a faint shimmering, a flash of light, and he was gone.

The room was silent. Stirring at last, Allic used his communications crystal to call the watch officer.

"Allic here. Control code: Moons Larna and Rega. Alarms off, all in control. Prepare my escort and inform Pina that we are leading a patrol out to him shortly."

Arising from his chair he walked out of the room and through his private chambers to the balcony that overlooked his capital city.

The sun called Yirtan washed the city of Landra with morning light. Already the merchants and street vendors were astir, their voices crying out, filling the city with the bustle of life. The golden light shimmered across the river, giving it the appearance of a river made of that most precious metal.

The pure white marble of the temple to Jartan caught the light as well. From its high rounded turrets came the blue-green clouds of incense which the temple priest alighted each dawn. The sweet scent wafted through the air, giving it a smell of pine forest and mountain air.

Allic smiled, wondering if Jartan had dropped in for a moment to scare the daylights out of the acolytes who tended the fires. His father always enjoyed such things.

Looking down from the castle keep, he could see both the east and west sides of his city with the river in between. Already the river was aswarm with commerce as vessels ranging from scows to schooners set out for the distant sea.

This was all his realm, and he felt a surge of love for this city of Landra. Landra of the thousand domes. Landra of the ten-league walls, made of polished limestone, which ringed the city in a girdle to the height of twenty men. All his to control—but now there could be war with Sarnak over the betrayal on his borders, since in his mind it had to have been

Sarnak. And conflict as well over the powers that these strangers had brought into this world.

He touched the crystal again. "Allic here. State of readiness increase to level three. Have a mounted escort from the outpost nearest to the incident join me for a ground surveillance patrol. I'll return before sunset, new code word, Jartan's Voice. Acknowledge."

The voice of his central command post replied with an affirmative.

Smiling, Allic drew upon the Essence and his body began to glow. As he soared in the air, five triads of sorcerers flew up to surround him. They flew with increasing speed towards the south.

Chapter 5

"Mistress, we await your command."

Patrice turned away from the crystal, pushing back her flowing red hair. She turned to face the sorcerers she was sending after the outlanders in Allic's realm.

"You know where to go then?"

"Yes, my mistress."

Patrice examined the witch and two sirens before her. They were perfect for the task. The sirens were silent, under the control of the witch who would command them when the time was right to weave their song of seduction. The witch had already created around herself the image of an innocent maiden. Patrice could see the cold hardness underneath—the power that could lash out and paralyze weaker forms. But that was hidden beneath silky red hair which cascaded to her waist; hidden in a slender girllike form, pale doelike eyes, and a gentle expression.

It was a mirror, Patrice realized—a mirror of herself from a time so distant she could barely remember it. She forced that thought away. It would only bring back the pain of things long lost.

"Capture as many as you can—and don't fail me in this. Your reward will be great, but your punishment will be greater if you do not succeed."

The witch bowed low, attempting to hide her fear in the presence of the demigod.

"I will watch through your crystal, but I cannot direct: to do so would reveal me to my cousin Allic and to Sarnak." Patrice pointed to the crystal around her throat. "Go then, and succeed."

The witch beckoned for the two sirens to follow, and the throne room was empty.

Patrice turned back to her seeing crystal and held it with her gaze, searching for clues about these strangers. There was some power here to ponder. She couldn't quite place a finger on it. It was not the Essence alone of the men that caught her. There was something more—a vague reawakening of an older memory which she had tried to turn away, but its haunting presence would not let go.

Pina stood before the assembled offworlders.

"Let me explain the situation to you, so you can see that Lord Allic is offering you something in return for your services. There are powers in this world that far surpass those feeble weapons you carry." Pina waved at Lieutenant Mokaoto's pistol, lying on the ground where he had dropped it. In a flash the gun was sliced in half by a beam of light that snapped out from Pina's hand.

The men looked at each other nervously.

"You have made an enemy of Sarnak the Accursed," Pina continued. "Not a wise thing to do, even for experienced sorcerers of this world. To ones such as yourselves . . ."

He fell silent for a moment, letting the reality sink in.

"You have little food, no water, no shelter, and wounded to heal. What will you do when his demons come again this evening?"

The offworlders muttered among themselves. A breeze stirred the trees and brought the stench from the smoldering demons lying on the ground. Mark looked from the alien sky to the beasts, suppressing a shudder.

Pina smiled inwardly at Mark's anxiety. He knew a simple way of demonstrating his intentions and power. Walking over to José's stretcher, he gestured for the humans to draw back. The men looked to Mark, who ordered them to obey with a wave of his hand.

This would be a drain to his power but Pina took one of the crystals from his belt, cupped it in his hand and laid it on José's wounds. Though he did not have the talent to completely heal the wounds, he could at least stabilize the injury and end the pain. José's eyes flickered open and met Pina's, and then turned towards Mark.

"Captain, where are we?"

Mark shook his head and smiled. "Later, José, later."

The Americans and Japanese were divided into two groups facing Pina. The conference had been going on for over an hour.

Finally Ikawa said, "Enough! You say that in return for three of your years' service, you will assist us in this world."

"That is correct. My lord and master Allic will provide you with food, shelter, and training in return for your enlistment under his banner. If you serve honorably, you will be treated honorably."

"Our duty is to serve the emperor. We cannot serve him if we are dead or stuck here." Ikawa cast a steely eye at his men and barked a command. Each Japanese snapped to attention and bowed. Turning back to Pina, Ikawa continued, "So we will swear fealty to your Lord Allic for three years and then we will try to return home." And he bowed.

Pina, using the knowledge he had assimilated from their minds, bowed back at the correct angle, and they straightened at the same moment.

Conversation had ceased among the Americans while this took place, and as Pina turned to face them, Kochanski burst out, "I just can't believe this. Not only are we in a nightmare, but we're going from the twentieth century back to the middle ages and now we gotta swear to serve some feudal lord. It's too much."

"Look at it this way, Sergeant," drawled Lieutenant Goldberg. "You're just enlisting in another army."

"We sure as shit don't have much choice," agreed Walker.

Mark heard them and said, "If anybody has any negatives, let's hear them now, 'cause we're going for it otherwise. Remember, this guy saved José's life." He pointed to where their comrade peacefully slept.

No one spoke.

Mark turned to Pina. "All right. We also agree to serve for three years. But no fast ones."

"Elaborate, please."

"I will not command my men to pull any bullshit like massacring innocents or if..." Mark floundered for a mo-

ment, then continued, "your treatment of us leaves anything
to be desired. If you get too nasty all bets are off and we try
to make it on our own."

"You are giving a conditional acceptance then?"

"Yes."

Pina stood straighter for a moment as if in communication
with someone not present and then continued, "Allic has
agreed, but rest assured, we do not massacre innocents, and
your treatment will be honorable."

"So what happens after this?" asked Walker.

"We'll take you to Landra, our province's capital, and
find you quarters. Then you'll start your training."

"What kind of training?" Ikawa asked.

"All of you outlanders have the potential to be sorcerers.
The force you call magic is simply the ability to control your
will, and then to draw upon the Essence and shape it to your
desire. Very few here have this ability, because most humans
are genetically unable to draw upon the Essence. Only the
gods themselves, their heirs, and sorcerers like myself may
use it."

"You mean that you're a mutant, and this magic crap
comes from the gods," Kochanski scoffed.

Pina's gaze hardened, and the aura of diffused light that
surrounded his body grew much brighter.

Kraut kicked Kochanski lightly and muttered, "Don't piss
him off, asshole."

Mark was more blunt. "Kochanski, shut the fuck up!"
And he stepped between Pina and his man, protecting him
with his body.

"Pina, a lot of what you're saying is hard for us to swallow."

Ikawa joined in, "We deeply appreciate your enlightening
us. Please continue." Mark shot him a grateful glance.

Pina was still staring hard at Kochanski. "The ability to
use the Essence is so rare and precious that families and
clans thank fate when a child is born with it. It occurs in only
one of a million births."

He paused. There was another benefit to using the Essence, but he didn't want to mention it yet. "And the gods
are not like your god. Our gods are here with us, enormously
powerful, and a permanent fixture of our world of Haven,
When you swear fealty to Allic you are also swearing loyalty
to his father and liege lord, Jartan, ruler of this whole region
of the planet, and one of the Creators."

There was silence as the men absorbed what he was saying.

"I will see to it that you eventually meet Jartan, Kochanski. And we will see if you still have doubts."

There was silence for a moment and Pina continued, "Once we get you settled in quarters, you will start your training."

"Does that mean we're going to have to live with the slants?" Lieutenant Younger pointed contemptuously to the Japanese.

As one man the Japanese turned, ready to face the challenge.

"Unwashed foreign pig. Our ancestors were civilized before your forebears crawled from under rocks. Why should we want to live with you?" hissed Sergeant Nobuaki.

A crack like thunder brought them back to reality. Pina brought his arms down and said quietly, "I grow weary of this. You are from the same world, fighting for survival in a hostile environment. I order you to put aside your hatreds. Failure to treat each other properly will be severely punished. I trust I am making myself clear."

The two groups fell silent, eyeing each other suspiciously. Pina looked the two groups over for a moment and then indicated that the men should settle down and rest.

Pina strode over to his two assistants and relaxed beneath the shade of a low hanging tree.

"So none of them were aware of the Essence in their own world?" one assistant asked incredulously.

"Remarkable, isn't it?" Pina replied quietly. "Apparently no one in their entire world has ever been exposed to the Essence in its pure form, and thus they have no built-in immunity to wielding it. A strange world, that."

"Wait until they find out what having the ability to use the Essence means," the first assistant said, chuckling softly. "As off balance as they seem to be right now, which do you think is going to affect them more—the powers of a sorcerer or the increased lifespan?"

"The latter," Pina said softly. "A lifetime of a thousand years will truly stun them."

Both assistants nodded.

"The problem for them," Pina continued, "is how that will affect their desire to return to their own world, and lose the gifts of power and extended life."

* * *

The dawn had been magnificent. The sun now rose to its zenith, flooding the savannah with a fiery light. Sounds from birds and animals had reached a stunning crescendo at dawn, but were now mute—lulled by the noonday heat.

The men were in various stages of repose, and no one had said a word for some time.

"Bogeys!" screamed one of the Americans. "There's a formation coming this way from the north."

Everyone was on his feet in an instant, weapons ready.

With his binoculars, Ikawa could count sixteen men flying in formation. Each wore the same style of dress as Pina and his men, with a glowing belt of crystals about their waists and wrists.

Mark's voice came from behind Ikawa. He hadn't even heard the American approach. "Pina says that it's Allic and his escort. He said they're flying over a ground force. I'm betting we see something come around the side of the hill very shortly."

Ikawa lowered his glasses for a moment and noticed that the other Americans had come over to watch.

"They're banking in," commented Lieutenant Goldberg.

Just then a force of mounted riders came into view.

"Looks like we are stuck in a pretty primitive society," Walker said. "If they use horses for cavalry instead of jeeps or tanks, then you can bet they've never heard of the internal combustion engine. Maybe we can strike it rich by selling a little modern technology."

Ikawa raised his binoculars again—and gasped. With his face a careful blank he handed the binoculars to Mark while remarking to Walker, "You may be right about the modern technology, sergeant, but not about the horses."

Mark focused in on the rapidly approaching party. "Jesus! Those aren't horses. They look like . . ." He lowered the binoculars and turned to look at Ikawa.

Both men stared at each other, and Mark continued, "They are riding what appear to be giant Dobermans."

Silence. Then one of the Japanese said, "What is a Doberman?"

Mark, who hadn't taken his eyes from Ikawa's, answered, "It's a dog. Only what they've got is the size of a Clydesdale, and looks mean enough to kick the shit out of a pride of lions."

He shuddered and handed the binoculars to Ikawa. "And there is a guy flying in the center of the column that makes

Pina look about as fearsome as a four-year-old."

Ikawa nodded. "We had better get ready. I think the next five minutes are going to be very important."

"My Lord Allic approaches," Pina announced, and he bent one knee to the ground. "Kneel as I do."

"Say, look," Goldberg interjected, "the Goldbergs haven't bent a knee to anyone since we left the cossacks behind. I'm an American, remember that."

There was a murmur of agreement from some of the others.

"Bend your knee to your lord," Pina commanded. And he looked toward the sky in the direction from which Allic was approaching.

Mark looked over to Ikawa. The Japanese had already followed Pina's command, but the Americans hadn't moved.

Ikawa gave Mark a beseeching look as the Americans gathered around their commander.

"Bend your knee!" Pina shouted.

Mark had to think quick. "All right, men, do you remember that asshole colonel back at the base?"

"Yeah, dipshit Guest," Welsh mumbled.

"Dipshit Guest," Mark agreed. "*You* had to salute him, *I* had to salute him—even though he was a stinking coward who pissed his way out of every combat mission we ever flew. But still we saluted him."

"I'd like to have saluted him with my foot up his ass," Giorgini replied.

"Right, Giorgini, so would I. Here in this place bending a knee is the same as a salute. Now, this Allic guy strikes me as a man with some balls. Just look at that guy fly." Mark quickly pointed towards Allic, who was already coming in for a landing.

"He's got Pina's respect; he's got mine. I'd rather salute him than that asshole Guest any day of the week." Mark went to one knee and looked reproachfully at his men.

One after another they followed his lead. Mark looked over to Ikawa, who wore a look of relief that was a reflection of Mark's own thoughts.

Allic landed by Pina's side and touched him lightly on the shoulder. Pina arose and gave a quick nod of respect.

"You have done well, my friend."

Pina started to go back down on one knee in response.

"No, stand by my side."

Ikawa was watching this closely. This one knew how to

command men, and had a presence as well. He was half a foot taller than any of the others, with a full mane of golden hair pulled back and held in place by a crownlike thing that had glowing crystals in it. His face was dark, tanned as if accustomed to being in the field. This was no palace princeling. This was a warrior, a man worthy of his sword.

Allic recognized Ikawa's appraisal with a nod. "You are men of qualities," he began. "Pina has told me of your fight with the demons. You will be men that I wish by my side."

"You understand the agreement that Pina has given to you and in your pledge to me, and through me, to my father Jartan, from whom you will find protection."

"On our world," Younger put in, "that's called a contract and it's made in writing."

Pina stepped forward with an oath and Younger recoiled.

"Damn you, Younger, shut up!" Mark hissed.

With a wave of his hand Allic ordered Pina to step back.

Allic swept them with his gaze and there was a hint of anger in it. "Listen, outlanders, and listen this one time. You are no longer on your world, wherever that might be. You are on my world, and in my fiefdom. The rules are mine, the game is mine. I approach you now in good faith: I will do it only once. Those who pledge their loyalty to me will have mine in return. Here on Haven we still honor our word. If a man does not keep his word he is *unta*, unspeakable. To call against a man's given word will always result in the death of one or the other. I will however forgive you this. Just this once."

He fixed Younger with his gaze and Younger lowered his head.

"Do you understand me?" Allic asked.

"We do," Ikawa replied. "Forgive him his mistake; he is not used to your ways."

"We understand each other, then. Do you have any questions?"

"Is there any hope of our ever getting back?" Mark asked.

"I cannot answer what I do not know. I can only pledge to you that after your three years of service I will do what I can to aid you in that quest. That I now swear to you."

"Then I am willing to swear service in return," Mark said quickly.

"I therefore accept you as my vassals. I shall command and you shall obey. In return for your service I will give you shelter, comfort, and protection from your enemies, as you will give me protection from mine. At the end of your service I shall aid you in your quest to return. You may stand, my warriors."

The ceremony impressed the Japanese, and just as predictably, the Americans groused. One by one they were all brought forward and blood was taken from a vein in their arms while they recited an oath of allegiance to Allic and the god Jartan. The blood was poured on crystals, two to each man. Surprisingly, the blood was absorbed immediately. For José, who was still unconscious, the crystals were gently pressed against his wounds. Each man received a wristband with one of his crystals fixed within it. The other crystals were stored within boxes that Allic kept.

"These are your first crystals," Allic told them. "They will provide you with basic protection. Do not take them off without cause. You are very vulnerable to spells right now."

Allic looked closely at Ikawa, realizing that he already liked him. He had the strength of command—as did the leader of the other group. Pina had said that these two bands were enemies. Looking from one group to the other, Allic hoped he could control the animosity that both parties held repressed. Now that the immediate danger was past, their hatred might boil over. These were good men; it would be a shame for them to waste themselves on each other—and it would require some attention on his part to prevent it.

After the ceremony, Pina brought over the wounded demon that his assistant had restrained in the field of light.

"So, Chaka, a little too zealous in carrying out your master's orders this time," Allic said sarcastically. "Three hundred years you have annoyed me, and now you are mine."

"Loose the field that surrounds me, Allic, and I'll spit in your eye," the demon responded in a voice that sounded like a landslide in a gravel pit. He turned to face the outlanders. "It is because of you that I face more bondage, and I curse all of you. I swear one day to rip your bodies open and eat your livers in front of your dying eyes."

Chaka reared up to his full ten-foot height, his glowing red eyes filled with malevolence. He opened his mouth to reveal twin rows of sharp yellow teeth that glistened with saliva. His breath stank of corruption.

He tried to extend his leathery wings, and groaned in pain as the holding spell prevented it. Chaka's face contorted with rage, and he shook his taloned fist at the offworlders.

"If it takes a thousand years I'll not forget," Chaka roared, fixing Mark with his gaze. "I'll hunt you in this world and the next until I find you."

The offworlders were clearly terrified, though they tried to hide it.

All of the sorcerers and riders, however, broke into harsh laughter.

"I call that bold talk from someone who will spend the next thousand years in the mines," one of the riders jeered.

"Chaka always was bombast and birdshit," called another. "If you have any real power, Chaka, why are you allowing yourself to be held by such a little field of light?"

And the entire assembly started laughing again.

The newcomers watched uneasily, like children trying to comprehend a conversation beyond their reach.

Allic's body began to glow brightly and he floated into the air.

"I'm going back immediately. Pina, you'll take command here. Keep the calvary escort and all the triads except my personal escort; fly my new vassals back home, and then detach one triad for a wide sweep to the south."

Looking over the travelers, he continued, "We'll give them the rank of acolyte initially and upgrade them as they earn it. Quarter them in the guest estate next to the palace wall. Bring them to me as soon as you arrive in Landra to start their training. The way the Essence is growing in them, they may turn out to be first-class sorcerers."

Speaking to the newcomers, he continued, "Pina will accompany you back to Landra, my capital, where you'll get settled. I will see you to do the initial testing. I'm also taking your wounded comrade back to my palace, where our healers will attend him. Good day to you."

He turned in the air and smiled at Chaka like a cat staring at a trapped mouse. "I'm taking Chaka with me too. We have a lot to talk about."

With that he shot into the air, and as he rose heavenward a pulsing beam of blue-white light shot from his hand, circling Chaka with its soft diffused glow. A cry echoed from the demon as he was pulled aloft with light that wrapped around him like fiery coils of rope.

Allic's escort surrounded José with the same field of light

and rose to join their commander and his prisoner. Within seconds they had crested the far ridge and were out of sight.

"Shit!" It was Walker, standing off to one side. He was trembling, a look of panic in his eyes.

Mark went over to him. "What is it?"

"Captain, you won't believe it. You just won't believe it!"

"Try me."

"Look, Captain, there was this damn wasp. It just kept flying at me and I got pissed off, waved my hand at it, and Captain, I blew it to hell with my finger. Here's another one!"

Walker pointed towards a droning insect. There was a flicker of light from his fingertip. A thin shaft of light snapped out with an electric crackle, and the wasp vaporized with a tiny puff of fire and smoke.

Incredulous, the men backed away from Walker, who stood in shocked bewilderment.

Pina looked at Mark and the others, then turned back to Walker. "So soon," he whispered.

China

The cowards hid out on the open slope, none of them daring to approach the entryway to the temple. "Motherless dung-eating curs," he cursed, realizing that he'd have to go in alone and finish it.

Chang Shin, warlord of the Hing bandits, stepped into the narrow defile, breathing heavily, his face soaked with the acrid sweat of fear.

His own men had come close to killing him as it was. If he did not go through with this, the survivors of his band would turn on him and slaughter him out of fear and anger over what had just happened.

He crept forward, bent double under the hundred-pound satchel charge. Chang reached the right-angle turn and crept past the 37mm gun, now a twisted pile of wreckage.

His throat was tight; his heart felt as if it would burst out of his chest. He pushed on. There was one of them. He wanted to turn away but his morbid curiosity forced him to look again.

Truly it was a monster from the nether regions—a demon of night. As they had charged the temple, expecting to slaughter the Japanese and white-skinned foreigners, these monsters of the night had greeted them. They had killed his men by the dozens, tearing the hearts out of quivering bodies and burning others with gouts of flame from their mouths.

He prayed to his ancestors, begging for protection, as he crept up to the smoldering temple. The four demons had died, cut down at last in a wild fusillade, but not before they had wiped out a quarter of his command and melted down the precious gun so recently taken from the Japanese.

The Japanese and the foreigners. Where were they? Damn them to the realm of nightmares, he hoped they suffered the anguish of a thousand cuts for all eternity.

Chang pulled the fuse, staggered to the temple door, and heaved the charge inside. Turning, he sprinted away, leaping over the smoldering bodies and puddled remains of the artillery piece.

He paused in the corridor only long enough to pull the fuse on the other two satchel charges that he had crammed into a fissure in one of the overhanging walls.

Just as he reached the entrance there was a roaring thunderclap, and another. A giant's hand of concussion hurled him down the slope. Rolling to one side, he watched as the canyon walls trembled then came dashing down, sealing the temple under a million tons of rubble.

"Curse them all," he whispered. "May they suffer in the nether regions forever."

Chapter 6

"Sir, time to awake. The first bell will soon strike."

"Damn." Mark rolled over, trying to hang on to the last vestiges of sleep. There had been that strange, haunting dream again. It had come to him half a dozen times since their arrival on Haven over a month before. The dream would start with a roiling thunderhead building in the distance, until it seemed to rush across the landscape, filling the world before him with its elemental powers. It washed over him, covering him as if he were floating in the air. And then within the raging torrent he would sense something else, a presence that could almost be touched, if only he knew where to find it.

"Sir."

"All right, all right." He opened his eyes.

It was Yamir, his aged and balding body servant. What an ugly face to wake up to in the morning, Mark thought, and he wanted to return to the dream, but Yamir stood silent, that annoying look of superior reproach in his eyes. How Mark hated morning people, who happily awoke in the hour before dawn and looked down their noses at anyone who was not bounding about when they were, as if late wakers were morally corrupt, or at the very least, suspect.

"God, I wish you could get me some coffee."

"You've asked me that before, sir. You know I've never heard of such a thing called coffee."

Mark closed his eyes. It was beyond him how any civilization could survive without providing its citizens with two scalding cups of java before starting the day. It was yet another reminder of just how far from home he really was. His mind filled with the memory of Alice, who always woke before him and brewed a pot and set the steaming cup by his bedside before leaving for the hospital. English nurses, he thought longingly. She was most likely in France now, somewhere with the British Eighth Army, and he was . . .

"Sir, your robe."

It was best to start in. Yamir was not only a body servant, he was a trained observer. The men called him a spy, but Mark preferred the other term, since Allic was only following good judgment by having his new men closely watched to get a better understanding of how they acted.

Taking the robe Mark followed Yamir into the main corridor of the manor. Ikawa came out from the opposite room and the two commanders exchanged nods. They then followed their servants to the bathing hall in the guest estate in Allic's citadel which had become their home. Over the last month the Japanese soldiers had started to lose the faceless anonymity of enemies and started to take on distinct personalities. Mark knew that while his mood was bad in the morning, Ikawa's was downright fierce.

Turning into a side corridor, Mark could feel the warm moisture in the air and hear the sounds of running water and muffled voices, punctuated occasionally by peals of laughter.

They stepped through a wide doorway and into a large circular room which was open to the garden outside. Opposite the doorway a bubbling stream cascaded out of the wall and down a smooth stone culvert into a round, steaming pool. Half a dozen Japanese and several Americans were sitting in the pool, and they shouted a cheery round of greetings which they knew their grumbly commanders would ignore.

Removing his robe, Mark braced himself and stepped beneath the cascade. It was always too damn hot at first, and he gasped as the steamy water thundered over him. Mark found it fascinating that the city sat above a geothermal spring which not only provided hot water for all its inhabitants, but was also used for heating when cool weather came. As near as he could figure, the climate was like southern California:

almost perfect weather with a short, mild winter.

It had rained heavily the day before and as a result the derusa trees has flowered again during the night. Dozens of bright red blossoms were scattered across the pool—the footwide blooms filling the room with a scent like lavender. Mark had decided that the derusa trees were like huge gardenias, genetically designed to bloom all year. Hell, according to the lectures he'd been attending, even their food crops were like that, producing harvest after harvest all year long. This world was really something.

Servants appeared from a side alcove and began to scrub Mark and Ikawa with pumice stones that always stung initially, but soon left them feeling loose and tingly. The public nature of all this, and the casual acceptance of nudity in Allic's court, still left Mark uneasy. But to the Japanese it was almost like the communal baths of home.

One of the servants finally gave Mark a gentle nudge out of the cascading shower. It still made him feel like a little kid as he sat down in the mirror-smooth culvert that went into the hot pool below. It was like riding the sliding board into the pool at Coney Island.

The hot tub made him feel like he was melting. He floated lazily for several minutes, wishing that he could slip back between the warm sheets and pretend today was Sunday morning, and breakfast in bed would soon be served, along with the Sunday *Times*.

But there was the responsibility, always the responsibility. Opening his eyes a crack, he saw that several of the men were already out of the pool. Yamir stood stoically to one side, but his impatience was already apparent. Reluctantly Mark swam over to the far side of the pool, and finding the exit hole, he ducked under the water.

With a quick push he slipped into the current and let it suck him along for its short length until he reemerged into the cold water pool in the adjoining bathroom. With vigorous strokes he crossed the pool and stepped out on the far side next to another cascade of water. This was the tough part.

Holding his breath, he ducked under the shower and let the icy water splash over him, shocking him into full consciousness. As he stepped out on the far side, more servants greeted him with towels and gave him a quick rubdown.

Now he was ready at last—but damn it, how he craved a cup of coffee.

"Thinking about coffee, sir?"

"Kochanski! I'd like to get back home just so I could have a cup and a pack of Luckies."

Kochanski was looking over a smiling dark-eyed redhead walking by outside in the garden, who boldly returned his gaze.

"I don't know about that, Captain. I bet this bathtub's better than anything I'd ever have back on Earth." His gaze returned to the girl. "It'd take more than a cup of coffee to get me to give this up. Like this age stuff. Now, I still don't know if I believe it or not, but according to what we've been told, people who can use the Essence can live for a thousand or more years if they stay here. Why would I want to leave?"

"But what about home?"

"Home to beautiful Trenton, New Jersey?" Kochanski said softly. "Home to getting my ass shot at by Zeros?"

"Or ducking ten tons of bombs from a B-29."

The two turned as Ikawa and Sergeant Saito came up beside them.

"Just talking about home," Mark said evenly.

"It's what we're all thinking about," Ikawa replied as he reached for the light blue tunic and breeches that one of the servants presented to him. It was the standard dress for Allic's sorcerers.

"If we start talking about that again," Saito interjected, "it will only remind us both what stands between us back there—or could still divide us here."

A single bell sounded in the distance, interrupting any response. Dawn had come, and with it the start of another day of training.

The elderly sorcerer who stood on the dais reminded Mark of one of his old briefing officers, but Valdez was far more of a perfectionist.

"As I have told you before, you must learn to focus your thoughts. That is the key, the source of your strength, to focus."

Allic had ordered him to finally start with the offensive training, but Valdez felt it was far too early for that. He looked at his charges for a moment then, exasperated, turned away. Thirty days of this, he thought. The ones called Japanese were learning at an acceptable rate. It seemed that their minds were better trained for what was needed—it must have something to do with how they worshipped their god. But the ones called Americans, they were too haphaz-ard, they would not force their thoughts sufficiently inward, or worse yet, they had the annoying habit of acting like they already knew it all.

As Allic's master trainer Valdez was entrusted with pre-paring these men to use the tremendous potential that they all had, but Allic wanted miracles. These men were out-worlders, barbarians without any social graces.

"Now watch me."

Valdez took the crystal wristband off his right wrist and handed it to his daughter, then looked back at the out-landers.

"Damn it, Walker, watch me, not my Liala. She's not the one with the gift, I am."

"I'd say she's got gifts enough," Walker mumbled.

"What was that!"

"Nothing, sir, nothing." The men around him chuckled.

"All right you clowns, knock it off," Mark ordered. "This could save your life someday, so listen up." He nodded for Valdez to continue.

The old trainer ignored Mark. Raising his hand, he turned to a straw dummy that was propped up across the courtyard. The audience grew quiet as a pulsing shimmer seemed to encompass the old man.

Several seconds later a sheet of light snapped from his hand and towards the dummy, which burst into flame.

"That is the power of the Essence," Valdez said, looking back to his audience. "It is part of the very fabric of this world. When Jartan and the other gods transformed Haven, they gave of their own creative spirit and their Essence, brought with them from the Great Void. The gods and their descendants may draw upon this power to create and to de-stroy."

"Does that mean," Giorgini asked with a touch of sar-casm, "that you claim to be a descendant of a god?"

"No, damn it. And don't blaspheme," Valdez replied. "The genetic pattern of all humans who were brought to Haven thousands of years ago has been subtly altered so that we mortals cannot draw upon the Essence. Occasionally someone like me is born who does not carry this genetic trait, and thus we can work what you call magic.

"It seems that your god did not leave any Essence in creating your world, or perhaps attempted to make too much, and thus the Essence was dissipated, spread out too thin to be of use—for even a god is limited in how much he can create.

"Without the direct presence of the Essence it seems probable that your god did not bother to give your race the genetic trait that our gods chose to give us. Therefore you have the ability to use the Essence here like few others, but it takes practice and concentration. Otherwise you'll be more dangerous to yourselves than to anyone else."

"Ah, but burning that dummy is easy. I've been practicing this stuff on the side," Walker replied.

Standing, he extended his hand and pointed. A second target dummy smoldered and gradually burst into flames, while his comrades and even the Japanese cheered his performance.

"Just fine," Valdez replied sarcastically. "But inelegant and crude. Now watch me."

Valdez snapped his fingers and his daughter handed back the wristband which he clicked into place. A second later there was a blinding crack of light. The head of the dummy Walker had ignited disappeared in a lightning flash. Valdez swung his hand around towards a row of dummies mounted in a line. Two holes were drilled where a real man's eyes would have been, the next one exploded in a gout of flame, the third was decapitated by a fiery sword of light, and the fourth simply disappeared into smoldering ashes.

Valdez swung around, and before anyone could react, the Air Corps insignia on Walker's hat congealed into a flowing puddle of fire. The frightened tailgunner whipped off the flaming headgear.

"That is the power of the Essence," Valdez said coldly. "Think of your body as a sponge drawing in Essence, expelling it as energy as you squeeze, and then refilling. It is the crystal that focuses my power. I send the power of the Essence through it—to narrow it, to magnify it, and then to use it. But to do that I must first learn to control it. Those who have the gift to use the Essence can use it at any time, but it usually is dispersed and can only be projected short distances. Only with the crystals can we focus it, send it to distant targets, and turn it into a finely balanced weapon or tool.

"Without the ability to calmly control the Essence, you will never receive a crystal of attacking power. We know you have the innate ability to focus your Essence for attack. That is why you men have been chosen to learn under me. Attack and defense all of you will learn, but some of you will also reveal your powers in additional ways; some for farseeing, some for healing, creating, or any of several other skills. But for now you will be trained as warriors.

"A moment of anger, even a careless thought, and you could do damage to yourself, or worse yet, to someone innocent. You must learn to be able to turn the Essence on and off as it flows through you.

"You must learn to use the Essence for defense before anything else. Lord Allic has given you defensive crystals which you should all be practicing with."

Valdez walked over to the group and approached Walker, who looked warily at him.

He grabbed Walker's left wrist and held it up so that the crystal in the wristband was before Walker's eyes.

"Why didn't you use this when I attacked you?" Valdez snapped.

"Well, ah, you see . . ."

"No excuse . . . There is no excuse if you're dead. We've been over this many times. You must learn to divert part of your thoughts to your defensive crystals even while attacking your foe. Visualize a sphere around you that lets nothing in. A blast will bounce off a good shield and save your life."

Valdez suddenly brought his hand up as if to strike Walker and the lanky tailgunner crouched down low and brought his left hand up. A dull crackling hum filled the air as what appeared to be a protective sphere materialized around Walker.

"Good, very good," Valdez replied. "You must train your instincts to focus your Essence into the crystal of defense. It should be done in a blinding flash, without thought, but by instinct alone. Remember that pointing your left hand towards the blow will focus the energy of your shielding to better deflect or absorb a strike from that direction.

"If you wish to live long enough on Haven to take advantage of the longevity that the Essence provides, you better learn this quickly. The sorcerers you face might have five hundred years of training, and they'll not excuse your slowness and retire with apologies until you are ready. They'll leave you dead.

"Another thing you must remember. If your opponent diverts more of his strength to the attack, you must equal that energy with your defense. But know that once that happens, if he is stronger or more skillful than you, you're dead."

Valdez turned and walked back to the dais. "Now you remember our lesson on bows, don't you?"

The men mumbled an affirmative.

"Good." Valdez reached down to a low platform to one side of the dais and stood back up again, a heavy longbow in his hands. With a single fluid motion he snapped an arrow out of the quiver, nocked it, and then pulled the bow to full draw and pointed it straight at Walker's chest, whose shielding went up to maximum power.

"Now watch, damn you," Valdez roared. Turning, he pointed the bow at the last dummy in the line. A tiny defensive crystal hung around the dummy's neck. With the bow still drawn, Valdez stared at the necklace, and a defensive shimmer developed around it. He released the arrow.

The arrow streaked to its target and with a thunderclap explosion merged with the glowing defensive light.

Fragments of the dummy arched into the air, and the courtyard walls reverberated with a roar like the burst from a flak shell. As the smoke cleared, the men gaped in amazement at the six-foot-wide crater where the dummy had stood.

"Damn you, why did you turn on your defensive shield when I pointed the arrow at you?" Valdez roared.

"Seemed like the right thing to do. Anyhow, I figured you wouldn't shoot."

"Figured, so you *figured*, eh? Suppose I was a turncoat, a traitor? If I'd fired that arrow I would have killed you and half the men sitting around you—that would have been damn good service for one of Allic's enemies.

"Remember, your shield will turn an ordinary arrow, except perhaps for one fired at very close range. But damn it, there is one sure way for an ordinary man to kill a sorcerer, and that's to possess an arrow tipped with a sliver from the red crystal of fire. When a red crystal hits a shield, it's converted to the pure energy of the Essence. The bigger the crystal, the bigger the blast. A catapult bolt tipped by a large enough crystal can blast down an entire wall if it is shielded. They're hard to forge and facet, but in any flight of arrows, always assume there's one of them coming in. You can spot it by its red glow, and through concentration you should be able to sense it even before you see it. Remember that!

"Some of you might be bodyguards to Allic and it will be your job to always watch for a red-tipped arrow. You'll only have a couple of seconds to react and blast it down, but react quickly, by the gods, or your lord and you are dead. It's one of the favorite tools of an assassin.

"I keep hammering and hammering that all of you must learn the art of concentration. You must be able to react in a second and come to full defense while preparing your offense, and at the same time be able to sense the presence or approach of a red crystal. I look at all of you here now, and only hope that you'll be alive a year from now."

Valdez fell silent for a moment and they looked at one another uneasily.

"Enough. There are more practice dummies on the other side of the courtyard, and for the rest of the morning I want all of you to practice with projection of the force to create fire. I want control, damn it! And I want focus. A good sorcerer, even without a crystal to focus his energy, should be able to ignite a human size target at thirty paces. Now move it!"

As the men assumed their practice positions, Mark could only feel anxiety. Walker and a number of the Japanese soldiers made it look so easy. But damn it, every time he tried to focus his power he found himself breaking into a cold sweat.

As if to add insult to injury, Walker called for everyone's attention.

"Hey, watch this!"

He turned his back to a target dummy and projected an over-the-shoulder shot at his straw opponent. Valdez was all over him in an instant, but Mark decided not to intervene. He was having enough trouble just trying to work up enough energy to equal a Zippo lighter.

Back in the real world he never had any real anxieties about command. He was a damn good pilot, one of the best, and the men wanted to fly for him, believing that he had "the luck"—that indefinable ability to always bring a crew back safely.

The luck, he thought sadly. Well, that ended on a hillside back in China. Was he finished now in this new world? He couldn't control this thing called Essence for attack, while all around him his gunners and the Japanese soldiers were proving their superiority. Would he be nothing but a fifth wheel here, his ability to control the respect of his men gradually drifting away as a new leader emerged, for a new world?

He looked over at Lieutenant Younger. As if Younger

were reading his thoughts, his copilot snapped out a narrow focused beam at his target, then smiled at him with a sarcastic grin, as if challenging Mark to do better. Younger turned away from him and started to speak softly to Sergeant Giorgini and the two of them laughed.

"Captain Phillips."

It was Varma, the dwarf companion and jester to Allic, who had come up to stand by Mark's side.

"How goes your training?" Varma asked in a friendly voice.

Mark was tempted to bark a sarcastic reply but realized that Varma was only trying to be friendly. He liked the jester. Some of the men thought his strange appearance amusing, but Mark had already noticed that Varma possessed a brilliant mind, and beyond all the jokes and foolish rhyming he was one of Allic's most trusted advisors.

"Oh, quite well," Mark replied quickly.

Varma looked up and smiled at him. "But of course. Well, not to worry about it, that's what I say. Anyhow, my Lord Allic requests the presence of you and Captain Ikawa, so let us go." And turning, Varma scurried over to Ikawa's side.

With a sigh of relief Mark left the firing line and followed Varma. He could not help but notice that Younger and Giorgini followed him with their gaze and continued their quiet conversation.

There would be problems with them, he was sure of that now. But being without their ability, how could he ever respond?

"So how goes the training?"

Damn, everybody has to ask the same question, Mark thought.

"My lord Allic, your Valdez is a good trainer," Ikawa replied.

"Please, when there is no one else present, we can drop the 'my lord' routine," Allic said, a smile lighting his features. "It gets tiresome after a while. Here, have a drink."

He pointed for the two soldiers to sit by his side and handed them a couple of goblets.

"A little early for that, isn't it, my lord?" Varma inquired.

Allic gave his jester a silencing stare. "I've lived my first thousand years without too much of a problem, but apparently I still can't have a friendly drink in the morning without some lackey interfering."

"Just doing my job," Varma said.

"Then, do your job and bring Hort in here, and stop nagging me. I'm a demigod, damn it, and I should be able to take a drink without some fool dwarf interfering!"

With his hands raised in a mock display of terror, Varma backed out of the room, bowing low.

"Some people think that being the son of a god has all the advantages," Allic said, looking into his wine cup, "but let me tell you, gentlemen, it can be a downright nuisance at times. They're always checking up on you and passing down some admonishment."

Mark gave a sidelong look of amazement to Ikawa. He still wasn't used to the idea of a flesh and blood man calling himself the son of a god. There were times when he thought all of these people were insane blasphemers. But he realized it was best not to challenge such a thing here. Demigod or not, this man had saved him, and he was obviously a prince of great power. If Allic wanted to call himself a demigod, let him

The Japanese, with their god-emperor, took such things as a matter of course. He'd have to make sure that Goldberg, who was Jewish, and Smithie, who had a strong streak of the fundamentalist, were kept under control. The last thing Mark needed was a damned religious debate.

Allic drained his cup and tossed it on the table. "There, that's better. Now, to business." He rose and went to the door.

"Bring him in, Varma!"

The door swung open and both Ikawa and Mark rose to their feet. In an instant Ikawa's defensive shield was up, glowing softly in the darkened room.

Bending low at the waist, a towering form cleared the doorway, then straightened to its full three meter height. Its eyes were like two glowing coals; its face a bizarre and chilling caricature of a blood-red skull that had been covered with scorched parchment. The creature stood in the doorway surveying the three before him and extended its arms to reveal two batlike wings that glowed with a faint phosphorescence and seemed to fill half the room. Seeing Allic it bowed low, its head coming down to eye level.

Allic looked over at Ikawa and Mark and smiled.

"No need for the defense, Ikawa. Hort is harmless."

"But that's a demon," Ikawa blurted.

"Sure it's a demon, but it's well trained. Why, he's even

housebroken," Varma piped in as he planted a swift kick on Hort's shin. The demon grunted and pushed Varma away with a gentle backhanded swing.

"I've decided to assign him as a guardian to your households. It will give a certain prestige, and protection, to you and your men. And while acting as a protector, he can also teach you the lore and customs of his race," Allic said.

"But I thought demons were the enemy." Mark was clearly puzzled.

"Tell him, Hort," Allic replied.

"I am in service to my lord Allic," Hort said with a low grating voice. "Allic rescued me from certain death when he journeyed to my dimension years ago, and thus I returned with him to Haven, for I pledged him blood debt of a thousand years in repayment. Even demons must keep their word," he finished with a low chuckle.

"Don't worry," Allic said, noticing the offworlders' anxiety. "I have half a hundred like him in my service. Some are willing, such as Hort; others are prisoners, such as Chaka. All of them take the oath. Occasionally one will break his pledge—but tell them, Hort, what happens to an oath breaker."

Hort growled. "Never would Hort do such a thing, Lord Allic. For if I did, you would either hunt me down or burn our pact, causing my death and everlasting damnation."

"If done correctly," Varma interjected, "Allic could make the burning last for years, keeping Hort in constant agony. I like the slower way myself."

"You would, little one," Hort said coldly, then turned to Mark and Ikawa. "If you are my new lords, know that I, Hort, slayer of forty-three of my foes, will serve you for the remaining six hundred and twenty years of my service."

Mark was at a loss for words. It wasn't every day that someone offered you your own personal demon to be your household guard.

"Remember, Hort," Allic commanded, "these two are outlanders. I expect you to teach them well about your people and how to survive against them. But don't trifle with them. They are sorcerers, and I suspect their power will soon be that of masters."

"But of course," Hort replied, bowing low again so that his wings fluttered and covered them with a scent that was not the most pleasant.

Turning, the demon lumbered out of the room, while

Varma followed him, imitating the demon's movements in an incredibly accurate mime, causing the other three to chuckle.

Allic turned to Ikawa. "I can feel enormous turmoil within you. What's wrong?"

"I can learn to deal with Hort," Ikawa said slowly, "but it's just that he looks so damn reptilian."

"Why would that bother you?"

Ikawa hesitated. "It's just that I've had this terrible fear of snakes since I was a child, and Hort made me think of them. I'll get use to him, my lord, it will just take some time."

"That's why I gave him to you. I want you to be familiar with demons, and through Hort you can learn their ways and how to control them. He's loyal, if only through fear of me and the power of his oath. However, he'll test both of you, seeing just how far he can go. Learning to control him is a part of your training. And speaking of your training, tell me, Mark, how goes yours."

There was a moment of embarrassed silence.

"I don't seem to have the ability," Mark said sadly. "My men, and Ikawa's soldiers too, are out there right now with their beams of light and I can barely work up a flicker. I just don't know."

Allic smiled at him. "It comes at different times and speeds. I can see into you, Mark Phillips, and know that you, like your comrades, can use the Essence of power. Walker has his control because he learned it as a warrior back in your world. Ikawa and his men were warriors similar to Walker, and thus they have the ability to fight as well. But remember that the Essence in a master sorcerer can manifest in several different ways. Great masters can control the Essence in half a dozen ways or more. Perhaps you will never control the blast from the offensive crystal that destroys an enemy. There are other skills."

"Such as flying?" Mark asked. "I've seen you and some of your sorcerers flying, and yet none of us can get an inch off the ground."

Ikawa nodded. "To fly like the birds," he said, his voice full of hope, "that would truly be a mastery of power. Among my own people there are Zen masters who, it is said, through long years of practice have mastered the ability to float in the air. Since coming here, that has been my dream. I have spent countless hours alone in my room trying and trying, but with no success."

Mark smiled at Ikawa. So the two of them had been up at night trying the same damned thing.

"It just takes the proper motivation," Allic replied. "Just the proper motivation, that's all."

"Well, how in hell are we to find this motivation? Are you saying I need some Dale Carnegie course to fly? Damn it," —Mark's frustration started to boil over—"I'm useless on the ground. I want to get back in the air where I belong."

He was already cursing himself for a fool even as he spoke, for he was letting his frustration show. Never show frustration to a commander, Mark realized, or he'll doubt your ability to command in turn.

But Allic only shook his head and laughed.

"Good, good. If you want it, then don't worry, the motivation will be found soon enough."

Allic drained off another goblet and smacked his lips in appreciation. "Good stuff, this pawinda. Laid it up myself nearly eighty years ago, but the two of you don't strike me as connoisseurs of the finer things. You're men of action, and I like that. Life here, with training all the time, must be getting a little boring for you."

Mark felt he had said enough already and remained silent. They had been locked away for three tendays of Haven time. There was a whole world out there and he wanted to see it.

"How about a little mounted patrol this afternoon?" Allic ventured with a smile.

"Excellent!" Ikawa replied. "I've been waiting to try one of your mounts."

"Ride?" Mark inquired. *Oh no,* he thought nervously, *not another crisis.*

He knew Ikawa as a Japanese officer took riding as a matter of course. But those things weren't even horses. The creatures called Tals looked more like one-ton Dobermans with leonine fangs.

"Sure," Mark said, gritting his teeth, "sounds just great."

"Fine," Allic said, his face alight with a mischievous grin. "After lunch, have Valdez direct all of you down to the stables. My people have chosen suitable mounts for you. I'll meet you at the east gate about half a turning after that."

Mark had long ago roughly calculated that a turning, or a bell, was almost an hour on his old watch. So half a turning...

Allic stood up as if to signal that the audience was ended,

and escorted Ikawa and Mark to the doorway.

"By the way, Varma reminded me that I've neglected one important part of your comfort." He broke into a broad grin.

"Oh, we're quite comfortable," Mark replied politely.

"No, no, if you men are anything like the people of Haven, there is one important detail."

"I can't imagine what," Ikawa replied. "The training is the best, and for creature comforts our surroundings are magnificent."

"Not all of them," Allic said. "Varma, get in here—I know you're listening on the other side of that door!"

The door swung open and the dwarf stepped in. "Only awaiting your command, my lord."

"Gorm meat. You're eavesdropping again."

"I'm innocent, my lord, honest."

"Enough. Do you think you can arrange a little diversion this evening for our new friends?"

"Of course, of course." Varma looked mischievously at Ikawa and Mark. "What will it be, gentlemen, women or young men?"

"What?" Mark roared.

"Well," Varma replied, "I've heard some conversations between your men. Always sex, sex, sex. I don't know what you people do back on your Earth, but on Haven sex is just another form of casual fun. Everybody does it until they make a life pledge to a single partner. And even then..." The dwarf chuckled and looked over at Allic, who roared in appreciation.

"Dozens of women are dying to spend the night with you outlanders," Varma continued. "They think you might know a new trick or two. But Allic here said to wait until you'd all settled in. So what will it be, gentlemen? Women, or perhaps young men, or both?"

"Are you calling me a..."

Ikawa pushed in front of Mark.

"Ah—why don't you just ask some of the girls to stop by tonight," Ikawa said smoothly. He grabbed Mark and hustled him out the door.

"Just one woman for each man, then?" Varma asked as they hurried down the hall.

"More than enough." Ikawa kept a hand on Mark's shoulder until they had turned into a side corridor.

"Did I say something wrong?" Varma asked, looking at

Allic. But his master was bent double with laughter as the two outlanders disappeared from view.

"That guy," Mark began, "that guy was calling me . . ."

"Different people, different customs." Ikawa tried to suppress a laugh. "Don't insult our hosts. They'll catch on to our preferences soon enough."

"Yeah, but I never thought—"

"Don't worry about it," Ikawa said. "We'll tell the men about the party later. We want their minds on the patrol this afternoon."

"Yeah, but . . ." Then his thoughts turned back to the patrol. Damn, one-ton dogs with foot-long fangs—and why did they have to look like Dobermans? *God, give me strength,* Mark groaned inwardly.

The rest of the outlanders were listening to a lecture from Pina who stood in front of a wooden apparatus that held the largest crystal any of them had ever seen.

That sucker must be at least the size of a basketball, thought Kochanski.

Pina stopped suddenly in the middle of a statement. He nodded as if acknowledging something, and addressed the Japanese and Americans who were listening to his lecture. "Allic has just informed me that after talking to Mark and Ikawa he has decided that you will all go on patrol this afternoon. The fresh air and a change from boring classes should be well received, heh?"

A satisfied murmur answered him.

He smiled and continued, "Now, however, I want to finish my explanation of how our crystal cannon or wall crystals work. They are far too large to be moved about comfortably by an individual and require a much more elaborate aiming device since we use a tighter beam to insure longer range. They are capable of holding a far greater charge than your wrist crystals, so you can pour more and more energy into it, aim, flip the aperture, and fire a blast over a hundred times more powerful then a standard shot.

"Questions? Yes, Kochanski."

"This is all very impressive, but limited in many aspects, including line of sight. If we were to introduce gunpowder you would have the advantage of mortars and rockets in addition to rapid-firing machine guns. Don't you think that would revolutionize warfare around here?"

Pina shook his head and murmured something to Valdez

who walked away. Pina continued, "This has been discussed since your arrival and we have decided to delay any development for a while. First, as a sorcerer you never have to worry about running out of ammunition, you just draw in more Essence. Second, your weapons are very finely machined. We can't match such precision without a major expenditure of resources, and we're not sure it's worth it."

"You're kidding."

Valdez had returned with one of the Americans' .45s and handed the pistol to Kochanski.

"Please stand and take a few shots at one of the practice dummies."

Kochanski looked at his companions and shrugged. He walked out a few steps and turned to face the targets. A quick check to insure there was a round in the chamber, and he flicked the safety off, aimed, and fired.

The shot kicked up dust beside the target and Kochanski lined up again, trying to correct his aim.

All the others were watching Pina who had moved in back of him and whose eyes suddenly glowed as Kochanski squeezed the trigger for his second shot.

Nothing happened. Puzzled, Kochanski cocked the hammer back and tried again. Nothing.

Pina then resumed his lecture to a captivated audience. "Finally we decided that all an opposing sorcerer has to do is use a little creativity and change the chemical structure of the explosive to render it totally useless. Mind you, we think it might win a battle or two before it is countered, but we haven't decided yet whether it's worth a long term investment."

Kochanski resumed his seat, feeling like an ignorant child.

"Any more questions?"

Saito raised his hand. "Here, sir. The patrol we're supposed to go on this afternoon made me think of it. Just what will our duties be when we finish training?"

"Well, you never really finish training. I'm seven hundred forty-three years old and I still need improvement in a number of areas. A lot of it is simple. Anger and adrenaline will give any sorcerer enough energy to blast someone else; just as fear and self-preservation will enable your shield to absorb or deflect almost anything as long as your will and strength hold. The rest of your talents can be developed in time. For now, you are warriors.

"Your responsibilities will be guard duty, patrols, garrison duties, caravan escort, and other special assignments. Of course you will continue to develop your skills throughout. You have much to learn."

"I know we're sworn to Allic and all that, but do we get any kind of pay for our services?" Younger asked.

Pina looked at him intently. "You are already lodged in an estate where you have all your food and drink, servants, and clothing provided. But yes, Allic has you listed as drawing pay with the rank of acolyte. If you want cash, simply go to accounting. Most of us just use our communication crystals. If you wish to buy something you call in the details and accounting takes care of the payment. It's all very simple."

Chapter 7

Lieutenant Mokaoto fought for his crust of bread, kicking the larger slave in the mouth and retreating to the full distance of his chains. With a roar the other man bounced up and tried to reach Mokaoto, earning another crippling blow to the throat.

Able to eat in momentary peace, Mokaoto choked down his food. He knew he was barely hanging on to his sanity. Weeks of living in these pits had tried his reason to the utmost. The room seemed to stretch on forever in the dim light, and scores of others were chained as he was, living in their own filth.

It was Ikawa who had brought him to this, Ikawa the traitor. Without realizing it, Mokaoto began to scream his hatred and frustration, his cries joining the moans and shouts of all the others.

And his body began to glow as the Essence responded to the draw of his subconscious needs.

Sarnak, who stood unobserved in the shadows, left the stench of the dungeon and walked back out into the morning air. With a smile he turned to his pit master. "You say he's been showing the Essence ever since his arrival?"

"Yes, my lord. It is still weak, but every day it grows. I would have thought by now that it would have reached its limit. If he ever realizes that he could use it as a weapon he would be dangerous. He's almost insane with rage, a danger to us all."

"Leave me. You have done well to break him so quickly."

As he continued to walk the battlements in contemplation Sarnak motioned to Ralnath. "I see a use for Wika at last. You will go to him and tell him I planned to execute him, but that you begged me to give him another chance."

Ralnath nodded as Sarnak continued, "I need this outlander developed and trained quickly and Wika will have the responsibility. Tell him that you judge that hatred will temper the outlander's metal even more quickly. If Wika can force him to pass through the trials in three tendays I will spare his parents and siblings. Otherwise their heads will join those of his wife and children."

"You make the judgment as to Wika's fitness for this, Ralnath."

Ralnath smiled in appreciation of the plan, and asked, "His crystals, my lord?"

"By all means return Wika's crystals to him. But you will make sure that both his offensive and defensive crystals are secretly flawed."

"Understood, my lord."

"And one more thing."

"My lord."

"The offworlder will need to focus his initial hatred. When you feel the time is right be sure that he believes that his imprisonment is Wika's fault, and that I was not even aware of how he was taken, for Wika kept it a secret."

Smiling, Ralnath withdrew, hoping that Sarnak's anger over the previous failure was no longer directed at him, and that Wika alone would pay the full price.

The Americans and Japanese stood uneasily in front of the stables.

"You must clear your minds of all fears," Valdez said quietly. "These Tals are from Jartan's private breed, and the family line has served his house for over five thousand years. The Tals are proud of their heritage and would die before harming any of Allic's warriors. But they have complete contempt for any coward that sits upon their back, so show some courage."

Cursing a steady streak under his breath, Kochanski held himself under rigid control as a Tal was brought before each of the outlanders.

Christ, what a monster, he thought, and was stunned when a thought was projected into his mind.

I am Nar-Talon, of Dar-tal's line. Very strong, good fighter.

"Uh, I'm Stan Kochanski, U. S. Army Air Corps," Kochanski responded, and the others looked around at him as if he was crazy.

"Look guys, the thing talked to me," Kochanski said defensively. "Honest!"

"Ah, bullshit," Goldberg replied even as a trainer brought one of the Tals up to his side.

"Hey, what was that? Who the hell was talking?" Goldberg cried, stepping back.

"Batha was merely introducing himself," the trainer replied, looking at Goldberg as if he were an ignorant peasant without any manners.

"What?"

"Tals are intelligent creatures," Valdez said in an exasperated tone. "I told you that before we came down here, but you laughed at me."

"But he spoke in my mind!" Goldberg looked warily at the Tal next to him.

"Precisely," Valdez replied, as if to a group of idiots. "You don't just ride a Tal, you become a battle partner with him. He's an extra set of eyes, and though limited, an extra brain that can help make decisions in the heat of combat. Tals can speak telepathically with whomever they please. Treat them with respect and affection and they'll be loyal until death. In the months to come each of the Tals will choose the man it prefers, and then you'll be a battle team."

"You mean they'll pick one of us as a partner?" Kochanski asked.

"Yes," Valdez said wearily. "You don't want to be atop a Tal that doesn't like you. They want a partner they can trust."

"I'd hate to be on the wrong side of one," Goldberg responded.

"Aye, their mouth is a mean one, to be sure. Why, 'e can rip a head off with a single bite," a stable hand said, affectionately stroking a beast on its muzzle.

Private Matsumoto stepped forward from the assembly and approached the Tal directly in front of him. He rubbed the Tal's flank and to the surprise of everyone placed his arms around its neck and gave it a hug.

"I had a dog back home," Matsumoto said softly. "How I've missed him. And now I have a friend again."

The trainers, who obviously held the same affection for the beasts, smiled approvingly.

Without another word Matsumoto vaulted into the saddle and leaned forward, patting the Tal on the shoulder.

"His name is Onta-Talon," Matsumoto said happily, "and he claims he can outrun all the others in this pack. So let's see!"

With a whoop of delight Matsumoto hung on as Onta broke into a run and charged out of the stable. The other Tals, having heard the challenge, approached the men with loud growls and short jumping movements, like oversized puppies eager to play. Their growls echoed and roared, and their leaps shook the stable.

"Well, let's go, Nar-Talon, or whatever your name is!" Kochanski cried as he grabbed hold of the pommel and swung himself into the saddle. The others, struggling both with their courage and the Tals, finally gained their saddles as well.

Kochanski grabbed hold of his peaked flying cap and waved it in the air.

"Hi-ho, Silver, away!" Kochanski roared as he galloped out of the stables in hot pursuit of Matsumoto, with the rest of the pack thundering behind him.

"Damn fools," Valdez mumbled, shaking his head.

"My lady, a messenger hawk has returned to the aviary."

Patrice turned from the window and looked at the young witch standing before her.

"Let it in, then leave us."

Bowing low the girl backed to the door and held it open. A small hawk fluttered into the room and landed on the windowsill beside Patrice.

It was such a beautiful creature, she thought, extending her hand to lightly stroke its breast. It was a special breed, a secret known only to herself and a handful of servants in the court. Not even her uncle Jartan knew of this little sideline of interest that she had developed.

Bending low she fixed the creature with her gaze and stared into its unblinking eyes.

If anyone had been in the room they would have seen a light shimmer from her hand encircle the bird, so that its bright red wings and dark orange body seemed to glow with fire. For several minutes she held it with her gaze, then smiling, turned away.

"So my impetuous cousin thinks his new allies can be safely let out of the castle. Now we can begin to play the game. He has too many of them already, and I think it's time the wealth was shared."

"Magnificent, simply magnificent."

Mark brought his Tal alongside Ikawa's and eased into a slow canter.

"Did you say something?"

"It's just I never could have imagined anything as beautiful, as stunning as this," Ikawa replied. "I thought Fuji in the springtime, still snowcapped, with the cherry blossoms around it, was paradise. But this . . ."

Mark leaned back, relaxing a little bit after the hard gallop of the last half hour.

Comfortable ride now, sire, stay slow?

He still wasn't used to a voice in his mind. The Tal turned its head and looked back at him with an appraising gaze.

"Ah, yes, that's fine, Gukha-Tal," Mark said out loud.

The Tal fell into an easy stride. Mark realized that the creature undoubtedly knew his anxiety and was responding by giving the gentlest ride possible. He leaned over and patted its flank. The creature growled softly, like a playful dog.

The wild beauty of Allic's realm spread itself around them. A high ridgeline, which they had been climbing for the last half hour, dominated the view in front. Turning in his saddle, Mark looked back down onto the open, fertile plain. Derusa trees dotted the countryside from horizon to horizon like great elms, their spreads a hundred or more feet across, and covered with blossoms. Deep red was predominant, but the colors shifted in some groves from pale pink through burgundy. The warm air was awash with a heady scent like lavender and new mown hay.

The fields were laid out checkerboard fashion. The crops appeared to be primarily grain, but here and there an ancient well-ordered vineyard was evident, the arbors heavy with fruit. There was some mechanization in the form of reaping machines pulled by oxlike creatures and occasional water- or wind-powered mills, where wagon loads of grain were waiting to be ground and logs were ready to be cut. In all of this there was a sense of organization and pride in labor that was well done. In many ways it reminded Mark of old Currier and Ives prints of American farms in a simpler and happier age.

They passed through small, well kept villages of white-washed houses made of masonry and split timber, peaked with brilliant tile roofs that more often than not were laid into multicolored designs of winged birds or swirling geometric patterns. The houses, large and comfortable looking, were decorated with intricate wood carvings depicting pastoral scenes.

The farm holders and villagers were a healthy lot, not at all Mark's image of medieval peasants. The men wore loose fitting trousers, open shirts, and broad-brimmed straw hats. The women who worked in the fields wore trousers as well, while those in the villages were dressed in bright skirts embroidered with arabesques. Almost all the women wore loose peasant blouses pulled in with a small waist cincture or corset.

Their eyes were bright and they called out cheery greetings to Allic, who returned their cries with a happy wave. He stopped occasionally to inquire about the crops or accept a beaker of wine, and Mark could not help but notice Allic's easy relationship with his people. There was a note of deference, to be sure, but it was the deference of a proud people who respected their leader and expected respect in return. No bowing and scraping: these people were yeomen, not serfs.

The outlanders were a source of curiosity, and when walking their Tals, a number of shouting, laughing children would run by their side. From more than one second floor window a young woman, and sometimes several, would lean out in their low-cut blouses and shout suggestive offers.

The Americans responded in typical fashion, and by the time they left a village behind, the children were already imitating their wolf whistles or shouting outlander slang.

Soon they had left the last village behind, as the trail led into the forest. It seemed they rode through a tunnel of green and sun-soaked red, the derusa trees creating a canopied tunnel that appeared to stretch forever. The path beneath their feet was strewn with fallen blossoms. The outlanders rode as if in a trance, soaking in every detail.

The forest was alive with great flocks of small birds with golden wings and lavender bodies that wheeled and darted around them, chirping rhythmically in an ever-varying song.

Many of the nobles in town kept a dozen or more of the birds as pets, since each one would respond to a call from the other by singing on a different note so that a group of them would weave an ever-varied tone poem. Its effect was hypnotic when just a dozen were singing, but out in the wild the gentle calling of hundreds seemed a symphony of changing harmonics.

As they emerged from the forest onto the high crest of the ridgeline, more than one of the riders looked back longingly at the magic they had just left behind.

But the view that now confronted them was even more breathtaking.

As far as the eye could see, the countryside was alight with the shimmering red-greens of the forest, checkered with the neatly arranged fields, orchards, and vineyards of Allic's people. Far away to the south and west, as the countryside swept downward, they could almost see where areas of cultivation reached the edge of the escarpment, which dropped away for thousands of feet down to the open savannah of the distant horizon. Far to the east was another ridgeline which marked the edge of Sarnak's realm, the distant mountains a shimmering dark blue line against the afternoon sky. Looking down and to the north, they could see the city of Landra, its great temples, palaces, and manor houses laid out along both sides of the river, all of which was surrounded by the shimmering limestone walls.

"Not a bad looking fiefdom, is it?" Allic asked, his pride obvious.

"I never thought I would see anything more beautiful than my homeland in the spring," Ikawa replied softly. "But now I have; it will hurt beyond measure when finally I leave this place."

"Let's not talk of leaving now," Allic said. "You still owe service to me, and I brought you here because I wanted to show you something. Please dismount."

Following Allic's lead, the Americans and Japanese dismounted, talking excitedly of the wonders they had seen.

"Would you men come with me," Allic called. "Don't worry about your mounts, they can take care of themselves."

The men fell in behind Allic, following him up a narrow, winding path that cut between a series of rounded boulders.

"Ah, the rest of you can head back to the castle," Allic said, gesturing to Pina and the dozen or so sorcerers who had accompanied the party. "Your mounts will find their own way back."

Without comment Pina nodded to his lord, a smile lighting his face. Effortlessly the dozen rose into the air, hovered for a moment, then with a wide sweeping turn they darted over the edge of the ridge and swooped away, disappearing from view.

"Damn," Mark mumbled, wishing that he could follow them. He started to turn his thoughts inward, ready to try again for the hundredth time, but Allic's command interrupted him.

"This way, all of you. We're almost there."

The path weaved up the ridge to end suddenly at the edge of a cliff. Allic stopped at the precipice. "Gather round, gather round, all of you."

The men came up to his side, forming a half circle around him, and stopped.

Ikawa came up to the very end of the trail and felt his heart climb into his throat. They were standing on the edge of a sheer cliff, thousands of feet above the wooded valley below.

The men were silent. Some went to the edge and looked down, but most stood several feet back.

"Now, you're probably wondering why I've brought you to this spot," Allic began. A faint shimmer encompassed him, and he rose a dozen feet into the air. "Gentlemen, I was talking with your commanders today about motivation."

Ikawa and Mark looked at each other, trying to recall the context of the conversation.

The shimmer around Allic grew in intensity. He held up one hand. "Gentlemen, we're here for a little motivation," he said, barely suppressing a laugh. "It's time for flying lesson number one!"

A beam of light shot out from Allic's hand, slamming into the rock directly behind the party. With a shattering roar the ground collapsed beneath their feet.

"Shit!" Mark screamed as the ground fell away beneath him. He was tumbling in space, falling to certain death. The wind rushed past him, plucking at his clothes, shrieking in his ears. He looked down to the ground rushing up. No, not yet. Not yet, damn it!

"No!" Mark held up his hands, willing the ground away to keep it from smashing his body. "No, goddamn it! No!"

Suddenly the ground was dropping away, the horizon rolling up before him, and the terrifying sense of falling had stopped.

"What the hell?" He was flying!

"I'm flying!" Mark screamed. His arms were straight ahead, the air screaming past him, while the ground rushed by several hundred feet below. He extended his arms out to either side, and looked off to his left.

The earth wheeled beneath his feet and he banked into a turn.

"I can fly!" Mark felt exalted. This was flying—flying with the wind in your face and no hulk of steel around you, no stench of gasoline and thunder of engines. He looked straight up and there above him several men were drifting through the air, one of them doing a series of low, lazy rolls.

He wished to be with them and even as the wish formed, he arched upwards. So that's how, Mark realized. *Think it or look at it, and the Essence responds.*

He soared towards the men above him and recognized Kochanski and Walker, both roaring with delight.

Most of the Japanese still were terrified, drifting wobbly in the air. But the Americans knew this element—it was their love. Reaching the height of his two comrades, Mark continued straight up, noticing that the climb had cut his speed to practically nothing. He arched his back over in a fair imitation of a loop and swooped back down, coming in on Walker's tail.

"Hey, tailgunner," Mark screamed, "somebody's on your ass."

"Jesus, Captain," Walker cried, tears of laughter clouding his eyes, "we're flying . . . Damn it, we're flying like goddamn Superman!"

One by one the Americans sought out their comrades in the sky, as if the old instinct of flying together in a B-29 still held form here, an unimaginable distance away.

"All right, *Dragon Fire*," Mark cried, as Smithie, the waist gunner, finally came into the formation.

A form snapped past them overhead then turned back and drew up alongside. It was Allic.

For a moment Mark forgot himself. "You madman," he cried, "you scared the shit out of us!"

"Didn't I tell you this morning," Allic replied, ignoring the insult, "that all you needed was a little motivation and you'd be flying? So I gave you the motivation the same way a hawk teaches her young."

"Yeah, fly or die."

"Precisely. Why are you complaining? It worked, didn't it?"

"Damn near shit my pants," Kochanski said.

"Bet some of those Japs did shit their pants." Giorgini chuckled.

Most of the Japanese were flailing around below them, bobbing this way and that.

"And suppose we didn't fly?" Mark asked. "We'd be dead."

"I wouldn't waste such a good investment," Allic replied. "Look over there." He pointed, then dove towards the cliff where Pina and his companions were hovering.

Several of the sorcerers were carrying terrified Japanese soldiers, while Pina and a couple of others flew slowly alongside the weakest flyers, ready to intervene if something went wrong.

"Say, let's buzz some Japs!" Giorgini started to break formation.

"Knock it off," Mark swung in front of Giorgini. "We got enough problems as is without rubbing this in to them. You want to start a fight or something?"

"Yeah, why not?" Giorgini was defiant. "They're Japs."

"They're allies of Allic, the same way we are," Mark roared. He could feel a terrible rage building, and for the first time created a noticeable aura around himself.

"Get back in formation," he said, "and that's an order!"

Giorgini looked at him for a moment, then silently lifted back up and swung in beside Younger. Circling over the cliff they saw Allic swing in beneath them, motioning for the group to re-form.

Effortlessly the Americans landed as a group on the precipice. The Japanese staggered in after them.

Ikawa suddenly rose into view. With a dash of bravado he attempted to roll as he came in for a landing, but his timing was a bit off and he landed sideways and collapsed on his backside.

Mark came over and gave him a hand, pulling him back to his feet.

"Not bad for your first solo," Mark said quickly, before any of his men could make a sarcastic remark. He could understand Giorgini's comments earlier: the temptation had existed for him as well. But if he ever let it show, the alliance would collapse in seconds.

"Most exhilarating," Ikawa said evenly, but Mark could see that his eyes were wide with fear. Only his iron control kept him from shaking like a leaf. Mark felt a wave of understanding: they both had to put on a show, to act fearless. He clapped Ikawa on the back.

"You should have seen my first landing back in flight school," Mark said, lying in what he hoped was a convincing manner. "You did okay."

Ikawa looked into his eyes for a moment, then smiled back.

"So, flying lesson number one is over," Allic said smoothly, as the last of his sorcerers came in bearing Takeo, the only one who had not managed to fly.

"You'll need practice, lots of practice, to learn complete control," he continued. "Now it's time to head back to the castle. Are there any here who would prefer to fly? The Tals know their own way back, so don't worry about your mounts."

In an instant several of the Americans leaped into the air shouting like children kept too long from recess.

Mark looked over to where the Japanese who had failed to fly stood alone. Allic went to his side, and producing a wine sack, he offered the man a drink.

"Some do not have the gift," Allic said soothingly. "Others will learn it as time passes. Do not be ashamed of your fear."

Takeo, humiliated, refused the wine and looked at the rest of the group. Most of the Americans, except for Mark and Kochanski, gazed at him with mocking contempt. And a fair number of the Japanese, who only moments before had been equally terrified, lowered their eyes.

Takeo walked up to Ikawa and bowed from the waist, "I am sorry if I have shamed you, sir," Takeo said, still trembling.

Before Ikawa could reply, the boy turned and bowed to Allic, as well.

He closed his eyes and hesitated for a second. "Banzai!" Takeo screamed. He was over the cliff before anyone could stop him.

"Get him!" Allic cried, and Pina leaped into the air and disappeared over the side.

The others looked over the edge.

"He'll never reach him in time," Kochanski said. They could all see the boy tumbling, and Pina desperately trying to close the distance.

"Jesus Christ," Mark whispered. Then, at the very last second, the boy stopped falling and swept out, rushing low across the landscape.

A cheer went up from the Japanese, and the Americans joined in, as the boy arched up into the sky. Pina came in alongside, ready to help the wobbly flyer as he regained altitude and finally came back to land on the cliff.

The Japanese clustered around him, slapping him on the back as he came up to bow to Ikawa.

"You have Bushido," Ikawa said proudly.

The boy gave him a weak smile, then with a gentle sigh he keeled over—out cold.

The men around him laughed, but there was no malice in their tone as they gathered around and worked to revive their comrade.

"Your kid has guts. I'm proud to be serving in the same group with him," Mark said, coming up beside Ikawa.

Ikawa turned and Mark could see tears in his eyes. This did not fit any notion he had ever formed of the so-called cold-blooded, unfeeling Japanese officer. To save Ikawa any further embarrassment, he turned and walked away.

Allic was obviously delighted by Takeo's courage. Kneeling by his side, Allic touched him lightly on the forehead. Takeo's eyes fluttered open.

"This thing your commander calls Bushido," Allic said, "it sounds like something to be proud of. Come, fly by my side as we return to the castle."

Allic stood up and looked at the men. "I don't know if your commanders told you, but there is a little gathering planned for you this evening back at the castle."

The men looked expectantly at him.

"You see, certain young women have been begging to meet you since you arrived."

There was an electric tension in the air—but in the presence of their lord they were silent.

"There's one girl with flaxen hair that I'm particularly interested in," Allic said, "but the rest are fair game."

"Does that mean we're getting laid?" Walker shouted.

"Interesting phrase," Allic replied, smiling. "We prefer the term 'making joy,' but I guess it's the same thing."

"So let's go make joy," José cried, and the men broke into lusty cheers.

"Follow me then." Allic laughed, and he rose into the air.

The others followed, shouting happily. Allic turned and flew back down the trail.

Mark suddenly understood where Allic was leading them, and his heart filled with anticipation.

They swooped over the Tals who barked excitedly and galloped behind them as they passed.

Allic turned into the arching tunnel of flame-red trees and the men followed one after the other. Mark broke out of the column, pulling a loop, and then swung into the rear of the line alongside Ikawa.

Side by side they drifted slowly beneath the canopy. The golden-winged birds darted around them, chirping excitedly, their cries mingling with the happy shouts of men who were learning to slip from the iron hand of gravity. The lavender scent washed over them, flooding their senses.

Mark looked over at Ikawa, who flew unsteadily by his side. He smiled encouragingly, wondering why he would feel this sudden warmth for a man he would have killed without a second thought only weeks before.

But for the moment that was forgotten. There was only the ecstasy of flying, and with it the first true sense of a bond, as they floated together through the cool shadow-washed tunnel of red-green light.

The light grew stronger as the end of the tunnel came into view. Together they flew out of the shadows into the broad, sunlit countryside that stretched to the far horizon.

With a cry of unspeakable happiness, Mark soared upwards, rushing straight towards the heavens. He extended his hand outwards to the sun, as if for that moment he could reach out and touch the light above.

Sarnak came into the map room and stood for several minutes reviewing the changes that had taken place since his last visit, several hours before. The map almost entirely filled a large, shallow pit and was so well made that every time Sarnak stood over it he felt like he was flying over the real thing.

Even as he watched, more of Allic's patrols were noted and shifted to their new locations. Macha, who ruled the land of Torm along Allic's southern border, had very heavy patrols out, he noticed.

Ralnath walked into the room. "My lord, I have been checking on Wika's progress with the outlander, as you ordered. Wika is driving him right to the edge trying to make your deadline of three tendays. The outlander is learning, and they already hate one another, as I'm assuming you wanted."

Sarnak raised an eyebrow. "How refreshing to be so obvious. What's my next move, then?"

Ralnath hesitated, cursing his loose tongue, then forged ahead. "You will want someone to befriend the poor lad eventually, learn his true worth, and make your plans accordingly."

Sarnak nodded, said, "The assignment is yours," and turned his attention back to the map. "Allic has finally moved his forces so that we have a clear path to our next target. This move will give Allic more pain than he's had in over fifty years, and could very well send him blasting his way into Macha's land before he's even thought about it.

"Signal Quarth to lead his strike team over the border tonight. I want the attack made at dusk tomorrow. Target: Dirk. And remind him that I want no one left alive."

Chapter 8

"So, how was last night?" Allic asked, looking across the table at Mark and Ikawa. He had been wanting to ask all day, since half the town was buzzing with details of the party, but thought it best to wait until evening when he could share a drink and find out about the previous day's amusements.

There was a moment of embarrassed silence. Mark was not the type of man to share the details of his bed. Upon their return to the castle he discovered that a feast had been prepared in the garden near the bathing pools. The girls had been stunning beyond his wildest imaginings—and the imagination of a bomber pilot could get pretty wild.

Her name was Chloe and it was obvious that she had picked him out long before the party started. Tall and slender, her hair a tawny auburn, she was the female sorcerer he had talked to at the House of Healing, where he had stopped to check on José the day after their arrival. It was apparent he had made a most favorable impression because her approach was very simple and direct, leaving no doubt in Mark's mind how the rest of the evening would turn out.

The men had been decidedly nervous at first, especially with Allic present. He had been all courtliness, but once he left with the blonde, the party soon turned into a raucous affair, eventually ending in the bathing area where they went skinny-dipping in the hot spring.

Mark had heard some outrageous stories about the "great Hollywood orgy," as the men were now calling it, but he had barely listened. It had been quite some time since he had stayed up until dawn 'making joy.'

Mark looked over at Allic, wondering what to say to his lord. He had had a great time, but the whole thing was still a little bit shocking. Somehow the men had hit it by tagging it a Hollywood party. Things like last night only happened to guys out in California, or to rich mob chiefs on Long Island. It didn't feel quite right somehow.

Mark finally broke the silence. "These—ah, well you see, these young ladies who were with us last night—"

"Yes . . .?"

"They all seemed like they were from . . ." and he fell silent.

"I think he means good families," Ikawa interjected.

"Some of the best—nobles or sorcerers all."

"I mean, I don't want to cause any embarrassing situations here," Mark said quietly.

"What's embarrassing?" Allic asked, not helping in the slightest.

"Well, ah, you know."

"No, I don't."

"Well, it seemed kind of wild there. I mean, back home things like last night only happen in Hollywood, what with the girls taking their clothes off and then swimming together in the pool."

"What's this Hollywood? Is it a kingdom?"

"Yeah, you could call it that. But like I was saying, we were kind of loud there, and I'm worried that others in the castle would find out and the girls' families might get upset."

Allic threw back his head and laughed. "Most of their families encouraged them. Your Chloe is Pina's daughter. And I must say, Pina was delighted."

"Pina allowed that!" Mark cried. "And he calls himself a father?"

"One of the best," Allic said evenly, as he poured another round of drinks. "Look, Mark Phillips, it sounds like the people of your world have some problems. Here our young people are encouraged to freely associate and to make joy. There's no stigma to that."

"But what about children and such?" Mark asked lamely.

"What about it? You must have noticed that people here live longer. Even those without the Essence normally reach a hundred. A good sorcerer such as yourself can make a thousand, maybe twelve hundred years. Self-rejuvenation is not difficult with the power.

"Now, if we didn't have some forms of control," Allic continued, "there would be far too many for the land to feed. The mugata root solves that problem. A woman or man merely has to make a tonic from the root once a month and childbearing is prevented. Besides, here it is considered very bad form for a person to have more than two or three children. Someone who has more is considered selfish. Unless of course you are a sorcerer or demigod."

"Why is that?"

"Because every parent desires a child to be born with such powers. One sorcerer in a million comes from the common people without the Power. Now, if one parent has the Power of the Essence, the chances increase significantly. If both parents have the Power, the chances are even greater. Therefore, those with the Essence are encouraged to have any number of children, for it is only through sorcerers that the strength of our realm is maintained and our people protected. In my entire realm there are only four hundred; and there are less than a hundred who can use the power in battle and are pledged to me. That is why your arrival was so important. That is why your celebration of last night was viewed by all with favor."

"But what about this sleeping around?" Mark asked, still unsettled by it.

"Healthy, clean fun. How else do you know who your chosen mate will be? Once you have found one special person, many take a vow of oneness. When it comes to the bearing of children, this is very important, for every child should know both his parents, and both parents should take responsibility for raising their child. To do otherwise is viewed here as behavior worthy only of contempt. Parents who do not do the best for their children are shunned by the rest of the community."

Well, damn, it did seem reasonable, Mark thought. And after six months of abstinence in China, and twenty-five years in chaste America, it was paradise.

His only concern now was facing Pina. Somehow fathers of women he slept with always made him feel uncomfortable, especially the father of a girl he had met at an orgy.

Their conversation was interrupted by a cry in the hallway. Yarma burst into the room without bothering to knock.

"My lord, a message has just come in! Dirk reported that he was coming under attack, and then there was silence."

Instantly Allic stood, an expression of growing anger tightening his features.

Several of Pina's sorcerers burst into the room, Valdez leading the way.

"What's this?" Allic roared.

"It's true, sire," a sorcerer replied. "The report came via a message crystal which was overloaded and jammed. They must have come in using a spell of protection, for we've sensed nothing amiss here."

"Who's attacking him?"

"Unknown, sire," Pina replied.

"Damn all to hell," Allic screamed, smashing his goblet on the floor. "I want everyone, every damned sorcerer in this city to report to the courtyard in one turning."

"But my lord," Pina interjected, "all the sorcerers?"

"You heard me," Allic roared. "One turning. Mark, Ikawa, your people too."

"But their training," Valdez protested. "They're barely pass the apprentice level. They don't even have proper offensive crystals yet."

"Damn it! I said *everyone!* Valdez, suit them for combat. The hell with the ceremonies, I want them armed with offensive crystals right now. They can learn how to shoot them in battle."

"Shouldn't we leave some men behind to protect the city?" Valdez asked quietly, obviously attempting to inject a note of rational calm. "This whole thing could be a subterfuge."

Allic stared coldly at the men before him. "The city can take care of itself," he said, his voice chilly and low. "That's *Dirk* out there, and by all my powers I'm bringing everyone with me. Do you understand?"

Mark could feel the tingle of fear in the room. He was used to Allic as an almost jovial character, but there was no lightheartedness now. Anyone who crossed Allic at this moment, might very well end up dead.

Without another word the assembled men and women bowed and filed out of the room.

"Get your men quickly," Pina whispered as they stepped into the corridor.

"What the hell is going on?" Ikawa asked, coming up by Pina's side.

"Looks like a raid on one of our border marches. Happens a couple of times a year. Usually just a bandit group hoping to pick up a couple of crystals as loot from a dead sorcerer. Occasionally it's a skirmish with one of our neighbors. But there have been far too many of these of late. There's been a lot of tension on our borders and we all fear that one of these incidents might be the start of something worse."

"Who is Dirk?" Mark asked.

"An old and trusted marchman. Dirk has been in service to Allic for nearly a hundred years."

Pina stopped for a moment and looked at Mark and Ikawa.

"He's also Allic's son." Turning, Pina ran up a side corridor and disappeared.

The room was crowded with the Japanese and Americans being briefed by their respective commanders on the forthcoming action when two sorcerers entered carrying large cases.

Silence fell as Derson and Jeen opened their cases on the table. The husband and wife team was in charge of Allic's treasury and crystal vault. Ander, Allic's First Sorcerer of the army, came in behind them.

Jeen spoke first as Derson continued to organize the contents of the boxes.

"We have been ordered to give you your full allotment of crystals. There isn't a lot of time, so shut up and listen."

"These crystals were all made by the House of Master Craftsman Richur de Mornya," Derson interjected. "He does superior work; Allic has been dealing with him for over a thousand years."

"Bear in mind that these crystals are owned by Allic and are being loaned to you by your liege lord. If lost, you are held accountable and can have up to thirty years service added to your contract. Guard them as closely as they will guard you."

"You talk of them as if they were alive," scoffed Giorgini.

Derson looked up and replied, "There are those of us who believe that certain crystals do have a very rough sort of sentience. We believe that the Elder Gods grew them in the ancient days for their own unfathomable purposes. However, they are only found in one area of Haven: Jartan's Crystal Mountains. Which is the source of his wealth and the reason for contention by any others of the gods and their descendants.

"Crystals are our most precious commodity; they are passed from generation to generation. They are the spoils of battle, and the bottom line of any treaty or trade agreement."

"Sounds like Jartan has a choke hold on the rest of the world. How come he isn't emperor or whatever?" asked Younger.

Ander smiled at Younger. "A good question, but too difficult to answer quickly. The gods have agreements among themselves, and Jartan trades freely with other realms to ensure long term economic growth."

Jeen cleared her throat and Ander smiled, saying, "Jeen's reminding me of my tendency to lecture."

"To return to our subject: You will find your blast crystals have the improved spinel cut, and your shield crystals have the standard brilliant cut. These offer far more refinement than the ones you used in training.

"We will also give you belts with other standard crystals, including communications, creativity, farseeing, healing, and others. Please take your old basic defensive crystal and put it in one of the slots on your belt. Your new shield crystal goes in the wristband on your left hand." He started to pass out the belts and wristbands.

Jeen spoke up. "I suggest you ignore all but the offensive, defensive, and communications crystals for now. Those are the ones that will save your life. Now, out to the courtyard for some quick practice before we go!"

"Close it up there. Hurry, damn it, hurry. It's just on the other side of this hill!"

Pina banked away from the formation of Americans and Japanese and swooped up to the head of the column.

Mark was straining to keep up speed, but he was damn near exhausted. They had been flying for several hours and he soon realized that to fly full-out, hugging low to the ground, took every bit of his concentration and strength. He estimated that they were flying at well over sixty miles an hour, and but for the protection of his crystal shielding the wind would have buffeted him into numbness long ago. Larna, the larger of the twin moons, had set long ago, and only the light from Rega guided them across the open savannah and low rolling hills. The rich farmlands of the escarpment were now an hour or more behind them. The crisp air of the high plateau had been replaced by the sultry heat of the savannah, and it was as if the descent had brought them into another world.

Allic had wanted to forge ahead, leaving his slower companions behind. It was only the combined protests of his advisors, warning that it might be a trap, which had finally restrained him.

There was a flash of light ahead. Allic turned his defensive shielding on high and rose to gain altitude for the attack.

Valdez came alongside Mark and spoke to him through the communications crystal, which broadcast his voice to everyone.

"We're the reserve for this," Valdez cried. "The trained sorcerers will go in first. You offworlders, led by me, will hold back until they need us."

"So what the hell does Allic want us to do if we attack?" Mark asked.

"Draw fire, if nothing else," Valdez replied, and banking to one side he signaled for Mark and the others to follow.

Damn it, draw fire, Mark thought. Now he knew what the pilot of an unarmed scout plane must have felt like. He looked back over his shoulder. The hundreds of hours each of the Americans had logged on bomber missions back on Earth must explain their affinity for flight because, while they looked as tired as he felt, all his men were still with him. Whereas only a couple of the Japanese were still with Ikawa; the rest had been straggling back ever since they left the castle. Pina had finally ordered a triad of sorcerers to act as rear guard, and to ride escort on those who had fallen behind.

Mark was seeing a new aspect of Allic. When angry, he became impetuous. If Allic's enemy knew him well enough, this could easily be a trap.

More flashes of light appeared in the sky as the other sorcerers activated their shields to combat readiness and disappeared over the ridge towards a soft, ruddy glow that bathed the eastern sky like a false dawn.

Valdez slowed and the group came up around him. They worked their way up the ridgeline, not a dozen feet off the ground.

Cautiously Valdez rose and crested the hill. Turning to the outlanders he shouted, "Allic wants us to come in. The enemy is gone."

They crested the hill and started a long sloping glide down

into the valley. There was nothing on the other side except several dozen sorcerers slowly wheeling and circling above a smoldering ruin.

A flame-blasted wall suddenly loomed out of the shadows before Mark. Rising over it, he crossed into the central courtyard of a large parapet-encircled fortress.

There was the stench of scorched wood in the air, mingled with something else, and the memories flooded back. A hospital back in London had been hit with incendiaries. He had been in the neighborhood and pitched in to help—and then the wave of smoke had washed over him. It was the smell of burning bodies, and the memory of that nightmare stench had never left him.

He landed near Allic, who stood silent in the center of the courtyard. The men around him were spreading out, rushing towards the smoldering keep at the far end of the courtyard, while others still circled overhead, alert for a trap.

There was silence, total silence. Mark and his men followed Pina in the rush towards the keep. The heavy iron doors to the sanctuary were blasted off their hinges.

He tried to go through the doorway but the stench stopped him. Gagging, fighting for control, Mark stepped into the keep.

"Oh merciful god," he groaned. Scorched bodies littered this side room. He turned away and went to the next. It was the same—this time they were mainly women and children. He saw how most had died, and he staggered out of the room, trying to keep from retching.

"Dirk! Dirk!"

Mark looked back to the main doorway. Allic was there, his entrance blocked by Valdez and several sorcerers.

A flash of light—and the men were thrown against the wall, and Allic came in.

Pina stepped out from a side room and stood silent.

"Dirk!"

"My lord Allic," Pina said softly, and Mark could see the tears in his eyes.

"Dirk?" Allic asked softly.

"He's dead, my lord," Pina said, and he gently placed his hand on Allic's shoulder.

"Allitia?"

"She's gone as well."

Allic started to press past him.

"Don't, my lord. Please don't. We'll take care of them."

"Dirk!" Allic pushed past him and rushed into the room. Pina followed him, and Mark, as if drawn in, joined them.

An aged and graying warrior lay in the center of the room, sword still in his hand. His body from the waist down was burned, blasted. Mark turned away. A woman was lying by his side, but Mark did not look.

"Oh, Dirk, my son, my son."

His son, Mark thought. Here was a man who looked in his healthy prime, as vigorous as himself, weeping over a man who looked old enough to be his grandfather.

Mark left the room and walked out of the keep.

Valdez stood to one side, the outlanders gathered around him. Valdez looked at him hopefully.

"They're all dead," Mark whispered.

Valdez braced himself, his face blank. "Dirk was the son from Allic's most beloved consort, Liona," he said softly. "She was a mortal—no Essence. And died fifty years ago. He still mourns her. Dirk was their only son, and to the heartbreak of them both, he too was born without the Essence."

Valdez looked away for a moment.

"And you, all of you. You take your gifts so casually, when it cannot be certain that even the son of a god can give the Power to his heirs."

There was a faint stirring behind him and Mark turned to see Allic coming out of the keep, a broken, scorched body in his arms. Pina followed, carrying a cloak-covered body that must have been Dirk's wife.

Gentle hands reached out to Allic and took the body away.

"Take them back to Landra," Allic said softly. "Make a resting place for them beside Liona."

Allic looked over to Valdez as if seeing him for the first time.

"Who did this?" he asked grimly.

"There's been no evidence so far of a message crystal. We must assume the attackers found it and took it with them."

"Then what evidence *do* we have?"

Valdez nodded to several sorcerers who stood to one side.

The three stepped forward and dropped an assortment of spears and shields by Allic's feet.

"Macha?" Allic asked incredulously.

"It would appear so, my lord. Those are weapons of the Torms."

"And do you believe it?"

"No logic to it at all, sire. We have had problems with Macha in the past, to be sure. But Macha knew that Dirk was your son. To attack Dirk is to directly attack you."

"Then if that bastard wants war," Allic said coldly, "he'll have war."

"It isn't logical," Valdez ventured.

"To hell with your logic. We go in tonight."

"My lord, we should at least wait till morning and check the ground. We might find more evidence then."

"I want revenge!" Allic cried.

"My lord." It was Pina, who was still standing inside the keep, and pointing at the wall beside him.

Allic turned.

"Please come here for a moment. I've found something."

Allic walked over to Pina and bent to examine the wall.

The others gathered closer and Mark turned to Valdez. "What is it?"

"Looks like battle code," Valdez replied. "All our commanders and sorcerers learn a symbolic battle code so that a message can be left. It's one of our best kept secrets. To any untrained eye, battle code looks like random scratches. A gate portal is one of the places we use to leave such messages. Maybe Dirk was able to scratch something before they broke in."

Valdez pushed closer and looked over Allic's shoulder.

"Sarnak," Valdez said, looking back at those beside him.

There was a growl from the assembly. Allic straightened and stepped out into the courtyard.

"Then it was Sarnak," Valdez said coldly. "That bastard tried to make this look like Macha's doing. They swept the place for message crystals to make sure, but they didn't see the message."

"We go for them now!" Allic cried, and several of the sorcerers cheered.

"My lord," Valdez interjected, "it could be a trap. Perhaps Sarnak wants to provoke a war between us and the Torms, but he must also expect that you might outguess him in this. If you charge into his realm without an army for support, his defenses will be too strong."

"I don't care," Allic roared. "I will be avenged!"

"Besides, my lord," Pina said, "if you should openly attack him he can turn that to his advantage. Our only proof is the scratchings in the battle code. Before all the other demigods and gods you will look like the aggressor."

"Damn them all," Allic cried. "Is not the death of my own son enough proof? What are you, simpering cowards and whining diplomats?"

"My lord!" Ikawa stepped forward. "I am new here, but I was a warrior long before you knew me. I too want revenge for what was done here. Let me propose a plan, my lord, that will catch your enemy by surprise."

"You're good at sneak attacks," Younger sneered from the back of the crowd.

Ikawa looked over at him.

Mark quickly stepped forward. "Ikawa is right, my lord, and so is Younger. Ikawa's people once hit mine with a surprise attack that even we must admit was effective. Listen to him, my lord."

Ikawa nodded respectfully at Mark, then turned back to Allic.

"Tell me then, and quickly," Allic said coldly, "but you better not be wasting my time."

The hour was very late but Ralnath knew his master would still be working. He knocked on the door and entered immediately.

"My lord, we've just detected two of Allic's triads crossing our border."

Sarnak laid down the report he was reviewing and stretched. Rising, he walked to his master crystal and activated it with a wave.

"Very curious. Why send such a weak force to reconnoiter my border? Is Allic with them?"

"No indication, my lord."

"Could it be that he is already attacking Macha?"

"Very likely, sire. Here, let me show you something." Ralnath meshed his mind with the crystal and shifted the perspective. "Right here is a very large, shielded mass heading towards Macha's realm. It's quite powerful, must have at least fifteen to twenty sorcerers to generate something that strong."

"Excellent. Step by step we approach our goal." He paused, watching the pattern of light heading farther and farther away, then switched back to the first scene with the two triads cruising slowly at the edge of his land.

"My normal pattern would be to react violently to a border violation," Sarnak said, speaking slowly, "and everything must appear normal so Allic will not suspect me of this night's work. Therefore"—his voice sharpened—"have them destroyed. Send the forces that just made the attack on Dirk —they're already in position near the border."

Chapter 9

"You're doing an excellent job," Pina said, banking over to Mark's side.

"How's that?"

"Your flying. That's it, keep up the erratic movements, wander out of formation. We want to make this look weak."

Mark wasn't sure if Pina was serious or joking about his clumsy flying techniques.

Damn, he could lead a flight of B-17s or 29s and have them wingtip to wingtip for a thousand miles. Most pilots hated tight formation work, but he loved it. But there was no stick here, no throttle to gently work up and down. This was formation flying by pure willpower. If he let his attention be diverted for just a second, he'd start to drift. Worse yet, if his attention turned to some object on the ground, the next thing he knew he was dropping towards it.

Mark realized that to fly with precision he needed to have his mind running on two different tracks simultaneously—one looking for signs of the enemy, the other maintaining formation and listening in his mind for the faint whisper of a voice when Pina projected a direction or flight change to him through the communications crystal.

Aboard a bomber there were eleven men working together as a team, to help with the flying. This must be what a fighter jock feels like when out on the prowl, Mark realized, and he could see why they loved it, once they had mastered the techniques of staying alive.

Acting as bait for Sarnak's sorcerers and demons wasn't Mark's idea of a fun time, but, he admitted, he would rather be out here with his ass on the line than be along with most of the Japanese and their escorts forming the decoy group headed towards the south. Mark was feeling more and more comfortable with his flying. If only he could feel as confident about his ability to fight. . . .

"Your offensive crystal that Allic gave you," Pina said, "just remember to concentrate your fire through that."

"Okay, got it."

"Okay?"

"American slang. . . means all right."

Pina smiled at him. "Okay," and signaling for a turn, they banked back on a more easterly course, heading straight for a horizon that still showed no sign of dawn.

"I'm still not detecting anything. How about you two?" Pina glanced over at Mark and Kochanski and saw they didn't understand.

"You should be using your different senses to detect danger. Hasn't Valdez gotten that far with your training yet?"

Both shook their heads. They had no idea what he was talking about.

"This is something you should have learned already, damn it. All right, using normal vision I want you to look over at our other triad. Can you see them in the starlight?"

Mark and Kochanski struggled to make out the figures over a hundred yards away.

"Yeah, but not very well," Mark said.

"Fine. Now I want you to shift your perception to a different level. Look for heat coming from them. Tell your vision to go to red. Take control, and use the Essence to will your eyes to see heat waves."

Kochanski said, "Jesus, I'm seeing three bright red blobs."

"Now look at the ground—look for the herd of animals below us."

This time it was Mark who responded, "There's almost a solid mass of red down there. No, wait, if I look harder I can see individual dots."

"That's infrared. It's a very useful detection device. Now I want you to tell yourself to look for details in the dark. Look into the shadows at the base of the hill up ahead. Will your vision to seek reflected light, even starlight. What do you see?"

As Mark forced his gaze into the shadows everything became clearer. "Everything's green. Different shades of green."

"Just so. That is starlight vision," responded Pina.

"Christ," swore Kochanski, "I can even see a bird eating some animal it caught. This is incredible!"

"Most sorcerers can see up to several leagues away, depending on conditions. It's a talent to be developed, as early detection of an enemy can save your life." Pina smiled and continued, "You need to learn much more. There are several different kinds of vision, and just as many kinds of hearing. It will take time, but you will learn to expand your horizons."

They had been flying the box formation for an hour, experimenting with their newly discovered talents. Eventually it occurred to Kochanski to try to visualize himself using his old skill as radar operator: throw out a signal and see what bounces back.

"I'm sensing something," Kochanski shouted, coming in close to where Mark and Pina were flying.

"What's that?" Pina cried.

"Something's out there. I'm picking up a mental image. There's something rolling in on a sweeping turn to the northeast."

Pina did a quick search. "I don't sense anything." He looked over at the other formation and projected a low intensity thought through his crystal.

In response the other formation banked in. The two Americans, Walker and Goldberg, struggled to keep up with Valdez.

"They're coming in fast. Dozen or more bogeys at two o'clock!" Kochanski shouted, falling back into the old vocabulary of a different war.

"I can sense them now," Pina replied. "You're right, at least twelve of them, more like fifteen. Hang on just a little longer."

"Damn, they're coming in fast," Kochanski shouted. "Should have visual any second now."

Mark scanned the morning sky to the northeast... "Bandits two o'clock high!" he shouted.

"I've got them," Kochanski replied, "coming in fast."

"Ready to retreat," Pina cried.

There were fifteen sorcerers, and twice that many demons below them, flying low to the ground. Suddenly the sorcerers clicked up their defensive shields, and the glow of their protection looked like shooting stars across the indigo sky.

"Get your shields up," Pina yelled.

Mark diverted his thoughts for a second and the faint shimmer of light surrounding him increased in intensity.

"Dive now!" Pina cried, as he rolled and went into a swooping dive that brought him out in a run towards the west.

Mark arched over, with Kochanski by his side. They plummeted straight towards the ground a half mile below. Pulling up, he leveled out into a shallow diving run back towards the western horizon.

Mark looked over his shoulder. The other triad was swinging in beside them a hundred yards to his left. A mile behind him the approaching enemies were diving to pick up speed, while the demons further down slowly pulled forward.

Pina drifted back, coming up alongside Mark and Kochanski.

"That's it, that's it, keep it erratic and let them start to gain."

Damn it, he was flying flat out. For nearly a quarter turning they ran, the enemy slowly gaining while the demons rose higher into the air to join their companions in the pursuit.

"Good formation, that," Pina shouted. "They kept the demons low while they hovered above on the edge of a cloud bank. That way, if we'd seen the demons first, we'd have dived into the attack and then they'd break on us from above. A good job, Kochanski. Now let them get closer."

Ever so slowly Pina dropped his speed; the men followed suit. The sorcerers behind them started to gain, until they were less than a quarter mile away.

A beam of light shot past Mark to his left. Another arched high, snapping over his head.

He broke right and dove then came back up again, banking left. Another beam shot past, this one uncomfortably close, so that he had a sudden whiff of ozone.

Damn, this was getting hot.

Another burst shot between Mark and Kochanski. The two broke to either side, then rolled back in, cutting to either side of Pina, who was holding a straight and steady course.

"That's it!" Pina yelled. "Act scared!"

"Goddamn it, I am scared!" Kochanski shouted.

"They couldn't hit the side of a castle at this range."

"Yeah, I've heard that line before . . . usually it's somebody's last line," Mark replied.

"Lower," Pina cried, and tucking in he started for the ground, with Mark, Kochanski, and the other triad following closely. The ground rushed up to meet them and at the very last instant Pina leveled out, so that they were skimming along at sixty miles an hour, not ten feet in the air.

Except for the fact that they were being shot at, Mark would have found the moment exhilarating. They hugged the dips and folds of the open savannah, swooping up dry creek beds, rising to clear a line of trees, and cutting back down so that the high prairie grass whipped by, striking the edge of their shielding so that their passage left a wavering track in the grassland behind them.

Clearing a low ridge, they startled a herd of giraffelike creatures, which scattered wildly in every direction. For a brief instant Mark found himself in the middle of the herd, weaving and dodging as the animals stood higher than his flight path, looking at him with wide, panic-stricken eyes.

He felt like he was racing through a forest of telegraph poles, while all the time crystal blasts shot past him, igniting the prairie with thunderclaps of smoke and flame.

"Exciting, isn't it?" Pina shouted.

Mark spared him a momentary glance as if he were crazy.

"Next ridge," Pina yelled, and pulled away in a burst of speed.

They cleared the herd and started up a long, sloping hill. The climb slowed them down a bit, while the pursuing sorcerers and demons were still flying straight, thus gaining on them from behind.

"Christ!" A burst of flame licked the edge of Mark's defensive shielding.

The impact caused him to career off to one side. For an instant he thought he'd fly straight into the ground. His stomach fell away as he arched up high and rolled, cutting between two trees that stood silhouetted on the crest of the hill.

"Those bastards!" Mark roared as his fear changed to rage. Shooting past the hill, he saw Pina starting a shallow bank to the right as he picked up speed.

He looked back over his shoulder and saw the first of the

sorcerers crest the hill, then another, and seconds later the enemy unit came up over the top with the demons swinging out to either side to close the flanks. Even above the roar of the wind he could hear the booming shouts of the demons, closing on their quarry.

A blinding flash cracked from one end of the ridge to the other. An instant later half a hundred shields flickered to life as Allic's hidden force rose from the high prairie grass. Ascending, they delivered a devastating volley to Sarnak's battle group, which had already shot past them.

A dozen demons tumbled from the sky, trailing inky plumes of smoke and flame until they impacted to ignite a series of fires in the dry grassland.

The pursuers were now the hunted, as panic-stricken, they broke formation.

Two of the surviving sorcerers and several demons broke towards Mark, Pina, and Kochanski. Mark pulled up high, Kochanski at his side, while Pina continued to bank low, skimming the tall grass.

The sky around them was torn by a hundred bolts of light as the battle became a series of swirling engagements.

Mark shot past a demon who fell by him end over end, his left wing gone from half a dozen bolts. Flying through the demon's smoky trail, Mark pulled up high, straight over the top of the battle.

To his right Walker was swinging in behind a panicking demon, who dodged in a desperate attempt to escape.

A bolt of light shot from Walker's hand; the demon smashed into the ground, trailing fire. Walker swung low as if to confirm his kill, then soared and pulled a victory roll.

"Mark, behind you!" a voice shouted in his mind. Mark pulled hard left and he felt a rush of foul smelling wind sweep past him. A demon shot by, not half a dozen feet away.

Mark rolled up but a blast of light cut in behind him and the demon disappeared in an explosion of fire and scorched flesh.

How? Looking down, Mark saw Pina watching him. Damn, it was just like having a wing man with a radio. Waving his thanks he banked in low, looking for a target.

There was one bright light in the action, however, that outshone all others: Allic. For the first time Mark was seeing his leader truly display his power. Beam after beam shot out, first from one hand and then from the other, as he smashed his way through the battle, outshooting and outflying anyone who dared to approach him. If Mark had ever doubted Allic's ability to lead in a close-in battle, that thought disappeared as Allic racked up kill after kill.

Mark turned away from Allic and looked for a target. He saw Pina flying low to the ground, pursuing and then blasting an enemy sorcerer out of the sky, not sensing another of Sarnak's sorcerers closing in behind him. A bolt of flame slashed out from the sorcerer, hitting Pina's shielding. The impact sent Pina into a skid, so that he brushed through the high grass. He came up wobbly, and his shield shimmered bright red as two more blasts hit and finally overloaded it, snapping it off.

The enemy sorcerer swung in close for a killing shot.

Before he even realized what was happening, Mark had tucked into a dive. Pina, stunned by the impact of the shots, weaved and dodged to throw off his enemy's aim. But the enemy kept on his tail, lining up for the final shot.

Mark was still several hundred yards away.

"No!" He held up his hand as if trying to block out the image of what he was seeing.

A bolt of light slashed out from his hand and slammed into the sorcerer's back, sending him tumbling. He rolled to one side and regained control, but his shield shimmered red from the impact.

Mark rushed in behind him as the sorcerer pulled straight up, struggling for altitude.

Mark lined up another blast. As if sensing his move, the enemy banked hard to the left in a rolling turn and came straight back at him, dodging Mark's bolt. The sorcerer fired even as Mark pulled a tight roll, and they shot past each other.

They both pulled straight up, looping over, and traded another round of blasts without effect.

The enemy sorcerer banked left, trying to come in behind Mark— but he had seen that old trick a hundred times in the skies over Europe and China. With a short upward pull he extended his arms, willing himself to stop.

His airspeed cut to practically nothing and he rolled to one side, ready to throw off another blast if his foe should try it.

His enemy flew past him not a dozen feet away, and for an instant Mark could see the terror in the man's eyes. The sorcerer desperately fought to kill his airspeed in a last ditch attempt at preventing Mark from getting behind him.

Mark waited until his aim was sure. "Eat this, asshole!" Mark screamed, and he extended his hand. A bolt hit the sorcerer square in the back. The defensive shield flickered off, and with a loud scream the wizard fell, his last shot arching high over Mark's head.

Another bolt shot from Mark's hand and the wizard ignited in a blinding flash. As he fell, Mark followed, hitting him again and again.

The body hit the ground setting the grass aflame. Mark pulled up, coming past at full speed, and as he pulled up he victory-rolled over his fallen foe.

He looked for another target but all was quiet, and he suddenly realized that the battle was over, and that, in fact, Allic and all the others had been watching his performance.

Still high on the adrenaline of combat, Mark soared in low towards where they were gathering on the ground and zoomed past, circling high in a loop and coming to a running stop near the other sorcerers.

Allic approached, and offered Mark a drink from the wine sack which he always carried with him, even in combat.

"Masterful, Mark Phillips. Why did you ever doubt yourself?"

Mark looked at his lord, and even in his praise he could still see the pain.

"Your revenge is my revenge," Mark said truthfully. The hatred over what he had seen earlier had finally exploded when Pina was threatened, and he realized that it had been the desire to protect a friend and to avenge the anguish of another which had enabled him to fight and win.

"But never let hatred or vengeance be the sole source of your power," Valdez said, stepping forward to clap Mark on the shoulder. "It is powerful but erratic."

Walker pushed through the crowd and came to Mark's side. "Two kills, Captain," Walker exulted. "Damn it, there's no plane to paint them on, but once we get back I'm having two demons embroidered on my sleeve. Two kills—am I good or am I good?"

The men fell into a round of good-natured jeering.

"Strip the bodies," Allic finally said, interrupting the celebration. "There are enough crystals on the dead to at least balance some of the debt for tonight." He cleared his throat and continued, "I wish to tell all of you how proud I am to have you with me."

A roar of approval went up from the entire group.

"Let it be known that the outlanders now have the rank of Sorcerers of the Realm. You are acolytes no more."

Allic looked around the gathering as if searching for someone. "Ikawa, step forward."

From the back of the crowd the Japanese commander advanced.

"From now on," Allic said, "you are one of my Achmen, my battle advisors. I am pleased to have one such as you serving me."

Ikawa looked around at the assembly and the men broke into a spontaneous cheer. He started to bow low in response but Allic stopped him.

"You are never to bow to me again. You are like Valdez: your words come from the coldness of logic rather than the heat of passion. I need such men. Next month I must go to my father's court, and as reward, you are to come with me."

"And you too," Allic said to Mark. "It's time that the two of you met a god."

The looting of the dead sorcerers completed, Allic's men gathered together and prepared for the flight back. Several of them had taken hits, but no one had been seriously injured.

Allic lifted into the air. One by one the others followed.

Pina walked over to Mark's side. "I wanted to thank you, as well."

Mark waved an acknowledgment.

"Why so embarrassed?" Pina asked.

Mark was silent.

"Ah yes, I see. You outlanders have such strange mores!" He chuckled. "I dare say when word gets around the castle how you bested that sorcerer and saved my life, Chloe will be more than happy to reward you."

Laughing, Pina lifted into the air and banked over to join Allic.

Oh god, would he ever get used to these people's customs?

"Come on," Valdez shouted, flying past Mark. "Allic might praise you, but you've got a damn sight more to learn before I'm done with you."

Shrugging, Mark ascended. He was exhausted, weak, and shaking. It was that way after every battle, when he climbed out of a plane ready to collapse.

Valdez and then Chloe. Well, maybe he could sit in the back of the room and sleep, and at least get ready for the evening.

As he soared, the Americans and Japanese fell in around him. When they cleared the shadow of the ridge, the group was washed by the first glowing red of dawn.

Upwards they climbed, plunging into a low ceiling of puffy clouds awash with a soft pink light. Mark burst through the gentle cloud into the clear light of dawn, arched over, and set a course for home.

Ralnath waited until he was sure that Sarnak had calmed down before he spoke.

"I can't believe Allic could be so cunning."

Sarnak's reply came through clenched teeth. "He isn't. Allic is a bull. This came from someone else—probably that damned Valdez."

He watched through his crystal as Allic and the others flew back to Landra.

"My time is coming, Allic. You'll be dead and your city will be mine, and there isn't anything you can do to prevent it."

Chapter 10

Allic's party was flying over a rolling countryside dotted with fields of golden grain, vineyards, and low hilltops covered by eldar trees that reached two hundred or more feet into the sky.

Mark's favorite, the derusa trees, had shed most of their blossoms. He still found it fascinating that the fallen petals retained some of their iridescence, so that here and there a green canopied forest would rise out of a carpet of fading red.

To his right, a dozen leagues away, the Crystal Mountains soared to the heavens, their eternally snowcapped peaks piercing the banking clouds—promise of a late afternoon storm. From horizon to horizon the mountains shimmered in the sunlight. It was easy to imagine that mountains and clouds were one, both forged from one of the radiant crystals which were hidden beneath the snowclad range.

Mark, Ikawa, Kochanski, and Allic traveled at a leisurely pace, while the escort flew overhead in a protective circle. As they passed over a village or a group of farmers out in the fields, Allic would call out his greetings, and the villagers would look up, astonished, then shout a friendly reply.

Mark could hear the conversations of those below as they slowly cruised along; and the sounds of rushing brooks, laughing children, and the gentle sighing of the wind.

The scent of the land came up to him, as well: the last dying fragrance of the red blossoms, or, where another grape crop was being brought in, the heady bouquet of the freshly pressed juice.

Kochanski asked why it always seemed to be harvest time on Haven, and Allic explained that the gods had done genetic work on plants and crops. Grains matured quickly, and different strains matured at different times. So by alternating crops to replenish the soil, and timing them to maximize yield, a farmer would always have a harvest. The same was true of vegetables and fruits. Indeed, Allic had a difficult time comprehending that because things were not as well arranged on Earth that famines occasionally occurred. Whole provinces actually *starved*? Unthinkable.

Upon reflection the outlanders agreed that it made perfect sense. In Allic's land, with a climate similar to Southern California where it just got a little chilly during the short winter, and where any drought could be corrected by a team of sorcerers using creativity...of course you would have year-round food crops.

When the time came for the noonday meal, Allic led them over to a narrow valley, set against one of the foothills to the Crystal Mountains, in a region of vineyards held in the highest esteem.

Landing in an open field where the vine masters were supervising the harvest, Allic and his traveling companions were met with a hearty round of good-natured greetings. A crowd gathered, and the visitors were soon escorted to an outdoor tavern at the edge of the village.

Mark had believed that the feasts at the palace were extraordinary, but this friendly meal, set upon rough-hewn tables shaded by towering eldar trees, was beyond compare.

The sweet richness of the freshly harvested grapes mingled with the pinelike tang of the eldars. The narrow valley before them seemed to climb almost to the clouds, step after step of terraces dotted with villages, groves, vineyards, and pastures.

The abundance of the land was matched by the generosity of the meal. It was plain country fare, but there was a remarkable variety: a dozen different cheeses and a score of meats and breads.

And as the platters of food were passed and the women of the village pressed their choicest selections upon the honored guests, the village's men uncorked bottle after bottle from what they thought had been the best year. Then a loud argument would ensue as dates and vineyards were extolled or attacked, while at the other end of the table someone would uncork yet another bottle, and another argument.

The sun shifted in its course, the shadows starting to lengthen across the field. Bawdy songs filled the air, joined in by both men and women, and more than one couple had excused themselves to disappear into the bushes. Half a dozen feasters had simply tipped over backwards, to collapse sprawling on the ground. Mark found himself staring into the bottom of his goblet, not sure if the last drink had been a light well-rounded white or a hearty, full-bodied red, or was it that brandy one of the vine masters had brought up from his special stock?

Finally Allic rose from the table, raising his hands in a friendly gesture as he tried politely to decline the shouted invitations for him to stay for a day or week or two.

Taking several bottles that were pressed into his hands, he beckoned for the rest of his party to follow. The guards, who while on duty had to abstain, were immediately at his side. Mark was almost tempted to stay behind, for a girl with light blue eyes and golden red hair which flowed to her waist had made it more than clear that making joy, if only briefly in the nearest hayloft, would be a pleasant way to end his visit.

Mark looked over at Ikawa and Kochanski and saw that they were wrestling with the same desires. A slender dark-eyed girl stood close to Ikawa's side, while Kochanski, to his obvious delight, had two young blondes, one on each knee, vying for his attention.

Allic was looking at them, bemused. Mark sighed, and patting his new friend on the backside, he joined Allic. Ikawa and Kochanski reluctantly followed.

With a polite wave and "Thank you!" Allic ascended, his half-inebriated companions behind him. As they rose, Mark looked down again, seeing his disappointed friend giving him a look that clearly said, *You don't know what you're missing.* He waved again, then followed Allic as he turned, banking out from the valley to return to their northeasterly heading.

Mark realized yet again how much the tragedy of the previous month still hung over Allic, who enjoyed the visit in the valley, but had not plunged into the celebration with the wild abandon that he was famous for.

Ever since their return from the fight, Allic had been

somewhat distant, and on several occasions Mark had noticed him flying alone to the top of the hillside which rose beyond the castle, to the place where Dirk now rested beside his wife and his mother, who Allic still remembered as a young mortal girl of sad doelike eyes and slender body.

How strange this near-immortality was. How strange that Mark could watch as Allic, who looked no older than him, cradled a gray-haired warrior and wept for an old man who was his son. Or to love a young girl who one day would be an old bent woman, an honored grandmother, while her lover stayed forever young.

Mark thought about this in his own life, as well. If Allic, as a demigod, was almost immortal, Mark still viewed his own increased life span as damn near forever.

At night he would lie awake contemplating the knowledge that if he stayed here on Haven he could live a thousand years or more. The thought was still so numbing at times that he tried not to contemplate its implications. How would it be when a girl, like that redhead, was eighty and looked eighty, while Mark was still young?

He looked again at Allic, understanding a little better the mercurial nature of his lord, who could live with such abandon, and lapse into such melancholy.

Since the fight Allic had been quiet, distant. It was not just the loss of Dirk, Mark realized. There was also the growing concern about the southern marches. There had been half a dozen incidents in the last thirty days, with villages being raided by unknown bandits on both sides of the border between Allic and the Torm nation to the south. Now the Torms were pressing claims for alleged damages, and hinting at stronger action since Allic couldn't really prove Sarnak's guilt.

They flew on in silence for nearly a turning, but at last a bit of the old Allic started to show.

He began by pulling out one of the three bottles. Uncorking it in flight, he drained off most of the contents and then let the bottle drop.

He looked over to Mark, a gentle grin lighting his features, and plummeted, weaving through an open stand of trees and then beneath a bridge spanning the river that they were following north. For Allic's companions it became a lively game of follow the leader.

The afternoon progressed, and the game became more difficult as Allic searched out interesting feats to perform.

Ikawa finally gave up, laughing and shaking his head in amazement when Allic dove and had to roll sideways to fit between two buildings. Mark and Kochanski followed him, and as Mark flashed down the narrow alleyway, he rocketed past an open window where an old woman looked out at him, wide-eyed. Pulling back up, Mark laughed with joy. Allic then pulled straight into the sky. Mark followed him through the clouds until finally, at what he estimated was about a mile high, Allic leveled out and uncorked another bottle.

"Now, let's see some real flying!" Allic cried. Rolling onto his back, he put the bottle to his lips and took a long pull.

Jesus Christ, Mark thought, but caught up in the spirit of the game he took the bottle and drank. Kochanski got it next, and they passed it around until they drained it; then they drank another.

A clear patch appeared in the clouds and Mark spied a barge floating with the river current a mile below.

"Dive bomber," Mark cried, and held up a bottle. He started into a dive and the two came up beside him.

Downward they shrieked, the wind blowing past them. Allic, roaring with delight, pulled ahead.

Damn, they were coming in fast, Mark realized—but still Allic held his course. They dropped below a thousand feet. The crew of the barge saw them and started to run around the deck of the vessel.

Five hundred feet.

Allic laughed uproariously as he steepened the dive into a near-vertical fall. Mark hung with him, his fear blurred by wine and exhilaration.

Two hundred feet, and suddenly Allic started to pull up as he released his bottle. Mark continued on, seeing Allic's bottle splash off the port bow. He released and started to pull up.

The river rushed up towards him and desperately he strained to overcome his rate of fall. He rocketed past the boat even as his bottle impacted dead amidships.

Damn, he was going to hit, and he felt his body brush the water, kicking up a plume even as he pulled back up.

"Scratch one flattop," Mark shouted as he rolled up and away.

"Damn crazy sorcerers," one of the boatmen screamed.

Laughing, Mark, Allic, and Kochanski banked away and

rejoined Ikawa, who had been shaking his head and watching from a safe distance.

A little shaken by Mark's near crack-up, Allic eased off a bit. Finally, after another hour of flying, they sighted a white-walled fortress by the riverside.

"Tonight's stop," Allic announced, "my cousin Gerel."

Mark's disappointment showed—the day's flying was over.

"Would you care to stay up a bit longer?" Allic asked, looking at Mark with understanding of his passion to fly.

Mark felt like a teenage kid whose old man had just given him the keys to the car, with a full tank of gas.

Allic looked past Mark to a bank of thunderclouds forming in the distance.

"I've always loved the flow of a thunderstorm myself," Allic said. "Why don't you try it out?"

Smiling, Mark gave a cheery wave and started to bank off to the east.

"Besides," Allic said as Mark flew away, "you might find something interesting there."

Mark rode through the first pocket of turbulence, rising and falling with the wild swirlings of the wind. The storm rose above him, cutting from horizon to horizon with its churning fire and shadow. Green-black clouds scudded by, flickering and trembling. A steady drumroll of thunder crossed the heavens.

He soared, riding a sudden updraft, and then cut an ascending path across the face of the towering thunderhead.

The high anvil of the storm rose thousands of feet above him, so that he felt he was climbing the face of a mountain of swirling dark ice.

Bolts of lightning arced down to strike the ground. He knew that there was little chance of being struck, since any object in the air carried the same charge as the cloud. Because of the wind shears, however, no pilot in his right mind would willingly fly into this. But Mark was no longer a pilot of metal and pounding engines, he was flying as a god, and the power of the elemental forces around him seemed to draw him in. He powered up his shield to maximum and cut a sharp banking turn directly into the heart of the storm.

It was madness, sheer magnificent madness. Sheets of icy rain lashed past him, slipping around the shield's protective cone so that only a fine misty spray, smelling of ozone and clean windblown air, reached him.

The turbulence was sharp and unexpected as he soared from updraft into downdraft and then into updraft again. So rapid was one of the upward rushes that his ears popped repeatedly, and he felt the first faint symptoms of oxygen depletion. The clouds thinned for an instant and he came up into the afternoon sky, as though rising into the bottom of a canyon, for he was surrounded by towering walls of cloud that rose yet twenty thousand or more feet on all sides of him. As quickly as the canyon had opened, the towering cliffs closed over him, flickering with fire and thunder.

Screaming his joy, Mark arched back over and dove into the heart of the storm. Sheets of lightning tore the darkness, blinding him.

He felt as though each flash somehow increased his own power, and as the thunder roared, he shouted in wild delight, challenging the storm.

He was banking sharply through a rolling wall of turbulence when a bolt of lightning shot past him, slicing the sky. Laughing defiantly, Mark raised his hand and shot a bolt of power, as if answering the storm.

He fired again and again, and when he stopped for a moment, he realized that the storm had become strangely quiet.

Mark suddenly had the vague feeling that something was watching him. Slowing, he looked from side to side, but saw nothing. However, that uneasiness was growing stronger. There was something else with him, and whatever it was, it had a definite power to it.

He started to increase his speed, and with a sudden rapid climb, pulled up and rolled over to change direction.

There was another flash and with a cry of pain Mark closed his eyes.

"Who are you to tamper with the power of my storm?"

Damn. It was like his dream about the storm and a beautiful woman.

She floated before him—he wasn't sure whether she had a physical form or not. The clouds swirled through her black hair; her loose windblown gown seemed to merge with the clouds about them—or was it the clouds themselves that cloaked her?

Her eyes shimmered with light, matching the storm's power.

Stunned, Mark watched her warily, not yet sure whether this was a hallucination.

"You still haven't answered me." Her voice drifted past him like a gently flowing wind.

"I'm Captain Mark Phillips of the United . . . of Allic's princedom," he finished lamely.

She laughed, and with her laughter the sky around them crackled. "Ah, so you're the one who travels in dreams to see me."

How did she know?

"Well, miss, you see . . ." He paused, embarrassed at the memory and her knowledge of it.

She smiled knowingly at him, and her eyes seemed to burn into his soul. Her gaze riveted him; he felt as though she was seeing right through him, probing his thoughts and his hidden desires.

She closed her eyes and with a nod turned and started to float away.

"I shall see you again, Captain Mark Phillips," and she was gone. The storm exploded about him.

Shaken, Mark tucked into a dive, the storm crashing around him. Downward he soared, outracing the lashing rain that tumbled from the clouds. The sky grew brighter and he burst from the wall of the storm into the light of a setting sun that turned the sky into a fiery cloud of reflected red.

The storm had taken him some miles from his friends, and racing in front of the advancing cloud, he searched for some minutes until he finally spotted Gerel's fortress gleaming in the sunset. Diving low, Mark came in for an approach, turning down his defensive shield so that those below would not suspect him of being hostile.

Coming in over the high parapet he saw Allic, standing alone on the battlement wall, as if watching the approaching storm. And swinging around, Mark landed by his side.

"Beautiful storm," Allic said.

"I'll say. Allic, you won't believe what just happened to me up there."

"Try me."

Mark gave him a quick recounting of his unusual encounter. As he spoke, he wasn't sure if Allic was laughing at him.

A smile crossed Allic's face.

"Do you think I'm nuts or something?" Mark asked, still a bit shaken.

"Nuts?"

"You know, crazy. I mean, I just saw a woman floating in the middle of a thunderstorm, which she claimed was her creation."

"Might be 'nuts' for your world, but on Haven—" Allic shrugged in what Mark realized must be a gesture common to more than one world.

"Damn, she was beautiful," Mark whispered, turning from Allic to gaze at the thunderhead.

"I know," Allic replied softly.

Before Mark could inquire further, Allic patted him lightly on the shoulder, and smiling to himself, left Mark alone on the battlements. Well, chances were the woman had already come to Allic's attention. Two such as they would naturally be drawn together—and with that thought Mark felt a surge of jealousy and resentment for Allic's power.

Lightning crackled across the sky, illuminated the distant hills with a sharp electric flash, and his thoughts turned away from Allic.

"Beautiful," Mark whispered, as the first heavy drops of rain lashed across the castle walls, carrying with it the clean-washed scent of a summer storm.

A very tired but triumphant Lieutenant Mokaoto was brought before Sarnak in his throne room. Word of Mokaoto's success at his trial had preceded him, and even some of the experienced sorcerers of the court watched with a new wariness. This stranger had completed the last step of his training, having demonstrated his ability to fly, to communicate through crystals, and finally to fire with such accuracy that he had knocked his testing partner unconscious with a single blow. What had stunned them all was the fact that he had accomplished in weeks what had taken most of them years.

"Most impressive, young man," Sarnak said, obviously pleased with the results, and his initial judgment of the offworlder's power. "You are a tribute to your race and ancestry."

Sarnak watched Mokaoto closely, and saw him almost swell with pride. Ralnath's readings on his character were correct. He had discovered the offworlder's pride of race, honor, and something of his history as well. Now to set the hook.

"The truth about your situation has just been brought to

my attention, and I'm forced to conclude that you have been treated most unfairly. I had no idea of the nature of your capture and the fact that you were so foully thrown into prison. I do believe that you were the victim of court politics, since it is obvious that someone did not want you to come to my attention.

"And then, when I heard of your own honorable people and their current situation, my anger was even stronger." Sarnak stepped from his throne, walked to Mokaoto, and spoke softly, as though sharing a confidence with a trusted friend. "You see, my realm is in somewhat the same situation as your own lost country: cut off from vital resources and denied its rightful place in the sun. My just attempt to break the stranglehold and free my oppressed people is quite similar. Do you understand?"

Mokaoto stared momentarily and nodded savagely, a faint glow beginning to surround him as his emotions churned.

Sarnak continued, "I cannot directly help you and your country at this time, but in return for faithful and loyal service I will make your enemies mine and raise you to your rightful place in society." He stepped back from Mokaoto and spoke again so that all could hear. "Are you willing to pledge to me and serve as my loyal retainer?"

Overcome with emotion and pride Mokaoto bowed and said, "My lord, I swear to take you as my liege and master. I am samurai!"

Moments later, the brief ceremony over, Sarnak awarded Mokaoto his wristbands and crystals and snapped them in place with his own hands.

"Now, my loyal retainer, I have been told who it was that so foully treated you, and kept you locked away, and then humiliated you in your training."

Instantly Mokaoto's shield snapped on as his hatred for Wika threatened to overwhelm him.

Sarnak unsnapped his own offensive crystal and held it high. All in the throne room immediately knelt in reverence to the relic.

"This, Mokaoto, is a gift from my revered grandfather, the Creator Horat, to my own father, and passed down from him to me. I lend it to you to remove the stain upon your honor and mine." He placed it in Mokaoto's trembling hands.

Almost weeping Mokaoto swore, "My lord, I am yours!" Turning, he left the room to find Wika.

Sarnak dismissed the crowd and gestured to Ralnath to join him as he walked out onto the balcony. He didn't say anything, just tilted his head and raised an eyebrow.

"Yes, my lord. I made sure that Wika's crystals were flawed."

Sarnak nodded.

He stood for a few minutes overlooking the river valley far below. The final act was about to start. With proper planning he could win it all, taking Allic's princedom out from under him with a single blow. But even if that did not come to pass and he lost his own land in the bargain, still he would win, for realms and conquest were nothing compared to the ultimate prize.

"Our spy in Jartan's court has informed us that everything is ready."

"Then you still plan to throw in with your Uncle Tor on this?" Ralnath said, his nervousness obvious.

"If you want much, you must risk all," Sarnak replied coldly.

"My only wish is to serve you," Ralnath replied quickly, afraid of Sarnak's implications.

"But of course," Sarnak replied softly.

"But if Tor should lose . . . After all, his opponent . . ."

"The war with Allic is nothing more than a screen to hide our real intent. I've always planned it that way. Tor and his army of sorcerers will be here in two days, and our army is already in position to move into the tunnel."

The tunnel, always the tunnel, Ralnath thought. For nearly a thousand years that had been his task, supervising the security for the hundreds of miles of tunnels dug clear from their capital to the edge of Allic's city. It had been a nightmare of work, drafting the labor, sending them below, and making sure that no one could ever breathe a word of it once they could no longer work. He shuddered inwardly at the thought of how he had solved that part of the problem.

And even within his own security net he had never known of the side branch to the main tunnel, the branch that led straight to the heart of Jartan's Crystal Mountains, for that operation was a secret that Sarnak had managed on his own, until the final planning had been revealed and Ralnath's position was shifted to be liaison to Tor's staff.

For a thousand years Rainath had labored believing that this was Sarnak's master stroke to take Allic's realm. But in truth the attack on Landra was only a diversion. For Tor,

Sarnak's uncle and sole surviving son of a fallen god, would launch his own attack into the Crystal Mountains—to steal the great crystal hoard of Jartan himself while attention was focused on Landra. Even if the attack on Landra failed, the captured hoard would give Tor and Sarnak the power to face even a god. With such power the other gods might even be bargained with or turned against each other.

Ralnath's fear was obvious as he looked at his master.

"I take it you don't approve?" Sarnak asked.

"No, my lord, it is just that I fear Jartan's wrath."

"If we win, then we ourselves will be like gods, and your power will rise a hundredfold."

"Yes, my lord," Ralnath replied quietly, his greed for such power balancing his fear to some degree.

"The attack against Macha is planned?"

"They fly once darkness has settled."

"Good. Make sure that Mokaoto is in the forefront. Be sure as well that he is seen by at least one survivor. The whole area knows of Allic's new sorcerers and Macha will be sure it is Allic attacking him.

"Once you return from the attack my army will start its move into the tunnel. You and the offworlder will go with the van. I've heard reports that the offworlder has suggested improvements to my communications control. He claims that he learned such things back on his world. Let him work on that as the army moves up."

Sarnak turned away and walked to the balcony overlooking his citadel. From the courtyard below came the sound of angry shouting. Sarnak leaned over to watch. There was a flash of light, and then another, followed by a shout of triumph.

Sarnak smiled wistfully as the attendants rushed out and took Wika's body away.

Chapter 11

Far to the south, across the border of Allic's realm, was the land ruled by Macha, Prince of Torm and son of Minar. It was a land of herds and savannahs, with lazy rivers and quick-tempered spearmen. Each village on the plains was fortified, and even the fields were surrounded by thick thorn fences. Life was harder here than in the temperate climate above the escarpment, but the rains came regularly and the herds were prolific, and the beauty of the open savannah made it all worthwhile.

On this day, however, clouds of smoke and ashes and the smell of carnage brought home the dangers of living so close to the border.

"This, this is the price of my trust!" With a cry of rage Macha cradled the small body to his chest.

"My lord," a voice whispered behind him, "please, my lord, give the boy to me."

"No!"

"My lord, we must send him to his rest. Please, my lord, the men are watching."

Could he have no rest? Could he never have the quiet of solitude with his grief? Even the son of a god could feel pain. But no, his people were always watching, drawing their strength from him. As the son of Minar, one of the Creators, his followers wanted to see him as a source of forbearance and strength. Even as he held the scorched body of his nephew, still the men of his guard would expect him to be the leader, the stern judge without passion.

Trembling, he came back to his feet, and Batu, his first commander of the host, approached him. With a look of infinite pain Batu extended his arms to take the burden.

Macha closed his eyes and let his feelings show again as he kissed the boy on the forehead.

"Sleep, my little one. May your spirit rise now to join your father. Sleep, little one, who was like a son to me."

Macha looked to his friend and nodded. The burden was lifted from his embrace and Batu took the body away. Macha knew he should attend the body as it went to the flames, but that was far too much for him right now. Later, after the revenge, he would come back here and make the offerings of his own blood upon the ashes.

Turning, he left the ruined fortress. They had flown through the night, guided by soaring flames which could be seen fifty miles away. But too late, far too late to save his half brother, to save his beloved nephew, or the hundred families of the border marches.

Smoke swirled around him as he strode through the gate and into the early morning light. From all directions units were coming up, rallying to the messages that had arrived at the other garrison points.

From above, the last of his sorcerers were circling down to land. From across the grasslands to the southwest he could see his elite regiment of a thousand mounted warriors eager for his command.

They were all too late to save this place. But they would not be too late for what was about to begin.

From out of the smoke Batu came up to his side and nodded in response to Macha's inquiring gaze. The boy was upon the pyre now. As the son of a god, Macha knew that the spirit would go to another house of the million realms of the gods, there to walk again beneath a different sun, and there to live out, he hoped, a life into old age. But never again in this realm would Macha see the youngster's shining eyes, or hear the peals of laughter at the simple magic performed by his beloved uncle, who was also the prince of the Torms.

"Never again," Macha whispered.

"My lord?"

"Why?" Macha asked, looking straight at Batu.

"There is no logic to it, my lord."

"Have you found any messages to confirm the evidence?"

Batu looked back at the blazing fortress. "It's been swept clean, my lord. They hit it hard—at least thirty sorcerers, the survivors claim. Our people never knew what hit them."

"They should have been ready," Macha roared. "Damn it, this is a border march!"

"But it's on Allic's border, my lord. You yourself knew that your brother dismissed the reports of raidings into our territories as coming from Sarnak, not Allic, and thus he was lax."

"And now we have paid for that trust," Macha said coldly. "You heard what the survivors said. The attackers were led by one of the new outlanders, and only our so-called friend Allic has those accursed outlanders with him. Oh, they tried to make themselves look like Sarnak's men, but they weren't good enough at their doooit."

Macha turned and looked back at the raging inferno that darkened the morning sky. It was all so obvious to him now, and he cursed himself for being a fool.

"I can see it clearly at last," he said, his voice edged with bitterness and self-reproach. "Those outlanders are his new allies, summoned from another realm. And it was no mistake, as he now claims. They're all trained sorcerers who give him a powerful edge. Allic thinks to provoke a war between Sarnak and me, and then with those new sorcerers he'll move in and clean us both out once we've exhausted each other. Oh, most clever of him, staging this attack with the hope that I'll believe Sarnak is behind it. With the crystals captured from our two realms, he'll have near the power of a god himself.

"But I am the son of a god, as well," Macha said, "and if this is to be a war between the sons of gods, then so be it. And if this is to be the start of a war between the gods themselves, then so be that, as well."

"My lord, we only have the evidence of this one attack," Batu cautioned. "Somehow it still seems out of character for Allic. I know he gets into his cups a little too much, but even when drunk, I don't think Allic would conceive of such a drive for power."

"The evidence is here, right here—" Macha pointed to the blazing fortress. "There's been half a dozen incidents on our border in the last month, and our ambassador reports that Allic is crying that we have attacked him on several occasions.

"Can't you see it? He's building his excuses with faked attacks upon himself, so he can whine to his father and neighbors about my perfidy.

"The true evidence is all around us," Macha shouted, his arms sweeping toward the ruins. "The evidence is the ashes of my nephew, rising even now over our heads. What more do you want for proof? Do you want me to go to Allic's court, crawling on my knees, begging to hear his lies? When I see him again it will be to spit on his corpse."

Macha looked towards his sorcerers and chieftains. "Gather the host," he roared. "We march tonight!"

"Jesus, Mark, will you just look at that!"

Mark didn't need Kochanski to point out the splendor before them. For several hours they had been increasing their altitude, following the terrain's gradual sweep into the snowcapped mountains. Now the air was sharp, invigorating, and Mark had realized just how much he had missed the cold, bracing winters of Pennsylvania. For years now, ever since the war started, he had either been in the drizzly winters of England or the near tropical warmth of south central China, followed by the seemingly eternal spring of this land.

Flying with Allic and his retainers, he crested the last of the snowclad peaks, and as if a curtain had been drawn back, the distant peninsula beyond and the city of Asmara atop it were at last revealed.

The walls of the city shimmered in the morning light, so that they seemed to match the pureness of the mountaintops the flyers had left behind.

Picking up speed, the party dove, running low over a broad highland forest that soon gave way to pastures, vineyards, and well-tended orchards. However, now the air was filled with not only the sound and smell, but also the feel, of the nearby sea.

The roads below were filled with travelers heading towards the city. Obviously it was festival time, for all were dressed in their finest, so that the paths and highways seemed to be awash with a thousand colors.

As the formation passed by, the mortals who could only dream of flying looked up and shouted their greetings. Politely the flyers returned the courtesies, but the three off-worlders barely paid attention: All they could look at now was the city and its wonders.

Jartan had built his capital city, Asmara, on the end of a peninsula that extended a dozen leagues into the Central Sea. This was the center of Jartan's realm, of which Allic's province of Landra was only a small part.

The outer series of walls passed by a hundred feet below, and at last they entered the first belt of the city proper.

The walls were set off on either side by open parklands a hundred yards across. One could follow the high limestone barrier as it stretched away for leagues in either direction, marked off by the surrounding ribbon of green.

The shimmering white wall set in a field of green created a stunning effect, but Mark realized that it was not merely for esthetics, since the open space provided clear fields of fire both in front of the barrier line and behind. He knew that Allic and all the others referred to Jartan as a god, but it struck him as curious that a god would still rely on medieval defenses for his capital city.

As they flew towards the heart of the city, a second barrier a hundred feet high lay before them with the same open space of gardens laid out in front. Following Allic's lead, the party rose and passed over the second line of fortifications into the city proper. With a wheeling turn they followed the wall for several hundred yards and then turned again over an open thoroughfare a hundred or more yards across.

"The Avenue of the Gods," Allic said, falling back to fly by Mark's side.

Buildings of limestone and marble rose half a thousand feet into the air, so that it was like flying down a canyon of burnished stone that shimmered, reflected, and rereflected the morning sun. Some of the buildings were shaped like great pyramids or giant obelisks, while others appeared like Greco-Roman temples, with massive fluted columns and broad stairs that were now crowded with people. More than one building even had a vaguely modern look to it, with huge sections of glass and polished metal.

Mark slowed for a moment, fascinated by a unique arrangement where a huge mirror, turned by a clock mechanism, caught the light of the sun and sent its image to a relay of fifty or more mirrors positioned down the length of the street. The mirrors in turn reflected the light to other mirrors or to giant prisms, so that rainbow splashes cut into every corner of the avenue, generating a lively interplay of color that darkened for moment with the passing of a cloud, then exploded with dazzling intensity so that it seemed as though rainbow after rainbow arced across the thoroughfare.

Music drifted on the breeze, the chanting of priests from one temple counterpointed by a wild pulsing roar of bagpipes from another, which mingled with a hundred different songs from the crowds, musicians, and street vendors.

The air was filled with a shifting patina of scents—incense from the temples, cooked food from street vendors, the smells of a vibrant city full of life, and the scent of the not so distant sea.

Yet Mark sensed that all this was but a prelude. For at the far end of the avenue he could see the inner core of the city, surrounded by a wall that was nearly twice as high again as the one they had passed over minutes before. The gate facing out onto the Avenue of the Gods was yet to be opened.

"Now we enter my father's true court," Allic said, and motioned for the others to swing behind him in single file. Slowing, he drifted up and over the wall.

The sound of a waterfall filled the air, and as Mark crested the barrier he saw a magnificent array of fountains arranged around the sides of a large hexagonal pyramid in the center of a vast courtyard. Atop the pyramid was yet another clock-driven mirror which reflected to more mirrors and prisms. The light in turn was reflected back to the fountains, so that the entire courtyard was awash in brilliance.

Dozens of jets of water leaped a hundred feet into the air, swirling in a pattern that shifted with every passing second. Mark could not help but laugh as Allic swept downward, cutting in and out through the high arcing jets of liquid, and then he noticed that there were others flying through and about the fountains as if this were an elaborate game.

Below in the courtyard he could see hundreds of upturned faces calling and laughing as the sorcerers circled in and out, dodging as new jets erupted.

There was a gentle pulsing of music in the air, and Mark realized that he sensed it more than he heard it. It held a wild, haunting beat that resonated in him.

Diving, he swung in behind Allic, and as the tempo of the music increased, so did the changing pattern of water jets.

A cheer came up from below, and looking over his shoulder, Mark saw that a sorcerer had been tumbled end over end by a blast of water. The crestfallen flyer regained his control and swung out of the play area to settle on one of the small islands in the lagoon that surrounded the fountain.

So, Mark realized, it was yet another game of flying.

Faster and faster the jets switched on and off. He visualized it as dodging streams of flak coming from below. Suddenly as he raced in close along the pyramid wall, a concealed jet erupted and struck him hard in the chest, sending him tumbling. Regaining control at the last moment, he skimmed low across the water and alighted at the water's edge, where a laughing spectator offered him a goblet of wine.

"Outlander, hey?" the old man inquired.

"Guess you could say that," Mark replied politely.

"The whole court's been abuzz about you folks. Ah, there goes another one."

Mark looked over towards where the man was pointing, to see that Ikawa had been knocked out.

Faster and faster the jets played on and off, and the haunting music grew louder, echoing in his mind. The hundreds of spectators had picked up the beat and clapped their hands in rhythm to the song, each clap signaling a change to the pattern of water. It all had an intoxicating, sensual feel to it, like a dreamscape.

The beat kept increasing and one after another the flyers tumbled, each fall met by another cheer, until only Allic and Kochanski were left. In and out they darted, weaving and turning, skimming low then high, racing across the surface of the lagoon, a stream of jets arcing up behind them in a chain of watery explosions.

Kochanski pulled up sharply to the left, barrel rolling in a tight series of loops, while Allic circled around him in his climb. It appeared that the two would collide when a jet of water arced down from the top of the pyramid, catching them both at the same instant.

As they fell, it seemed the entire lagoon and the pyramid in the middle exploded in one showering cascade of water, while the eerily half-heard music thundered to a climax. The water showered down, the light from the mirrors casting rainbows over the crowd, as everyone broke into a wild ovation.

Allic pulled up low over the water with Kochanski at his side, and reaching out, prince grabbed the hand of vassal and held it high in a sign of mutual triumph. Together the two descended to Mark's side, where the crowd surged around them, shouting greetings and praise.

"Welcome to my father's court," Allic laughed.

Servants came forward with towels and goblets of wine.

"How the hell did you do that?" Mark asked, looking at Kochanski.

"Beats me, Captain. It was like in my mind I could see where each jet was, and where it would cut, and all I had to do was weave through it. I felt like I was watching one of those slow-motion movies."

"Useful in a fight, I dare say, dodging the blast of an enemy," Mark said quietly.

"You see then," Allic said, "here all things are but shades of others. Games train for war; the words of court mask the speaker's intent. This is my father's court, but it is also the court of those who serve him, and wish to gain in his sight, as well."

Allic fell silent for a moment and looked at the two of them carefully. "We had best go and prepare. The god Jartan will wish to see you at once."

The god Jartan, Mark thought. If only his father could have heard those words, how his Baptist preacher's soul would have been aroused. It was bad enough when his father was in the same room with a Unitarian minister or even worse, a Catholic priest, ready to debate some obscure point of doctrine. But a god?

He felt a cold stab of fear. Was he really about to meet a god? Mark was reminded of his father's fire-and-brimstone sermons. Would this be a fiery god of Old Testament wrath?

"You look a little nervous," Allic said.

"Listen, if you were raised a Baptist, you'd be damn nervous too, meeting someone who thinks himself a god," Mark said anxiously.

"He does not think himself a god," Allic said, a note of caution in his voice. "He *is* a god. And he awaits our presence. It's not wise around here, Mark Phillips, to keep a god waiting."

Mark felt that it was beyond even the wildest designs of Cecil B. de Mille. Allic walked before him, his golden cloak shimmering in the strange, haunting light that seemed to fill the great hall yet came from no visible source. He, Ikawa, and Kochanski walked behind their prince, wearing their old army uniforms which had been freshly pressed and mended, the brasswork polished by servants to a glow that would have pleased even a boot camp sergeant.

The corridor was more than a hundred yards in length, broadening into a great triangle to a high dais at the far end of the chamber. Along the walls the chosen of Jartan's court stood in groups, talking and drinking with the ease of long familiarity. The music was stirring and majestic at the same time. Everywhere there was the shimmering light, so that the assembly seemed to glow with an inner radiance.

Mark tried to ignore the curious stares, keeping his eyes straight ahead, looking towards where he expected Jartan to wait. But there was no throne on the dais, no great bearded figure sitting there. The far end of the audience chamber was empty save for an enormous pillar of shifting light. Glancing surreptitiously out of the corner of his eye, he could see a dozen other columns of light around the walls of the chamber.

So, what is this? Mark thought, suddenly disappointed. Here he had been all geared up to have the shit half scared out of him by a towering presence who spoke with *thees* and *thous* like somebody from the Bible, but there was nothing. Just an empty dais and what was probably a searchlight or something buried in the floor.

All right then, Mark thought. *We'll bow down before the unseen god, make some public intonations of piety, and be on our way.* He could only hope his father wouldn't ever hear of this breaking of the First Commandment about false gods.

Allic came to a stop and extended his hands as a signal to the men behind him.

Mark looked out of the corner of his eye at Kochanski. The old history student was really getting into this. He realized that for Kochanski this was the stuff of dreams—of ladies dressed in silken robes and warriors fair, of distant lands that most likely never were, but should have been.

"My father, I have come again to pledge myself and my realm to you," Allic announced, raising his arms.

He lowered his arms, and turning, looked at Mark and the others.

"He is here," Allic said evenly. "Jartan now wishes that you announce yourselves."

Damn, this felt a little ridiculous, Mark thought. Growing up he could never get into all the glorying and praising god stuff of his father's church. In fact, since the day he left his parents' home, he had never again gone to a service. He could remember how his old man had loved it when Grace, his kid sister, would "get the spirit" and start speaking in tongues and calling on Jesus to help her. Mark had found the whole thing rather embarrassing. But he had to do something.

He stepped up to Allic's side and came to attention. Trying to suppress a grin, he snapped off a salute.

"Captain Mark Phillips, pilot 306th bombardment group, serial number 15677432, at your service, my lord."

Ikawa and Kochanski, following Mark's lead, did the same.

Well, that ought to take care of it. If he ever got back home this would be a hell of a good story to tell the guys—that is, if they ever believed him in the first place.

"Do you not consider it dangerous to be flippant in the presence of a god?" a voice boomed through the audience chamber.

Before his terrified eyes Mark saw a fiery form taking shape within the light. The figure swirled in upon itself and with a blinding flash ignited into a pulsing tower of blue-white flame.

God almighty, what've I done? Mark thought.

The tower of light whirled like a tornado of flame. "I am not amused by your thoughts," the voice boomed.

Mark felt his knees turning to jelly. He thought for a moment that he should abase himself before this presence. But that probably wouldn't work, and anyhow, if he was going to get blasted, he'd prefer to face it standing up.

"I am Jartan, one of the Creators of this world. And you will either obey me or die."

Gritting his teeth, Mark stared into the coiling fire and waited stoically for damnation.

"Good, very good," the voice whispered. Mark kept staring straight ahead, not daring to move.

"My son has told me of you and the others. He claims that despite your faults, you have potential."

Mark did not respond. At this point it was best to keep his big mouth shut.

"We'll talk again later," the voice whispered, and the tornado of flame pulsed ever smaller, until the figure in the light flickered out.

Mark felt a hand on his shoulder, and turning, looked into Allic's eyes.

"Don't ever press your luck with him," Allic said, his features cold. "Remember, he can sense your very thoughts. It was obvious that at first all three of you had angered him.

But he admires courage—he never could stand grovelers—and that was your redemption."

"I'm sorry," Mark whispered. He could see that this might have turned out badly for Allic if they had too greatly angered Jartan.

The sound of other voices now echoed around them. Mark felt as though everyone in the room was watching him, which undoubtedly they were.

"Let's join the others," Allic said. "I've brought you here for a reason. Part is my promise to help you leave after your service, and I dare say, only my father could arrange that. But also to let others know that my strength has been increased by the addition of you and your men. Do your part. But if you should embarrass me . . ."

Mark knew better than to inquire about what had been left unsaid. For the first time he was seeing Allic as a cold and, if necessary, hard politician who could call his underlings to account. He had at times suspected that Allic might be a little too free and easygoing with his responsibilities, but not now. Mark felt a new level of respect for Allic, and he nodded, accepting the warning.

Turning, they walked towards the crowd that filtered in around them, eager to examine the three new wielders of power who had aroused the interest of a god.

Mark found himself being presented to a dizzying array of princes, sorcerers, healers, warriors, philosophers, and priests. Already he could see how most of them were maneuvering, trying to get a grasp on these new creatures, evaluating whether they could be allies or possibly enemies to be dealt with.

Several priests cornered Mark, and he had to tread lightly when they quizzed him on the nature of his god. Knowing that Allic was watching, he maneuvered and ducked, and after nearly a quarter-turning had not made a single statement with any real content.

"Mark." Allic put a hand on his shoulder. "If your worships will forgive me," Allic said smoothly, "there's someone here who insists that I introduce Mark to her at once."

Allic led him through the crowd to a small knot of people standing in the far corner of the room. Allic broke away from Mark's side and came up to the back of a woman and slipped his arm around her waist.

The woman slowly turned, placing her hand on Allic's shoulder.

Mark went numb as her dark blue eyes bore into him. Her raven hair flowed over her shoulders, covering her full breasts. The sheer blue silk of her gown clung to every curve of her long slender body.

The faintest of smiles crossed her lips and she drew closer, Allic still by her side. Mark coolly held her gaze, struggling to suppress the instinct to activate his defensive crystal.

"Yes, you are as I remember you, young flyer," she said softly.

"Mark Phillips, may I present Storm."

Mark looked at Allic with a tug of jealousy. Never had he met a woman like Storm, yet she triggered a defensive wariness in him.

"Oh, we've already met. Haven't we, Captain Phillips?"

He had seen that look before, but never with such a frank openness of invited pleasure. He looked suddenly at Allic. It must be obvious to everyone, especially to his lord prince, how this woman was looking at him.

Allic stared at Storm, then at Mark, threw back his head and started to laugh.

"Ah, my poor friend, too much has already happened to you today. Don't worry though, I'm on your side with this particular issue, and I have to say that I almost feel sorry for you." He pulled Storm closer with a playful hug.

"She's my sister, Mark."

Mark couldn't help but breathe a sigh of relief, and a smile crossed his face.

"Would that be on your father's or your mother's side?" Kochanski asked, coming up to join the conversation.

"Why, on our father's side," Storm said evenly, still looking straight into Mark's eyes.

"Then you are the daughter of a god," Kochanski said quietly.

"But of course," she replied, holding Mark with her gaze.

Oh no, Mark thought, struggling to keep his features calm.

She stepped even closer, her warm fragrance washing over him; she smiled at his obvious discomfort.

"Does my being the daughter of a god intimidate you, Captain Phillips?" she asked, her gaze still fixed on him.

"Well, ah, no, not exactly," he lied, struggling not to lower his eyes for a quick look at her cleavage. The low cut of her imperial-style dress made it rather difficult to ignore.

Damn, the last thing he needed was for Jartan's daughter

to think that he was checking her out—then the shit would really hit the fan. But try as he would, human nature won out and he sneaked a quick look downward.

Christ, what a body.

"Well, do you like the way I look?"

Mark could feel the blood rushing to his face. The women back home would never have been so damn direct.

All right then, Mark thought, *if she wanted to be that way about it . . .* "Yes I do. You're a knockout."

"I take it that is one of your outlander terms meaning that you like the appearance of my breasts."

Storm smiled at how her response caught him off guard, and slipping her arm around his, led him off to a quiet corner of the reception hall.

"Allic's told me about your customs regarding women. Sounds rather restrictive to me. Gives no credit to a woman to make her own choices."

He looked at her out of the corner of his eye. Damn, she was beautiful. Her long black hair swayed softly with her every step, complementing the feline grace of her body.

But this was the daughter of a god, he kept reminding himself. He knew what the hell his Baptist dad would say about this theological question. Damn, screwing around with a goddess—even the thought was blasphemous!

Together they slipped into the quiet shadows of an archway leading into a side corridor.

"Would I be too forward," Storm whispered, drawing closer, "if I said that I found you very appealing?"

"Ah—not at all," he said woodenly. Was she propositioning him?

"You seem very nervous."

"It's just that this type of thing doesn't happen to me every day," Mark said. "I mean, I almost get fried by a god and later the most beautiful woman I've ever seen is telling me how appealing I am. Now, don't get me wrong, your highness, but . . ."

"Storm, just call me Storm."

"All right then, Storm. It's just that I'm feeling a little overwhelmed by all of this."

Then he found himself throwing all caution to the wind. "Two months ago I was a flyer. I was fighting in a war and I knew that we were right in what we were doing. I knew, damn it . . . I knew how things worked, and why things were the way they were.

"And now all of this. I don't know what the hell I'm doing here. The whole world is turned upside down. I came from a place where all this stuff you attribute to the Essence was nothing more than fairy tales. According to the way the game was played in my old neighborhood, I should have died back in that crummy temple. Who knows, maybe I really am dead, I still think that at times. . . ."

She looked at him as though he were talking a foreign language, but he didn't even notice. His frustrations at last were coming out.

"Then I meet this incredibly beautiful woman in a lightning storm that she claimed was hers, and two days later I find out she's the daughter of a god and I think she has the hots for me. Are you following me?"

"I think so."

"Look, Storm, you are *really* attractive, but I just don't know how I can handle another complication."

"Does that mean you're not interested in making joy with me?"

Be careful here, Mark thought. This girl could fry him if she got pissed off.

"No, I wasn't saying that at all," he replied cautiously. His eyes wandered again, and his pulse quickened.

She drew closer, pressing him against the wall. Her body seemed to melt against his.

She held his gaze with an unblinking stare that seemed to look deep inside him. His body reacted to her with a vigor that made him lightheaded.

She smiled, closed her eyes and kissed him. He responded with intensity, and held the embrace for what seemed an eternity—or a moment.

At last she drew back, her face flushed, her breath coming in short, shallow gasps.

"I was right about you," she whispered. "I have felt your presence since you first came to Haven and I could feel your affinity through your dreams and our encounter in my storm." They gazed at each other for a moment and she nodded.

"I think we should return to the gathering," she said, but it was obvious to Mark what she'd prefer to do. His common sense was glad that her reasoning was overcoming desire, but he was still frustrated. In spite of his fear, he wanted this woman.

"After all, they'll already be talking about my leading you away as I did."

"I'd think around here someone in your position could pretty much do as they please."

"Hardly!" she said, laughing. "Don't you have a little game called politics on your world?"

"So, it's that way here too."

"I wanted to stake out my claim to you right up front," she said evenly, as though the passion of the last minute had never occurred.

"After all, you outlanders are a prime interest around here. Not only has your arrival significantly shifted the southern power bloc in my brother's favor, but we've got the guilds who want to get new ideas and products from you, the priests who either want to try you as heretics or investigate any new truths your society might have developed, et cetera, et cetera. Besides, I dare say half the women in the court would be more than happy to make joy with you, if only to experience an offworlder."

Mark couldn't help but feel a conflicting emotion of excitement at the prospect, mingled with anger at the thought of being considered only a morsel for bored court ladies. He looked at Storm and wondered if that was all that he represented to her as well.

"Ah, I can see by your expression what you're thinking of me," she said, drawing her arm through his.

She forced him to look into her eyes.

"Believe me, Mark Phillips, my interest in you is far from casual. Don't take our different standards and apply them to your values. I'm interested in you, and I plan to find out what you really are."

Storm smiled, and Mark could sense the genuineness of her words. He smiled in return.

"Anyhow," she said softly, "I wanted to get to you first, before anyone else caught your attention."

Storm led him down the corridor and back to the brightly lit audience chamber. Mark noticed that more than one head was turned in his direction, and a low murmur filled the room at their reappearance.

"So, now you've laid your claim to me publicly, is that it?" Mark said, not with anger but as a statement of fact.

"Of course! Though more than one of the lovelies out there will try and get to you, as a challenge to me.

"Just a word of caution, if Allic hasn't already given it to you. Watch everything you say or do. Each person here has their own game. Some of the people in this room would gladly kill their opponents if given but half the chance."

"I'd think with a god and demigods like you around, that would be kind of hard."

"What do you mean?"

"Well, where I come from, our god has a tendency to severely punish any people who do wrong, or at least those who don't follow what he thinks is right and wrong."

"Rather narrowminded of him," Storm replied.

Mark couldn't help but chuckle. "Doesn't Jartan punish wrongdoers?"

"Occasionally, when somebody really crosses him, but he isn't the only god, and blasting someone might create political problems."

"Politics among gods?" Mark asked incredulously.

"Of course. Don't your gods engage in the game?"

"There's only one all-powerful god in our world."

"Sounds rather boring to me."

"I've never taken it up with him," Mark replied, trying to keep a straight face. "He isn't noted for his sense of humor."

"I can't understand this god of yours. How can a god have unlimited powers? Wouldn't unlimited powers create unlimited boredom for their wielder? Our gods placed part of their powers into this world, creating it, generating the forces so that life can flourish, and perhaps surpass them. With that comes a certain randomness, which is the focus of existence. For, if everything were preordained, if everything were controlled, nothing would be left but infinite boredom.

"Jartan has power, as do I, and even as do you. But your power is independent, and not even Jartan can foresee all that you might do or become. If it were otherwise, he would have gone mad eons ago."

"In other words, there really is free will," Mark stated.

She looked at him uncertainly.

"Never mind. You're saying I might already have enemies here."

"You're vassal to Allic; you've been linked with me. Need I say more?"

As they came back to Allic's group, she was hailed by an older lady across the way, who waved her over.

"Maybe tonight, maybe tomorrow, but rest assured, Mark Phillips, I'll be looking for you when we have time to be alone."

She gave his hand a playful squeeze and turned away. For the moment he was alone, and he looked around for a familiar face.

Kochanski was nowhere to be found. He noticed Ikawa off in a far corner, drink in hand. Suddenly feeling somewhat isolated, he started across the room towards the Japanese officer, who looked over the shoulder of the woman he was talking to and noted Mark's approach.

With a bow and gesture in Mark's direction, Ikawa broke off his conversation and joined Mark.

The look they exchanged was communication enough, and they quickly went to a table set in a quiet corner.

"I noticed you disappearing with that woman," Ikawa said, smiling. "Half the people here noticed it, and the other half was told within seconds."

"She certainly came on strong. By the way, she's Allic's sister."

"Ah, that explains why he was laughing when you wandered away."

"What about that number you were talking to?"

"She also came on very strong."

"Yeah, they all do around here." Mark chuckled ruefully. "By the way, where's Kochanski?"

"Oh, you missed that little stir. Right after you stepped out with your new friend, I saw two women in blue robes leading him out of the room. Allic said he had been singled out for a significant honor."

"What's that?" Mark asked.

"Just that Jartan summoned him for a private audience. Seems like quite a high honor."

"Honor, yeah," Mark said nervously. "Let's just hope he doesn't get all our butts in the wringer with some stupid question of his."

Chapter 12

The game of Gō had been in progress for hours when Sergeant Saito ruefully shook his head. "Takeo, you have won again. I have played better than ever and still lost."

Takeo bowed and asked hopefully, "Another? I'll give you a six stone handicap?"

"No, not tonight. I think I'll relax and finish my glass of wine before I retire."

Another of the Japanese refilled his cup, showing good manners, as Saito stretched back on the couch. "Who would have thought that we could go from the worst pesthole in the empire to this?"

The Japanese wardroom was a sitting room overlooking the pool, and just now it was filled with soldiers at their ease. They had been a little slower than the Americans to adjust to the luxury of their surroundings, but were enjoying their new life enormously.

Private Shigeru stirred and spoke deferentially. "Sergeant Saito, are we to work on 'creating' again tomorrow?"

Saito stretched and replied, "Yes, we have another session in the morning, with a lecture on using communications crystals after that. I think Pina has something special for us in the afternoon."

"I will never be able to create," Shigeru said ruefully. "Give me a load to lift or a task a man can see, and I am

148

happy. I am no good at making things that aren't there."
And then quickly, "Of course I will keep trying, honored
sir."

Private Yasuma broke his customary silence and said
softly, "All my life I have dreamed of being able to create the
things I see in my mind. I watch the American José bring
things into existence, beautiful things, and I know that if I
could only match his talent I would be complete."

Sergeant Nobuaki's voice was filled with rage and contempt. "You are unworthy to be Japanese, Yasuma. The
Americans are a race of mongrels! How dare you speak of
them so? I long for the day when we can kill them all."

The men froze in surprise. They had sworn to put the old
animosities aside, and for weeks no one had dared to speak
of the past. For more than one of them, it was no longer
simply a question of orders. Both sides were starting to es-
tablish friendships with their former enemies.

Saito jumped to his feet and screamed, "Attention!"

Instantly every man was on his feet rigidly staring straight
ahead.

Saito, as senior man present, walked over to Nobuaki and
slapped him across the face. "You are the one who is unworthy. You disobey both Lord Allic and Captain Ikawa." And
he slapped him again.

"You will this instant come with me to Pina's quarters and
repeat your statement to him."

After they left the room the other Japanese stared silently
at one another, torn by conflicting loyalties.

"Would anyone else like to try a game of Gō," Takeo said
quietly, trying to break the tension. His question was greeted
by silence as the others retreated into their own thoughts.

Takeo sat alone in the corner of the room.

I wish Imada were here, he thought sadly, wondering how
his friend was and what he was doing out on patrol.

"I tell you, Imada, you trust him far too much. You're
just like that fool friend of yours Takeo, always trusting what
Ikawa and Saito say."

"Why shouldn't I? He's the officer," Imada replied defensively, turning in the saddle to look towards his companion.
"Anyhow, he got us out of that scrap with the Chinese, didn't
he?"

"Got us out of the scrap, is it? What do you call where we

are now?" Yoshida said sarcastically. "How will we ever see our families again?"

Imada fell silent, lost in sad reflections. Yoshida was right. There was a war back home. What of his mother and his sister in Tokyo?

"But Ikawa knows what he's doing."

"Knows what he's doing," Yoshida barked. "Trusting Americans? Do you call that honorable, or even sensible, to trust our enemies?"

Imada was silent.

"He trusts the Americans." Yoshida drew his mount closer. "He trusts these people as well.

"Just look at them," Yoshida whispered, nodding towards the half dozen men riding across the open steppe ahead of them. "Do you see any like us? No! I see only people who look like Westerners."

"But I've seen no Westerners or black men, or Orientals, either," Imada replied. "It seems like all the races were blended here to form one."

"But do you see any like us—any of the divine race of the sun?"

Imada shook his head.

"There, that proves it then," Yoshida said, as if he had presented an unshakable argument. "We are alone here, surrounded by enemies, and our own leader has sold us out."

Imada couldn't reply. Unlike the world he had left, this one at least did not seem to be driven by any racial hatreds. If there was illogical hatred, it seemed to be fueled by who followed which god or demigod.

They rode in silence for some minutes. After nearly a week out, Imada was finally getting used to being mounted. He would have preferred to fly like the single sorcerer who hovered above them as air protection, but he knew that riding was part of their training. Air patrols might be more fun, but the only way to really patrol a border was by mounted units which could see every detail of the land up close and spot a track or sign missed by someone only a dozen feet above.

The mounted patrol crested a low hill and halted. The flankers, far to either side, rode in to join the rest of the group.

"The Golka Springs." Urba, the group leader, pointed towards a virtual garden, blooming in the middle of ocean-like steppes.

The oasis was tucked into a narrow fold of land, and its warm scent beckoned to them. It was a smell heavy with the promise of water, flowers, and quiet repose.

The Tals needed no urging. The sweetness of the spring water was known to them, and they were eager to reach it.

"We'll camp here tonight," Urba announced, "and start back for home tomorrow."

The Tals went straight to the nearest pool of water, and were drinking even before their human companions had dismounted.

Imada felt that he was walking in a dream. The oasis was a riot of blooms that completely covered the ground and coiled overhead, hanging down from the branches of the trees, forming a cooling canopy of shade.

The shadows of evening had long drifted into the mantle of night. Yoshida had the first watch, and the rest of the patrol was already asleep. But the seductive beauty of the oasis would not let Imada rest. He could remember the scent of the courtyard garden at home in the spring. He could remember sitting in the moonlight, dreaming of what he would be when school was done, dreaming of having a lover to sit beside him in the evening stillness.

Rising from his blanket roll, Imada slipped out of the encampment. Yoshida barely nodded to him as he walked into the darkness. The sound of running water attracted him, and he pushed through a sea of flowers to the edge of a small pool fed by a tiny waterfall that cascaded down from another pool above. The pool glowed with a soft phosphorescent shimmer that seemed magical. The night air was warm, each breath a delicious joy.

Slipping off his clothes, Imada stepped into the pool. To his surprise it was not cold but warm, as if heated. Lazily he floated out. Lifting his arm out of the water he laughed with amazement as the shimmering water rolled off him, as though light had turned liquid.

For what seemed eternity, Imada drifted, letting the warmth wash away his fears, his memories.

A hand touched his shoulder.

He turned, splashing, ready to cry out. A girl floated beside him, her head above the water.

"It is said that the Golka springs," she whispered, "can enchant until all sad memories drift away, like snow melted by the morning sun."

She drew closer to him, and before he even realized it, her lips brushed against his. Then, laughing softly, she pushed away.

She was the most beautiful woman Imada had ever seen, and her red hair floated around her like a darkened halo. He wanted to ask who she was, why she was there, but he almost feared that if he spoke, she would disappear.

Her face shimmered in the pool's soft phosphorescence, and her dark eyes smiled at him. His gaze lowered and he saw that she was as naked as he.

She drew closer, and this time her arms drifted around him.

Smiling, she kissed him again, with a searching passion that made the blood pound in his ears. Imada had been too embarrassed to join in the parties back at the castle; he had wanted things to be different. And now this mystery, who had seemed to drift to him out of a dream, coiled her body about his.

He felt the sandy bottom beneath his feet as the two of them stood chest deep in the water, locked in passionate embrace.

Her hands drifted down his arm, her lips slipped away from his for a moment, and he saw the wristband holding his protective crystal drop into the water.

For the first time he spoke to her. "You shouldn't," he whispered. "I've been told that I should never take it off."

"To protect yourself from me?" she asked innocently, and she leaned forward again, kissing him eagerly, her body pressed up against his.

Imada heard a muffled cry in the distance. He tried to turn his head but she held him locked in her embrace. His passion almost drove him to ignore the distant shout, but there was another, closer, a scream of pain.

He struggled to pull away from his enchantress. He couldn't tell if she was responding in passion or if in fact she was struggling to hold him.

There was a flash to one side, another scream, and then an entire series of flashes.

Wild with panic he looked into her eyes. He could see the passion but there was a look of bemusement, too.

Her foot slipped behind his, and with a splash he collapsed beside the pool. The girl leaped on him, pinning his arms. She touched his neck, and Imada felt as if someone had struck him a paralyzing blow. He was incapable of moving.

"Wilenta?" It was a soft whisper, coming from the direction of the encampment.

"Over here, Ophrea," the girl replied.

A rustling of flower vines—then a shadowy form stood above them.

"We got one of the offworlders. Is that the other one?"

"It was so easy, I almost felt guilty. He's such an innocent, trusting boy," Wilenta replied. "I had his crystal off before he even realized it."

The other woman chuckled. "Looks like you had some fun doing it."

Wilenta grinned. Leaning forward, she kissed Imada on the cheek.

"Don't worry, offworlder. Our mistress Patrice has plans for you and your friend."

"What about the others?" Imada asked weakly, feeling like a complete fool.

"Oh, we killed them," Ophrea said. "They're no use to us. But your friend is all ready to join you for a little trip."

Ophrea had spoken easily, offhandedly, about killing his companions, and Imada felt a knot of pain in his heart. He had never taken the dangers of Haven seriously, and now good men were dead and he was captured. With his powers he should have sensed the danger.

"I almost wish we could have finished our little encounter. I guess Patrice will get you now instead." Wilenta sighed, leaning forward to brush her lips against his. Several feminine voices joined in laughter at her comment.

She kissed him lightly; then her hand started to glow and his thoughts fell away into darkness.

Kochanski stood nervously in the center of Jartan's private audience chamber staring at the column of pulsing light.

"Look, I might as well be honest. I'm not sure how to approach your presence, especially after the way we messed up earlier."

The shifting pattern of radiance laughed. "Kochanski, isn't it? Am I pronouncing that the way you want?"

Kochanski smiled and nodded. He'd heard a hundred different ways to butcher the pronunciation of a good Polish name. Even some of the Irish priests in high school had mangled it without ever bothering to check, and now this god was trying to be polite.

"There's a chair over there—yes, the smaller of the two in the corner. Just go on over and be comfortable."

Be comfortable, Kochanski thought, and realized that he should avoid even a joking thought, for if this being could read minds . . .

"In fact, I can read minds, and when I feel like it I can probe your deepest memories. But I prefer to talk, not eavesdrop, so please relax and be at ease."

Relax? How in hell am I to relax?

There was no reply to his thought. Kochanski settled in to the chair, and noticed a tall glass of beer on a side table. At least it looked like a beer . . . He picked it up and sipped. To his amazement it didn't taste anything like the heavy beers and meads common to Haven. It almost tasted like a Schaefer served straight from the tap down at the old Polish-American Democratic Club back in Trenton.

"Now how did you do this?" Kochanski asked, holding the glass up as if in a salute.

"Oh, that. Well, I picked up your inner wish for a 'cold one,' as you put it, at the start of the reception. Your taste memories were easy to read, just a little work at creating, and behold."

As Jartan spoke his image formed in the chair across from Kochanski. The form was human, though up-scaled in dimensions, so that he would stand nearly nine feet tall.

At least in this respect, he thought, Jartan was playing out Kochanski's image of a god: larger than life, a long white robe cinched with a golden cord, and, of course, the flowing beard that cascaded to his waist.

"I did tap into your thoughts for this image too," Jartan said with a rumbling chuckle. "I hope I didn't disappoint you."

"No, ah, no, not at all, my lord."

"The 'my lord' can be dropped in private, Kochanski." He paused to study his own image. "Interesting, very interesting. Have you ever considered the social and historical implications to this shape?"

Kochanski had to smile. Jartan was almost Falstaffian in his mood.

"You must be wondering why you're here?" As he asked the question, Jartan's body reverted to a pattern of light, with a brightly glowing figure inside that was still seated in the chair.

"Yes, sir. I've been curious ever since I was asked to come here."

"Progress reports from Landra showed the uniqueness of the way the Essence was growing in you. Now, you might doubt that, since your skills in combat were far below some of your other comrades. But combat is only one way to use the Essence. Pina said that you were the most intellectual and inquisitive of the lot, and he was correct. In you I can see the mind of a scholar, forever searching, looking around corners, wondering. I like that. So I chose you to teach me."

"Teach you?" Kochanski was incredulous. "But you're a god!"

Jartan's booming laugh echoed through the chamber. "Maybe our definitions aren't the same. Tell me what you think a god is."

"Why, I guess most of us back home believe that God, and I mean the one god, is all-powerful, all-knowing, and all-seeing. That from Him all has come and will go. He is the beginning and without end, forever eternal, the Maker of all."

He rattled off the lines as if reciting it from his old catechism for the approval of Sister Lawrence, back at St. Hedwig's Elementary.

"Interesting. Where did you learn that?"

"The priests and nuns of my god taught me."

"I see. Well, I guess we have a little problem here."

"I had a feeling there'd be a problem. You see, sire, from my viewpoint you don't quite fit into what I've been taught is the nature of the universe."

Jartan rumbled with laughter. He enjoyed this man. Almost all humans he ever came into contact with simply groveled at the sight of him, or worse yet, became whining sycophants.

"I need to learn some things from you," Jartan said bluntly. "I could probe your thoughts, but that can result in something being missed. It's best if I ask and you answer."

"Right... There is one major problem for me," Kochanski replied. "You see, I believe that a god, or gods, however you want it, are all-powerful and so already know the answers."

"Think about that," Jartan replied softly. "If I truly could know all, see all, across all eternity—consider what that would mean."

"I've wondered about that long before I came here," Kochanski replied. "I think, for myself, it would drive me mad."

Jartan paused. "For some of us, it nearly has."

"Do you mind if I ask some questions first?" Kochanski said, his curiosity overcoming him.

"Ask."

"First of all, I was taught by the priests that there was only one god, and the rest were false."

"That's pretty narrow of him, if I do say so."

"Then how many are there?"

"I don't know."

Kochanski stood and started pacing. Even as a child he had wrestled with the paradox of praying to god for one thing, while in his heart of hearts he desired something else. Though his cautious side warned him to be diplomatic, he figured he might as well get it out in the open.

"You know, ever since I've come to Haven, wherever it is, I've been hearing about gods and demigods. But I don't believe you guys fit the definition. A god should be all-powerful, and you just admitted that you aren't. How can this be?"

"Ah, so you think a god is all-powerful. That is your paradox. You think there is one thing that controls all, and you call that god.

"In a way that is true. Each of us has a part to play in what could be called a dream. But that dream is not conscious or separate from the whole. It is simply that which we are all part of. Each of us is an indestructible part of the whole, but the whole is not separate or self-creating—and certainly does not control everything."

"Then what is a god?"

"Now we're getting down to the particulars. You see, there are an infinite number of realities, or places of existence. Your world is one; through a gateway you crossed into Haven and its cosmos. At that moment you passed into another reality.

"This is my domain as a god; along with my remaining siblings, I control this realm. But it is merely control of the physical, and while occupying this place, those beings of life that should decide to pass through here.

"I can change the force of life, I can terminate its existence in this particular plane, but I do not have the power to create life from nothing or to send it into final oblivion."

"Then you are not all-powerful?" Kochanski asked softly.

"Who is?" Jartan replied.

Kochanski was stunned. Intellectually he pondered the sometimes illogical nature of his own religion. But with one comment Jartan had pulled out all the props, the mooring points which had been common to almost every belief he had ever encountered. No one was all-powerful; they were all in this game together, but no one was running it.

"You seem a little shaken." Jartan reached out and touched Kochanski on the arm.

"It's just . . . well, it's just that you've told me there is no father, no guide, no supreme arbitrator or judge."

"Your god claims that distinction?"

Kochanski nodded.

"Such things are what a child needs, Kochanski. A child needs to know that someone decides what's right or wrong, and will punish or reward. But when you become an adult your parents should no longer do that for you. If a parent does attempt to think for his child, then he is stealing life itself from him. Finally, a parent should be an advisor, not a judge, and so too with a god. I'm merely saying to you that in the realm of the universe, Kochanski, you are an adult."

Kochanski smiled weakly. It would take some getting used to.

"Then, what can a god do?" he asked.

"For one thing, I can not create or unmake you. You are as eternal as I, in your own way. You've heard my son speak of the Essence?"

Kochanski nodded.

"It's a crude word to describe what words cannot describe, but it is good enough. The Essence, or what some might call energy, is the fabric that holds everything together. It is the very fabric of time, forever coiling in upon itself, forever renewing."

"Our textbooks say that energy can neither be created nor destroyed, but used again and again in some form or another."

"Exactly."

Kochanski settled back in his seat. He looked at his empty glass of Schaefer and gestured to Jartan. The god laughed, snapped his fingers, and as if pouring from an invisible pitcher of beer refilled the glass.

"If only the guys back at the club in Trenton could see

that," Kochanski said, raising his glass again in a salute.

"There are questions that I wish to ask, as well," Jartan said, "so let us finish this. As I was saying, the Essence is the power. Quite simply, a god is someone who can control it completely. Thus it was that ages ago, I, along with those who became my brothers and sisters, eight of us in all, combined our Essence and broke through the barrier out of the Great Void and into this universe. When we mastered our powers, we chose this world and shaped it, made it into the Haven you see now. In the shaping of it, our own Essence became part of the very fabric of the world.

"In time, we brought others like you here, to play out the dramas of their existence. We as gods can thus interact with them. At times we have walked among them, played in their lives, fought their wars, loved, lived, hated, and even died."

"Died?"

"Yes, even a god may die. Oh, he is not destroyed, but his spirit goes back into the Sea of Chaos, the Great Void, to wander through the emptiness and begin again. Such partings are bitter," Jartan said sadly, "for loved ones are lost forever in this life, though if one tries they can be reunited in another reality, vaguely knowing that they have loved each other before." Jartan seemed lost in a melancholy darkness. At last he roused himself, looked down at his companion, and smiled.

"Even a god can know sadness and remorse."

"I've heard the War of the Gods mentioned several times," Kochanski asked quietly. "Am I allowed to ask about that?"

Jartan hesitated. "It's still painful, but yes, it is something you should know, since the repercussions are still being felt today. The god Horat was always the most driven of the Creators, and as eons went by, he became obsessed with ruling not just his region, but all of Haven.

"Finally, he met with our brother Borc over some border dispute. Borc was tricked and betrayed into lowering his defense." Jartan paused. "Horat then murdered and devoured our brother."

"Devoured?" gasped Kochanski.

"Not the flesh, but the Essence. He sent Borc back to the Great Void an empty husk.

"Of course all of the Creators knew instantly, for we felt Borc's agony."

Jartan was silent for a few moments.

"The rest of us banded together and made war on our insane brother. The conflict took years, killed untold millions, and sent most of his region back into the sea. The final confrontation cost my brother Danar his life as he saved mine. We finally were able to drain away Horat's Essence and send him back to Chaos.

"That was three thousand years ago, but the pain is still fresh, the hatreds are still just below the surface. Sarnak the Accursed fought in that war and was instrumental in Borc's betrayal. But in the settlement treaty Sarnak's life was spared in exchange for prisoners. Sarnak is a grandson of Horat, while Tor is the last surviving son. Those two have not forgotten, nor have I nor my kin."

Kochanski felt it best to leave that topic untouched for now. "Pina told us that you've placed a genetic block in humans against using the Essence. Why?"

"We brought humans into this reality eons ago for companionship and as subjects," Jartan said, his features relaxing with the change of topic. "At that time we thought it was heresy for mortals to dare to use our Essence, so we changed them. But over the years our children, and then their children, spread and interbred, and we decided to ignore it. My last census showed almost one in every milion will be a sorcerer, and that's up from just a thousand years ago."

Jartan could see Kochanski running figures through his mind, and continued, "From what I can gather it seems your god has left your reality and took most, if not all, of his Essence with him. Do you have sorcerers at all on your world?"

Kochanski reflected for a moment. "We have legends from our ancient times, and occasional unexplained phenomena, but no sorcerers."

"Precisely. Your god obviously took it with him when he left, or held all the Essence to himself in jealousy, and had no reason to change your ancestors."

"And when we came here we could naturally use the Essence," Kochanski finished, his aura glowing brightly. He was happy here, with powers that he could only have dreamed about before.

A moment later his aura dimmed to nothing. It had occurred to him that if they ever did find their way back to Earth, they would automatically lose their powers.

Jartan nodded. "The bitter with the sweet," he said softly, as he watched Kochanski staring gloomily at the floor and muttering to himself. *Some of Kochanski's cursing is truly imaginative,* he thought.

"You are depressing yourself over something that may never happen, Kochanski. Haven't you been listening? You have all eternity and life after life to live and enjoy."

"So in a way the Japanese are right after all."

"I don't know about that," Jartan said, "but if you've been taught that you only have one go around, then you have been misled."

Kochanski found himself laughing. The full implications of all that he had just heard were beyond comprehension.

Draining off his beer, Kochanski held up his glass for another, which was instantly produced. Why, this was even better than his kid brother fetching beers for him back home. Taking a sip, he settled back in his chair, looked up at Jartan, and smiled.

"Now it's my turn," Jartan said, smiling back. "Tell me about your god and his realm."

"Have I got a story for you," Kochanski said, trying to keep a straight face while debating whether he should provide the Catholic, Fundamentalist, or Jehovah's Witness version of reality.

Mark felt like he had been on a roller coaster for hours. Storm was the most beautiful female he had ever seen, much less picked up! Only who had picked up whom? Back where he came from it was the guys who were supposed to be doing that. This independence of women was confusing him.

He felt a nudge at his elbow and turned to see Ikawa's admiring grin. "Brought you another drink, Mark. Although I never saw a man who needed one less. You look like a kid getting set to unwrap a present. I must say your behavior is almost adolescent."

Mark glanced at Storm again. "She is stunning, isn't she?"

Storm turned from Allic to stare directly into Mark's eyes and smile.

Again Mark felt a current running through his body, like an electric shock. *If I don't get laid tonight,* he thought wickedly, sensing that she might be tapping into his thoughts, *I'm going to need a wheelbarrow to haul it around with tomorrow.*

His musings were interrupted by Ikawa's chuckle, as he looked over towards Kochanski, who was coming up to join them.

"You Americans and your courtship rituals," Ikawa said.

"For the last couple of hours your captain and that young lady over there have been doing nothing but staring at each other, and thinking heaven knows what. I remember attending dances in your country where whole roomfuls of people would be engaged thus." And all three smiled, Mark a tad ruefully.

"Weren't you supposed to have a private meeting with Jartan?" Mark asked Kochanski .

"Yup. Just got back. You wouldn't believe me if I told you, so I'll just say it was incredible."

"Did you keep your mouth shut?"

"Hardly, Captain. I started the conversation off by telling him I couldn't believe he was a god."

"You're kidding me?" Mark groaned.

"Nope."

Mark and Ikawa darted glances at one another, not sure if they would kill him now or later.

"Not believing around here is very dangerous, Sergeant," Ikawa said, not wanting to cross too far into disciplining one of Mark's people. "Please refrain from such idiocy in my presence, as I will be sorry to see you go. But I would be even more upset if I was blasted because I was merely standing near you."

Kochanski smiled at him as if he was part of some wonderful private joke.

He's definitely cracked, Mark thought, *but this isn't the place to kick his butt.*

"How about we find a john," Mark temporized, as he put his empty glass on a passing servant's tray and grabbed a full one. As they moved away he smiled at Storm and got a glance that sent another shiver down his spine.

Kochanski rolled his eyes at Ikawa as they walked toward the door. "I think you're right. Reminds me of when I was in the eighth grade."

As the three offworlders walked back into the room ten minutes later, they paused once again at the magnificence of the vast domed chamber which soared half a thousand feet into the air. Mark looked for Storm but she was gone.

"Can you really believe that we're part of this?" Kochanski muttered. "My old man works in the Trenton gashouse. To him a high class night was knocking down beers at the Democratic Club, or when he got to dress up for the Knights of Columbus polka dance. And here his son hangs around with gods and has powers that would seem near god-like back on Earth."

"Considering all we've learned about the various power blocks, guilds, black sorcerers, and demons," Ikawa replied cautiously, "we're like innocent children in a Byzantine court, too ignorant to know our danger."

"Quite right, Captain Ikawa," Kochanski replied, still smiling, "but three months back any insurance agent would have said my life would be up after twenty missions. I bet the odds for your people fighting in China weren't much better. I can handle the odds here after that, and I'll be damn sure to be a fast learner.

"Anyway, Mark," Kochanski whispered, leaning closer, "tell me about Storm. Looks like you two have got something going!"

Mark shook his head. "God, I hope so. I've never been so horny in my life."

As he finished speaking, he noticed that one of the pillars of light around the walls of the chamber had suddenly shifted in intensity and was now coming straight towards them.

"Jesus Christ, it's Jartan," Kochanski said, his voice edged with fear.

Mark tried to stay calm as the column came rushing at them.

"He must have overheard us," Kochanski said, drawing back.

Mark could see a figure in the light as it drew closer, much too close for comfort. Jartan extended his arms and the pillar spread to include not only Mark but also Ikawa and Kochanski in the light, shutting out the rest of the room. By squinting, Mark could see a brightly glowing figure with luminous eyes, fluid and graceful as the wind.

A voice appeared in their minds. *I seek him who speaks with the intent to defile a demigoddess!*

It took all of Mark's self-control to keep from pointing at Kochanski and saying, Him, him, he's the one who made me say it.

A quick glance at Kochanski showed a person seemingly in shock, incapable of response. Mark mustered his courage and replied, "Great god Jartan, we are new to your world and have not adapted totally yet. Please understand."

The light grew immeasurably brighter, forcing their eyes shut, as a world-consuming voice shouted with laughter. Suddenly the light was gone, and they were in a comfortable drawing room with Allic and another being who was still in the column of light. Chuckling, Jartan let his form coalesce, so that Mark saw a brilliant humanlike pattern of light. Jartan settled into a chair next to a blazing fireplace.

"Very good, Kochanski," Jartan rumbled. "Your little prank went very well."

Mark and Ikawa looked at Kochanski, whose smirk vanished instantly.

"Come on, Captain. He said he wanted to talk to you guys. We both knew you were a little interested in Storm, and, well . . ."

"You're dead meat, Kochanski." And Ikawa snarled in agreement.

Jartan and Allic started laughing again.

"Come over and drink some of Kochanski's beer," Jartan said good-naturedly, pleased at the way his joke had turned out. "I want to get more information about your world, Mark. Kochanski tells me that you are the one to ask about why your sexual customs have evolved as they have."

Mark closed his eyes and vowed to get even with Kochanski if it killed him.

An hour and a half later Mark was watching in amazement as Kochanski downed his drink and launched a verbal attack on Jartan's last statement regarding government's role in society. How could anyone be that resilient?

One of Jartan's pet demons deftly refilled their glasses, then stirred and replenished the fire. *The perfect butler,* Mark thought, *except he's the size of truck.* Then, as Jartan smiled and prepared a crushing counter to Kochanski's latest sally, Mark sensed something on the fringe of his mind. He half raised his hand before remembering where he was. Jartan, ever-perceptive, nodded and snapped his fingers.

Storm appeared through a side door. With a cheerful nod she acknowledged Mark and then slipped over to a couch and reclined gracefully while accepting a glass of brandy from a bowing demon.

"How goes the party?" Jartan inquired.

"Frightfully boring," came the reply. "And ten days to go of this. I know it's important, but there are times when the petty arguments drive me near to distraction." She paused and looked at Mark.

"Well, Father," she said softly, "how well do you think the two of us are matched?"

Father and daughter turned to study Mark, their eyes glowing.

Damn it. Mark tried to control his thoughts. This was worse than any damned date where the father would give him that I-know-what-you-want-to-do-with-my daughter look.

He felt anger growing. They were looking at him as though he was only the latest amusement to be examined.

For a moment Mark wrestled to control his mounting rage. *The hell with it,* he decided, *and if she doesn't like it, the hell with her too.*

Jartan nodded in acknowledgment and lowered his gaze.

"My apologies, Captain Phillips. Again you have shown me that you are a man of courage and pride. So often the men who approach my daughter conceal their true intent, which is only political advancement. You strike me as a man with too much pride for that type of concern."

Storm gave him a glowing smile, sensing his anger. "Will you walk with me this evening?" she asked, almost shyly.

Mark forced his gaze to the floor. He wanted to go with her, but he'd be damned if he was going to be mesmerized, or probed again, or anything else that had to do with powers and magic.

"You two mind if I leave you guys for a while?" Mark asked, looking at Ikawa and Kochanski.

"Christ, I should be so lucky," Kochanski mumbled, nodding.

Mark stood and held his hand out to Storm. Turning, they left the room.

Jartan was quietly studying the reaction of the two friends left behind and noted that where Kochanski merely shook his head with a feeling of friendly envy, Ikawa was in a profound depression. Perhaps he should also have someone of his own. He could see that honor was the driving force within Ikawa, but a tie to Haven would make him stronger and happier. An instant later, Jartan knew.

Mark could feel the desire burning in them both as they walked through the gardens to her rooms. He almost felt as though there were an actual current running through the air, ready to strike off sparks.

His mind was a maelstrom of emotions. At the same time

he was receiving a direct flow from Storm through their clasped hands, and it was a match for his.

The moment the door closed she was in his arms, her breasts against him, his hardness against her loins. He slid his hands up the smoothness of her back and caressed the back of her head as he kissed her. She pressed against him as he undid the clasp of her gown.

I want you to be as deep in my body as you are in my mind. Her thoughts came to him as she gestured and his clothes seemed to liquefy and flow to the floor.

"Now that's a handy parlor trick," he responded as he lowered her to the thick carpet.

Time seemed to freeze as the combined waves of their passion flowed over them, and their minds began to mesh as completely as their bodies.

Ikawa was finally drunk enough to really enter into the give-and-take with Jartan, Allic, and Kochanski, and had just finished destroying the logic of one of Kochanski's truisms with a wicked little parable that left them all laughing helplessly, when a tremendous flash of lightning snapped across the sky. There was a rolling boom of thunder and both Allic and Jartan looked at each other for a moment and broke into fresh gales of laughter.

Ikawa rose and walked to the window. Leaning out, he saw a pulsing light from a tower at the opposite end of the courtyard. There was another flash of lightning, followed seconds later by a third and then a tremendous fourth.

"Four so far," Allic roared. "I say, he must be quite good."

"I just wish I could have seen his expression when that first flash hit," Jartan boomed.

"Is this what I think it is?" Ikawa asked.

"Couldn't be anything else," Allic replied, wiping the tears from his eyes.

"And each of those flashes means . . . ?" He was embarrassed to ask.

"But of course," and as if in reply there was another flash and boom of thunder, and they looked at each other and started to laugh again.

Jartan finally fell quiet and looked back to Ikawa, who wasn't sure how to react.

"Don't worry," Jartan said softly. "There is a power in

you which will soon be matched, as the sun is by the darkness of night."

Allic stirred at that. He glanced at Ikawa, and nodded to Jartan.

Another flash of lightning crossed the sky, causing father and son to look at each other, and then to Ikawa, and smile.

Lieutenant Younger knew the gross pig opposite him was perhaps the wealthiest man he had met on Haven so far. Allic and his party had barely left Landra before the invitation to dine at this man's manor house had arrived. The overstated richness of the manor showed Younger that there was a social class other than the gods and sorcerers with money and position, and he wanted to learn more about the great merchant guilds.

When he had met Redfa at a castle reception for Allic just before the departure for Asmara, Younger had surmised that the fawning good will and curiosity were a ploy to get potentially valuable information and knowledge. Hell, he didn't mind. He was always looking to get ahead himself, and this was the first tycoon he had met on Haven. So he had let his interest show, and wasn't too surprised at the invitation which arrived for a "private meal where we can discuss concerns of mutual interest."

Redfa looked shrewdly at Younger. "Would you care to take a walk in the gardens? I would be interested in hearing more about your home world."

Younger smiled lazily and nodded. "I've a few questions of my own. Are all the sorcerers in this land tied to feudal lords, or can a man have a few enterprises of his own?"

The sharp eyes tightened for an instant, then Redfa smiled and rose, taking a snifter from a servant as he led the way to the door.

"Less than half of all sorcerers with your power are in service to any lord at a given time. Oh, to be sure, if there is an emergency most of them can be impressed into service, but many of them belong to their own guilds or work in the service of various merchant guilds.

"To a man such as you," Redfa continued, "there are limitless potentials. All you need is a contact with someone who can help to show you the way."

"And benefit by my powers," Younger countered, not wanting to be negotiated down at the very start.

"But of course," Redfa replied smoothly. "I am a merchant of rare fabrics, artifacts, gems and, ah, collectables of unusual quality."

Meaning he probably was a fence for stolen goods, Younger thought.

"I could always use your services, as you could use mine. I believe that we can make an arrangement to our mutual benefit."

"What's the percentage, and what do I do?" Younger said evenly.

"Ah, my friend, formal percentages are difficult to discuss as Allic's tax collectors will eventually find it in my contracts and books. My own thought is to make this more of a profitable friendship—both you and I can gain much from knowing each other. Do remember, my friend, that you are new here, and there is an old saying amongst us that he who runs with the gods might one day find himself under their feet, crushed and forgotten."

Younger looked at Redfa, his features expressionless, but Redfa could see that he had hit a nerve.

"Of course, service received will not only build in the bank of my good will, but can produce more tangible and immediate returns."

Redfa continued to walk beside Younger, waiting for some kind of response. When none was forthcoming, he mentally gave the outlander credit for being a hard bargainer and tried a different tactic.

"Before we get down to details I'd like to share with you one of my special little collections."

Reaching the far side of the garden Redfa guided his companion into a darkened corridor. There was a faint scent on the breeze that Younger recognized as norna, an opiate forbidden to those in service to Allic, as an intoxicant and aphrodisiac too powerful for most to handle. He had smelled it before, while wandering Landra's back alleys, but had never dared to try it.

"Ah, yes, my little collection knew you were coming, and they wanted to be ready to entertain us."

Younger looked at his companion and smiled.

Chapter 13

Tor, the only surviving child of the Creator Horat, stood with his nephew Sarnak before the entry of the tunnel. Tor had brought his army of sorcerers with him from his realm in the north, ready at last to spring the trap on Allic and Jartan.

"The time of our destiny and vengeance has finally come," Tor said coldly. "For three thousand years I've dreamed and planned for this day. Soon we will avenge the deaths of our divine ancestor Horat and my brother Orsta, your father."

"All has been prepared, uncle," responded Sarnak. "Ralnath will be stationed at the tunnel fork to pass information between us."

Both stood in thought. Sarnak's responsibilities were fairly straightforward: attack Landra with most of his army and sorcerers while Allic's attention was diverted to the war with the Torms. Treachery had neutralized the neighboring province's armies, and there were more traps to spring should help arrive. In spite of all the wealth in crystals that stood to be gained, Sarnak realized his primary goal was to act as a screen for the main effort against the mines of the Crystal Mountains.

For thousands of years Jartan had been carefully excavating a monstrous crystal called the Heart. Bit by careful bit his engineers had freed it from the mountain. It was now in the final stages of the rough faceting prior to its journey to Jartan in Asmara.

Sarnak had been ready to implement his plans for over a century. All he had needed was word from their spies that the Heart was ready to be moved.

A crystal of its magnitude could surely maim or even kill a god if properly used.

For this, Sarnak's realm might be sacrificed—it would never stand up to the wars that were coming. He was even prepared to sacrifice his son, if that particular trap could be set. He had not expected the loss of his land to bother him, or what he had planned for his child, but it did in his deepest self. Tools are to be used, Sarnak thought, and with the Heart in their hands he would be more powerful than even Horat. At last his family would have one of the great weapons, and their revenge.

When we have won this war I will reclaim my land, he vowed.

Sarnak glanced over at Tor to whom he owed familial allegiance and felt a surge of pride.

"Soon we will have our vengeance," he whispered.

Tor met his gaze and nodded. "I won't attack until I know that all attention is fixed on you. You know the sacrifice. If you win against Allic, so much the better, but primarily you must divert them. With your assault Jartan's attention will be turned aside from the Heart. Once we take that, your sacrifices will be repaid a thousandfold."

Sarnak merely nodded. He had accepted this plan as part of the greater goal, but perhaps more than the Heart, he wanted to strike down Jartan's son with his own hands. Only then would he have atoned for the whispers about his cowardice in the last war between the gods.

Allic and his party were watching the games from Jartan's private balcony, relaxing and arguing about the last contest. In the brilliant sun the clothes of the multitude in the arena were bright against the shimmering white sand.

The winners of the last game were being crowned, and the losers were helped from the arena, dusty in defeat.

"It was obvious even before they crossed swords that red would win," Allic said as he leaned over to collect his winnings from Mark.

"But green looked so much stronger, quicker," Mark replied sadly, counting out his losses.

"It was in the eyes," Ikawa said, and Allic nodded.

"I didn't see anything," Mark replied.

"But to a swordsman," Ikawa continued, clearly enjoying himself, "it was obvious from the start. You could see the way his eyes kept flickering from red's face to his feet, and then to the point of the weapon. The man knew he was outclassed, and fear breeds desperation. Desperation can make a man dangerous, but usually it makes him foolish. It's a wonder green didn't kill himself out there."

"Red was chivalrous," Storm said quietly. "If he hadn't pulled his blade back, green would have impaled himself. Remember that Lord Wester—in the red—had been insulted more than once by green, and this was a challenged duel match. I just hope the humiliation keeps the fool quiet from now on."

It had all happened so quickly, Mark thought. It looked like the green swordsman was moving in for the kill with a quick diving lunge, and the next instant red was stepping back, the alarm echoing throughout the arena, indicating that green had been hit for the second time.

This had been Mark's first morning at the games, and the pageantry and ritual of deathstriker had fascinated him, even as its darker side made him uneasy. The object of deathstriker was to twice cut the embroidered heart on your opponent's uniform. A cut anywhere else, even if it drew blood, was a forfeit. Ninety-nine out of a hundred matches ended with what was called a white win: so good were most of the duellers that a forfeit was rare. But the red win was entirely different. If an opponent was fatally stabbed through the embroidered heart, which was placed over a man's unprotected heart, it was declared a win, and no criminal charges would be leveled. Most duels were between professional swordsmen, who performed for the entertainment of the crowd, the same as sorcerers who dueled until one shield went down and the match was over. It was a display of skill —not for blood.

It was also the chief form of gambling in the realm, complete with complex analysis forms, professional bet advisors, and sporting syndicates that trained and fielded the professional swordsmen.

But once a year, during the festival, any long-standing feuds that had not been settled by arbitration could be settled in the arena. In the parlance of the street it was referred to as "stepping onto the sand." Most of these duels finished with a forfeit or white win, honor was met, and that was that.

But this helped to breed a small underclass of petty nobility that thrived on the challenge and danger offered by "stepping onto the sand." They were tolerated in court, since it was felt that every individual was responsible for his own actions. If they wanted to die on the sand, no one would stop them.

With such combats there was a high enough incidence of red wins, either by accident or design, to fill each match with tension.

"It makes me think of ancient Rome," Kochanski stated, making a dramatic show of eating a bunch of grapes while reclining on a couch. "You know, baseball and football never got to me as a kid. I used to fantasize about going to the ancient colosscum to watch the gladiators, but I hated their masters. But the guys down there want to be there, and I must confess that sometimes it's the simplest way to settle an argument."

"My father told me of your conversation regarding the Roman games the other night," Allic replied, looking appraisingly at his new sorcerers. "I knew the history of your world had its dark moments, but some of the things your ancestors did would almost equal the actions of the Accursed."

"I could tell you about this one fellow kicking around right now," Mark began, then looked at Ikawa and realized the difficulty he had placed himself in by alluding to an ally of Japan, but Ikawa smiled and shook his head.

"Don't worry about it," he said quietly. "Even some of our people find him repulsive."

There was a moment of embarrassment as the three tried to find a way around a difficult turn in the conversation.

But it was something totally unexpected that broke the tension as Ikawa suddenly turned in his seat and stared intently at a slender dark-haired woman who stepped into the booth next to theirs.

"By my ancestors," he whispered, "who is that?"

Allic turned to see. "My half sister, Leti," he said, trying to sound casual. Ikawa's eyes had not moved from her graceful form as she settled into a chair.

"She is so very beautiful," came the quiet reply.

"Hers is a tragic story." Allic drew closer. "Each festival is a time of humiliation, but her honor demands that she bear the pain without comment."

Ikawa turned and Allic knew what would come next.

"Tell me of this honor," he whispered intently, as Mark and Kochanski excused themselves so that they could go and meet with some of the fighters from the previous match.

Several turnings later Mark and Storm found Ikawa sitting moodily on a bench in the corridor.

"What's up, pal?" Mark said good-naturedly. "I figured a man with your interest would be enjoying the games."

Ikawa slowly shook his head, then gave Mark a look of determination. "Captain Phillips, I am far from any of my own. Would you do me the honor of being my second in a duel?"

"What the . . . ?" Mark glanced at Storm, but she looked as perplexed as he was.

He turned back to Ikawa. *Christ, what now?* "I don't understand, Ikawa, but I'll stand by you through hell or high water."

Ikawa's eyes were shining. "We go to right a wrong."

"Let's see if I understand this," Mark said somewhat later. "This guy killed Leti's brother in a duel and won his crystal. And he keeps trying to get hers as well?"

"It's deeper than that," Storm replied. "Leti's mother, Ilea, was one of my father's wives before I was born. She was a descendant of the Creator Danar, who sacrificed himself to save my father's life in the final confrontation with Horat, three thousand years ago. When she married my father, Leti's mother received two crystals, shaped by her father as her wedding present. To one who had learned true mastery, the crystals could be used as a pair: the first to create light and heat; the other, darkness and cold. When Ilea left this existence to enter the Great Void, she gave one crystal to her daughter Leti and the other to her son, Vilmar."

"You mean that even as a demigoddess she still died?"

"Even a demigoddess can weary of this realm in time," Storm said sadly, as if revealing a part of existence she wished not to think about. "Ilea did not die, but voluntarily entered the Sea of Chaos. She left a portion of her strength at her temple, at the Oracle of Derr in the south, and so Leti hopes that through the power of the two crystals Ilea might someday return. It is hopeless, especially because Cinta took one of the crystals some centuries ago."

"And Cinta is . . . ?" Mark asked.

"Cinta is one of my distant cousins," Storm said distaste-fully. "He's always coveted both crystals, and Leti besides. He provoked a duel with Vilmar, with the crystal as a wager, and won it fairly."

"So why doesn't Vilmar try to win it back?" Mark already half knew what the answer would be.

"It was a red win," Ikawa replied. "Cinta knew Vilmar was no match, and the win was an act of barbarity."

"Vilmar knew his chances," Storm said. "He knew Cinta was a sword master who hated him. He took his risk; that was his own fault."

"But there is no excuse for Cinta's taunting of Leti, or the way that he openly moves to possess her," Ikawa argued.

"No," Storm replied, "everyone finds that ill-bred. He won the crystal fairly, but no one approves of how he puts his crystal up as a prize to humiliate her in the arena year after year, taunting her to match hers to his."

"Why hasn't she appointed a champion?" Mark asked.

Turning to Ikawa she responded to him, as well. "Leti has never appointed a champion because if he lost, she would be lost as well. Many have entered the contest on their own, hoping to win the crystal on her behalf, but all have failed. Cinta is the master of the deathstrike, and most of his wins are red wins. As the years pass, fewer are willing to try. Cinta believes that if he waits long enough, Leti will eventu-ally come to his bed, hoping to regain her brother's crystal."

"It's repulsive," Mark said angrily, but with a wave of fear for Ikawa.

"Jesus, what makes you think you're even in his league?" he asked.

"I studied under two masters of kendo: One in my youth and one during the long months of garrison duty in China."

"You're kidding me."

"No. Private Yasuma is a master of both kendo and kar-ate."

Mark thought for a moment. Yasuma was the quiet one. Hardly ever said a word, but when he did it cut right to the heart of the matter. *God, there's so much I don't know about the Japanese.* He shook his head and continued, "What can you put up as a prize against his crystal?"

"The sword of my ancestor," Ikawa replied proudly.

Allic was irritated. This whole thing was foolishness. He and his father had thought that Ikawa would be drawn to

Leti, and perhaps draw her out of her shell. But never had he thought that Ikawa would get embroiled in this damned foolishness with Cinta. Not only would this embarrass him in front of the whole court, but he could lose the services of one of his best sorcerers should Cinta decide to go for the kill.

"What makes you think you can defeat a master swordsman?" he shouted.

"Have you ever fought against a left-handed sorcerer?" came the quiet response.

Allic was puzzled, but Mark grinned. "I get it. It's like boxing a lefty. His style is so different that it's hard to adjust to."

"Just so," Ikawa said, smiling. "Kendo will be as hard for him as his style is for me." He shrugged and continued, "My lord, when did you ever worry about the odds when you wanted to do something?"

A frown crossed Allic's face; then he began to laugh. "I know when I'm being manipulated, Ikawa. Sometimes you're too clever for your own good. Do you honestly think you can match him?"

"I hope to give him a hell of a fight, my lord. I have fought in the deathstrike with several of your own garrison back in Landra and—"

"Did you ever fight Stede, my master of the sword?"

"I beat him, my lord."

Allic mused for a moment. "Stede is damned good. He's fat, but no one is quicker and more deceiving in the deathstrike . . .

"All right, let's do it. I could never stand Cinta anyway," Allic growled. "This will be easy. I'll just pick a fight with him, and by the time I finish telling him how great a swordsman you are, he'll be challenging you to get back at me."

"Now, let's have a drink before we go," he continued, pulling the cork from a bottle. "I'm always a lot nastier when I'm drunk."

Mark stood nervously beside Ikawa down on the arena floor. He couldn't understand why it was so damned hot all of a sudden. The heat seemed to come off the sunbaked sand in waves.

The crowd in the stands was cheering them lustily, like people everywhere who will always identify with an underdog, although very few were willing to bet their money on the outlander.

Word of the challenge had swept through the city the night before—how Cinta had howled with rage at Allic's words and had actually pressed to fight Ikawa right in Jartan's courtyard during the reception. Mark could only hope that rage was so blinding that it would help Ikawa now, for in watching Cinta up close he had seen a man with incredible strength and wiry agility.

Mark glanced at Ikawa, and could not refrain from grimacing at the Rising Sun headband Ikawa had made. *Old memories die hard.*

Ikawa was staring into the stands trying to find Leti. His look of determination hardened as he finally saw her, sitting by Allic and Storm. Seeing that she had caught his attention, she stood up and gave him a formal bow, which set the tens of thousands in the arena to their feet, shouting their approval. In all the years of her trials, this was the first time that she had even acknowledged a challenger, and the crowd took notice.

"Who would have thought we would be lucky enough to meet women like those two?" Mark said, his voice barely audible above the roar. "I seem to recall a remark about adolescent infatuation from you less than a week ago. How the mighty have fallen." They exchanged a smile.

The cheering started to die off; then Storm stood and bowed towards Mark, setting off another round.

"Thunder and lightning, thunder and lightning!"

For a moment Mark thought they were acknowledging her power, then realized what they were actually referring to. His embarrassment showed, and the crowd roared with delight, while Storm shook her fist jokingly at the spectators.

The far door of the arena slid open to reveal Cinta and his second, and the laughter died away. Cinta was by no means unpopular, having the respect of many an aficionado. An ovation went up as the nobleman and his second who was his brother-in-law, strode into the arena.

He moved with grace and speed, making his overweight in-law seem clumsy by comparison. They made their way to the far side of the battle circle drawn in the sand.

A gong rang and the crowd fell silent. Sumar, the ranking master of ceremony, stepped from beside the tower of shifting light that was Jartan, and using his crystal, addressed the crowd.

"We have a challenge!"

A roar went up again from the crowd.

"Ikawa of Landra, what do you offer as trophy to this event?"

Unsheathing his sword with a movement almost too quick to see, Ikawa held it high. "I offer the sword of my ancestors, who have been samurai for uncounted generations. It was made by the master craftsman Miyoshi-Go, and is without blemish."

A hushed silence fell over the crowd. The standard weapon for deathstrike was a narrow, almost foillike sword. The blade of a samurai was shining for the first time in Jartan's realm, and the spectators were trading guesses as to how this new sword would match against the lighter weapon standard for the game.

"Cinta of Darthe, what do you offer as trophy to this event?"

Cinta stepped forward and held up a crystal as big as his fist, which seemed alive in the sunlight.

"I offer the Crystal of the Sun, made by the Creator Danar. And I spit on the ancestry of his people and the worthless piece of metal that he presumes to offer as a trophy!"

Ikawa's face grew white with anger, and his hands flexed and unflexed around the hilt of his blade. He took a deep breath and held it, and Mark could see calmness come over him as he went into the light, focused trance of a samurai.

Jartan's voice rolled across the arena. "Both offerings are accepted. Let the contest begin." And the crowd's roar was deafening.

Mark looked Ikawa straight in the eyes. "Go cut his balls off."

Ikawa nodded and walked into the ring.

Ikawa's entire being centered upon his enemy as they slid across the ring at one another. Cinta's right shoulder was facing him, his left arm back for balance, and the target over the heart away from Ikawa's advance. Almost like a Western fencer, Ikawa thought, except that Cinta's sword was longer than a rapier. Good slashing ability and a superb stabbing weapon, but maybe a little too thin for repeated shocks? And if he could get inside that long blade . . .

Unlike the traditional dueling of the samurai, he knew he would have to use his blade to block his opponent's lunges. That would give an advantage to Cinta. Stopping near the center of the ring, he held his blade up, vertical and drawn back behind his left shoulder, both hands on the hilt. It was a style unknown to Haven. Cinta hesitated for but a moment and then closed.

They met, and the swordplay was almost too quick to follow as each probed the other's defenses. Cinta was much more aggressive, and obviously held his opponent's square stance and two-handed sword style in contempt.

They wove their blades in deadly earnest, perspiration falling upon the sand in showers. Finally, when he judged that he had exhausted Ikawa, he set up an elaborate double feint and confidently slashed for Ikawa's heart.

Only Ikawa wasn't there. His left hand met the flat of Cinta's blade and beat it aside just enough for his body to twist away His right hand swung his sword in a glittering arc that met the heart on Cinta's chest in a shower of sparks.

The entire arena burst into wild applause that almost drowned out the whistles of the referees as they stepped into the ring. The contestants lowered their blades and glared at one another.

Cinta's second came sputtering into the ring and addressed the referees. "I call a foul. The damned outlander deliberately allowed himself to be cut upon the hand to distract Lord Cinta, and cause a forfeit. This is rank cowardice."

"Why don't you get your head out of your ass, fatboy, and look at Ikawa's hand?" Mark sneered. "There's no cut!" he shouted, holding up Ikawa's hand.

A moment later the head referees announced, "The first round is awarded to Ikawa of Landra." And the crowd went wild.

Mark handed a towel to Ikawa. "I thought he had you for a second. Nice sucker punch!"

"He is incredibly quick. I can't handle his thrusts as well as I should. That blade is too long for an effective stop-thrust on my part."

The comments came out between gasps, as Ikawa tried to dry his hands and arms. Mark handed him another towel and he continued, "I was hoping to break his blade by landing a solid shock, but he's too fast."

The gong sounded and both fighters reentered the ring.

Cinta's blade was everywhere. Ikawa retreated slowly from his onslaught, breaking the rhythm with feints and ripostes, but still forced to the defensive. Suddenly he stumbled and Cinta's sword struck towards his heart.

Turning desperately, and falling backwards, Ikawa dodged the blade. It struck the red heart but at such an angle that it continued up the shoulder, slashing his tunic open.

Once again the referees' whistles were heard as soon as the flash was seen, and they awarded the round to Cinta amid the applause of the crowd.

"Jesus, how did you avoid that thrust?" Mark wiped Ikawa's wound with a towel.

Ikawa gasped, "I wanted him to go for the opening I gave him, but I never dreamed he would be so quick."

A referee came over and examined Ikawa's tunic. It was obvious that the cut had started dead middle in the heart zone and then had skidded across Ikawa's ribs, out of the red area, and up to his shoulder. By the rules, as long as the strike first hit in the red, it was legal, blood or no blood. By the drawing of blood, however, Ikawa could concede the match.

The crowd grew quiet in anticipation.

The referee looked from the wound up to Ikawa, who grimaced and shook his head.

The crowd roared approval. The game would continue.

Mark glanced at Cinta, who was pacing restlessly, waiting for the gong, and then he looked back to Ikawa, who was bent over double, gasping for breath.

"Let me guess. You want him to think you're already beat, right?"

Ikawa continued to gasp, but paused long enough to give Mark a quick wink as he staggered back to the edge of the circle. Only by leaning on the sword which he thrust into the sand was he able to stay erect, and the whole arena believed that the next strike would be a red win.

The gong sounded and Ikawa moved two paces forward and waited, his sword swung back, exposing his chest as if challenging Cinta to strike and finish it. Cinta was not a fool and approached slowly, but confidently.

Ikawa called upon the spirits of his ancestors, and by use of koan, attempted to achieve the state of *mushin*, where his spirit would be free of all feeling and his body and sword become a unity, a single instrument of the unconscious.

Cinta hesitated momentarily, seeing a change in his opponent, then launched his attack.

The instant Ikawa's sword met his, Cinta was fighting for his life. Blades sang in a fury as the berserker who was Ikawa forced him back across the circle, parrying desperately. The crowd was standing cheering.

Within minutes Ikawa began to regain normal consciousness and realized that he still could not get through Cinta's defenses. But those efforts were designed to guard the heart!

He slashed for Cinta's chest, instantly changing his cut to evade the parry, and sending his sword flashing straight towards Cinta's eyes. In a contest where an accidental wound other than the heart meant forfeiture this was shocking, and Cinta jumped back with a cry.

Ikawa deliberately burst out laughing, followed immediately by Mark, and gradually by the crowd.

Cinta screamed and leaped at Ikawa, who had half turned his body away while laughing. Cinta's thrust was a flash that stopped all laughter.

Only Ikawa wasn't there. His spin and parry were as quick as thought, and his slash at Cinta's unprotected heart ended in a flash. In an instant the whistles of the referees were drowned by the crowd, which was already on its feet, thundering its approval.

Cinta, however, was too far gone in hatred. Ignoring the whistles he turned the full fury of his blade on Ikawa, determined to kill him no matter what. A moment later he was blasted off his feet by the head referee's crystal. Lying there stunned, he heard Ikawa proclaimed the winner on points and awarded the Crystal of the Sun.

Mark was supremely happy. Grinning from ear to ear, he baited Cinta's kinsman as the grotesquely fat man shrieked his protest at the referees.

"Damn it," the nobleman roared, "he tried to hit Cinta in the face. That's a breech of the rules."

"Lord Heberlin, control yourself. It is only illegal when he cuts him, not when he startles him."

Mark chimed in cheerfully, "You've got no case, porkie. In fact, you ought to be thankful that Ikawa didn't finish him off when he overextended on that last lunge."

Heberlin turned on Mark and snarled, "Keep your mouth shut when your betters are speaking, you—"

Mark's fist stopped his comments and stretched him out on the sand.

"I'll kill you for that," Heberlin promised as he struggled to pick himself up.

They were in the shadow of the arena entrance; the crowd

was watching Ikawa accept the crystal. No one had even noticed the little altercation that had just taken place, although Mark was surprised to note how near one of the pillars of light in the arena had drifted.

"I'm still new here, and I don't want a whole lot of fuss," Mark said to Heberlin, loud enough for the referee to hear. "Why don't we just go outside and take a piss together?"

Heberlin hesitated, so Mark turned to the referee. "He's got his offensive crystals and I've got mine. Maybe you'd even like to come along, in an unofficial capacity, and take a leak yourself?"

The referee was obviously delighted at the challenge. He glanced at the pillar of light, then nodded. "As a matter of fact I would thoroughly relish such a trip. Lord Heberlin, surely one of your girth would also appreciate a trip to the jakes?"

The portly nobleman tried to assume an air of dignity. "Let's go, then. I suppose I ought to be grateful for the chance to kill him in private."

And the three turned and walked side by side out the tunnel, angling towards the vast gardens beyond.

Ikawa held the Crystal of the Sun in his hand, glorying in its feel. Already he seemed to have an affinity for it. It seemed to surround him with brilliance far outshining his force shield.

He made his way across the arena, heading for Leti, and the crowd parted before him: the day's entertainment had been the best of the festival, and it looked like the drama was continuing.

Ikawa went to the private balcony and came over to stand in front of Leti. Again he was struck by her beauty—hazel-green eyes and short black hair, with ivory skin. Her white gown was trimmed in black and she wore the biggest, darkest crystal he had ever seen in the sash around her trim waist.

"You fought magnificently, sir," she said admiringly. "Never have I seen such swordplay."

He held up the Crystal of the Sun, and its light washed over them.

"I have been told that this should belong to you."

"It is the mate to my crystal of night," Leti replied softly, pointing to the crystal on her belt, "and is part of my family's heritage. What price do you demand for it, my lord?"

Ikawa paused and smiled. "I demand nothing. It is rightfully yours," and he placed the crystal in her hand.

Such was the power and intensity of his gaze that she still stared into his eyes, not even looking at the crystal in her palm.

"I demand nothing," he repeated, "but I ask for the right to court you, Leti."

Conversation rumbled around the court.

"You have earned that right, and I grant it, my lord." She extended her hand to him.

He froze. Was he supposed to kiss it, or bow over it, or . . . Her voice came into his mind.

Custom calls for you to take the ring off my first finger, the voice whispered, *and wear it as a token.*

As he was carefully sliding the ring onto his smallest finger, she gracefully wrapped her arm through his and said, "My lord, you must be thirsty. Will you join me for refreshments?" Arm in arm they walked back into the palace.

Cheers echoed after them as they left.

Chapter 14

The light from the setting sun came through the stained glass doors, illuminating a low center table covered with the remains of a feast. Relaxing on seats in various stages of repose, the group flowed along with the inner currents created by the mind singer who was building his symphonic piece to a crescendo.

In counterpoint the mind weaver was leading the group through a soaring journey seen only with the inner eye. Together the group floated through distant star fields, racing at impossible speeds past pulsing red giants, skimming over blue-green planets, and swirling clouds of aurora light.

As the song of the mind singer reached even higher, filling their universe with its joyful wordless symphony, the mind weaver formed the image of a pulsing core of light—and together the group fell into its core. With a blinding flash, woven into the final crescendo of the mind singer, the core burst.

The image faded as a billion suns were born while the wordless song drifted away into night. The group stirred from its collective dream.

The mind singer and weaver quietly withdrew. Their audience was still somewhat dazed by the symphony and visual extravaganza that the two master sorcerers had projected into their minds.

"Even better than Scriabin's *Poem of Ecstasy*," Kochanski said admiringly to Mark, who could only shrug noncommittally, while wondering if he could teach the mind singer a little bit about the Big Band sound.

"This is the life," Mark drawled, looking over to Storm, who lay on the couch alongside. "I can't recall ever being this relaxed and happy."

"It's one of the most satisfying festivals I've ever known," Leti said quietly, looking over at Ikawa, whose hand she was holding. "My one regret, is that you didn't cut his heart out," she said in a matter-of-fact voice.

"Jesus, Leti," Mark said, trying not to sound startled, "remind me never to get you mad at me."

"She's right," Storm said. "Cinta is not to be treated lightly. He'll want his revenge, and he'll plot it out, even if it takes a hundred years. You should have killed him and been done with it."

"I was only interested in the crystal," Ikawa replied truthfully.

"And speaking of enemies," Allic interjected. "Mark, better look out for Heberlin."

"He's not to be trifled with either," Leti replied. "His type doesn't have the courage to kill outright. They do it with poison."

"But anyhow," Allic continued, "they knew the risk, so it's their own responsibility."

A grin lit his features as he looked at Mark, then, unable to contain himself, he burst out laughing.

"The referee told several of his friends," Allic roared gleefully. "The whole city's buzzing with it. 'Let's go take a piss together!' By the gods, I'll not be surprised if that's how the alleyway toughs will challenge each other from now on! Everyone knows how you simply flew circles around him, shooting him again and again on his fat ass until he finally smacked into the ground and gave up. He probably won't sit for a week!"

"Aw, I couldn't kill him," Mark said, almost defensively. "He was so clumsy it was a slaughter. Anyhow, I'd like to know how someone like him gets to be a nobleman. Or do you just get to be one because you're born into it?"

All three of Jartan's children stiffened.

Allic responded first. "Heberlin was just a sorcerer until he married into money, and used that to buy a title from Cinta's family. Granted, it's venal, but are you telling me that in your old world such things never happened?"

Storm was next and did an admirable job of holding her temper. "Where ever did you get the idea that Jartan would allow us to grow fat and lazy? If you want to be part of his court, you owe him service. That scum Heberlin only gets in here because he's part of Cinta's clique."

Mark could see he was treading on dangerous ground, but the whole subject of nobility bothered his grassroots sensibilities, and he felt like he finally had to get it out in the open.

"But I've seen some nobility here that are nothing more than drones, living off their subjects."

"You don't have nobility in your country," Ikawa told him, "but when I was living in Boston and going to MIT, I saw hundreds of spoiled brats of the richer class, who had never done a day's work in their life, living off the wealth created by their ancestors. Granted, many of them would become productive, but I met many who were obnoxious bores, who didn't care one bit for anything other than their own pleasure, as if it was their right."

Mark had to concede that point.

"I've served my father for over 600 years," Storm replied, "and have done everything from diplomacy to assisting in the mines to spending thirty very dangerous years on a research team trying to control the focal points by the Sea of Chaos. I believe I've earned my titles."

Mark wished he had thought a little before opening his mouth. He nodded at Storm and turned to Leti.

"I meant no offense," he stated quietly, "but it's your turn, so let me have it."

Leti stared and slowly shook her head. "Mark, I won't be nasty, but there's a lot you don't know. I fought by Jartan's side in the war against that monster Horat, three thousand years ago, and lost my mother and grandfather before it was all over."

She again shook her head as if trying to shake off a dark mood.

"I served then and I serve now," Leti continued. "I leave tomorrow for a tour as inspector general of the northern coastal defenses."

Leti looked over at Storm. "You did this several years ago, didn't you?"

Storm nodded. "Pirates getting out of hand again?"

Leti stretched and yawned while answering in the affirmative. "Still, I won't be gone more than two or three months," and she turned to smile at Ikawa. "Allic may I pay you a visit once I'm done?"

Allic got a mischievous gleam in his eye and replied, "Of course, Leti. I'll even attempt to keep Ikawa off garrison duty or patrol during your visit."

He paused, trying to keep a smile off his face. "Still, there could be conflicts in the schedules . . ."

He got the reaction he hoped for: Leti threw a roll at him and they all broke into laughter.

"I was planning to go back to Landra with you and Mark for a short visit," announced Storm. "I suppose Mark has a tour of duty coming up too?"

Mark saw the quick grin before Allic lowered his head and started pantomiming sorrow. "I don't know. These damned schedules . . ."

"How about a barrel of wine from my estates to change the schedule?"

"Two barrels."

"Robber! Done."

At that moment the door burst open and one of Jartan's officers came into the room.

"My lord, we've received a message from Landra," he said, trying to control his voice. A situation has developed . . ." He looked nervously at Allic.

The mood in the room was still somewhat lighthearted as Allic set aside his goblet and looked at the messenger.

"What situation?" he asked.

"My lord . . ." He seemed to be grasping for the right words.

Suddenly the room was silent with tension. Allic was on his feet looking at the messenger.

"My lord, there's been a report that your province has been invaded by the Torms. My lord, your country is now in a state of war."

Mark looked over at Ikawa, who returned his worried gaze.

"So again it has found us," Mark said quietly.

Trembling with exhaustion, Mark cleared the ridgeline and breathed a sigh of relief. The city of Landra was finally in view.

Mark looked over towards Ikawa, who was struggling to stay in formation. He swung alongside the Japanese captain.

"Only a matter of minutes now," Mark said, trying to encourage him.

Ikawa grunted in reply.

The duration and fatigue of the flight reminded Mark of more than one occasion when he had coaxed an ailing plane back to base with little more than fumes in the tank by the time he landed.

Storm was up ahead with her brother. Mark knew that when it came to flying she had nearly limitless strength, and that knowledge made him push even harder to keep up the grueling pace.

A patrol of sorcerers, dropping out of the cloud cover, swung into an escort position above Allic's party and approached cautiously.

Killing off their altitude, the party followed Allic's lead and turned onto final approach, heading straight towards the main battle gate. Now that war was on, flying parties had to enter the city down this one narrow corridor. Any other approach would be viewed as hostile, drawing immediate fire from the wall defenses.

Mark could see the heavy crystals mounted on the main towers tracking them. It was unnerving—and what a perfect setup this could be for an assassin. But a group of sorcerers with sufficient power could disguise themselves, so even Allic's approach had to be treated with caution.

The aerial security team came close enough to touch them. There was a perfunctory salute from the head of the security team, and pushing forward to the main battle tower, he gave the signal to allow Allic to pass.

Clearing the wall, they soared over the city to land in the main courtyard of the palace, while the security team pulled up and headed back into the clouds.

The courtyard bustled at the approach of the lord. Servants rushed forward bearing refreshments, and were shouldered aside by staff members and court attendants, each one pressing to be heard. Allic and Storm pushed through the crowd, signaling for the staff to follow into the throne room.

From the far side of the courtyard Mark saw Younger and Giorgini and several of the Japanese rushing forward to greet their leaders.

"How was it?" Younger called. "And where's Kochanski?"

"More important right now is—what happened here?" Mark replied.

Ikawa came to Mark's side, and the question that had been burning in him ever since Allic mentioned it during the flight back finally came out:

"Imada and Yoshida," Nobuaki answered. "They've been reported overdue for nearly a tenday. Valdez said they were most likely cut off due to the invasion and that it was the least of his worries at the moment."

Ikawa grunted. It was war again and he had to harden himself. Always he struggled to harden himself, to not get attached in any way to his subordinates. But still it hurt, especially with Imada.

"Where are the rest of the men?" he asked.

"They were sent to join the southern army," Nobuaki replied.

"Who sent them?"

"Valdez. He also ordered Younger and Giorgini and the three of us to stay behind," Nobuaki's voice trailed off as if it was an admission of guilt that they had not been sent into the fight.

Ikawa could see why. Valdez probably realized that it was best to keep Younger and Nobuaki away from the heat of combat while their immediate superiors were not present. Fire at Macha's warriors could just as easily be directed against a former foe. And as for Shigeru and Denzo, they just were not experienced enough with flight. Again Valdez had shown his superior judgment of men under arms.

"What reports are there on the fighting?" Mark demanded.

"There's no sense in my going over this twice," came a sharp voice from the back of the crowd. The men parted as Valdez pushed through.

He gazed at Mark and Ikawa, judging their exhaustion after what must have been a harrowing high-speed flight in Allic's wake. The faintest flicker of a smile crossed his lips. These men were tough if they had kept up with Allic when he was angered.

"Come on. I'm making my report to Allic right now. You might as well get it straight from me, rather than a collection of half-witted rumors from this rabble."

Valdez scanned the crowd for a moment and could sense the bristling at his insult. Good, they were toughening. They'd have to be tough if they expected to survive what was coming.

*   *   *

"How bad?" Allic asked quietly, looking across the table to Valdez.

Valdez pointed at the map on the table and Ikawa was struck immediately by its similarity to combat situation maps back home.

"They hit across the border six days ago," Valdez began, "and are estimated to be in excess of thirty-five thousand. The southern army was overwhelmed by the end of the second day, losing half its total force, and was forced to completely abandon our holdings below the escarpment."

Valdez looked towards Allic, but the ruler said nothing.

"They hit us hard, full surprise, and managed to put out a jamming screen so messages could not get through. A number of their demons and sorcerers were posted as a curtain behind our army so that no information could get in or out.

"Without your presence here, my lord, there just wasn't the power to detect what was happening. They had already broken our forces before I learned of the attack."

Allic nodded. "What have you done in response?"

"I sent them any reinforcements we could spare. Eight thousand foot, which cut our city garrison in half. Fortunately they were on maneuvers two days march north of the pass. They should already be there."

"Sorcerers?"

"All of the offworlders except five, and the two who are missing. I also sent along all the sorcerers whom I could hire from the guild, though the price was high. Our primary battle team stayed here. The others, I hope, will be able to buy time for us." Valdez looked across the table to Mark and Ikawa, expecting a response.

"Why our people?" Ikawa asked coldly, not caring at all for the comment about "buying time."

"They're servants to Lord Allic," Valdez said sharply. "Your men were available and I used them. I will not commit my elite reserve in a battle which might only be the opening stage of a wider war."

"You did correctly," Allic replied smoothly, and he gave his two lieutenants a gaze of warning not to challenge Valdez's decision.

"Has the enemy crested the escarpment?" he asked, pointing to where the blue lines representing his forces were traced in.

"Our last report came in yesterday, saying that our force

was being flanked on both sides at the base of the escarpment, and was starting to pull back. We were lucky to even get that information before their jamming stopped us again. We haven't had word since. I gave the orders for the reinforcements to start digging in at the top of the pass and prepare fortifications for our retreating forces. We've been in the blind since then, my lord."

"Let's assume the worst," Allic said.

"It could be quite bad, my lord," Valdez said softly. "Assuming the worst, the position has already been overrun. They could already be through Wolf Pass and coming into the realm. I've already taken the liberty, my lord, of recalling our armies stationed on the eastern and western frontiers. But neither army can get back here for nearly a tenday.

"I'm afraid to say, my lord, that if the southern group is finished, Macha could very well sweep right up to the city, burning and looting the entire province. We could lose everything there, thousands of lives, along with the entire wealth of the region. Macha knows that he doesn't have enough sorcerers to beat our defenses from above, but he certainly could make it hell out in the countryside."

"Damn them to the fires!" Allic roared. "Why this knife in the back? I've lived to our agreements."

"It could be an alliance between the Torms and Sarnak," Storm suggested. "Macha alone we can handle, but the two of them together... You know the figures—we've looked at them often enough. If Macha goes over to Sarnak, they'll have superior numbers in the air."

"Macha? Never. I've always thought him a bit too cold-blooded, but he's nobody's fool."

"But you must face the question of Sarnak in all of this, and plan for that possibility," Storm replied.

Allic looked at Valdez who nodded.

"We've always known that we don't have the people to match the combined strength of Patrice and Sarnak, while also keeping a watch on Macha as well. We thought our diplomacy could keep him out of a fight or even swing him in on our side. Damn it all, I can't imagine what pushed him into this; he hates Sarnak nearly as much as we do. We now have to assume Patrice is in this too, and waiting like a vulture to help pick over the corpse." He grimaced.

"We do have the tactical advantage of the offworlders," Allic replied.

"Wait a minute," Mark interrupted. "There's something

here I still don't get. What about Jartan? He's your father."

"True. And he'd trigger a full conflagration in the process," Storm replied. "If he comes in, Minar, who is Macha's father, will come in. Or if Jartan should move against Sarnak—and we all know that he wishes he could—that would bring Tor into the fight."

"So what? This Tor isn't a god," Mark said.

"But he is the only surviving child of Horat," Valdez told him. "Tor came from the marriage of a god to a demigod, and his power is nearly as great. Jartan must not move against any other god's descendant, not even Horat's. It is a delicate balance that has managed to keep a semblance of the peace."

"The balance," Storm continued, "has managed to keep for thirty centuries. So my father will stand out of this one as long as the other gods do. Besides, we're not children. It's up to us to fight this out."

"Damn it," Mark replied, "this isn't some game. Real people are dying out there. If the gods have all this power, at least they could stop it."

"You still haven't grasped it," Ikawa said softly. "In the end it *is* nothing more than a game, an illusion. That is why we Japanese can die in battle without fear, for what we believed back on Earth has been proved to us here. All that counts is honor, Bushido, which we carry with us into the next world."

"Easy for you," Mark said. "Remember I'm still an American at heart."

"I know," Ikawa replied, looking straight into Mark's eyes.

"Enough of this," Valdez growled. "There's a battle to be fought."

"The answer is obvious," Allic said evenly. "We leave before the middle of the night."

"What do you plan to commit?" Valdez asked.

"Everything here, every sorcerer, except for you and the oldest men of the reserve. Ander will be coming back in from patrol and when he does I want him to handle air cover over the city while you prepare the town for the worst. I plan to put the rest of my sorcerers there." Allic pointed to the position at the edge of escarpment.

"But my lord, the forces there might already be annihilated. Logic demands that we keep our main complement of sorcerers here in reserve until the rest of our ground armies move up. Then we can drive Macha back. The southern army at this point can only slow them down, not defeat them."

Ikawa felt his anger rising but kept it in check. This man had sent nearly all of his people out there, and it seemed as if he had simply written them off as a delaying force. The cold-blooded logic of it was correct: to put out enough to slow the enemy down while your dispersed forces were pulled back in. But this was not an exercise, and his men, nearly all that were left from his old world, were out there.

As if Allic was reading Ikawa's mind, he said, "Valdez, go tell the men out there that logic has written them off."

"Never reinforce defeat, my lord."

"You did by sending up the contingent of offworlders."

Valdez was silent.

For the first time Ikawa felt a vague sense of disquiet about this man. Could it be that he wanted the outsiders pared down a little bit? Was there a fear that the new group was growing too powerful? Or was there another reason?

"All right, I'm taking half the wall crystals and I'll leave twenty sorcerers of the reserve to hold the city."

"That leaves Landra all but naked," Valdez warned.

"The first contingent from the western army will be in the city in eight days. We'll keep Macha's people in front of us, and fight our way back through the pass. With the additional sorcerers, we might even push Macha back."

"But what about Sarnak or Patrice?" Valdez argued.

"Look, damn it. I know who the enemy to my front is: Macha." Allic's voice rose so that all could feel his anger.

"I go to the enemy. I'll not hide back here waiting for a possible threat to materialize while there is a threat for all to see to my south. I want Macha's head for this; Landra will have to take care of itself. Prepare to leave at once. This discussion has ended."

Without waiting for a response he turned and stalked out of the room.

Valdez shot a quick glance at Mark and Ikawa, as if expecting a challenge.

Mark was tempted to say something, but in his heart he knew that Valdez had only followed the correct logic. It might mean the lives of his men—but command could not be swayed by the question of lives. He nodded towards Valdez, signaling that there was no challenge. The battle chieftain turned and left the room.

"Not to hurt your masculine pride," Storm said, approaching Mark, "but will you be able to keep up? I mean, I can take you two in tow if need be."

"As a matter of fact, it would hurt my masculine pride," Mark said, trying to smile.

Storm turned away and looked at the map.

"I hope he knows what he's doing," she said softly. "Allic tends to charge ahead the moment he sees what he thinks is his foe. Someday it'll be his undoing."

Mark would remember that comment in the days to come.

Chapter 15

"Christ almighty, here they come!" Walker shouted.

Goldberg looked over his shoulder. He wanted to rise for a better vantage point, but the Torms had air superiority now and anything that moved even a foot off the ground this close to the battle line was hit by concentrated blasts. After they had lost several sorcerers, word had come down from Pina that men could only go airborne to protect the ground troops if they were attacked from above.

He could hear the chanting growing ever louder, "Torm, Torm, Torm," as the crescent-shaped battle line started its advance, the two flanks encompassing a front nearly half a mile across, gradually closing in as they funneled into the pass.

The solid wall of humanity advanced at an inexorable pace, never faltering.

"Hold steady," Goldberg ordered. They were deployed atop a low rise in the middle of the pass. Anything that advanced would have to come over them first. He looked to his left where the thin line of Japanese were deployed in open battle formation, their Nambu machine gun concealed in a hurriedly dug bunker, while to his right were the rest of the Americans with two Thompson submachine guns anchoring the flank.

Goldberg looked back over his shoulder to the low ridgeline in the middle of the pass, a hundred yards away. The last of the stragglers had pulled back, and from the flurry of activity he could see the flash of axes as trees were felled for protective barricades, while men dug, sometimes with their bare hands, to throw up a fortified position, started earlier in the day by the desperately needed reinforcements.

"Buy time," Pina had said to the offworlders. "Just a turning of the glass, that's all. We need to keep them back while strengthening the line."

Buy time, goddamn them. They'd been buying time now for three days. A bloody trail of buying time that stretched back across thirty leagues of running.

Thirty leagues and five thousand dead. For Goldberg it was like something out of a history book, or perhaps some British movie like *The Four Feathers,* where the regiment formed a square and the native armies would swarm in, an ocean of men as endless as the sea.

But this morning the Torms had come up against something new: the power of a Japanese machine gun. The retreat had finally been slowed when the weapons, which Pina had held in reserve, were released in a desperate bid to buy time for the fortification work. This was the final step back: if they were pushed out of the pass the Torms would be able to pour onto the high plateau and overrun the province.

"Five hundred yards," Saito shouted.

The ground beneath them shook to the marching cadence of the enemy host.

Goldberg looked back over his shoulder.

"Pina, goddamn it, you better give me some fire support and keep those flying bastards off our necks."

A single shot sounded.

Goldberg looked up the line. It was Smithie. Goldberg wished he had waited a bit longer, but the man was an expert with a rifle, and besides, it was impossible to miss, so tightly packed was the advancing army.

An officer in the enemy's front line crumpled. There was a momentary pause at the shock of this new weapon, and then all hell broke loose. Forty thousand voices rose in one long scream of anger, and the Torm host broke into a rolling charge. Behind the enemy line a score of sorcerers rose, firing at the thin defensive line.

One of the sorcerers weaved forward, daring Allic's men to meet him. Walker stood up from his slit trench, aimed his Thompson, and squeezed the trigger. The sorcerer's shielding slowed several rounds, but one got through and the impact sent him staggering. He barely made it back to the protection of his lines.

The Japanese Nambu opened with a staccato burst. The team worked like experts: a burst, tap the gun on the side to move it a fraction, and then another burst—all of which were hitting home.

"Hold your fire," Goldberg screamed to his men. The Japanese were combat infantry, they knew their business. But he wanted them close, real close, for his own people.

The wall moved closer. *Damn, damn they're getting too close!*

White flame shot over his head, fired from half a dozen sorcerers at the same time. Goldberg ducked instinctively into the trench. The ground a dozen yards away exploded.

Another burst of flame, and then another. It seemed the ground would melt around him.

He felt a flicker of pressure. A flame bolt had nicked against his shielding, causing it to glow as the energy was absorbed.

Angry now, he flicked the safety off his M-1 carbine, sighted on the leaders of the charge, and yelled, "Fire!"

It was impossible to miss. He squeezed off round after round. Even when he missed his intended target, a man to either side would crumple and go down. So tightly packed was the charge that one round would cut down two, even three men before its power was spent.

The Nambu crew was really hammering it now, holding down for long sustained bursts.

Fire flashed overhead, rifles and now even pistols cracked, the world was engulfed, overwhelmed by the roar of battle, as twenty held against a rush of thousands. Finally they got support from Allic's longbowmen. Sheets of arrows rose heavenward, the shadow of a thousand bolts racing across the ground. The arrows would seem to hover for a moment and then come hurtling down, slashing into the enemy line with devastating impact.

The Torm line faltered, slowed, then stopped, and from out of the host a triple line of skirmishers advanced, their shorter bows, which did not have the range of Allic's weapons, at the ready. If the archers got close enough, Goldberg realized, they'd have to cut out the defensive shielding, since it was always possible that the Torms would hazard a red crystal or two.

The archers rushed forward fearlessly. As one fell, another rushed to take his place, while all the time the Nambu cut its bloody path.

To either flank Torm skirmishers hugged the high ground, working their way towards the flanks of Pina's main force. Goldberg was tempted to call for fire to pin them down, but thought better. Firing straight ahead, every shot counted and delayed the main advance.

For long minutes the battle was stalemated. The Torms could not advance any further, but were increasing their pressure on the flanks. Goldberg looked back over his shoulder, hoping for a signal to pull back, but no signal came. They were out there on their own.

The Nambu fell silent. Dodging enemy fire bolts, Goldberg rushed over to the Japanese position.

Saito looked up to him, his eyes full of despair.

"We've got one box left, and that's it," the Japanese sergeant cried. "I need to hold something in reserve."

Goldberg looked back to where the enemy line had faltered.

They were starting to pull back!

A hoarse cheer went up from Pina's men, who were still feverishly digging in.

God let it end, Goldberg silently prayed.

But it was no rout. The center of the Torm line pulled back grimly, but the pressure on the flanks was still building as unit after unit of slingers, light infantry, and archers filtered along the clifflike walls of the pass. They did not stop to engage the delaying force but pushed on, intent on cutting off the main defenses at the top of the pass.

The pullback in the center slowed and finally stopped. So close were the Torms that Goldberg could clearly hear the shouted commands as the enemy's rage grew.

"Your men," Saito asked, looking at Goldberg. "How much ammunition?"

"José, whatya got left?"

"Twenty rounds."

"Welsh?"

"I'm out."

Damn him. What good is an empty Thompson?

"Smithie?"

"Twenty rounds."

"Walker?"

"Thirty rounds."

"Kraut?"

"Maybe ten rounds."

Goldberg looked back to Saito.

Even before the question started to form a roaring shout came up from the Torms. It crashed against them like thunder, washing away all other sound.

"Torm, Torm, Torm! *A tu* Macha!"

"Christ, they're charging!"

Goldberg turned to look. It was an irresistible tide, a crashing wall of armed men rushing forward at the run. They were only several ranks deep, while behind them, moving at a steady trot, came the rest of the army.

They could use the rest of their ammunition and knock out the charging line, but then the rest of them, shielded by flesh and blood, would push on over.

There'd be no stopping them this time.

"Let's get the hell outa here!" Goldberg roared.

Straightening, he pointed to the rear. The men needed no prompting. Grabbing their weapons, they scrambled out of the trenches and burst for the rear. A triumphant cry came up from the Torms. The ground beneath Goldberg's feet trembled with the weight of their advance.

Goldberg turned and leveled his carbine to fire another burst. There was a blinding flash.

He felt as if every nerve in his body had been touched with fire. He tried to scream, but no sound would form. And then his thoughts slipped away and he fell into darkness.

"Captain, I don't know if I can keep this up."

Mark glanced at Younger, who was struggling to maintain formation. For that matter, Mark wondered how *he* was managing to hold on. After less than four hours of exhausted sleep in a corner of Allic's conference room, Storm had roused him. Allic and the others were ready to leave.

For a moment Mark had been tempted to say the hell with it and ask her for help with the flying, but pride had stopped him. He knew that she could undoubtedly sense the exhaustion, but she had wisely refrained from offering any help.

"Not much longer, Younger. You can see the glow, there on the horizon."

They were flying now by the light of the twin moons, which bathed the world in an eerie double-shadowed light. For the last half hour they'd been able to see the shimmer on the horizon. It put him in mind of the time he had gone as a liaison with a British night bomber team and had been able to see the flames of Hamburg from two hundred miles out. All hell must be breaking loose on the edge of the escarpment.

"Not much longer." It was Storm, swinging up on his side. He smiled grimly at her.

"Perfect time for an ambush," Storm called. "Allic wants cover up above. We're it."

"You hear that?" he shouted. "Open formation, we're going up."

In a process that still amazed him, he willed the direction, arched his back, and started up, climbing at a forty-five degree angle, the Americans and several of Allic's sorcerers following Storm's lead in line abreast.

Within minutes they were several thousand feet above the main formation. The Ventilian Hills were now below them, and as they pierced a scattered bank of clouds, Wolf Pass finally came into view.

"It looks like a bloody nightmare down there," Giorgini yelled, approaching Mark.

To Mark it looked more like the gates of hell: The pass was ablaze with light, bolts of magic fire snapping across the landscape and reflecting on the clouds about them so that it seemed they were flying through a sea of flame.

As the party drew closer they could see by the moonlight and reflected glow where advanced raiding parties of Torms had already skirted the edge of the defensive fortifications and were sweeping into the open plains beyond. Here and there freshly kindled fires marked where yet another farmstead was being torched.

"Three o'clock, fifty plus bogeys," Younger shouted, pointing. "Below us, dropping out of the clouds."

Mark could see two formations of twenty-five demons, and the first was already diving toward Allic.

"Bandits, definitely bandits," Mark cried. "Coming in three o'clock high on Allic."

Storm was already warning her brother via her communications crystal. Allic's party broke formation and wheeled straight into the attack.

"Let's get into it!" Storm shouted.

"Not yet," Mark cried. "There might be a second wave from another direction. Hold formation."

Mark had snapped the orders as if still back on the

Dragon Fire. Now, he looked to see how this demigod would react to such a perfunctory command. He relaxed when he saw the look of acknowledgment in her eyes.

Good. Mark was getting sick of arguing with these people about the power of fighting in large formations instead of breaking up into small groups or individual contests once a battle was joined. If in the minutes to come Storm would stick with him, the others might start to listen when they saw the power of a coordinated strike.

He looked over towards his crew. They were holding tight formation as he expected them to.

"Twenty plus bogeys coming in," Giorgini yelled, "nine o'clock low. They're bandits, look like sorcerers."

"That's the one for us," Mark cried.

All weariness was forgotten. He timed the moment, watching as a loosely scattered formation of sorcerers swooped down on Allic's party from behind.

They must have been waiting for this, knowing that reinforcements were bound to come in. It was a good plan: send in the first wave of demons to break up the formation and divert it, then drop the sorcerers in to pick off the lone flyers one after another from behind, while the second wave of demons is held in reserve.

"Keep it tight. Stay on my wing," Mark ordered. "Going down now!"

He pulled up, winged over, and dove. In formation, the others followed.

They would have one good pass. Mark would pull this like a standard fighter sweep: no fancy maneuvers—just come in high, drop through the formation, and slam them with everything as you shot through, hitting them with enough speed that it'd be difficult for them to follow.

The formation was right below him, and Mark picked the last sorcerer in the unit. He could almost imagine a ring sight silhouetting his target. The imagery seemed to help him concentrate, and he waited until his target filled the entire circle.

Now!

A blast of fire cracked from Mark's wrist, striking his opponent between the shoulder blades. There wasn't any doubt on this hit. The flyer crumpled, his back shattered. Trailing fire, he fell.

Instantly Mark found another target and fired as he dove past the startled enemy.

The strike was nearly perfect. The others got off their

shots, each striking a foe, and several enemies simply disintegrated in midair. Mark slammed out a third bolt, winging an enemy who was rolling into an evasive. The injured sorcerer tumbled end over end, disappearing into low lying clouds.

Following Mark's lead, his battle group continued to dive, weaving and turning to throw off the feeble return fire.

Mark pulled up into an Immelmann turn, ready to pounce on anything that was following. But the enemy formation had been broken by the onslaught. Their surprise thwarted, the surviving sorcerers fled back towards the southwest.

"They're in retreat," Storm shouted. "In after them!"

"Straight into their own air defenses?" Mark protested. "We don't know what they've got on the ground over there, and our surprise has been blown. Let's tighten up and keep our eyes open."

He looked towards Allic's formation, several hundred yards below, still fighting demons. He was tempted to order a dive into the battle, but felt it best to keep formation in case the Torms had more surprises waiting.

Anyhow, Allic was more than holding his own against the demons.

Thunderclaps echoed and rolled against the sides of the pass, counterpointing the shouts of the thousands below, who paused in their own game of slaughter to watch the carnage above.

The first formation of demons, shattered by the concentrated blasts of Allic and his companions, broke to either flank, their phosphorescent wings shimmering green. The second group swooped downward. While holding formation above the main fight, Mark's team fired into the advancing line. With an almost fatalistic determination the demons pushed their attack home, breaking through the line of fire. Within seconds they seemed to swarm over Allic.

A white-hot fire exploded in the middle of the fight, lighting the countryside bright as noonday.

"What the hell was that!" Mark threw an arm across his eyes.

Even above the roar of the explosion he could hear Storm's cry. For long, frightening seconds he flew blind.

Blinking, he looked down. Everything was reversed, like a photographic negative. The flare was still burning with blinding intensity, but through his squint he could see that the flaming object was dropping, tumbling away from the fight. Mark looked at Storm, and saw the terror in her eyes.

"What was it?" he screamed.

"Probably a red crystal hitting the defensive screen of someone powerful," she cried.

Allic! The flame was right where Allic had been. Christ, he wanted to go down, but not now. He had to hold position up here. If it was Allic, if Allic was dead, there was nothing they could do to help him now. He tried not to think of it.

Mark watched as the flare, once a living body, fell away.

"There he is." Storm's voice nearly broke with relief.

Mark followed to where she pointed and could see Allic still flying, his companions pulling in closer, a protective wall.

Mark, still blinking, scanned the sky above and to either side, wondering what the enemy might throw at them next.

But Macha's forces only pulled back to the protection of their own lines.

Storm, Mark, and the rest of his crew swung into air-support formation above Allic and followed him in as they made a low approach towards the embattled line holding the edge of the pass.

Half a dozen bolts of fire snapped out from the Torms as they came in across the field, but the shots, tossed out at extreme range, were wide. The enemy fire slackened and at last stopped as ground forces followed the lead of their superiors in the air, and grudgingly pulled back for a respite before the next battle.

Still scanning the sky above them, Mark weaved back and forth, waiting for Allic to land.

"He's on the ground," Storm called. "Let's get in."

This was the vulnerable time, Mark realized, as they went down. If anyone lurked in the cloud cover, they would hit now.

But all was quiet as they alighted near the center of the camp.

Exhaustion washed over Mark. The adrenaline rush of combat was past, and he trembled. All around him was chaos, shouting men, the cries of the wounded; and over it all the stench of fire, fear, and death.

Allic was off to one side, being led towards the tattered remains of a tent, and leaning on one of his sorcerers for support.

Together Storm and Mark pushed through the mob towards Allic, who smiled wanly at them.

"Sheena's dead," Allic said weakly. "I sensed the red crystal in his hand even as he tried to hit my shielding. There must have been a powerful warding spell on him—I should have noticed him much, much sooner." He paused.

"I thought it would hit me, and I tried to drain off my defense shield. Then Sheena pushed me aside and threw herself on the demon. She's gone, gone to save me."

Allic looked straight at Mark, and for a second he thought Allic was wondering if he would have made the same sacrifice for his lord. He hoped he wouldn't be asked.

Chapter 16

"Did you get him?"

The demon was still bent over, gasping for breath. Macha waited patiently.

"My brother did as you commanded," the demon gasped. "One of Allic's guards blocked him."

Macha gave a characteristic shrug and turned away.

"The pledge to my family to release the bond of punishment on our sire, will you still honor it?" the demon asked.

There was a grumble of anger from Macha's aides. The word of their lord had been questioned.

"Your brother failed," a lieutenant barked. "Your sire will burn forever in living torment as far as I'm concerned."

Without a word Macha walked away from the group and looked towards the encampment, strengthened now by Allic's presence.

Macha knew enough of battle to know that a plan, any plan, was fine when drawn up on parchment, or discussed around a table—but it was far different when placed in action.

These offworlders had been the most difficult part to judge so far. First, with their weapons that shot bolts of metal. He had hoped that the retreat would become a rout when Pina's forces hit the top of the defile. But the offworlders had slowed his advance long enough to allow them to dig in.

The fools—they should have fortified this pass long ago. That alone had given him cause for a moment of doubt. Valdez was nobody's fool—a man who plans an attack must also plan for defense—and he could not understand why Valdez had not seen to fortifying in preparation for war.

Macha shook his head. Allic was far too easy to read, and he had almost regretted the plan, knowing he was playing on Allic's famous impetuousness and foolhardy bravery. A commander, Macha thought, should lead with his mind, not with his heart. It had been a good plan, but plans unfortunately didn't guarantee success.

Macha shrugged. They'd wait for dawn.

He looked back at the demon, who glowered at him defiantly.

"Your family pledge is fulfilled. Your brother passed into the shadows with his attempt. I shall give the order to have your sire released from the mines."

The demon's look of hatred turned instantly to shocked surprise. Bowing low, it withdrew into the night.

Macha looked at the formation drawn up in the shadows behind his command tent, and to the unit commander who had come with reinforcements less than a turning ago.

"Zambara, your unit is ready?"

"They are eager to feed," Zambara answered.

"Good." Macha turned and looked back up the slope. "Pass the word to the handlers: With first light your regiment will advance."

He had been thwarted by things unplanned for—the skills of the offworlders. Now they would feel his wrath...and it would destroy them.

"Do you wish you had gone with your friends?"

Kochanski turned from the window. How quickly he had adjusted to all of this, he suddenly realized. He was facing a god, a pulsing tower of light, but he barely gave it a thought anymore, as he bowed in acknowledgment. In the Old Testament men usually groveled, whined, or at least took off their sandals and crawled around on all fours. Instead he found himself looking towards the side table where he knew Jartan's usual offering would appear.

Sure enough, a chilled pitcher of Schaefer's materialized on the counter with two glasses. For more than a week now,

that had been the signal that Jartan wanted to talk. He realized, as well, just how much this being liked him. He was an
anomaly, a fascinating diversion. But Kochanski knew that
Jartan had also come to treasure the conversation that was
devoid of worshipfulness and wheedling.

The shimmering glow coalesced into a brilliant, luminous
figure shining with an internal radiance. Jartan then strode to
the table, poured a couple of beers, and downed his in a
single gulp.

"Good stuff, that. I can see why you like it."

"I wish I had a clearer memory of some of the German
dark beers, but it's been quite a few years."

"Why's that?"

"Remember the war back home? German beer is politi-
cally suspect these days."

"Foolish. I'd like to try it sometime. But you still haven't
answered my original question about wishing you had left
with your friends."

Kochanski settled into the chair by Jartan's side.

"They're my friends."

"Even the ones you call Japanese?"

"Of course. It's kind of hard to blindly hate an enemy
once you get to know him. Why do you ask?"

"I have my reasons. But you think they're in trouble?"

"I've felt that from the moment they left and you ordered
me to stay here. If they're going into danger, it's my duty to
share that danger."

"Sometimes the hardest duty is not to share the danger,
while those you love bear the brunt. Remember, Kochanski,
I have two children going down there to fight."

"So why don't you intervene?"

"When you were a child and got into a fight, did your
father come and thrash your opponent for you?"

"That's not the point. A street corner brawl between kids
is one thing. This is war."

"No, it's not different. In many ways this *is* a street corner
brawl. And if I were to intervene directly, then Minar must
come in. You know the power of my son; that is but a
shadow of my own power in war, and Minar's as well. It
would be as if we brought the sun from the heavens and let it
burn the land till it became nothing but cinder and glass.

"No, we must not intervene, though at times I do wonder
if there is something beyond this fight, something darker."

"Can't you tell?"

"Kochanski, Kochanski, my friend. You give too much power, even to gods. Besides, the knowing can at times be blocked, cancelled by the power of others, if they set their mind to it. But sometimes what a god cannot see, a mortal can. Because your looking is unanticipated. It can also at times reach closer into the hearts of your foes."

"I can't help but feel that you want to show me something to put my mind at ease."

"Maybe not at ease, but at least to make you realize that even here, you can serve your friends."

Kochanski stood at the railing of Jartan's private balcony overlooking the sea and listened to the sounds of the surf hundreds of feet below. The gentle midnight wind swept through his hair, caressing him lightly with its touch. In the heavens, the Twins had set, and the sky was filled with the majesty of the Cloud shimmering from horizon to horizon. The Runner was at zenith, tracing its eternal race across the heavens, while forever beyond its reach floated the Maiden and the five stars of the Crown.

"I've yet to ask you," Jartan said, coming up to Kochanski's side, "are the heavens as beautiful on your own world?"

His own world, he thought. He could remember as a kid when he'd get out of Trenton for a week at scout camp up on the Delaware, he'd go alone into the fields at night, lie down, and soar into the heavens, his imagination riding the tails of meteorites and coasting the firmament of the Milky Way. Was that the Milky Way, the cluster of stars overhead that was simply called the Cloud? If so, where was Earth, the blue-green speck of home? Was his old girlfriend now looking across the endless sea, dreaming of a heaven, and thinking that he was somehow floating there above her? The wind chilled him and with a wistful sigh he looked back to Jartan.

"Not as beautiful, but just as distant," Kochanski replied.

"Come over here and sit down for a moment," Jartan said, beckoning towards an ornate, oversized chair that looked like a throne.

Kochanski settled uncomfortably onto the throne, his dangling feet barely touching the ground. He placed his hands on the armrests, grabbing hold of the griffins' heads mounted to either side. A tremor went through the chair, and it started to rise.

"What the hell?" Kochanski yelped. If he was going to fly,

damn it, he'd prefer to do so like everybody else did, arms outstretched.

The absurdity of his fear caught him. The way anybody else did—yeah, just like Superman. He settled back, and through gentle experiment he realized that pressure on the griffins' heads raised and lowered the chair. But movement was slow. He concentrated his power on the chair, but still it drifted heavenward at a leisurely rate.

He looked over to Jartan, who was floating in the air by his side.

"All right, my lord, it's obviously not for flying. What's the real purpose of this thing?"

Jartan laughed. "I call it the god chair, and its purpose is to explore. Lean your head back."

Kochanski settled back.

"Close your eyes."

Again he did what Jartan requested. But he could still see!

With a start he nearly jerked out of the chair, which was now floating several hundred feet above the palace.

"Ah, startled you." Jartan laughed. "Now close your eyes and relax."

Warily Kochanski leaned back and closed his eyes. Again he opened them in a near panic, but trying not to show his anxiety, he closed them again. His gaze lifted upwards. The stars! The sky from horizon to horizon was ablaze with light, as though the night heavens had crackled into white-hot blaze.

"Just relax," Jartan said, "and turn to the southward."

Kochanski did as he was directed. It seemed as though the world beneath him had grown pale, like a photo too long exposed. He almost wished that he could close his eyes against the light, and chuckled at the absurdity. His vision shifted to the world beneath him, where he could see a court-yard, and two young girls walking in the shadows. Curious, he watched them, wishing he were closer to see who they were.

The chair seemed to fall away beneath him, rushing him in a blinding instant so that he now hovered directly before the two. Not only could he see them, but he could see through them, sensing in one a pure flaming light, while in the other there was a darker thought, a feeling of jealousy for her companion who was talking of her lover.

Embarrassed, Kochanski started to speak, to explain his

sudden intrusion into their privacy, but a deep rumbling laugh made him open his eyes.

"How?" Kochanski cried. "I didn't move an inch! Yet I was down there," and he pointed to the courtyard. But where was it? Leaning out of the chair, he looked all about him, but the courtyard, and its two lovely inhabitants, were nowhere to be seen.

"Where was I?"

"I'm not sure. I didn't have time to track you. In the chair one can travel leagues without moving an inch. You looked off towards the horizon for several seconds and then you started to voice an apology. Whomever you were trying to speak to could have been right below us, or could have been five hundred leagues away. At first the chair gives only one confusing moment after another. But with practice you can control where it takes you, to get a brief glimpse of a moment far away."

"I could see my friends, then."

"That is why I brought you here."

"Do you use this?"

"Not often," Jartan confessed. "I created it, gave it part of my own Essence. But it does not work well for me: my power overwhelms the chair's magic. But for someone like you, it can have its uses. First you must learn to control it—and no one has yet learned to do that completely. Without total mastery, the chair is only an amusing toy, since its visions can rarely be directed to a specific locus and held there.

"But you seem to have a strange gift, a rare turning of the Essence. I have heard how you can sense things from afar. You offworlders have brought abilities from your world which here combine with the Essence to give you rare and powerful talents. José, I am told, has it to a lesser extent. I understand that Giorgini has a similar power, but . . ." Jartan seemed unwilling to comment further.

Could it be? Kochanski wondered. Giorgini was radar fire control, José was radio, while he was the radar man. Could it be?

"Try it again," Jartan said. "This time turn your thoughts to one of your friends."

Kochanski did as he was told. Closing his eyes he settled back. The world shimmered softly about him.

Goldberg. Since late this afternoon his thoughts had turned to Goldberg, and the feeling persisted that something was wrong.

He felt the chair shifting again; the illusion of the land rushing beneath him.

"Goldberg!" he shouted, but it could not be heard.

Kochanski wanted to scream, to reach out and care for his friend who lay half buried in a blown-out bunker, surrounded by enemies. Was he dead?

Kochanski struggled for control. Goldberg was hundreds of miles away. If he was dead, nothing could be done. Kochanski was almost ready to curse Jartan for allowing him to see this. What good was seeing if there could be no helping?

For long minutes he fought to stay calm while gazing at his friend's body. Finally he pulled away.

His vision swept over the battlefield, the enemy host, Allic's beleaguered forces bracing for the threat.

The threat? His mind dwelled on that, and even as it did, he felt himself starting to drift away. What the hell was going on?

He wanted to stay, to find Mark and Walker, and yes, even Ikawa and Saito, to reassure himself. Then he would return to Jartan.

But it rankled that he should be here, safe, while his friends waited out the night. He belonged with them, facing the enemy who at this moment threatened Allic's realm.

Again, as if somehow prompted, his mind turned away, drifting.

Where was he going?

His mind scanned around him and he felt something that disturbed and alarmed his subconscious. Abruptly, the chair whisked him away, and the ground seemed to rush up towards him. He screamed, thinking he was about to crash, and held out his hands as if to ward off the impact—but the chair just continued into the ground as though it didn't exist.

He found that he could still see, almost like he could when swimming in clear water. Riding beneath the world he headed for the disturbance.

There was a burst of light that momentarily blinded him, and he found himself gazing down a tunnel that cut deep into the heart of the world. And it was swarming with life: sorcerers, demons, and the great machines of war.

He could feel the hatred and malevolence of their minds. And in an instant Kochanski knew.

This is the real threat!

He felt something sense his presense and he turned to flee. Back through the ground, rising heavenward to get away, even as a dark form probed and grasped at him, trying to pull him from the chair.

Struggling, he clung with both body and spirit, and as he rose the ground seemed to burst asunder.

Before him in the distance was Allic's city of Landra, stripped naked so that the supposed menace from the south could be contained. But that was not the real danger!

Beneath his feet an army was marshaling, and at last all the bits and rumors—Macha's strange attack, the reports of Sarnak's kingdom stripped of troops—at last it was clear.

Even as he hovered, wondering, there was a tugging from below. He looked down and his heart froze: He was gazing into the eyes of Sarnak, who regarded him with cold hatred.

"You know too late," Sarnak whispered.

Kochanski tried to form words of defiance, but Sarnak's power held him speechless, immobile.

"I might be tempted to let you leave and tell," Sarnak said. He hesitated, then shook his head. "But I think it better if your soul comes with me. I have a place prepared for ones such as you."

He reached towards Kochanski.

There was a blinding flash. With a strangled cry Kochanski tried to pull back. He felt hands gripping his shoulders and he shrieked. The hands shook him.

He opened his eyes. It was Jartan. Dazed, Kochanski looked around and saw that the two of them were still floating above Jartan's palace.

"Sarnak!" Kochanski cried. "He tried to . . ."

"I know," Jartan said soothingly. "With the chair you stay here, yet you travel far. But what you see can be sensed by one standing by you. I could see the shadow of torment closing over you, so I pulled you back."

"It's Sarnak!" Kochanski announced. "I could see it all. The war with Macha is nothing but a lure for Allic. Sarnak's dug a tunnel to within sight of Landra, and is sneaking an entire army through it. Even if Allic stops Macha, Sarnak will still win.

"Jartan," and he hesitated for a second, "all of them, Allic, Mark, Storm—everyone has walked into a trap!"

Chapter 17

Patrice stood by a large pool in her courtyard, watching flickers of light in the reflections. Her aura glowed as she strove to see how the war between Allic and Macha was progressing. Finally, she lowered her arms and the darkness of the night came back to surround her.

"What did you see, Mistress?"

"Nothing more than we already know," Patrice answered the witch. "I don't understand any of this. Why are Macha and Allic fighting? There is no logic to it."

She shook her head. "Mobilize the army. No matter who wins, I want to be prepared to intervene as an ally with the winner. And increase the watch on Sarnak's border. He is much too quiet."

The witch nodded and touched her communications crystal, sending the orders.

Patrice had turned her attention back to the waters of the pool. "By the way, how are my new toys?"

"The two outlanders are responding well to the drugs, mistress. Soon they will be as pliable as babies."

"Keep me informed. I can use them, no matter how this war turns out."

Patrice turned her mind back to the conflict. Her spy in Landra had informed her that the city was dangerously undermanned, but there were too many dangers for her to move before her own plans were ready.

She glanced at the sky. Dawn was coming.

"I think you better get your men up," Ikawa said, leaning over to wake Mark.

Stretching, Mark came to his feet. A light mist had risen, cloaking the field like a burial shroud. Mark rubbed the sleep from his eyes and looked to the men who lay on the ground around him. They were all here now, except for Kochanski and Goldberg. Where was Goldberg?

"Thinking of Goldberg?" Ikawa said, more as a statement than a question. Again there seemed to be that ability to almost read what the other was feeling, and he looked at the Japanese captain.

"He could still be alive," Ikawa said gently.

"Who? Oh, Goldberg you mean. Perhaps." Mark turned away.

"All right," Mark commanded, going to the men who were his only link to the other world, "time to stand to. Dawn soon."

The men started to stir, cursing.

Ikawa walked back towards his own command and Mark fell in by his side.

The mist around them was slowly dissipating, the sky behind them shifting from deep indigo to scarlet and orange.

"You know, Mark, at times I almost fear what I am becoming here. There are times when I can somehow see . . . see what is around a corner, waiting and lurking. And then I wonder if by seeing I am drawn to that path, or can still change it, and the seeing is nothing more than a warning."

"Go on, spill it. What's bothering you?"

Ikawa turned away from Mark and walked over to the barricade, Mark following in his footsteps.

Through the mist they could hear Macha's troops stirring, the noises for a day of slaughter.

"They have something over there." Ikawa's eyes were full of fear.

"I dread this day," he whispered. "There is something over there, something I can almost smell."

"And you think that death will take you today," Mark said evenly. God, how often he had climbed into a plane with that certainty of death hovering over him. Convinced that when he again touched earth, he would be trapped in flaming

wreckage. And yet at the end of the day he would climb out
of the plane, his legs trembling, only to lie awake that night
thinking that tomorrow would be The Day.

He knew what Ikawa was fearing, and no words could
drive it away.

Mark lay his hand on Ikawa's shoulder.

Ikawa looked back at him—then his gaze shifted past
Mark and his eyes grew wide.

Mark spun around. Nothing was there except the mist,
now burning away. A breeze came drifting across the field to
blow away the last of the mantle of grayness.

"I saw something," Ikawa said.

"What?"

"I thought I saw something rise into the air and come
back down."

Ikawa pointed to the sentries posted along the wall. Several of them were peering intently towards the enemy encampment, visible at last now that the mist was nearly gone.

"Whatever it was, it's back down now," Mark replied.
"Most likely a sorcerer or demon rising for a quick scan."

Ikawa was silent.

All around them warriors were forming into ranks. Pennants swirled and stretched with the coming of the breeze.
Morning was upon them, and with it the promise of battle.

"We'd best see to our people," Mark said. "I'll meet you
at Allic's tent."

"Our job is to hold," Allic said to his unit commanders.
"As long as we hold the top of this pass, Macha cannot break
out onto the high plateau."

"But a number of raiders have already worked their way
around us," came a voice from the back of the tent. "My
homestead is only a half-day's ride from here."

"Damn it, we can't stop all of them," Allic snapped.
"Some raiders are bound to work their way around. But the
main force is blocked. They don't dare to leave an organized
foe in their rear.

"I've detailed half a thousand Tal riders to hold the
raiders in check and to keep our communications open. But
here is where we have to stop their main force, until the
other frontier armies can join us. I've stripped Landra to
hold Macha here. Damn it all, it's here that we hold him, or
your farmstead and every other farm in the province will be
gone inside a week.

"Pina, what do you estimate their forces at?"

"Forty thousand, my lord."

From the silence in the tent Mark realized that Pina was only now admitting in the presence of his subcommanders just how bad he felt the odds really were.

Allic smiled, as though relishing the chance to prove his skill against an extra enemy or two.

"We've got the wall crystals here; that will cut them down," Allic said. "Have the ranks form the standard shield wall when the attack comes.

"Ikawa, are there any projectiles left for your weapons?"

The others in the tent murmured among themselves. The miracle of the guns had brought them the precious time needed to strengthen their position.

"Not enough to make a difference now," Ikawa replied. "We should hold what we have left as a final reserve."

"All right then, place your weapons in this tent. If need be I'll give the command to use them.

"Mark, I like the way your people fight when they fly," Allic continued. "When the battle is joined, can you lead the whole group of offworlders like that again?"

Mark looked over at Ikawa. His people had no training or instinct for the close formation fighting, but they'd have to try.

"Yes."

"Then I'll lead my sorcerers up. Mark, you command the offworlders. Fight them as you see fit."

Allic smiled at Storm. "Macha has no idea you're here yet, so when you . . ."

A distant thunder filled the air and rolled away. It pulsated again, louder than before, and then yet louder again.

"The drum roll of the Subata," Pina said quietly.

Mark saw the hesitation cross Allic's features.

"Full ground defense!" he snapped at the frightened trumpeter who had burst into the command tent. "Form squares with shield walls, sorcerers stay in squares."

The signaler rushed from the tent, and within seconds half a score of trumpeters were sounding the commands. The camp outside broke into pandemonium as the ground troops rushed to take position.

"Pina, all sorcerers are to man heavy wall crystals," Allic shouted, and then he turned his gaze on the offworld commanders. "Mark, rally your people here and hold the center square; don't go up or you're lost. Ikawa, stay with me but send your Saito to the next square with several men. "We'll need them to help fire one of the wall crystals."

As Mark and Ikawa emerged from the tent, an ominous pulsing washed over them. In counterpoint to it came a distant rolling chant: "Torm, Torm, Torm."

"What the hell is going on?" Mark shouted as Storm dashed out of the tent after him.

"The drums mean that Macha has brought up his regiment of Subata."

"What the hell is a Subata?" Mark cried.

"Look, here they come!" Storm pointed off to the south.

Ikawa was already staring in that direction, a look of primal terror in his eyes.

Mark turned southward, and his cry of fear echoed the anguished shouts of those around him.

"My lord, there should be no stopping them now. It has been long since their last feeding."

Macha looked to the commander of the Subata, and the sorcerer grinned at him with wolfish delight.

Macha felt a wave of revulsion. The Subata were needed, but they were a weapon of desperation, not a worthy one. A man should be met by another man, with spear, or bolt and shield. This bestial slaughter was not to his liking at all. But he had lost too many already; he wanted this fight concluded before Allic's other forces could unite.

"Just see that they don't turn back on us. If they do, I'll have you staked out for your lovelies to finish off."

The sorcerer tried to show defiance by refusing to turn away from Macha's gaze, but at last he broke. He feared not that the Subata would turn, but that somehow Macha would be able to read the other thoughts, the hidden work, the secret plan in service to another lord.

A shadow passed over them—a shadow that blotted out the sky. A foul wind blew across them from the beating of thousands of leathery wings. Macha gazed upward as the Subata host moved forward to the attack.

For a moment Macha almost felt pity for Allic. His army could never withstand the Subata. With luck, before the day was out the fools would be relieved of this renegade Allic, who could so brutally stab his neighbors in the back.

The plains and hills surrounding Landra were filled with Sarnak's army. His sorcerers and demons already had full command of the air since they far outnumbered the skeleton force Allic had left behind.

His engineers were already completing the pontoon bridge that would allow him to cross the river and attack the west side of the city, further dividing its defense.

Sarnak stood on the crest of the slope, his banners fluttering in the breeze, his cape swirling out in the wind behind him. The sun shone upon him and he was content.

I have never felt so alive, so complete, as I do at this moment, he thought to himself. *If only it could last forever...*

His field commanders were doing well, maneuvering the men with practiced ease, sending out skirmishers to test the walls, drawing the fire of Allic's heavy crystals so their positions could be marked.

Already he could see that Allic had played into the trap, for his spies had reported nearly two dozen of the heavy weapons but a month ago, but only twelve could now be spotted. So the fool had left his city naked for the taking. Perhaps this plan could work completely after all.

"Soon you shall be the prince of Landra," Mokaoto said evenly. "Let me be the first to congratulate you."

Sarnak turned and gazed at the Japanese officer.

"Tell me," he said smoothly, "was it usually the custom in your army for officers to congratulate each other before the battle had even started?"

Mokaoto was silent at the reprimand.

"Perhaps following your logic I should congratulate you on what you plan to give your former commander once this fight is completed."

At the thought of his revenge Mokaoto smiled grimly.

"To achieve your dreams, you must first risk," Sarnak said evenly, "as I now risk. You may therefore have the honor of leading the first wave of sorcerers against their wall, signaling the general attack."

Mokaoto did not flinch or look away.

Whatever this man is, Sarnak realized, *he does have courage. Useful, but also a liability.* He had sensed that this man's power was still growing. *Courage, combined with cunning, could be a benefit, but it could present problems, too.*

"Now go," Sarnak said coldly.

Mokaoto lifted into the air, shouting the signal for the attack.

A tumultuous shout came up from the throats of tens of thousands.

The first wave started in.

Within seconds the walls of Landra were wreathed in fire and smoke as wall crystals fired, and heavy battering crystals, dragged all the way through the tunnel by gangs of laborers, fired in reply.

Even as the thousands rushed forward, more men poured from the opening of the tunnel which had been blasted out of the hills, a league beyond the city wall. The reinforcements emerged in joyful anticipation of the pillage about to begin.

Sarnak also laughed. The two armies which should be allied against him were tearing the life out of each other, far to the south.

"Christ in heaven," Walker screamed. "What the hell are they?"

Mark stood riveted in terror, as his men and the Japanese formed up beside Allic. All around them sword- and spearmen prepared to receive the attack.

At first it had seemed like a black cloud rising from the Torm camp, but it was a cloud made up of thousands of individual shapes.

"They're fucking snakes!" Giorgini cried. "Fucking snakes that fly!"

"Holy merciful god," Mark whispered. There were thousands of them, and the smallest were at least twenty feet long. Larger ones were two, even three times that size. Their bodies seemed to be shaped like airfoils, and they flew by means of an undulation combined with the flapping of thin, batlike wings that spanned a distance nearly as wide as they were long.

Now he understood Ikawa's foreboding. He turned to the Japanese captain, but Ikawa was rigid, almost catatonic.

Jesus, he was terrified of snakes, Mark remembered, and now this!'

"Ikawa," Mark yelled, "you've got to hang on; you've got to defend yourself!"

There was no response, only a blank look of despair.

All up and down the line Allic's men braced for the onslaught, forming into a dozen squares, one to each wall crystal, the formations checkerboarding the confines of the earthen-walled fortress. If there had been a hope for escape, panic would have broken the position then and there. But after the initial terror, all seemed to realize that in running there was no escape, for the Subata would hunt them one by one. Only through squared shield walls and a hedgehog of spears pointed upward could they hope to survive. Grimly the warriors fell into their positions.

In the center of each square a wall crystal was deployed, a sorcerer and several assistants behind it to aim the heavy weapon. The sorcerers, defensive shields could be seen turning up to maximum all along the front.

Mark brought his own shield up and looked over at Ikawa, who still was silent, without shielding of any kind.

"Private Takeo," Mark cried.

"Here, Captain."

Mark beckoned towards Ikawa and the young private went over to Ikawa's side. Standing next to his commander, Takeo brought up his own shielding to protect both of them. He would not be able to fight, but at least his commander would have some protection.

A lightning flash cut through the air from the first wall crystal; one of the snakes tumbled from the sky. In seconds all the wall crystals were in play. To Mark they looked like searchlight beams cutting through the morning air. Wherever a beam touched there was an explosion of flesh and another snake fell, hissing. There'd be a momentary pause as the sorcerers working the crystal focused their strength, and then another flash of light.

But it was not enough. The leading edge of the darkness swept over the embattled camp. The Subata were upon them.

Never had Mark heard such a mind-numbing cacophony —the screams of thousands of terrified men, the explosive snap of crystals firing, the steady thunder of the drums, and a shrieking hiss, almost like nails on a blackboard, that came from the Subata as they swooped in.

All around him his men aimed and fired, gathered their strength, and fired again. But so powerful were the snakes that many could absorb several blasts from an individual sorcerer before they finally went down.

The men comprising the square around Allic's command tent held to their positions. At first the Subata would drop singly, looking for an opening in the hedgehog of spears. Sharpened blades would lash up at them. More than one man would hook into a wing and then be borne aloft as the snake soared to escape. Mark watched in horror as a man refused to release his embedded spears.

The warrior was lifted up out of the formation. In an instant several snakes closed in, their joyful shrieks filling the air, the largest of them snatching the man whole with its gaping jaws. The two halves of the spearman's body fell back to the ground, spraying blood.

A score of Subata swooped in low, heading straight at Allic's square. Several of the beasts slammed into the shield wall, cracking it like a egg. Allic charged forward to meet them, Storm and Mark by his side, sending blast after blast into the press of beasts, some of which now folded in their wings and slithered across the ground.

A snake reared in front of Mark, its head as large as a horse, its basilisk eyes gazing at him with the look of death. Mark fired; the snake recoiled.

Suddenly its mouth opened and out sprayed a milky foam. Horrified, Mark watched as a spearman next to him caught the spray full in the face. Shrieking, the spearman fell clutching at his eyes—while a dark cloud that stank of burning flesh coiled up around him.

Mark aimed another blast, slicing off the snake's head. Still spraying its poison foam, the Subata fell backwards, headless body twisting.

All about him was madness. More snakes pushed in, trying to break the square, while overhead others hovered, pounced, withdrew, sprayed poison on their foes, and then positioned to pounce again. More men were dragged aloft, to be torn apart in an insane frenzy of feeding, their blood and shattered bodies raining down on those below.

"Saito's square!" someone screamed.

Through the wild press of battle Mark could see the square to his left going down, crushed by a hundred or more snakes. The wall crystal fired and fired, but it was not enough. Suddenly in mid shot the crystal spun around, the flame slicing straight into the ranks, cutting down a score of men. The square disappeared beneath a writhing wall of movement as hundreds of Subata moved in for the kill.

"Banzai!"

Startled, Mark turned to see Ikawa rising into the air, his defensive shield off.

The Japanese's eyes were wide with a wild frenzy.

"Jesus, Ikawa!" Mark screamed. "Grab him, grab him."

Several Subata immediately swung toward the sorcerer.

A flash snapped from Ikawa's hand, smashing his first attacker in the forehead. The snake crumpled, impaling itself on upraised spears.

Another snake came up behind Ikawa, who rolled in mid flight and struck it down with another single blast.

But the third closed in for the kill.

"No!" Mark soared upward, firing blast after blast. Behind him there was a wild shout: "Banzai! Banzai!"

Transfixed, Mark saw the battle frenzy take hold of the Japanese warriors.

As one they rose, rushing to the aid of their commander. Half a dozen bolts slashed the serpent even as his jaws closed around Ikawa. The beast fell away, hissing.

"Banzai!" The Japanese followed their leader, who cut through the serpents, driving forward to the next square which was disappearing under the attack. The Japanese cut through the press, slaying any that dared to oppose them.

All rational thought gone, Mark followed in their wake, desperate to cover their advance, firebolts all around him. His men were following, flying by instinct in tight formation.

For a brief flash Mark saw Storm in the middle of the melee. But this was another Storm, a woman more like the elemental fury he had first met in the sky. Darkness was gathering about her, a swirling cloud of power, flashing fire, and driving wind.

They were over Saito's square. Most of the footmen were down, the snakes giving themselves over to a frenzy of feasting. But in the center there was still a knot of defenders.

The Japanese swept in, firing repeatedly. So tight was the press that men and snakes died together in the fire from above, as the attackers cut through to their beleaguered friends.

"Banzai!"

From out of the few survivors, four Japanese, led by Saito, lifted into the sky as the square beneath them disappeared and was consumed.

Now the warriors pressed upwards, the Japanese in the center, the Americans flying a tight circular formation around them. Now they were more than a score, each protecting the other, screaming their defiance. The snakes gave back from this challenge and swarmed to other less risky targets.

With the instinct of a flyer, Mark pushed upward, knowing that safety could only be found by being above your opponents. The sky beneath them was covered in an undulating darkness of beating wings.

Leveling off at a thousand feet, they swung into a wide

arching turn, firing continuously on the combatants below. Mark realized they might be hitting their own men as well, but it was the only hope they had for breaking the attack.

"We got some bandits coming up at nine o'clock," Walker shouted. "Fifty plus!"

Mark looked off to his left and saw sorcerers and demons sailing out of the enemy camp. Beneath them the Torm infantry was slowly advancing, hesitating to come near the Subata.

Mark saw one of Pina's assistants in the formation with them, and he swung to Mark's side.

"This is why Allic wanted us on the ground," the assistant shouted accusingly. "There we can help defend! Up here we have to fight the snakes and Macha's sorcerers!"

"Can anyone control those bastards down there?" Mark shouted.

"Once their first blood lust is sated, the drumroll will stop. They've been trained to snatch whatever dead they want and withdraw.

"As they retreat, Macha's army will close and hit what's left."

Two of the formations below had been swarmed under; the others were just barely holding on. If the Subata could break another couple of squares there'd be a hole in the line so big that Macha's men could march through before Allic would be able to redeploy his men.

"Those Torm sorcerers are closing in fast," Walker warned.

Even as he shouted, the first bolts snapped through their formation.

"Shit!"

They could fight up here and perhaps hold their own, but they were needed at the battle below.

A shadow passed over the group, and with a strangled cry of fear they looked up, wondering how yet another formation of snakes could have gotten above them.

But this was no formation. It was a swirling cloud of night that flashed with light.

A bone-chilling wind lashed them. Bolts of lightning shot from the cloud into the snakes below.

"Goddamn!" Mark shouted. "It's Storm!"

His men looked at him in confusion.

The wind slashed past them and hit the Subata. Hissing and shrieking they were driven back from their feast.

The Subata could soar on rising drafts and float on the gentle morning wind but they did not have the power to battle a storm-driven gale. Within seconds the attack started to break apart. A wild shout came up from the beleaguered troops below.

Mark looked heavenward but his heart was full of fear. He knew the strength of his lover. She could take the power of nature and play with it as she willed. It was another thing altogether to conjure a storm out of stillness. She was pressing herself to the limit.

"Ikawa!"

Mark whirled around. "Damn him!"

Mark felt totally useless. His command control was disintegrating under the pressure of trying to decide where to engage in the battle. Now Ikawa had broken out of the formation, still wild with battle frenzy, and was diving straight at the Torm sorcerers, the rest of the Japanese following in a ragged line.

"Follow them!" Mark screamed.

His men winged up and over, one after the other dropping, pulling a perfect formation dive. Within seconds they were alongside the Japanese. Mark tried to signal them to close, but Ikawa and most of his command were beyond caring or comprehension. They were fey, convinced of defeat, and as if touched by the fatalistic spirit of their samurai forebears, they now sought death with the hope of taking as many of their foes with them as possible.

The charge bore down on Macha's sorcerers. Bolts of fire slashed the air. The Torm sorcerers broke with the onset of the attack, again following their old instinct to pair off against opponents and fight one-to-one. But the offworlders were presenting them with warfare of a different sort, as the Japanese in their madness still retained some memory of what Ikawa and Mark had taught them. Within seconds three of Macha's sorcerers were injured and out of the fight. And then a power stronger than any of them overwhelmed the field.

The sky grew black as night, flickering with fire. Wind borne, Ikawa drove forward, wreathed with incandescent flame, Mark and the others following in his wake.

Their formation sliced through the enemy sorcerers who scattered in every direction, both sides now firing ineffectively as all were buffeted by the wind. Within seconds the attacking force was over the Torm lines, which had stopped in their advance.

A blast of flame, the combined power of several wall crystals, came up from the center of the Torm lines. The flame seemed to merge directly on one of the Japanese privates flying a dozen feet ahead of Mark.

There was a flash. Horrified, Mark flew through an inky ball of smoke that stank of burning flesh. Private Matsumoto was gone.

"Evasive!" Mark screamed. "Break right!"

Another flame shot up, cutting where the formation would have been in another second if it had flown straight.

"Evasive, break left!" Mark screamed.

They cut another tight turn, firing back now, hoping to disrupt the enemy below. Damn, they could just stay up here drawing shot after shot, Mark realized, but every time they tried to cut in towards the center of the enemy position, the heavy fire drove them back.

They'd have to do something damn fast. The Subata attack had been broken, the winged snakes were retreating, some of them already beyond the rear of the Torm lines. But the ground forces were still intact. Even as the desperate struggle was waged overhead, the enemy surged into the attack. The change in fortunes had only been temporary. Within minutes Allic's forces would be overwhelmed as the enemy broke into its charge.

"Keep them busy," Macha shouted, pointing to where the offworlders weaved back and forth, dodging the powerful counterblasts of his heavy wall crystals.

It was still almost going to plan—except for that damned storm.

Then he realized: Allic's sister Storm had come into the fight.

Shouting with rage, Macha strode over to a heavy crystal, pushing the lesser sorcerers aside.

"My lord," Orma his battle advisor said, coming to stand by him, "we can handle them. You're needed to concentrate on command, to project the aura of strength which heartens our men against Allic's will."

"It's Allic's sister up there." He pointed at the rolling darkness that was now directly overhead.

"Another demigod," Orma cried, his voice edged with fear.

"So am I!" Macha roared. "A match for any of Jartan's damnable spawn."

A blast of fire arced from the heavens, striking an advancing company of spearmen, hitting their standard with an explosive roar. Dozens of men fell, the column reeling from the impact.

A blast, and then another blast snapped out, cutting the center of the advancing line.

The sorcerers around Macha drew back in fear. Their lord seemed wrapped in darkness as he called to the very source of his Essence, drawing in his power, forcing it to do his bidding.

His armies hesitated, sensing that they had lost the protection of their lord's guiding will.

A bolt of fire as brilliant as the sun shot from the crystal in Macha's hands.

At the same instant a flame of equal brilliance cut down from the heavens. The two met, blinding all who had looked. For a moment it seemed as though the two fires had merged into one, and then they shot past, each to its separate goal. The battle wavered, stopped, as tens of thousands stood transfixed.

Stunned, Ikawa still continued with his dive, the men behind him scattered by the shock wave from the twin blasts. He pulled up, skimming low over the Torm battle lines. Off to his left he saw a column of fire rising where the bolt from above had struck.

Out of the flame emerged a figure, his cloak smoldering. The man staggered, fell to his knees, then attempted to rise.

That must be Macha, Ikawa realized. the fatalistic fury that had seized him reasserted its hold, and he dove to the ground, skimming over hundreds who stood transfixed by the impact of the strike. Macha saw him coming and raised a wavering arm. The blast that snapped out was weak by former standards, but still powerful enough to nearly overwhelm Ikawa's defensive shield and knock him sideways through the air.

He knew he would never survive the next shot, but turned to charge anyway.

Macha's arm was poised for the final blast when he was struck from behind, his weakened shield flaring and fading as he almost lost consciousness.

*   *   *

Mark hit the ground hard, rolling away from Macha. Standing, he let loose with a tremendous kick, catching his foe square in the groin. Reaching down he ripped the offensive and defensive crystals from Macha's wrists.

The rest of the offworlder battle group came in around Ikawa and together they landed, forming a protective circle around Mark and Macha.

For the moment there was nothing to protect them against. The ground still smoldered beneath dozens of scorched and torn bodies. The entire command team, except for its leader, had been blasted to oblivion.

Mark looked over at Macha. "You bastard, I should kill you now," Mark roared. "But Allic probably needs you alive." Macha didn't reply as he lay on the ground, doubled up in agony.

"Captain, we better get moving," Kraut shouted. "They're reorganizing." Mark looked up and could see a number of enemy sorcerers and demons swinging in to protect their fallen leader.

Mark motioned to Ikawa and together they picked up Macha. Straining under the burden, they lifted, and flew just above the enemy host, racing to the protection of their own lines.

Screams rose from the Torms at the sight of their leader being borne away. The Torm sorcerers tried to cut them off, but dared not fire.

From out of the Landrian line, Allic and his entourage came, soaring above the offworlders to provide protection. The Torm sorcerers drew back as the Landrians jeered their contempt.

They crossed into the beleaguered fortress to the shouts of the embattled defenders. Alighting next to the command tent, Ikawa and Mark dropped their burden as Allic landed beside them.

"Mad heroics," Allic said grimly. A sad, almost bitter smile creased his face and he clapped Mark and Ikawa on their shoulders.

"Mad heroics, and damn admirable, as well."

"It was Storm," Mark said. "She broke his defense. We merely did the mop-up operation."

"Yes—Storm," Allic replied.

Where was she? Mark looked up and for the first time realized that the sky was clear, the air fresh.

"Storm?"

"She's in there," Allic said, and pointed to the tent.

Without asking leave Mark rushed into the tent.

He was almost afraid to approach. She looked small, fragile, as if somehow she had drawn in upon herself. As he drew closer he couldn't contain a low cry of fear.

Her face was badly burned, the injury streaking down her left shoulder to her flame-charred hand. He realized that Macha's blast must have overwhelmed her, bursting her defensive crystal.

"Storm?" he whispered, drawing closer. But she was silent.

A panic swept over him. She was dead!

He came to her side, his hand slipping under her tunic, trying to find a heartbeat.

"I am a little too tired for that kind of attention right now," she whispered, opening her eyes.

She tried to chuckle but it was obvious that every movement was an agony. She grimaced, trying to suppress just how badly she felt at the moment, but Mark could see the charade.

"The fight?" she whispered.

"We have Macha," Mark replied. *And I'll cut his heart out for this.*

"Good, very good. You must understand, Mark, that it was a fair fight between us."

"You make this all seem like a game. Sometimes all of you make me sick with this damned honor."

Her eyes started to flutter closed.

"Storm!"

Was he losing her? He reached out and shook her unburnt hand.

"Damn you, that hurts," she whispered. "I'm only resting. The Essence is gone from me; I must draw it back into myself. It'll take time—he almost pushed me beyond the edge. I'll come back, love, but it'll take time."

Her words slipped away. A deathly stillness came over her. Mark could barely detect the flutter of her heart, the gentle swelling of her breasts, as she drew in the shallowest of breaths.

He watched, still fearful that somehow he would lose her. In the background he could hear words of anger. Coldly he rose and strode back into the sunlight.

* * *

"You treacherous bastard," Allic roared. "I'll cut out your heart and stake it to the ground for this!"

Still on his knees Macha glowered up at Allic.

Half a dozen of Allic's sorcerers surrounded their captive, each focusing on a separate ring of containment, concentrating with all of their energy to hold the demigod in place, now that he was starting to recover from the shock of Storm's blow and the coup de grace delivered by Mark. Nearby, two of the remaining wall crystals were positioned to give support.

"Go ahead. I don't give a damn," Macha gasped, "but I'll still have the satisfaction of knowing that all of your carcasses will be heaped upon my pyre before the day ends. Maybe you'll live, though, Allic. It'd be like you to desert your retainers and fly off once you lose this fight, drunken scum that you are. You, the son of a god? You aren't worthy to wipe my ass."

"Damn you to fire forever!" Allic roared. "Bring me a sword!"

He looked to Pina. "You heard me. Bring me a sword!"

"My lord Allic," Pina said softly, drawing closer so that the others would not hear. "You can't just execute Macha, especially not like this."

"Can't I? I've lost more than a thousand here this morning. Are you telling me they should go unavenged? My sister lies near death in that tent because of him."

"All of it was a fair and open fight," Pina replied softly. "Restitutions and levies can be demanded from Torm as Macha's ransom. Our men fought with honor against his. Killing Macha will not bring them back."

"I don't care," Allic cried. "I want his head on a stake, with his damned black heart jammed into his mouth."

"My lord," Pina said, a note of pleading in his voice. "As long as we hold Macha alive, his people will not attack. The moment they know he's dead, they'll keep on coming till they all are dead, or we perish."

"Better that than to let this back-stabbing oath breaker live another minute."

"Me, an oath breaker?" Macha roared, struggling against Allic's sorcerers to come to his feet. "You're the back stabber. Your people crossed the river, raided my villages, and killed members of my family. If I had not struck back you'd probably have destroyed another dozen of my towns while still whining about your innocence."

"You lie!" Allic screamed. "A sword, are you all deaf? Bring me a sword! I'll not honor his body with flame."

Pina was motionless, the others around him frozen at the uncontrollable fury of their lord.

Allic looked around the circle. With a shout of rage he strode up to Sergeant Saito and snatched the pistol out of Saito's belt.

"Is this loaded?" Allic asked.

Saito nodded, looking to Ikawa for guidance.

Allic took the pistol, cocked it, and put the weapon to Macha's forehead.

"My lord, not like this."

Allic swung around. It was Ikawa.

"And who are you to challenge me?" Allic shouted, his face contorted. "You are my vassal!"

"Precisely why I speak, my lord," Ikawa replied. "A samurai serves and protects his lord, not only on the field of battle, but also in counsel. If you wish to kill me for speaking, then do so. But I must speak, my lord. Do not kill an honorable foe in such a manner."

A hush fell over the assembly. Ikawa dared a glance to Mark, but he could see the rage in Mark, as well. It must be over Storm, he realized. He braced himself.

"You are brave but foolish," Macha shouted. "Your lord is an oath breaker. He betrayed his treaty to me—why should he listen to you?"

"That's a lie," Allic cried, his gaze still riveted on Ikawa, who drew closer so that only Allic could hear his words.

"I respect you too much to see you thus dishonor yourself in a moment of rage," Ikawa whispered. "If I had known that this would be the result, I would not have helped bring this prisoner to you. I've spared prisoners who were my hated foe. Do the same now. Please, my lord."

Allic was silent, his gaze cutting into the vassal. Ikawa closed his eyes, bracing for the impact of the bullet, either into his skull or into the man who kneeled on the ground before them. As he waited he was amazed at the sudden clarity of it all: only minutes before he had risen into the air, driven by a terror beyond his imagining, praying for death to snatch him.

The fear of death still had clung to his heart when he dove to his confrontation with Macha, hoping only to take a foe with him into the void. But now...

Now he wanted to live. He felt death even closer here, but at last there was no fear.

The gentle wind felt unnaturally hot. As though from a great distance, Ikawa could hear cries of alarm. The breeze grew, hot and strong, buffeting him.

He opened his eyes. A pillar of fire was hovering before him, pulsing with flame.

Allic was looking to the light, and Ikawa followed his gaze.

The light pulsed, coalesced, and took the shape of a being Ikawa could recognize. Judging by the hawklike eyes, sharp brow, and narrow face, this must be Minar, the father of Macha.

Ikawa looked again to Allic. His commander, still torn with rage, stood before Minar's pulsing image.

"Come to save your son?" Allic taunted. He spun away from Ikawa and pointed the revolver at Macha's head.

"Both of you are fools," Minar said quietly

"If I even start to feel your intervention," Allic said coldly, "this offworld weapon will smash your son."

"I'll not stop you," Minar replied, "for if I did my son would live in shame. Better that he die than live as half a man, believing that he needs my power as a shield."

Macha looked straight ahead, and as the assembly looked to him they could sense the truth in Minar's words.

"Kill me or let me live, Allic," Macha said, "but do it of your own will. I don't want him here or need him."

A silence came over the group. Allic stared at his enemy. With a shout he swung the gun skyward and squeezed the trigger. The explosion echoed in the walls of the pass, then all was still.

Allic turned to Minar. "In the past I never had cause to doubt your words. If you have not come to save your son, then why are you here?"

"In the past," Minar said, "did you ever have cause to doubt the words and honor of my son?"

Allic looked back at his foe who was now standing, though Allic's sorcerers still kept their containment ring about him.

"Though we had our differences," Allic's voice grew cautious, "no, I never had cause."

"And you, Macha? Did you ever know Allic to deceive you?"

"No, damn him, though I thought him too driven by his passions, still I believed him to be honorable."

"Then why this war?" Minar asked, his voice now showing a flicker of anger.

Neither demigod spoke.

"You are both fools." Minar's rage showed as his form grew larger.

"But my border watches, my family, my friends—slaughtered," Macha protested.

"And Allic's too!" Minar barked. "Both of you lost much in the weeks before this conflict boiled over. But I ask you both to swear in my presence: did either of you ever attack the other, or know of attack launched by your underlings?"

The two stood silent, exchanging a look. The truth was becoming clear.

"There was a third, who brought down this shame upon your houses."

"The Accursed," Macha whispered.

"Do not run off for blood yet," Minar roared. "Both of you are guilty of that: you, Macha, for attacking. And you too, Allic, for not realizing that Macha would only attack with a justifiable reason, and that there would still have been room to parley."

"Is it the Accursed?" Allic asked.

"That is why I am here," Minar replied, his rage passing as quickly as it had come.

"Your father, my brother, reached out to me and told me how an offworlder had discovered that even now Sarnak is attacking Landra."

"What?" Shouts of rage exploded around Allic.

"Jartan knew that Macha would never knowingly serve the Accursed. But he surmised that my son could have been deceived into this war to decoy Sarnak's thrust. Jartan knew also that if he delivered this news, Allic might believe, but you, my son, would doubt. And thus I came as soon as I heard, to stop you hotheaded idiots from destroying each other, while the true culprit goes unpunished."

Allic looked at Macha, who stood trembling with fury. The sorcerers containing him withdrew at Allic's nod.

"We have both been taken for fools," Macha snapped.

"Landra?" Allic asked.

"Under attack at this moment."

"Will you help me?" he asked, looking at Minar.

"I'll help," Macha said quietly.

Allic turned to face him.

"Not out of love for you," Macha said coldly. "I started this war to avenge my kinsmen and my people. I attacked the wrong foe, and for that I will answer. But my enemy is yet unpunished, and I will have vengeance!"

Allic nodded silently. His rage was directed towards another target. Macha was, in his mind, now a comrade in arms.

"My army marches within the hour," Macha continued. "Hatred might still be strong between our men, so I suggest that your ground commanders meet with mine to plan our separate routes. I intend to stay with my army; you may do as you please. When the army reaches Landra, we'll plan our attack."

"Until we meet, then, after Sarnak's defeat," Macha said icily. He nodded to Allic, and then to his father. He started to turn, then looked back towards Ikawa.

"If ever you wish to serve another prince," he said evenly, "know that a place for a man of courage can always be found in my camp."

He hesitated, then continued, "Your actions make me glad that I spared one particular prisoner. I'll see that he is sent over to you as soon as he is able."

Mark looked up, hope etched in his features.

"The offworlder was stunned in yesterday's fight and unconscious when my people captured him. He's not able to fly yet, but should be ready to fight again by tomorrow."

Without another word Macha strode from the camp. As he emerged from Landrian lines, a triumphant shout rose from the Torm army, and some men surged forward.

Looking to the pistol in his hands, Allic snapped the safety into place and tossed the gun to the ground.

"I do not say this often," he said coolly to Minar, "but I'll say now that I was wrong about your son, and you."

"Enough of this," Minar said as his form dissolved into a glittering whirlpool of sparks. "Your city is threatened, your realm might still be lost. The others can be discussed later," and then he was gone.

"Break camp at once," Allic commanded. "We force march to Landra.

"Communications officers!"

Three sorcerers and their assistants stepped forward.

"Has there been any word from Landra?"

"Since we left there has been a jamming, as you already knew."

Damn! He should have known... except he had assumed that it was the work of Macha's men.

"Keep trying to break through it. Send messages to the frontier armies, and another to my father."

Allic glanced at the troops around him. "Trela, you'll take command here."

A tall, silver-haired female sorcerer stepped forward. Her face was lined with fatigue, but there was an energy and deadliness about her.

"You're to force march the army back to Landra. Send advance riders to rally the militias throughout the province and have them fall in your line of march. Pass the word that supplies are to be provided to Macha's army as it passes.

"I'll leave you half of my sorcerers and half of the wall crystals to protect the army on the march. Pick the ones you want. Pina will come with me as second in command."

Again his gaze flickered over the crowd. "Stede, I want you to take the remaining sorcerers and fly escort to the wall crystals. Sarnak's people will be just waiting to pounce on you carrying such a heavy burden, so be careful."

The bulky sorcerer nodded.

"Mark, Ikawa."

The two captains stepped forward.

"Gather your people. We fly straight to Landra and hold till the reinforcements come up."

The two inwardly groaned. Both were trembling with exhaustion. But there was nothing else they could do. Allic would continue to drive them and use them up until either the true enemy was dead, or they were dead from trying.

Both saluted and started to call for their men.

"Ikawa, come back here," Allic ordered.

Ikawa turned to face his lord.

Allic drew closer, and there was again a silence. "You were a fool," he said coldly.

"No, my lord, again I am forced to disagree. I was loyal."

Allic's lips compressed as he studied the offworlder. He had sensed more than once the doubt and fear inside this man, but that was gone.

"I'll say it twice in the same day." He hesitated. "I was wrong, and your actions were correct."

Turning, he strode into his tent.

The others gathered around Ikawa, eager to compliment him on his courage both in the charge and in the confrontation. He silenced them with a look.

"I was frightened beyond caring," Ikawa said quietly. "Now let's move. The real war is just beginning."

Chapter 18

The city of Landra was no longer the realm of beauty that Allic had left. Clouds of smoke and flame almost blotted out the sight of the ruined wall on the east side of the city which Sarnak's forces had taken half a dozen turnings ago. Valdez strained to see if any of the defensive towers along the wall, long since cut off, were still holding.

"High, swinging in from the left! First crystal stand clear!"

Valdez and those around him turned, protecting their eyes.

The wall crystal in front of the observation tower crackled, releasing a flash of light. The target, a lone demon, dived in an evasive move.

"Second crystal, clear!"

Another flash burst from the tower, catching the demon full in the chest. There was a puff of smoke and an explosion as flesh boiled and detonated from the heat.

A feeble cheer came up from the keep as the lone demon, trailing smoke, tumbled into the ruins of the city below.

"Down!"

Valdez and his fellow officers ducked for cover as a rain of fiery bolts snapped into the wall, shot from the enemy-controlled outer battlements. The protective shielding that encased the upper towers of the keep glowed red, pushed near overload by the concentrated blast.

"So the bastards have finally brought their own equipment up," Valdez growled, dusting himself off.

He walked over to the sorcerers commanding their main defensive battery.

"Balcha, be sure to keep those damned demons back. If one of them is carrying a red crystal and hits our shielding, we'll all be frying in the nether regions."

"I'll try, my lord, but without aerial support I can't promise anything."

"Don't try," Valdez snapped, "do it! Or I'll heave your worthless carcass over the wall and find someone who can."

"You've got a dozen sorcerers in reserve who aren't manning the heavy crystals," Balcha replied defiantly. "Just give me some air cover with them, and I can use these crystals as they were intended—for ground support and counterstrikes."

Valdez stared at the exhausted sorcerer, not sure whether a word of encouragement or of raging reprimand would be in order. Damn it, the old man was right. Without air cover the wall crystals were being wasted knocking down an occasional demon. The weapons should be employed to support the ground fighting or for an aerial counterstrike. But there simply weren't enough. Stripping the outer walls of crystals had been madness, he had tried to tell Allic that, and now they were paying the price.

In fact, at this moment he had to assume that they would lose.

"Just do it," Valdez said quietly, and turned to rejoin the unit commanders who stood waiting for orders.

"Down!"

He ducked again. There was another flash, stronger than before. The shield started to overload, crackling with the distinctive sound of cracking glass. The sorcerers working the defensive crystals were bent over with the strain, their eyes bulging, sweat standing out on their foreheads, trying to counter the blast. Some of the energy leaked through, smashing a part of the main turret.

The rock glowed hot, ripping apart with a thundering roar. Steaming fragments, some as big as a man's head, slashed across the battlement, catching Balcha with a full blast of red hot fragments. His personal shield could not block the impact. Before Valdez's horrified eyes, the old sorcerer was decapitated and fell, showering those around him with blood.

"Three more circling in low to the right!"

One of the reserve sorcerers rushed forward to replace his fallen comrade, while the defenses fired another reply.

"Signaler!"

An apprentice came to Valdez's side. The boy was trembling with terror, both of Valdez and the slaughter. He could not help but stare saucer-eyed as the decapitated body was dragged out of the rubble.

"Any word from Allic?" Valdez snapped.

"Nothing, my lord," the boy said, his voice breaking.

"From any of the other armies?"

"Every level is jammed; we can't get anything out. We've sent several messengers but the demons were upon them before they even cleared the city."

Valdez snorted and turned to look out over Landra.

The citadel was an island in a sea of fire. The entire eastern half of the town, except for the keep, was now in Sarnak's control. Fierce fighting continued in the western half across the river, and the defense was holding for the moment. Most of the refugees from the east had crossed the river for protection. He could only hope the western town would hold, for if it started to fall there would be a mad stampede to the citadel—a citadel he would have to keep locked. He pushed the thought aside, not wishing to face that horrifying possibility.

"Now, back to the rest of you." Valdez glowered, dismissing the signaler, trying to focus his thoughts on the task at hand. "This is to inform you *only . . .*"

He hesitated before continuing.

"Ander is down," he said quietly. "I'm now in command."

The various unit commanders looked at each other in consternation.

"It can't be," one gasped.

"Damn it, it's true. As far as we know, he's dead."

He didn't have time to spend on this, but he knew an explanation had to be given. "The sortie just before sunrise was led by Ander. They were hoping to hit the entry to Sarnak's tunnel and blast it shut. We lost eight of the ten sorcerers who went in. Sarnak second-guessed us."

Valdez stopped and stared at them. Damn it all, he had tried to talk Ander out of committing the precious few sorcerers they had left for an offensive action, but like his master, Ander was driven by the spirit of attack.

"Do you think there is a security leak?" Varma asked, sitting precariously on shattered rubble.

"Why in Jartan's name do you think I've called you here? We must assume that Sarnak has someone inside. If we have time, I want a truth-testing run on all your staffs."

"Bad for morale, Valdez. Especially now," Halnath, commander of the western town defense, said quietly.

Valdez stared at him. "I want it done, once we slow this next attack."

As if confirming his statement, a rumbling boom echoed from the north. The group rushed to see the destruction.

The two northern bridges connecting the eastern and western halves of the city were going down. They had been constructed with cunning, with just this possibility in mind. When certain key stones were simultaneously moved, a series of bolts shifted, collapsing the bridges. The team assigned to the bridges had done its task, and in the process plunged several hundred of Sarnak's elite troops to their deaths. The two southern bridges had been destroyed earlier in just the same manner.

"That just leaves the viaduct between the citadel and the western town," Valdez said quietly. "By all the gods, man, you must hold it open."

"With what?" Halnath snapped. "Where the hell is our illustrious lord? Where is the western army—or even the damn southern army, for that matter? Allic's been outmaneuvered—this is disaster, Valdez, plain unmitigated disaster!"

"If I didn't know you far better," Valdez replied quietly, "I'd have you arrested right here for treason."

"What can be called treason by one, is truth to another," Varma interjected. "But truth is always truth to a man of wisdom."

Valdez looked at the dwarf. The man was right, but truth so openly stated could only hurt them at the moment. He had to keep them fighting until Allic came up: that was his responsibility. What came after, he preferred not to think about.

"Do you propose that we surrender to the Accursed, instead?"

The others were silent. Sarnak had given the traditional demand of surrender; with the refusal, terms could no longer be asked for. Only complete submission would be considered, and he could imagine what would happen if an army with its blood up was set loose upon a surrendering populace.

"We still fight, then?" He looked to the others. Each in turn, including Halnath, nodded his agreement.

"There is no way that we can evacuate all the refugees into the citadel," Valdez said quietly. "Therefore the western half must hold, but you'll have to do it without fire support from this side or any reinforcements. The citadel must use what it has to defend itself. Barricade every house, Halnath —fight them street by street, house by house."

"Can't I expect any sorcerers as reinforcements?"

Valdez looked at him coldly. "No. I'm down to just a handful; I must keep them here in reserve. I drafted everyone out of the guilds, but in battle most of them are useless."

Halnath was furiously silent, although he knew that Valdez was right. But he, not Valdez, would have to go back and break the news to those on the other side of the river—news that might very well doom them.

"I understand."

"I'll try and divert two wall crystals on the south tower to pin down any attack across the water," Valdez said, knowing that he might not be able to keep the promise. "That's all I can offer."

"Down!"

Another blast rocked the tower. The stone swayed beneath them.

"Any questions?"

"Just one," Halnath said coldly. "Do you have any plan at all to get us out of this?"

"Yes," Valdez snapped. "To hold this city until relieved, or die in the attempt."

"My lord, I've just received confirmation. Twenty or more sorcerers are approaching from the south."

Sarnak stirred from where he had been sitting in quiet meditation, while the distant rumble of battle echoed through the scorched altar room.

He gazed about the remains of the temple. No wall was now more than shoulder high, the roof had collapsed, and rubble lay everywhere. It had once been known as the Temple of the First Sighting, a shrine to Jartan located on the southward road, half a league beyond the city wall, where travelers crested the last ridgeline and first beheld the wonders of Landra. Sarnak had taken great pleasure in watching the temple's destruction. He made the ruins his command post.

Now the pure white altar vestments had been stripped away, and the altar dedicated to the memory of Horat. Congealed blood clung to the altar stone, where several of Jartan's priests had been dedicated as messengers to the god.

"O Horat, do you now know?" Sarnak whispered.

"Do you now know that still there are some who revere your memory, and plan to avenge your death? Perhaps still we can bring you back, if the offerings are rich enough. Soon I shall give to you a worthy sacrifice."

Sarnak's features turned almost wistful. There was still time to change the plan that he had formed years ago. The body of Ander had been brought in and he could see it was perfect for what he was about to do. Ander's death made the plan far easier, for it would be the perfect bait. His features hardened again. Soon the altar would greet yet more. With luck soon Jartan's son would lie here.

"Who are they?" Sarnak asked his communications commander.

"We believe Allic is with them. The presence we've detected could only be a demigod in his wrath."

"The rest of the two armies?"

"A signal came in an hour ago from our spies in the Ventilian Hills. The armies are force marching; a number of stragglers are already falling behind."

"And the Subata?"

"Just now reorganizing."

"It could have gone better, but I have no need for complaint," Sarnak said softly. "True, we could have hoped that the Torms would have destroyed Allic and his men. But the fact that Allic left his city almost defenseless is enough. You have done well with placing your spies, Kala. Your reward will reflect it."

The young sorcerer bowed low, keeping his features set so that his pleasure would not show you. "All to serve you, my lord."

"Nonsense," Sarnak said coldly. "We all serve to advance our personal desires. It is merely in my best interst to reward success, as I would punish you if you failed. So don't flatter me with your pious mumblings. Do we understand each other?"

"Yes, my lord," Kala replied coolly, looking up to face his master. He breathed an inner sigh when he saw that Sarnak was not angry. With Ralnath detached to a secret command, Kala had found himself elevated to the post of controller of Sarnak's battle command center, with the offworlder as an advisor. He knew that this might be his chance to gain favor with his lord, as long as Mokaoto did not claim the credit when victory was won.

"Just a moment, my lord, something else is coming in," Kala said quietly.

He walked to the far corner of the room, responding to the quiet urging of a tiny paging crystal that rested in his ear. Curious, Sarnak followed him. The room's northern alcove was now taken over by the communications team. A table was covered with maps, sheaves of reports, and a series of communications crystals. Each crystal was worked by an apprentice who sat hunched over the glowing gems, receiving reports and forwarding orders back to the various commanders, sorcerers, and observation positions covering the various approaches to the city.

Sarnak gazed at this organizational masterpiece with pride. None of his rivals had such an organization. Mokaoto had suggested some of the changes, citing the system used back in the wars on his world. Now, there is where they truly understand how to organize fighting, Sarnak thought wistfully.

In the far corner of the alcove were half a dozen of his best sorcerers. Touching hands, they sat in a circle around a glowing blue crystal. Through their efforts they had so far been successful in blocking all communications into and out of the beleaguered city.

If only Jartan or Minar had not directly intervened, Allic would still be in the south. Still, Sarnak could use this to his advantage . . .

"My lord."

Sarnak looked up at Kala, who had returned from a hurried conference with his staff. "Go on."

"There's no mistaking it. Allic is less than half a turning away. Even now he's trying to break through to talk to Valdez."

"Very good," Sarnak said, a thin smile creasing his face. "Inform Verg and his demons that I want a full air assault on the southern approaches to the western town launched in a quarter turning. I want every one of them up. Verg will know what to do from there, he's been briefed.

"As soon as the attack is launched, lower the jamming so

Allic can talk with his people. Once you've done that, everyone here is to evacuate to my new headquarters. One of my guards will show you the way."

"My lord?"

Sarnak smiled. "I have my reasons."

"Yes, my lord." Bowing, Kala started to turn away.

"And one more thing," Sarnak said quietly. "My son is to meet me here at once."

Some of the communications apprentices, who had of course been listening to every word, looked up and exchanged quizzical glances.

"Your son, my lord?"

"Yes, damn you, my son. Are you deaf?"

"As you command." Kala hurriedly withdrew.

Sarnak stood watching as the orders were issued. Satisfied with the progress of his plans, he walked over to the altar and settled down to wait.

"Once you've done that, get out of here. I wanted this building cleared in a quarter turning!"

Their flight north from Wolf Pass had been slow, for even Allic finally had to admit that he and his sorcerers had been pushed past the edge of exhaustion. Halfway into their journey they had finally settled to ground for several hours of exhausted rest. Mark had been first to stir and had found Allic standing alone, looking off to the north.

"Perhaps too late," Allic had whispered. "If Landra falls, it will be all my fault. All those people—those thousands of people who looked to me for protection—all lost because I did not take the time to think this crisis through, but acted from blind instinct. Always before, that instinct worked. Sarnak knew precisely how to manipulate it. He bested me before the first battle was joined."

"You did what you thought was right."

"But was that good enough? I must turn this, I must turn it back or lose my life in the trying. Otherwise there is no honor, no joy left to me."

Mark wanted to help, but he knew that the burden of command could only be borne by one.

"I first served you because I needed to in order to survive in this world," Mark said firmly. "I serve you now, Prince Allic, because I want to. If you are defeated, that will be a defeat I'll share, for I believe that you fought to the best of your ability."

Allic laughed sadly. "I heard your Kochanski once repeat an old Earth saying about victory having a thousand fathers."

"And defeat is an orphan," Mark continued.

"Not here," Allic responded. "This orphan is mine alone." He turned away from Mark to rouse the others for the last leg of their flight.

Minutes later they were back in the air.

From fifty miles out they could see the columns of smoke rising thousands of feet into the air. Again Mark found himself thinking of a bombing run as they turned into a final straight-line approach. The only things missing were the black puffs of flak, and the never-ending passes of the fighters' winking death. Now just twenty-five miles out, individual fires, flashes from wall crystals, and the detonations that followed could be plainly seen.

But this time he was not lining up to bomb an enemy target. This was his home under attack. For the first time he found he could truly understand what it must have felt like for the fighter pilots he had faced, fighting desperately to beat back the waves of destruction.

Mark looked at Ikawa and the Japanese contingent. Ikawa looked back to him and nodded. Mark knew that his own men were thinking similar thoughts, and he wondered if the Japanese were having their memories thus kindled, as well. He hoped not, for any memory of their former enmity could not be afforded now.

The formation was in close order, Allic and Pina together in the middle, the Japanese slightly higher to port, the Americans to starboard. Allic's shield was glowing white hot. In spite of his earlier comments to Mark, it was obvious that he was working himself into a towering rage at the sight of his city being destroyed.

"I've just made contact," Allic roared, his voice booming across the open sky. "Their demons are attacking the western half; the east is already taken except for the citadel."

He surged ahead.

"My lord," Mark cried, trying to come alongside him, while the other Americans struggled to keep us speed.

"My lord," Mark repeated, "go to the citadel first. Talk to Valdez, find out more before we attack."

"The enemy is in the air!" Allic shouted. "We strike them as we come in. I'll have the advantage of surprise."

Mark wanted to argue. He looked over towards Pina who flew on the other side of Allic. Pina merely nodded, resigned.

"Bogeys, hundred plus," Giorgini announced.

"That's affirmative," José cried. "I'm seeing hundred—make that hundred and fifty plus."

"Bandits, bandits, look at them sweeping in along the wall," Walker countered.

Any hope of argument was gone. Allic pushed forward, far outstripping the others in his haste to reach the city.

"You provide cover for us," Pina shouted. "I'll try to keep pace."

Mark was tempted to try to stay with Allic, but thought better of it. His team might be able to keep formation, but the Japanese would soon be strung out behind and too vulnerable. The best that he could hope was that Allic's fury would be enough to sweep all before him, giving his support team time to come up and cover him from above.

"Damn!" José yelled. "I hope those hotshots with the wall cannons don't hit us thinking we're with Sarnak."

"There's nothing we can do about it," Mark responded. "Assume all fire to be enemy. Keep your eyes open."

They held straight in their flight for several more minutes. They sky was clear, so at least they wouldn't have to worry about being pounced on from above.

Mark could now clearly make out individual targets as the range closed to less than a league. The demons were in two groups, one to draw fire running parallel to the wall, while the second would sweep down from above, pick up individual men, and cast them down. Rolling clouds of smoke poured up from the walls, where shields had been overloaded, obscuring the view.

It appeared that the demons had yet to see the threat coming in from above and to their flank. Mark could only hope that their surprise would be complete, and his men could slash through them before being discovered.

"Get ready to go on my command," Mark said.

"They're breaking!" Walker shouted. "They've spotted Allic. Look at them scatter. Come on, let's go!"

"Are you ready, my son?" Sarnak asked, smiling almost wistfully at the young man before him.

Estin nodded excitedly, his dull face aglow.

"And then it will all be mine, isn't that what you said, Father? It'll all be mine!"

"Of course, my boy, of course. Now lie down."

"But it's covered in blood, Father. I don't like that."

"Never mind, my boy. You'll have fresh new robes once you've defeated him, robes worthy of a king."

"A cape of gold cloth! Promise me, gold, with silver thread, just like yours?"

Sarnak nodded and placed his hand upon Estin's forehead, covering his eyes.

"Are you changing me again, Father?"

"Yes, remember our plan? We looked together at the body of Ander and then I shared my plan with you."

"No. Should I?"

Suddenly he felt a moment of compassion, almost of doubt. The boy was excellent material for a changeling, with a power to draw on that could only have been a sacrifice from his own flesh.

"Hush now, boy. Close your eyes."

The spell took form, his strength flowing out to change, to shape, to deceive those who might approach. The face and body beneath his hands shimmered, shifting as muscle, bone, and sinew took that which was misshapen, a caricature of manhood, and made it into another form. *If only I had the power to make this forever, to shape not only body but mind, as well, then it would all be different,* Sarnak thought sadly.

His face bathed in sweat, Sarnak reached beneath his robes and produced a glowing crystal of deepest red, which seemed to swallow light itself.

He slipped it beneath his son's tunic.

"You now have the power," Sarnak whispered. "When he comes to you, all you must do is reach up and embrace him. Then will the red crystal touch its opposite. It will be drawn to it like metal to lodestone. When the two meet, Allic will be destroyed, and you alone shall be left to rule his realm."

The boy smiled—but it was Ander's face that was smiling.

"Good-bye, my son," Sarnak whispered, and he started to withdraw.

"When I am a king," Estin said in Ander's voice, "will you love me then, Father?"

Sarnak gazed at him in silence, hesitating. Then he remembered what had to be won, what had to be sacrificed, if he was to succeed. Only by using his own blood could he bait the trap properly.

"Of course," he whispered, his voice barely heard, and strode from the temple.

He walked down the sunlit corridor of the ruined temple. Emerging through the shattered doors, he saw that all was in place, the pennants of his court shifting slowly in the gentle breeze. His staff had not understood why he had wished to openly reveal his location. Before the glass turned again they would understand. Looking off towards the city, he watched for a moment as another volley of blasts struck the main citadel—but still the walls held.

He turned his gaze towards the western part of the city where the demons were attacking. One, then another broke away, and in an instant the entire force was flying low across the river. From out of the smoke above them he could see two forms emerging. Only a fool would not know that one of them was a demigod, his wrath visible for all to see.

It was time. Without another look back to the temple, Sarnak flew down the hill and joined his staff and waiting reserve of sorcerers concealed in the opening to the tunnel.

Shouting with rage, Allic dove for the kill. Pina was flying close in beside him, ready to block with his left hand any bolts that might be fired at them by the demons—whose assault had broken long ago.

They skimmed low across the river. An angry shot fired by Allic smashed into a demon. Howling, the creature tumbled into the water and disappeared in a cloud of steam.

Flying full out, the two crossed the river, charging through the plume of steam, and swept up the bank of the river, firing on the ground forces which scattered at their approach.

"My lord, I have Valdez," Pina shouted. "He's calling for you to pull in!"

"Tell Ander to sortie on me, now!"

Pina called in the command; then his face turned pale. "Ander was lost this morning, my lord!"

Allic paused, as if deciding. "Then Sarnak dies now! The temple of First Sighting—look, his damned pennants are there!"

"My lord, at least bring up support."

"I have the advantage of surprise," Allic cried. "Follow me!"

They swept up off the river. The demons scattered in every direction, but Allic's attention was now focused on the temple.

Already Pina sensed that something was dangerously wrong. Sarnak's headquarters should have been bristling with defenses, but no fire answered their approach. He followed as Allic pulled up and cut into a high banking turn directly over the burned out temple. Pina braced for the blasts from Sarnak's heavy crystals, but still there was nothing.

"Sarnak, you bastard!" Allic roared. "Come up to meet me. One to one, Sarnak!"

His only answer was the distant booms rumbling back from the city.

"My lord!" Pina pointed into the wreckage. "Ander!" Allic was already diving.

And at that moment Pina knew. Gathering his strength, he pulled into a dive, racing Allic to the ground.

"No, my lord, it's a trap!"

The temple disappeared in a fireball.

"Jesus Christ!"

Horrified, Mark watched as the temple ruins exploded.

For a moment the party slowed, stunned, unsure of what could be done. The fire burst rolled upwards, flattened out, raining debris.

"We've got to check." Mark fought back tears of rage.

"Check for what?" Younger snapped. "Let's just get the hell outa here—this fight's for suckers. Screw Allic, he got what he deserved."

"If you break one inch," Mark grated, "you'll be dead before you hit the ground."

He stared at Younger coldly. The lieutenant, his lips compressed with rage, finally nodded.

"Ikawa!"

"Here, Mark."

"Give us air cover. We're going in to take a closer look."

"Going down, now!"

The American formation dropped while the Japanese surged ahead. They swooped on the temple, debris raining around them.

"Look over there," Saito cried, "beyond that fold in the ground! It looks like a tunnel opening. Look, there's a group of sorcerers coming out."

"Hit it," Ikawa shouted.

"That did it," Sarnak said as the concussion washed over them.

"Your son," Kala said, looking at his master with fear and revulsion. "Your son was in there."

"Yes. My son," Sarnak said quietly. "He could be shaped as a changeling," he continued, as if justifying to himself the sacrifice. "He had the Essence in abundance, but was not fit to rule. Thus I had designated him almost from birth to fulfill this sacrifice. With his power, and that of a shard of a crystal of Horat, I forged the weapon. But to use it I needed sacrifice of my blood."

Sarnak turned and looked at Kala.

"Why do you object?" he asked.

Kala was silent.

"There're sorcerers coming in," an assistant next to Kala said. "Looks like the offworlders."

Sarnak looked back at his reserve sorcerers.

"Kill them. I wish then to go up and examine the ruins."

The sorcerers rushed forward to attack.

"They're coming in low," Kala shouted. "Get down!"

Firebolts snapped from Ikawa's formation, slamming the hillside, so that the lip of the tunnel glowed with energy. There should have been wall crystals here to defend this point, he realized, but perhaps Sarnak did not have enough of those weapons to go around and was using everything he had for the offensive.

The hillside suddenly slipped away, blocking the tunnel entrance. He had cut them off, at least for a couple of minutes. The demons were rallying a mile or so to the north. There were far too many of them, and even as he thought about the threat, the host wheeled in position and started to close. Mark and the others were low, searching the smoldering rubble. There wouldn't be much time to find the remains and get out.

Ikawa came in just above Mark and his men. "The demons are moving in," he shouted.

"Another minute!"

"Captain, over here!" Walker was on the ground pulling back a smoldering timber, digging furiously.

An arm was sticking out, covered with a light blue tunic trimmed with gold: Allic.

"It's him, we've got him!" Walker called.

"Mark, we've got to get out of here!" Ikawa shouted.

"Pina's under him," José said. Mark grabbed Allic's arm and pulled him out.

Mark had seen wounded men before, both on Earth and here on Haven, but still he wasn't prepared. The right side of Allic's face was crushed, teeth and bone showing through.

His eye, oh Jesus, Allic's eye. Mark turned away and retched.

"I've got Pina out," Mark heard José call, as if from a great distance.

"Mark, now! With him or not!" barked Ikawa.

A series of bolts flashed overhead.

Mark turned back, struggling for control. "José, Welsh, take Pina. Walker, help me. The rest of you up for support."

Mark looked again at Allic. He snatched a piece of charred black cloth that lay on the ground, and wrapped it around Allic's face, then grabbed him around the shoulders, while Walker took his feet. Struggling under their burden, with effort they lifted and flew back for the city, skimming the ground.

Allic dangled beneath Mark, while Walker flew directly below, supporting the lower half of Allic's body. Mark could feel the warm blood trickling over his hands and soaking through his shirt, where Allic's head rested against his chest.

Mark felt a slight stir. "He's alive!"

"You'll be dead if they cut us off while you're carrying him," Younger rejoined, pointing towards the swarming demons.

"I'm not letting go," Mark snarled. "Just keep them off."

The demons, seeing the burden that the party was carrying, roared their challenge and charged.

The Japanese pulled ahead, forming a tight wedge. A single volley slashed out. Seconds passed, another volley was fired, and then another, as if they were again infantrymen, lined up and firing on command.

The center of the demon pack broke under the blasts. On either side, and directly above, the remaining Americans positioned themselves, acting as top and side gunners, striking anything that started to close on the flanks.

The fight boiled over, slashing into the formation. Mark felt something slam into his back. Smithie pointed almost straight at Mark and fired a blast, the weight above him let go, and he heard the terrible shriek as the demon fell away.

It was still a quarter of a mile to the outer wall, and another half a mile to the citadel.

Bolts shot through the melee.

Oh Christ, Mark cursed silently. *Their sorcerers are coming in.*

The demons on the left flank broke off, turning back to the rear.

"A sortie," Ikawa shouted.

A dozen sorcerers led by Valdez were coming in low over the water, dodging blasts from the crystals in the outer walls, held by the enemy.

"To them," Ikawa cried.

The formation turned and cut out over the river. Valdez and his companions bypassed the formation to either side, disrupting the demons who were still trying to close.

Mark and Walker pushed straight ahead.

"Take the lead," Ikawa shouted. "We'll cover the retreat."

The Japanese pulled up in a rough attempt at an Immelmann turn. Even through his fear and exhaustion Mark felt that at last they had finally started to learn how to fight and fly like airmen.

The wall loomed closer.

Mark had a moment of panic when he saw two heavy crystals come to bear on him—and fire.

The bolts swept to either side. One of the sorcerers with Valdez disappeared in a blinding flash.

The wall was closer, closer, finally dropping away.

They were in the city, cutting over towards the western half of the town, away from the enemy. Flying low over the rooftops, they ran parallel to the river.

The extent of damage was stunning. Riverside warehouses crackled and roared. Villas had become armed fortresses under siege from a battery of Sarnak's heavy crystals on the opposite waterfront.

They passed directly over a blazing palace whose waterfront side was aswarm with Sarnak's soldiers. Companies of militia were rushing down narrow side streets, valiantly attempting to contain the rupture in their defensive line.

Mark heard a ripple of explosions and looked over his shoulder to see his escort firing a volley into the attackers as they passed over.

Finally they reached the one bridge still intact that linked the two halves of the city. Turning, they skimmed down the length of the structure, using its high side walls as protection from enemy shots fired from the eastern bank.

Straining with the last of their energy, Mark and Walker pulled up, cleared the outer wall of the citadel, and landed roughly in Allic's private courtyard.

Within seconds José and Welsh landed beside them. Mark looked over at them and for the first time realized that Pina's left arm was gone, his left side scorched to the bone.

"He's alive too," Welsh gasped, and collapsed next to the wounded sorcerer.

A shadow passed over them and they looked up to see the covering formation wing over. Most of the sorcerers flew back to the beleaguered citadel tower, but Valdez and Ikawa landed by Allic's side.

"Is he alive?" Valdez asked fearfully.

Mark nodded. Bracing himself, he pulled back the bandage that had covered Allic's face.

"Without his strength we can't hold," Valdez said numbly. "I had hoped that through his power we could yet turn the tide."

"What are you saying?" Ikawa barked.

"That it's over." Valdez was grim.

"Like hell it is," Ikawa replied. "It's not in my code to surrender."

Ikawa was staring straight at Mark, and for a second he thought that this was somehow a reprimand for the surrender back in China. But then he realized that Ikawa was merely looking to him for support.

"With what do you plan to hold?" Valdez asked. "I tell you, it's senseless to continue. I was holding out solely on the hope that Allic would be able to get us out of this. But not now. Once we can move Allic I will have him sent to Asmara. Then I plan to surrender this city. Perhaps we can still find quarter from Sarnak."

Chapter 19

"My lady Storm."

Storm came slowly out of her dazed slumber. Her bed swayed beneath her and she felt as if she were on a boat at sea, until she realized that she was riding inside a supply wagon. A murmur came from the outside, the all-too-familiar sound of an army on the march. Macha was leaning over her.

"Then we've lost, and I'm your prisoner," she whispered, sitting up. She felt her wrists and waist. Her crystals were still there.

"No, you're not a prisoner," Macha said ruefully. "In fact, at the moment we're in alliance."

"In alliance? Not before the sun freezes to ice."

Macha quickly explained all that had transpired since the moment the two had struck each other down, and Allic had returned to Landra.

"I still have a demon of a headache from you," he finished. "I thought for a moment that you had in fact defeated me."

"Next time I will," Storm grumbled. "And now we're supposed to be allies?"

"Storm, if you don't believe me, I have one of Allic's aides waiting outside this wagon."

She stared at him. There was no lie in his heart, she quickly realized.

"Very well," she said. With a groan she stretched, probing within herself to sense how much of the damage had been healed, how strong the Essence was within her. She realized there was still not enough to fly and to fight, let alone create another full thunderstorm.

Now that had been a masterful creation, a real sky smasher, and she smiled with pride. Rarely had she conjured a storm of such power out of still air. Given another few minutes, why, she might even have whipped up a small tornado to heighten the effect.

"Had you worried, didn't I?"

"Let's just say that I was somewhat impressed."

They fell silent. It had not been their first confrontation, but there was little animosity, for among their class a lasting grudge usually resulted in mutual destruction. They had been enemies before, and might be again, but political concerns had shifted, and with the polish of master diplomats, they could move with the tide.

"So it was Sarnak after all," Storm reflected.

Macha nodded, his expression set. She could sense his embarrassment over being made to look the fool. All politics aside, this was one grudge that would not be ignored, for Macha, like Allic, loved the people of his realm, and viewed it as his first responsibility to rule fairly and to protect them. Thousands had died through Sarnak's maneuver. Macha would demand payment in full.

Macha looked away for a moment, and she could sense that he had unpleasant news.

"It's Allic?" she said quietly.

His face was a mask.

"Or is it Mark?" she cried.

"It might be both," Macha replied. "The interference on our communications cleared a short while ago. Allic has been injured."

"He's alive, then?"

"I don't know. The report was garbled, and we didn't get a confirmation before the jamming started again. Allic is seriously hurt, he's been badly maimed. In short, he might die."

She absorbed this, trying to hide her emotion. She needed all her strength concentrated on healing if she was to be of any help. She could spare only a moment indulging in fear for her brother.

"Mark?"

"No word on him directly. Valdez said that the city will fall. He's planning to evacuate once Allic can be moved, but fears they will not be able to break out."

Landra falling to Sarnak. It was impossible. It had to be impossible.

"Is there a chance the communication could have been false?"

"Allic's assistant was with me when it came in. He spoke to Valdez, and their battle code was confirmed. It's true."

"Then we must fly to him at once!" Storm said, struggling to rise.

"And do what when you get there, wobble around in the air so Sarnak's men can pick you off?"

"Then you should go. You have at least thirty sorcerers with you right now."

"Not even for my brother would I do that," Macha said coldly. "My army fought a running battle for the last ten days. I've lost eighteen sorcerers already, and half the survivors are injured. I need my air cover over my own people."

"Against what?" Storm cried. "Sarnak has thrown everything against my brother. He doesn't have anything left to send against you. Your army and Allic's ground forces here could force march through the night and be athwart Sarnak's line by late tomorrow."

"As I have already planned. And when both our armies arrive, our sorcerers will be over them for protection, as good battle sense dictates. I will not strip my air protection from my army."

"Then if you're too much of a coward to go to his aide before it's too late, I'll go north myself with the sorcerers Allic left here!"

"I wouldn't advise that."

"And why not?"

"The Subata have gone over to Sarnak." Macha grimaced.

"What?"

"My lieutenant who commanded the Subata and his assistants had sold themselves to Sarnak before this campaign began. One of the Subata assistants deserted and came back last night to tell me.

"They'd reorganized their forces after they had finished

their feeding. Even now the beasts trail us not an hour's march behind. If I pull off the air cover, they'll strike."

"Then attack them first."

"Useless. They would just scatter, and Zambara would know that I am aware of his betrayal. Besides, he and his assistants are in hiding. If I can't find them, we can't put the Subata out of action."

"Then send out patrols at once!" Storm snapped, her anger increasing with every negative response from Macha.

He extended his hands in a gesture of exasperation.

"There have been reports of Sarnak's sorcerers shadowing us, and at least one report of spies in the hills. If I send people out too far from the support of the main group, they could be cut off. If I send too large a party out, stripping our defenses here, Sarnak could hit us hard from above."

She sat on her cot feeling impotent. She wanted to scream at Macha, but knew that the burden of the decision had been hard on him, as well. Unlike her brother he was being coldly rational about this. He wanted revenge, to be sure, but he would not risk any more of his people without just cause, and the possible loss of Landra, or even of Allic, was not his ultimate concern. She knew too that she was not yet in any condition to lead the remaining sorcerers from Allic's forces. They were needed to protect this army. How often had she heard Jartan speak about the obligation of rule. But he had never taught her how to deal with the pain of ruling.

"I'll stay with you till we reach the city," she said in a resigned voice.

"You should rest," Macha said gently, and he withdrew from the wagon.

But sleep came hard, although she knew that to heal for tomorrow's fight she would have to sleep. All she could think of was her brother, and of Mark who was bound to him—a bond, she knew, that he would honor, even if it meant his death.

"There is no sign of his body," Mokaoto reported.

"Then I must assume that he is alive," Sarnak replied. "That would match your report," and he looked at Kala.

"Remember, my lord, we only know a small part of their code. We do know the code word for Allic, and we believe his name was linked with statements concerning injury and escape from Landra."

"Are you sure Valdez was speaking?"

"That's been confirmed."

'If Allic is alive and they flee, the shame of his defeat and humiliation will kill him anyhow," Sarnak mused. "This sounds like the truth. Valdez is too loyal to Allic. He would put Allic's physical survival over all else, even if it meant a life of humiliation thereafter. The plan failed, but only in part."

But at least it had worked enough to put Allic permanently out of the fight, Sarnak thought. A berserk demigod like Allic could have turned the tide of battle. Now he was off the board.

Still, when you got right down to it, the war over Landra was only a game within a game. After all, Landra was merely a city. What Sarnak wanted was the prize hidden in the Crystal Mountains beyond. In a moment of insight Allic might have suspected, but now he was removed.

"Should we hold back the assault, then?" Mokaoto asked, disappointment in his voice.

"What for? If we do not press in, Valdez might think again. Besides, I want to destroy Landra. We must draw them here—and then we can crush them. Order the main assault to continue."

Smiling, Mokaoto bowed and withdrew.

"Damn it, that was close!"

A fine shower of dust sifted down from the ceiling and settled over the Americans.

Mark looked around at his men. They had been up on the citadel wall throughout the rest of the day after their arrival and long into the night, only to stand down for several hours until they were called back up for another eighteen hours of defense. But exhaustion had finally drained them completely, and Valdez agreed to send them down for rest, and their first hot food in days.

Most had instantly fallen asleep in spite of the bedlam, but Mark, burdened by worry, had not been able to doze off. Walker had sat by his side, and they now looked at each other for a moment, bracing for the next explosion.

"You know, Captain, I've been holding back on you guys..."

"How so?"

Walker reached into his pocket and produced a small package.

"I don't believe it," Mark said, laughing, "a pack of Camels!"

"Unopened, Captain. Been saving it for something special. Care for one?"

"Shit, yeah."

Walker pulled off the wrapper. Mark absently started to reach in a pocket for his Zippo lighter, then laughed. He didn't need the Zippo nowadays; he concentrated for a moment and the cigarettes were lit.

They both leaned back, drew deeply, and sighed.

"Preferred Lucky Strikes myself," Mark said.

"Yeah, Lucky Green's gone to war, you remember?"

Another explosion rocked the shelter.

"Here, Captain, take the pack, you look like you need it."

Mark looked at Walker.

"Go on, Mark. I always stuck half a dozen packs in my flight jacket before a mission back in China. Never knew where we'd land and figured they might come in handy with the locals."

Mark hesitated but Walker pressed the pack into his hand.

"Worried about this pull-out, aren't you?" Walker asked.

Unable to contain himself, Mark opened up. "It'll kill Allic, even if he survives. The healers are over in the next corridor trying to stablilize him and Pina enough so they can be flown out and taken north to refuge at Jartan's court. But goddamn it, Valdez is so intent on saving him that he's not even thinking about what will happen when they wake up. Landra will be gone."

He fell silent. Landra—this beautiful city, this fascinating place that had finally started to become his home, was coming down around them. And the people? All these wondrous, open people, given over to the sack.

His memory wandered, recalling the days spent strolling the city streets, talking with the merchants, sitting in the taverns. All of it would be gone, the city in ashes.

"We *can't* let it happen," Mark said, voice hard with conviction.

"There isn't anything more we can do, Cap'n. You, me, all of us, we're fought to exhaustion. Even the Japanese sleeping over there, they're plain used up."

Mark nodded wearily.

"Goddamn, I always did wonder what it was like on the

ground for the bastards we were delivering the goods to, back in our war," Walker said. "Now I wish I didn't know."

"How's that?"

"Just, when we were back on the old *Dragon Fire*. Shit, Captain, you couldn't see it the way I could, bouncing around back there in the tail. Why, we'd drop them eggs, and you'd be up front, pulling us around for dear life through the flak belts. But me, old Jimmy Walker, I'd be riding high in the back, looking down from thirty thousand feet, watching them babies just slam into the Japs.

"Boom, there goes a factory, boom, trains looking like my kid brother's toys go flying up in the air, boom, there'd go a whole row of houses."

He fell silent and looked over at the Japanese.

"Now I know," he said softly.

As if in counterpoint, another explosion rocked the room and more dust filtered down. Walker sighed and took another pull on the cigarette.

"Buy a bond and build a bomb, remember that one?" Walker whispered, looking over to see if his captain had finally fallen asleep.

"Huh?"

"Oh, just buy a bond and build a bomb, remember the advertisements in *Life*? Right there alongside a picture of Dorothy Lamour or Rita Hayworth, bonds pasted all over their luscious big kazooms while they posed next to a ten ton blockbuster."

Mark suddenly came to his feet.

"Goddamn it, wake everybody up," Mark said. "Ikawa's people too."

"What the hell, Captain?"

"Just do it!"

"What's going on?"

Mark grinned at him.

"The hell with Valdez, Mr. Walker. We're taking over this fight right now."

"But Valdez has given no orders regarding this," the old sorcerer roared.

"I don't give a damn if Jartan himself ordered you differently," Mark shouted. "Step back from those wall crystals right now, or so help me, my people will blast your ass right off this wall."

The sorcerer looked at the offworlders who surrounded

him. He hesitated and looked over at the small communications crystal set in the mount next to the heavy weapon.

"Go ahead and try it," Ikawa said. "Though it will grieve me, I'll not hesitate to strike."

Without wasting any more time by arguing, Mark shouldered his way forward, pushing the sorcerer out of his path, and went up to the stand that held the wall crystal.

"Bring those slings over," he orderered, wrestling the crystal from its mount and dropping it onto a sling.

"Take the other two, as well," Mark shouted, and Shigeru stepped forward. With one arm he scooped the second crystal up, and turning, used his other arm to reach out and take the third.

"But we were ordered to keep up fire until the evacuation. How are we to stop them from breaking in?"

"Once we pull out, they'd break in anyhow," Mark roared, turning to face the sorcerer. "Think about that, damn it! Look out there, just look," and he dragged the sorcerer to the edge of the wall and pointed to the thousands of refugees who now crowded the single bridge standing between the two halves of the town. Most of the western section of the town had fallen during the night. Even as he pointed a score of demons came low over the river, striking troops who were struggling to cross the bridge. As the crowds pushed and swayed, trying to get out of the way, dozens fell screaming into the swift currents below.

"We don't have the strength to protect them anymore," Mark shouted. "So we evacuate, and hope that Sarnak ends the slaughter."

The demon squadron rose, dragging victims aloft. Coming in high over the citadel walls, they dropped the men, who plummeted to their deaths.

"Well, do you think those bastards will be interested in quarter now that their blood is up?"

The sorcerer was silently looking down at the masses who struggled to gain entrance to the last stronghold.

"Well, answer me, damn you!"

The sorcerer looked at him, his face an image of pain.

"My family is down there, offworlder," and he spat the last word with contempt, "but I follow my orders."

"Well goddamn it, where I come from orders are orders till they no longer have logic. So either help or get the fuck out of the way."

There was a low cheer from the other Americans.

Mark turned toward the three massive crystals cradled in their individual baskets of woven rope. Each basket had three rope lines extending out from the center; the end of each rope was knotted around a short wooden pole.

"All right, Walker, strap the clay pots on."

"Detonators," Walker commanded, kneeling. He looked over his shoulder and grinned like a child about to light a firecracker in the school bathroom.

José came forward and carefully gave Walker three pots, their lids sealed shut with wax. Ropes dangled from the two handles on each of the clay pots and Walker quickly wrapped the ropes around each of the crystals, securing the pots to the softly glowing gems, still hot from firing. The slings were then bundled up, so that the entire affair of pot, gem, and sling was one tightly woven mass.

"Boy, when this thing hits the ground . . ." Walker laughed like an excited child.

"What's inside those pots?" the sorcerer asked with growing nervousness.

"Why, a red crystal, of course," Walker laughed.

"Sacrilege!" the sorcerer screamed. "It is blasphemous to use a great crystal like this. The gods themselves will surely curse us, for the crystal is their gift, that we might focus the Essence."

"They already have, asshole." Walker's voice was edged with sarcasm.

One of the communications sorcerers came through the crowd. "We've just got the word from Valdez," he announced. "Allic is still unconscious but will be evacuated in half a turning. Once that's done the city will be surrendered."

"Yeah, well, tell him to take a couple of minutes first to come up and watch the fireworks," Walker shouted back, his words barely audible as another series of explosions rocked the citadel.

The sorcerer was silent.

"Just tell Valdez to come up here and watch," Mark snapped, and signaled to his crew. They formed up on the crystals, three to a bundle with Shigeru being the ninth man. As one they lifted in close formation, wheeled out from the citadel and climbed into the predawn sky.

The city below them was engulfed in flames and smoke. Half a dozen wall crystals, mounted on the enemy-held outer wall, fired at them, then suddenly fell silent.

"Look out for air defenses," Mark cried. "They're holding back their fire."

"Here they come," Ikawa yelled, "five o'clock low!"

Mark almost laughed at the Japanese officer now using the terminology of the American air corps. But he could see where a dozen or more sorcerers, escorted by a score of demons, were ascending from just outside the outer wall.

"There's our target on the ground, approaching the citadel from the south." Walker was leading the third drop team, which was directly behind Younger.

"There must be thousands of them," Mark replied.

The enemy host was advancing down the main plaza, which ran from the southern gate to the fire-blasted citadel wall. At its fore were three heavy wall crystals mounted on wagons, firing into the citadel, where the shielding would glow bright red, overload, and another section of battlements would slide away. Above the roar they could hear the thousands of infantry chanting: "Sarnak, Sarnak, Sarnak!"

Another volley—but this time there was no defensive shield. The blasts sliced through the citadel like a white-hot poker through butter.

"Swing out over the outer wall, we'll turn into final, and then a straight run down the plaza," Mark ordered. "You got that?"

The team shouted.

"Walker, drop first, by the outer gate, try to hit the crystal mounted on the wall. Younger, you're second, in the middle; I'll drop third on their crystals."

"Captain, that's damn close to our own people," Younger said nervously. "We don't know just how big an explosion these things will kick."

"You wanna take the time for a few tests first? We'll just drop and find out. Ikawa, keep those bastards off us. Turn onto downwind now."

The formation swung around running downwind and parallel to the enemy column, several thousand feet below.

The enemy sorcerers charged upward, while from the flank more formations came up to greet them. The air hummed and flashed with firebolts. The Japanese stayed close to the bombing team, keeping the enemy at bay.

A wild flurry of shots roared up, again wide. Mark realized that the enemy was holding off, waiting for its forces to get into position before closing in. He could only hope that they would hold off long enough.

They passed the outer wall and crossed out into the open countryside. He wanted to turn immediately, but knew that every second further out would allow them just that much longer for a straight and level approach as they came back in on their bombing run.

Ten seconds, five.

"All right, turning left, now!"

The formation rolled into a perfect turn. The enemy sorcerers, assuming that this was a party carrying wounded in an escape attempt, had positioned themselves further out to meet them. But now their target had turned aside and was flying back in towards the city.

"On final!"

Ahead of them several wall crystals, mounted on one of the battle towers, were pointed straight up, sending flaklike bursts into the air.

It was like before, Mark realized. the enemy fighters, like trailing sharks, looking for the weak, the flak up ahead. Below was the flaming wreckage of a city, waiting for yet more death from above.

"All right, *Dragon Fire,* we are on final," Mark shouted. "Walker, you've got the lead. Concentrate!"

The city gate was before them, the heavy assault troops pouring through its blasted portals. *Another couple of seconds,* Mark thought, *just a couple more seconds.*

"Bombs away!" Walker cried. As the crystal fell, Walker and his team banked hard right to act as escort.

They were flying down the main plaza, packed with enemy troops. Straight ahead Mark could clearly see where Sarnak's wall crystals were pouring their fire into the citadel's upper works.

"Two away!" Younger shouted.

"Steady, steady now." Mark was looking straight down. He could imagine the bombsight, the cross hairs tracking the target. He had to be sure. A couple of seconds too late and it would hit the citadel wall.

"Steady, steady. Bombs away!" Mark released; a split second later Welsh and Giorgini, carrying the other two ropes, released, as well. The bundle dropped. They surged upward; their burden fell directly beneath them, growing smaller as it rushed to meet the ground.

"Don't watch it," Mark screamed. "Don't watch it!" The world behind them disappeared in a blinding incandescent flash.

"They're turning back," an apprentice shouted, pointing towards the mass formation that had flown over them several minutes before.

Kala looked back to where the apprentice was pointing.

"Ignore them," Kala shouted. "It must be Allic and two others that they're carrying like that. Sarnak has all ways blocked. Our job is to coordinate this break into the city. Back to your duty."

The heavy crystals next to them fired again. The enemy shielding had gone down completely; now it was simply a matter of cutting out huge sections of the wall, making a path wide enough that a hundred men could rush in abreast.

"Damn it, let's take it," one of the infantry commanders roared. "Enough with this sorcery—it's time for the sword."

Kala looked over at the commander. He could see that the man's blood was up. Allic would be a prisoner in minutes, either in that foolish attempt to flee, or if they were turning back, he'd be captured in the city. The battle was for all practical purposes over. He wished he had the power to order the infantry to stand down. Once the troops were released it would be a massacre. Damn these people, they were savages.

"Listen, sorcerer," the commander shouted, drawing closer, "raise your fire. Their shielding is down and I'm going in."

The commander raised his sword high, his heralds standing to either side lifted his pennant into the early morning light.

"Forward," he screamed. "No prisoners!"

"No prisoners!"

The host advanced, a surging ocean of armed men, their swords glinting wickedly in the light from the flaming citadel.

"They've dropped one of the bundles," the apprentice cried, grabbing Kala by the sleeve.

"What the . . ." He watched as the round bundle tumbled end over end.

"The second one!" the apprentice cried.

Those bundles couldn't have been Allic or anyone else. The men carrying them had not been hit. They were flying straight ahead in an almost stately, lumbering formation.

The third bundle dropped.

And then a memory came, of the offworlder, Mokaoto, talking about how wars were fought back on Earth. About how they rained death from . . .

"Run!"

Even as he fled he glanced back at the plaza, now swarming with troops. He could clearly see the first bundle coming down by the main gate.

"Kala, what is it?"

He turned to look back at the apprentice.

The world lit up as bright as the noonday sun. The apprentice, who had been staring straight at the blast, screamed, covering his eyes as the world was washed in light. Kala started to turn and the shock wave knocked him to his knees. Men were down, screaming; buildings on either side rocked and swayed, roof tiles falling off, heavy leaden panes shattering.

A second sun rose—the flash washing over them again—and this time the ground bucked beneath his feet, slapping him into the air, the concussion knocking the breath out of his lungs.

In the last seconds he had left, Kala saw his apprentice lying on the ground, a sliver of glass as long as an arm sticking out of the boy's chest.

Above the roar he heard a whistling sound, dropping in pitch, growing louder. He looked straight up and saw his death falling from the sky, growing larger, filling the heavens.

He never saw the flash.

Sarnak looked in stunned disbelief at the three pillars of fire. The concussion of the second explosion was still washing over him when the third explosion hit. Even from half a league away the roar seemed to be all-encompassing. The tower of flame was detonating and redetonating, soaring ever higher.

"They're blowing their own crystals," he said numbly, not quite believing what he had just witnessed.

Like everyone else he had assumed that the bundles must have contained Allic and two others. As they flew out on their wheeling turn towards their bomb run, he had thought again, realizing the burden being carried was too small and that this might be a diversion for the real breakout in another direction.

And then the bombs had dropped.

Mokaoto had told him about this thing called bombers. But they had destroyed the crystals, and from the size of the last explosion he could see that several of his own precious crystals must have been hit, and detonated, adding their power to the conflagration.

"Genius," he whispered, "I thought only I had the daring to thus defy the wrath of the gods."

But even as he stood in admiration his hatred burned cold and hard. The battle now hung in the balance. He might lose, he knew, but the offworlders would lose something, as well, if they tried the same maneuver again.

As he stood watching, a cold wind swept down from the north, snapping the pennants out by his side. He looked up at the wind-whipped flags, snorted, and returned to his command tent.

"Jesus almighty," Walker roared, "did you see that? That last one must'a touched off them others. It was like the world was gonna shake apart."

The formation, having swung wide, was circling back to land on the observation tower. Shigeru, along with Welsh and José, had already broken off to pick up another set of slings and three more "detonators."

"Looks like trouble, Captain," Walker said, coming up by Mark's side.

Valdez was waiting for them, his rage causing his battle shielding to glow brightly.

They landed even as a distant echo came rolling back from the mountains, repeating the roaring thunder that had swept over the city only minutes before. At the moment of the flash the battle in all quarters had stilled, defender and attacker paused in terror, wondering if the gods themselves had intervened. Now as the echoes washed down from the hills, the battle began anew.

As Mark and the others landed on the citadel wall, they ignored Valdez for a moment and walked across the battlement to gaze at the plaza below.

Massive craters, each a dozen yards or more across and just as deep, scarred the street. Each of the blasts had taken out everything within a hundred yards, leveling the buildings.

The carnage was sickening. Hundreds of bodies lay scattered, ripped apart so badly that they were not recognizable as human.

Thousands more lay upon the ground, wounded, screaming; or wandered in numbed shock. The assault had simply disappeared.

"You just destroyed in one flash what had taken dozens of sorcerers hundreds of years to shape," Valdez snarled at Mark.

"Listen, buddy, we have an old American saying," Mark replied coldly. "Never argue with success. We stopped their assault." He pointed down to the wreckage.

"That is temporary, tactical," Valdez snapped. "But the crystals, the crystals are finite, a gift from the gods. Destroy them and we have no more. They took hundreds of years to shape and you smashed them like a willful child."

"I'm going to save this city whether you like it or not," Mark said evenly, staring into Valdez's eyes. "I swore an oath to serve Allic till death. Well, damn it, we're serving him. In my mind, his realm, this city, the people of this city count more than all the damn crystals in this mad world."

Shigeru and the two Americans came down to land by the party, each of them carrying another sling and a clay pot.

Mark pushed past Valdez.

"Take those three crystals over there," Mark ordered, pointing at the topmost battery on the wall.

"What are you doing!"

"The enemy is still advancing on the bridge in the western half of the town. If we don't stop them, all those people," and he pointed to the thousands of refugees crammed onto the bridge, "are doomed. We're going to save them, and I plan to wipe out Sarnak's heavy crystals on the western side, which are supporting the attack."

"You've destroyed three wall crystals already. We need what's left for fire support when we break out," Valdez shouted. "If Allic knew you were doing this, he'd kill you himself."

"Then tell him to come up here and stop us," Mark replied. "But till he does, I'm going to stop Sarnak, and you better get out of our way. Walker, set up those detonators."

"Anything you say, Captain."

"Stop!"

Mark spun around.

"There is no choice!" Mark shouted. "Either help us, or

crawl away and doom your lord to a life of humiliation. Christ, Allic would be the first to stay and fight to the end. But if you try to stop us, it will be offworlders versus your sorcerers. And we'll slaughter each other while Sarnak laughs."

"This is mutiny!"

"No shit, Sherlock!" Mark contemptuously turned his back to check on the bombs.

"Shigeru, bring up more slings while we're out. Saito, take his place on the team. We're going to strip this wall of crystals and use them. Now move!"

Mark turned around to face Valdez again, but the sorcerer was gone.

"He went below," Ikawa said. "He might be bringing up his men to stop us."

"Then Sarnak will truly win this," Mark said grimly.

"How can I help?"

Mark turned and saw Stede appear through the doorway.

"You look like hell," Ikawa said, coming over to his friend who had taught him the art of the deathstrike.

"We wondered what happened to you," Mark commented. "The last I saw of you, you were preparing to bring back the wall crystals used in the fight against Macha."

"We ran into an ambush," Stede said warily. "We were pinned up in the hills until this morning. I lost ten sorcerers and two crystals. I had to hide the rest of the crystals in the hills—there was no hope of bringing them in. I probably would have lost the rest of my sorcerers, because we were trying to break into the city and were hit hard. Then everyone was distracted by the blasts and we broke through. I just overheard that exchange between you and Valdez. Has that man cracked under the pressure?"

"It's just that we believe the city can still be held."

Stede paused. "I'll get my people together." Turning, he disappeared back into the fortress.

"Damn, it still might work," José said, coming to Mark's side.

Mark knew they had the advantage right now, but it wouldn't last long. Sarnak would soon have all his people up, ready to swarm upon them. He could only hope that for the moment Sarnak still was divided in his plan, fearful that even this desperate act might be a cover to bring Allic out while his own forces were divided and stunned. With Stede's team

Mark realized that they might even be able to work a diversion.

Minutes later Walker stood up. "Ready and armed," he announced.

The north wind swept around them, blowing the smoke from the first three explosions off towards the south, cloaking the distant enemy lines.

"Let's go," Mark shouted.

The team lifted into the air. This time there was a ragged cry of triumph from below.

As they headed out towards the west Stede and his sorcerers rose, carrying several large bundles. The bundles were nothing more than rocks, and Stede swung out to simulate another bomb drop.

As they crossed the river into the west side of the city Mark and his team struggled for altitude.

"All right," Mark cried, "on the embankment promenade, first drop take out the troops, next two for the wall towers covering their advance on the bridge."

"Here they come," Ikawa roared.

Enemy demons and sorcerers were winging up from their positions in the western part of the town. But the diversion was working: nearly half of them were breaking towards Stede.

"Keep it tight," Mark ordered, "shields overlapping!"

The formation pulled in closer together, presenting a larger target. But at the same time the shielding of one reinforced the other, so that a hit in one place quickly dissipated. It would take a dozen or more bolts striking the formation simultaneously, or several slashing into just one man, to have an effect.

Mark felt as if he was flying inside a slow lumbering target as flash after flash struck them, the strain from the impacts not quite dissipated before another shot raised the strain even higher. No one alone could have survived that onslaught, but together they had hope.

Outside the tight formation the Japanese weaved back and forth, returning fire, disrupting Sarnak's sorcerers as they tried to concentrate.

"Turn left, now!"

"Smithie, tighten it up, tighten it up!" Mark cried.

Half a dozen bolts hit Smithie in rapid succession. With a

startled cry he dropped his end of the bomb and fell out of the formation, his shield glowing hot.

"Smithie!" Takeo dropped from the formation and dove after the American. Half a dozen of Sarnak's sorcerers broke off attacking the main group to fall upon the two.

Smithie struggled to regain control. Takeo swung in alongside, grabbing and providing support. Mark watched as the two raced towards the citadel, while Sarnak's sorcerers broke off the chase and turned back to the main target.

Younger and Welsh struggled to hold up their load. Mark slowed their flight, trying to keep them within the protection of the formation.

Bolts hit the two, who quickly fell astern and outside the protection of the formation. Suddenly Younger's shield overloaded and snapped off. A bolt nicked the heavy crystal dangling beneath them.

"Drop it!" Mark screamed. If the bundle was hit square on and the clay pot shattered, they'd all be gone in an instant.

The bomb dropped away. Mark averted his eyes at the last second, as the flash snapped out, raising a column of fire a thousand feet into the air.

"Fifteen seconds," Mark shouted, forcing his attention back to the flight.

Younger closed back with the group, seeking their protection, Welsh at his side.

One of the enemy sorcerers was now hit square on. His shielding disappeared, and a bolt from Ikawa cut him nearly in half. The formation flew straight through where the sorcerer had been only seconds before and Mark choked on the stench of burned flesh.

"Five seconds!"

The enemy sorcerers slashed into them again. A buffet ran through the formation from the impact, their collective shields glowing. Mark felt the formation waver, as if it was about to burst.

"Ready!"

"One away!" Walker and his team released.

"Two away. Break left!"

The formation surged upward, their burden gone.

Cutting through their turn, they dove back towards the

protection of the citadel, Ikawa and his men covering the retreat.

Mark led the group straight through the expanding column of fire and smoke from the first explosion. He knew it was a desperate act, but hoped that it would throw off their pursuers.

As he hit the wall of smoke he instinctively closed his eyes. They were buffeted by the violent updraft and several seconds later emerged from the other side. He looked over his shoulder. The enemy had broken off, cutting around the column rather than going straight through.

The second bomb hit, followed almost immediately by the third. The two towers disappeared, followed an instant later with secondary explosions from both that mushroomed out at almost right angles from the primary blast.

"No need for a photo recon on that," José cried. "One hundred percent destruction confirmed!"

Valdez, his eyes still stinging from the flash, watched from one of the casement windows as the explosions tore apart the twin towers holding Sarnak's heavy crystals. He felt a perverse fascination, like someone watching passively as a madman smashed a priceless work of art, yet he was unable to turn his gaze away.

The double shock ripped across the river, kicking up a wave that hit the battlements like a hurricane.

The offworlders appeared through the smoke, returning to the citadel.

He looked to the team of sorcerers poised and ready by one of the wall crystals which was pointed towards the sky.

"Do we fire, Valdez?" one of them asked.

To serve my lord unto death, Valdez thought. This had to be death, he realized. In the distance another sound came to him, louder than the first faint ripplings of moments before. It was the sound of thousands cheering. Not in hatred, nor in blood lust, but in hope.

What would Allic think when he awoke safely, but his city was gone? And Valdez knew the answer clearly at last. It was best at times to let one's lord die in the fighting than to let him live in shame. Better to die screaming defiance than to crawl into the shelter of night.

"My lord, I can hit them clearly," the sorcerer said.

"We're cursed and abandoned by the gods already," Valdez said coldly. "Take that crystal up and give it to the off-worlders."

"My lord? We only have three crystals left!"

"Damn it all, doesn't anyone around here understand an order when it's given? I said to take that crystal up and give it to the offworlders. We're staying here to fight."

Chapter 20

During the middle of the second night on the march, Macha gave up trying to beat stragglers back into line. Men were actually passing out from exhaustion in the middle of the road, their comrades dragging them to the side, placing them in the care of civilians, and then pressing on.

But as fast as the twin armies melted away from exhaustion, their ranks were renewed as each village's militia, which had been braced for attack from the south, now fell into rank and joined the host sweeping north—the Torm and Landrian armies marching on parallel roads, a league apart.

The armies were passing through regions of prosperous farms, orchards, and vineyards. The populace poured out to meet them: Word had raced ahead that this was the relief column, rushing north in a desperate bid to raise the siege.

At every farmyard gate women passed out pitchers of water and wine, while their children pressed bread, meat, and bunches of grapes into the soldiers' hands. In the waning light of the twin moons they had seemed like ghostly angels of comfort, hovering in the blue dark light, offering words of encouragement and compassion as the troops pressed along, their column a serpentine line of darkness, cutting through moonlit fields.

Now as the army pressed through the heat of day the women rushed up with buckets drawn from their wells, to see

271

them passed into the ranks and reemerge seconds later, to be refilled again.

Hollow-eyed Landrian officers and cavalrymen, mounted on lathered Tals, galloped back and forth down the line, urging the column to close up, and warning the villagers to secure themselves in their houses, taking the stragglers with them. For once the army had passed, the Subata would be overhead.

"Close up, men, close up, keep moving," the command was shouted until voices were hoarse, a litany endlessly repeated.

Over all hung a dense cloud of dust, kicked up by the advance of thousands of soldiers, wagons carrying supplies, the precious heavy crystals, mounted units, and the growing horde of militia.

Only at the very front of the column could the way ahead be clearly seen. The soldiers moved on, their pace heavy, grim, as they watched the growing pall of fire and smoke on the northern horizon. Macha rode at the front of the column to judge the distance and to try to maintain the pace.

Pausing for a moment to take a drink offered by a peasant child, he heard some excited shouts and turned to see a woman skimming above the treetops, another woman at her side.

Damn, he thought, *here she comes to nag me,* and he wished that she had been forced to stay at rest for a while longer. For a moment he almost felt a wave of pity for the offworlder who had succeeded where he had failed.

She came in low, landing by his Tal. Her companion, nearly breathless, alighted by her side.

"Fredna here has found them," Storm shouted.

Macha looked down from his mount. For a moment he was tempted to stay mounted, an obvious breach of etiquette. But he thought better of it and slid off the Tal.

"Found what?"

"Your traitor. He's encamped not a quarter turning flight from here. She spotted him while swinging back from a patrol I sent out."

"We barely have enough sorcerers to watch the approaches to our army, which is strung out from here to damn near back to the pass, and you're sending patrols out to look for that scum? Are you mad?"

"It's better than sitting here passively, knowing they're out there and doing nothing."

Exasperated, Macha turned away. He had given express orders that all aerial patrols were to stay within a quick return of the army to provide cover. The Subata host was easily visible, trailing them about three leagues off to the southeast. As they were drawing closer to the city there was the chance that Sarnak, having the advantage of being able to shift his forces on interior lines, could send out a coordinated assault and hit them with all his own sorcerers while the Subata moved in from the rear.

"Listen to me, Macha. I sent out those patrols on my own. They've got results. Are you going to throw the chance away?"

"This could be a decoy," Macha said cautiously.

"It could be? Yes, it could be. You were impetuous enough to attack my brother on what was only decoys. Have you now grown too cautious? But I know for certain that if we don't take the chance, there won't be much left up there by the end of this day."

A dull rumble cut through their conversation, followed seconds later by a second, and then a third. They looked to the north, and low on the distant horizon they could see three plumes of smoke jetting up.

Macha looked at the smoke as if studying it for some hidden clue. A moment later he turned back to his aide.

"Pass the word down the line verbally—no crystals. If anyone is listening, I don't want it known. I want all sorcerers to me! Now move it, damn you, or I'll flame your hide. Once we've gathered and taken off, you're to pass back down the line and tell the troops that we're going to slaughter the leader of the Subata."

Within minutes the army was behind them. Macha looked back at his troops, strung out over miles of roadway. They were marching themselves into the ground. He'd be lucky if a third of his forces were with him by the time they reached Landra. From his vantage of treetop level, he could barely discern the burning city on the northern horizon.

"Over there is the main host of the Subata." Fredna's comment brought Macha back to the immediate problem.

He could see them, some in flight, moving to the fore, while others had settled to rest for a while until at last they were at the end of the column, at which point they would rise again and move to the fore, like an endlessly turning treadmill.

"If they attack," Macha shouted, his voice carrying on the wind, "we immediately return to the army. Is that understood?"

Storm glared defiantly at him, but said nothing.

"I saw them over by that grove—there, just on the flank of that hill," Fredna called.

"You all know how this is to be done," Macha commanded.

There was a chorus of eager shouts in reply.

"Let's go!"

The formation dropped low, skimming several feet above the ground. This was Macha's favorite type of flying. Out on the savannah of his homeland he would fly like this for hours, hugging every fold of the land, skimming down dry gulches, dodging between the open stands of trees. Now he put his skills to the test, at one point dropping into a narrow forest path through a grove, the opening barely wide enough to pass through without turning sideways.

They came in low, placing themselves at the extreme disadvantage if anything was above, but trading that for the hope of surprise.

The payoff came as they skirted the edge of the hill, coming around the base. Storm's sorcerers broke to the right, while Macha led his group to the left. The second wave of Macha's sorcerers came straight up the slope, cresting it high and then slowing to hover above.

They hit the hidden encampment from both sides and above at once.

Before their target knew what had even happened, Macha was in the middle of their camp.

"Damn you all, come here, Zambara," Macha bellowed, landing to confront the terrified men.

"Why are you hiding here?" he roared.

Zambara looked around to his companions for support, but they blanched and turned away from him.

"We could not locate you," Zambara replied lamely.

"Then why aren't you with your beloved Subata, rather than skulking here half a dozen leagues behind them? You could have at least sent one of those assistants of yours out to look for me!"

Zambara fumbled for words.

"I'll tell you why," Macha roared. "You've thrown in with Sarnak. You hid here, knowing that my people would be watching the Subata and would search for you there and you thought you'd be nice and safe out here by yourselves. You were waiting for me to leave for Landra, and then you'd turn the Sabata loose upon your own people. You're a traitor!"

Zambara stammered, but there was no time to reply. Macha might have given benefit of doubt to the man, but for the fact that Zambara and his assistants had so obviously been hiding.

Macha pulled out his ceremonial short sword.

Zambara's head hit the ground before his body had even started to sag.

Macha turned to face the terrified assistants and pointed the dripping sword at them. "Which one of you is next?"

As one, the five acolytes fell to the ground, wailing.

"Durth," Macha called.

One of his sorcerers stepped out of the ranks.

"You're to take charge here. Take their control crystal and escort these five back to the Subata and get them under control. Do you think you can handle them?"

Durth looked at the five acolytes with disdain. "Snake handlers," he spat. "I soil myself by even being near them, but if you command it, my lord."

Macha stepped up to the acolytes and pointed at them with his sword. "You're to follow Durth's commands without hesitation, you traitorous scum. If but one snake breaks away and causes harm, either to my people or Allic's, you will be blamed. You still face charges of treason, but know my judgment will be far easier if you obey me now."

"Remember," he said coldly, "Zambara was lucky: his end was swift for I had no time to see it otherwise. But I can make one's death very slow," and his voice lowered, "very slow indeed, so that you'll grow old while still young, begging for death to end your torment. *Do you understand me?*"

The five were on their faces, cowering.

"Then obey me, and serve Durth." He spat on the ground and turned away.

"What do we do with this?" one of Macha's assistants asked, kicking at Zambara's body.

Macha looked back at the acolytes.

"Have them fly over the Subata and drop the carcass for their dinner. Make sure they stay long enough to watch the feeding."

Macha started to fly away and then shouted back as if an afterthought, "And don't forget the head."

* * *

Airborne, the contingent flew straight across the open fields back towards the armies. As they leveled out and started in to land at the head of Macha's column, all could see a flash snap across the northern horizon, followed seconds later by two more.

"What are they doing up there?" Macha asked, looking at Storm.

She was afraid to even wonder.

Macha nodded. "It's time. I'll have word sent to our ground commanders to push forward at a forced march while we fly on. Your Tal riders and mine will move out at once; they can be there in several turnings. The rest of us will pick up our wall crystals and head for Landra!"

"There could be spies in the hills," one of Macha's assistants cautioned, pointing to the distant ridgeline.

Macha looked at Storm for a moment and she feared that he might change his mind.

A smile crossed his features. "We'll leave six of our most inexperienced sorcerers behind. If that offworlder Goldberg is fit, have him fly as well—I don't think he'd want to miss the fight. We'll have those who stay behind fly back and forth over the columns and kick up a big stir."

"But the spies will see us leaving."

"Boy, don't you know anything about flying? Look at this land." He gestured at terrain checkerboarded with woods, fields and orchards.

"We'll do some ground-hugging flying like the world has never seen. If any of you so much as flies higher than a man's shoulders, I'll blast you myself. We'll cut through the woods, hug the streambeds, and weave down the orchard rows— they'll never see us. I'll lead the way. Now get ready to move out in a quarter turning."

He looked back to Storm.

"Think you can keep up with me?" he said with a grin.

Unable to contain herself, she gave him an exuberant hug.

"I should make dramatic gestures like this more often," he said self-consciously.

She kissed him on the cheek and drew back.

"That offworlder must be one unusual man to have caught your interest," he said softly.

"He is, at that," Storm replied. "If we can save him in time, I'll be forever in your debt."

Macha shook his head and remembered his encounter

with Mark. Damn, the audacity of that man. "I should leave him to the carrion caters."

"But I know you too well," she replied, still smiling. "Your honor would not allow you to do that."

"Come on," Macha growled. "Let's go in there and save those damned fools."

Mesmerized, Sarnak watched as the twin columns of smoke spread into a dark oily pillar thousands of feet high, dwarfing all the other fires in the city combined. From out of the darkness the formation reappeared and headed back to the citadel.

Whatever hope Allic had of gaining help after the loss of Landra, Sarnak now knew was disappearing with those clouds. Allic, or somebody in his army, was deliberately destroying crystals that should have been the booty of victory.

"Mokaoto!"

"Yes, my lord." The Japanese officer came to his side.

"Those men, are they the ones?" he asked, already knowing the answer. He merely wanted to show Mokaoto the quarry; there'd be time enough after the battle to let him have his fun.

"Yes, my lord," Mokaoto growled. "The Americans, and the traitors to my emperor." He clenched his fists with rage. "I want them," Mokaoto said coldly.

"Soon enough. But you must remain by my side to handle the communications, since Kala is gone. After all, you helped design it; now I need you to run it. Let the fools up front risk their lives for us.

"This could still turn against me," Sarnak continued, "but if they have taken the first sacrilege and destroyed the crystals that should have been mine, then I shall do the same in turn."

"But I thought the crystals were sacred," Mokaoto said.

"Those crystals, they are nothing." Sarnak now realized the implication of what the offworlders had unleashed. "The crystals in my possession are mere toys. If through them I can destroy all of Allic's sorcerers, we can still turn this to our favor."

Mokaoto turned to face his commander.

"Ah, you don't understand, do you?"

Mokaoto was silent.

"How will they react, do you think, when they believe

they have discovered my hoard of gems, now that they are decimating theirs?"

"They will fall upon it like tigers on a dying fawn," Mokaoto replied.

"Order my reserve group to stockpile our remaining crystals in the open, above the hill beyond our main tunnel opening. Have them put my great red in a container and place it, among them. Let the fools then come to loot my hoard. If they see it, they will flock to it like carrion. But once one lands and his shield touches the crystal, or the container holding the red is shattered..." Sarnak smiled. "Everything on and above that hill will be gone."

"And myself, my lord? When may I seek my revenge?"

"You are to stay here with me. That is your post."

One of the communications assistants came up to stand before Sarnak.

"What is it?" Sarnak asked.

"It's not good, my lord."

"Go on."

"I've just picked up two reports. We have a report of fifty or more sorcerers from the north. We believe they might be some of Allic's sorcerers who had been assigned to serve at the Crystal Mountains. They've most likely been released to return home."

Sarnak tried to suppress his smile. "More for the trap," he said quietly.

He had hoped to be into the city by the time reinforcements had come up and to use equipment captured from Allic to hold them off. But the trap could still be sprung, now that the offworlders had shown the way. No crystals of significant power would be left here when the battle was finished, but then there'd be no enemy sorcerers, either. It would be an even enough trade, and the reward from Tor in the Crystal Mountains would make up his losses.

"What about our man with the Subata?"

"Silence, my lord."

Something was wrong there, he thought. The enemy armies to the south were still a good six turnings away. This was starting to get close.

"Any report from our spies in the hills?"

"Just that the enemy is still strung out on the roads; the sorcerers were seen to fly southward for a few minutes and then they returned. Nothing since."

Something definitely wasn't right here. He looked at the

communications officer, feeling suddenly uneasy.

"Order everyone up," Sarnak commanded, "I want everyone on the offworlders. If they should dare to use their remaining crystals, strike them down. Now move."

"Do you want a patrol sent to the south?"

He hesitated. It would be prudent, but he was already stretched to the limit. He could not afford to send more sorcerers to a front already covered by his spies.

"No, I want everything here. Every sorcerer, every demon, here!"

"Will you be going up, as well?" Mokaoto asked coldly, staring straight at his commander.

Sarnak turned on him with rage. "No, damn you!" Sarnak roared. "Now go back to your post!"

Bowing, Mokaoto turned and left. Sarnak stared after him, barely restraining himself from blasting Mokaoto. No one had dared to cast doubts on his bravery in combat for centuries. Only Mokaoto's potential usefulness had saved him—this time.

Now, if Sarnak could only take Mokaoto's anger, channel it, and shape it, there would be a truly formidable weapon.

So, sorcerers were coming down from the Crystal Mountains at last. Excellent. He touched the communications crystal on his belt, sending Tor and his army in the other secret tunnel the signal to attack the Crystal Mountains. Nothing could stop Tor now.

Chapter 21

Two more columns of smoke filled the sky. The seventh blast smashed the northern tower, where Sarnak had mounted three of his own crystals, and the following one had annihilated a heavy troop concentration in the Square of the Merchants, where the enemy had made an attempt to storm the citadel from the north.

The ninth bomb, last of the heavy crystals, had never even gotten into the air, for as they cleared the citadel, Younger, Giorgini, and Welsh had been stunned by a concentrated blast. Wavering, they dropped. For a terrifying moment Mark thought that they would either slam into the citadel wall or drop their bomb and obliterate the citadel. Struggling, the three barely cleared the wall and landed behind the protection of the citadel shield, which was back in action.

It was only the addition of the sorcerers released by Valdez that had seen the rest of the team through the last bombing run, and even then it was tight, with barely enough coverage to keep the formation from breaking apart.

Coming in low and hard, Mark led the group to land inside the citadel where Valdez awaited them.

"I thought we were all doomed," Valdez said ruefully, shaking his head and looking at the scorched bundle of the last heavy bomb in their possession. A thin smile crossed his features. "You might actually have been right about this."

Knowing that this was the highest praise anyone could hope for from the old training master, Mark found himself breaking into a weary grin.

"How are they?" Mark asked, looking over at Younger and his team.

"In any other situation I'd order all of them to stand down for at least a day," Valdez replied. "But look out there," and he pointed out over the flaming city.

Mark nodded. They needed every man who could fly, injured or not. He turned away and walked over to the three shaken Americans.

"Too close for comfort," Mark remarked to them.

"We'd have been all right if those fucking Japs had been doing their job," Younger snarled.

"Stow it," Mark snapped. He looked over his shoulder and saw that Ikawa and several of his men had come forward to check on the Americans. All of them had heard the comment.

"You forget, Lieutenant Younger," Ikawa said coldly, "that one of my 'fucking Japanese' saved Smithie's life not an hour ago."

"Big deal," Younger snapped. "That little faggot Takeo did it just to run from the fight."

"Fatherless scum!" Nobuaki stepped forward, his shielding up.

"Nobuaki," Ikawa roared, leaping between his enraged sergeant and Younger, who was coming to his feet, hand up to meet the threat.

Mark jumped in front of Younger and pushed his arm aside, then slammed him against the wall.

"Goddamn it," Mark snarled, "the enemy is *out there*. Out there, and don't you forget it."

Younger looked at him with cold fury.

"We're going back up and I expect you to be flying with us as a team. Do you understand me, mister?"

For a second Mark thought that there would be an open challenge, but Younger turned away with a mumbled curse.

Mark walked back to Valdez and the rest of the group. The Japanese were silent. Ikawa was off to one side, giving Nobuaki a tongue-lashing. Mark could see that most of the men were ashamed and embarrassed by what had just occurred.

At last Valdez broke the tension. "Come with me," he

commanded, and pointed to a side chamber off the main tower. The men strode in as a group.

"Are they ready?" Valdez asked.

A group of young acolytes were huddled over a table working furiously. At Valdez's approach they stepped back.

The table was heaped with a hundred or more smaller crystals, most the size of a fist, some as large as grapefruit. To each was lashed a small dark bottle sealed with wax.

"This is most of Prince Allic's private crystal hoard. Resting on this table are thousands of years of work faceting and shaping. To each is lashed a bottle containing a small red crystal, our entire supply."

Valdez looked at the group, a pained expression on his face.

"It's dive-bomber time," Walker roared, rushing to check the heft of one of the smaller crystals. He looked back at Valdez and smiled.

"Pops, with this stuff we'll dive-bomb those bastards back to hell!"

Valdez nodded gravely.

As the men gathered round the table to pick up their loads, small padded satchels were passed around for each of the weapons, which were then slung over their shoulders, where they could be pulled out and dropped individually.

All the men handled the bombs with extreme caution, for if two should hit together and a bottle was broken, it could spell all their dooms.

"Your raids have stopped the enemy advance," Valdez said as the men were loading up. "In half a turning all our forces in the eastern half have been ordered to advance as one towards the south wall. We have the one large crystal left to take out the last tower and blow another hole in the wall. Our forces will already be rushing towards that position when you hit it."

"My people will try to support you from above as long as is possible," Valdez continued. "You are to ignore the fight above and use these." He pointed at some of the crystals on the table. "Once the heavy weapon has been dropped, you are to use the smaller crystals to smash the enemy line on the ground so our army may advance."

"But we're still outnumbered in the air," Mark pointed out. "If we split off, your own people could be wiped out."

"By that time I pray that the ground forces, with your support, will have broken out of the city. They've been ordered to pivot and push the enemy towards the river, at which point you're to destroy Sarnak's temporary bridge. It will cut his forces in half. We'll have the one remaining bridge in the center of town; we can shift our troops back and forth to defeat them in detail. When you are done, you're to climb back up and help those of us who are left."

"In other words, defeat their ground attack at the possible cost of you and your sorcerers."

"If you know of a better way, tell me," Valdez said quietly.

Mark looked at Valdez appraisingly. Their bombing runs had stopped the offensive, but had not given them victory. Valdez was very likely ordering his own death. Mark stared at him, wishing somehow to come up with an alternative.

"It is Bushido," Ikawa said quietly, coming to Mark's side, and bowing towards Valdez.

Mark nodded and turned away.

"Christ, they're coming up this time with everything they've got!" Giorgini cried.

"Cut the chatter," Mark snapped. "We can see them."

Mark was in the lead, this time with Jośc and Walker helping to carry the heavy bomb, while Ikawa and the rest of the men flew in a protective shield around them. At the last minute Ikawa had assigned Shigeru and Nobuaki, the two weakest flyers, to lead the ground assault which would hopefully break into the open fields beyond.

Even before the last of them cleared the tower, the enemy was upon them, diving in close and slashing out with bolt after bolt, for they now knew what was being carried in the sling, and hoped to have it drop back on the citadel.

It was worse than anything Mark could have ever imagined. The sky was awash in fire.

A sorceress tumbled directly in front of him, shrieking. Ally or enemy, Mark couldn't tell. All he could see was the smoke as the woman fell, and disappeared into the fires below.

Straining with the effort, Mark leveled out and headed for the tower. The three heavy crystals mounted within fired repeated shots at his formation. One of the bolts cut straight up at them, but it was intersected by one of Valdez's assistants. It was a suicide move—the sorcerer simply disappeared in a blinding flash—but the rest of the party was saved and pushed on.

Valdez came up close, flying only inches away.

"We're going in," Mark cried.

Valdez nodded and gave Mark a look that clearly said, *I'm following a madman.*

"Ten seconds!"

Yet another sorcerer placed himself between a heavy blast from the ground and the main formation. Mark looked over at Valdez and saw him screaming with rage. He realized that Valdez had given orders for that tactic to be used and knew, as well, the agony the man must now be feeling for ordering comrades to their deaths.

Directly beneath them they could see the ocean of Allic's men surging forward, no longer held down by the fiery blasts from the tower which were now aimed skyward. Shigeru was plainly visible at the head of the press, and Mark could imagine the giant bellowing with joy as he finally had the chance to close with his enemies while his feet were planted firmly on the ground.

A dozen sorcerers raked across the formation, all of them firing as one, so that for an instant Mark felt as if their collective shielding was about to overload.

Concentrate—he had to concentrate on the bombing and leave the flying to the others.

It had to be perfect, this one was it. Mark held his breath, looking straight down. The shielding around him went bright red again, hanging on overload.

"Ready!"

A buffet sent them surging as a wall crystal shot got past one of the protecting sorcerers who had tried to place his body before it. The shot nicked the edge of the shielding.

"Bombs away!"

The formation surged up and for a moment the battle stilled.

To everyone's shocked amazement four of Sarnak's sorcerers broke out of the battle, diving downward, firing blasts at the bundle.

Valdez's men fired at them in turn, hitting the leader so that two others were thrown off. But the last one pushed grimly on, trying to detonate the bomb before it hit.

The crystal hit the base of the tower, there was a split second of delay, the pursuing sorcerer turning desperately away—and then the world beneath them disappeared in a thunderclap roar.

Stunned, all watched as the entire hundred-foot edifice

seemed to lift straight up into the air, then vanished in two more white-hot flashes. The shock wave disrupted the battle overhead.

"Now in and after them," Mark cried.

The Americans pulled up, one after the other winging over into a dive, the Japanese following in their wake, while Valdez and his embattled survivors banked right to face the bulk of Sarnak's sorcerers.

Allic's ground forces pushed forward, ready to close with the enemy. But none were to be found. A zone of death nearly two hundred yards wide had been blown into Sarnak's lines. The triumphant forces surged through the break and emerged into the open fields beyond. Further down the wall, where the first break had been cut with the first bombing run, Sarnak's men came pouring out, some fleeing the city, the rest grim and turning to face their enemies, while from the positions back by the tunnel the last of Sarnak's reserves rushed forward to try and blunt the counterattack on the flank and throw it back.

"There's our target," Mark cried, pointing to the threat on the flank. One after another they winged downward, each man pulling a small crystal from a satchel. Walker pushed to the lead, going into a near vertical dive.

Walker lined up on what appeared to be a command unit and dove straight for it. At the last possible second he released and pulled out, skimming so close to the ground that he found himself in a hail of arrows.

The small crystal detonated behind him, cutting down everyone for nearly a dozen yards.

All across the enemy advance, bomb after bomb impacted, so that within seconds, along a front of several hundred yards, the entire column was down.

"Better than hundred-pound bombs," Walker yelled, coming up to Mark's side.

"On to the bridge," Ikawa ordered, pointing to their second major target, a half mile away.

Mark called for his formation to follow.

They cut across the open field, ignoring the confusion of battle beneath them. Pulling up to several hundred feet, they leveled out.

"Three for the bridge should do it—one on each end, one in the middle," Mark shouted. "Ikawa, hit the formations on either side!"

"In sequence," he went on, "me, Walker, then José. Then we form up and turn back to hit their flank!

"Ready, now!"

Mark winged over, diving vertically for the bridge. He released his crystal directly on the massive moorings that held the pontoon bridge in place, and pulled out. There was a wild eruption behind him, followed seconds later by thundering crashes from the middle of the river, and finally from the far side as José's bomb missed the bridge and impacted on the bank a dozen yards upstream. A staccato series of explosions rippled up and down both sides of the river as the rest of the Americans and Japanese slammed into the troop formations on either side. Even with the near miss the bridge was destroyed.

Seconds later they reformed and headed back towards the main part of the fight. Mark looked overhead and saw that Valdez was still holding his own, but the odds were getting worse. Already some of the enemy sorcerers were diving to intercept them.

"We got company from above," Mark shouted. "Let's rip the shit out of their lines and get the hell back upstairs."

"Captain, where's José?"

Mark looked over his shoulder to see Walker searching the sky over the bridge, looking for their missing comrade.

Jesus, the kid must have bought it back there, Mark thought angrily. *I never should have sent him out on the wing like that alone.* He searched the sky, hoping to see a sign, then looked towards the enemy formation closing from above.

"He's bought it," Mark yelled. "Push on with the attack. Open line wing abreast; we'll unload everything we've got. Now move it!"

The flyers came up in one line, Mark on the left, Ikawa a hundred yards to the right. They swept across the field several hundred feet up and lined up straight on the enemy formation which they had staggered moments before. It was now surging forward again.

The soldiers on the extreme left of the advance saw the enemy sorcerers who had tormented them earlier coming back in again, and they knew their purpose.

A shout of panic went up and within seconds had worked all the way down to the other end of the formation, a quarter mile away, as thousands looked heavenward and cried out.

Lining up, Mark dropped his first bomb, and kept drop-

ping them. Before he had tossed his last weapon he found
that he could no longer watch. The results of a hundred high
explosives dropping on thousands of men packed together in
a field was sickening. When they reached the end of their
run, the formation pulled up and over, ready to meet the
sorcerers coming in behind them. The sight that greeted
them was beyond imagining.

Where thousands had advanced only moments before,
there was nothing left but ruin. The field was awash in blood,
so that from the air it seemed as if the ground below had
been painted from end to end with scarlet. Thousands of
shattered bodies littered the field, and the stench of burning
flesh gave it the semblance of one vast pyre. Like maggots on
flesh, the survivors crawled about or writhed in agony, their
screams a rising cacophony of pain. The battle on this part of
the field was over.

"Let's go back upstairs," Mark said grimly, pointing towards the enemy formation chasing them.

"Captain Phillips," Saito cried, and pointed off towards
the northeast.

A group of fifty or more sorcerers, flying high, were
clearing the hills not a mile away.

"God in heaven," Mark whispered.

"Damn it," José cried, frustrated with his miss. He swung
high to the west, gaining altitude for another pass.

Rolling over and into another dive, he saw where the
other two hits had shattered most of the bridge, but he
wanted to make sure that his end of the deal was wiped out,
too, before rejoining his comrades. They'd be sure to tease
him later if he left the task undone.

Taking his time, he came in with deliberate intent, and
released.

As the weapon left his hand a firebolt slashed past him.

He dove for the ground while his last drop impacted on
the bridge, sending the wreckage skyward. Another bolt
slashed in front of him and he jinxed wildly, cutting to run
upriver. A glance over his shoulder showed him that three
sorcerers were cutting him off from his comrades, who were
already unloading their last bombs.

"Blessed Mary help me," he cried as the sorcerer closest
to him rolled in, firing repeatedly.

He turned straight into his opponent, firing a shot. Then,
defying all the rules of combat, he dove lower—cutting

straight underneath his opponent—just inches off the ground.

The sorcerer pulled into a tight turn, while the other two kept to his side, preventing any hope of regaining the protection of his friends.

Dodging and weaving, José drifted further from the main field of action, crossing over the scattered backwash of Sarnak's army which bolted in every direction at their approach.

Ruins of the temple where Allic had nearly died loomed before José. He pulled a tight turn, swung around them and cut straight up, hoping his opponent would cut around below him. The trap worked, and as the sorcerer came around a crumbling wall, he fired a blast. The shot went wide, striking the side of the building. The sorcerer dove to his right, rolled, and recovered.

Now fifty feet up, José started into a steady weaving climb, hoping to gain altitude above the two others who were still running to his left. The third sorcerer cut below him and came around in a banking turn, racing up towards his two comrades who were climbing skyward, rushing to get higher and then cut across above him for the kill.

Several hundred feet up they crossed over the main entrance to the tunnel and pressed on. José looked desperately around, hoping that the terrain below might offer some means of escape. His eyes fastened on a glint reflecting the early afternoon sun.

Crystals? He looked closer, wondering why such a hoard would be left out in the open with no guards in sight.

A firebolt slashed in front of him. Banking hard right, he tried to flee back towards the river, now nearly a league away.

He suddenly realized that he was lost. By climbing like this to nearly a thousand feet, he was wide open on all sides, without even the hope of using the ground cover to throw off pursuit.

Desperation seized him. He said a silent prayer, and set himself to turn on them, hoping at least to take one of his opponents before he tumbled to his death.

A series of blasts ripped across the sky. Where the three enemy sorcerers had been, there was now only a cloud of flaming smoke.

"Holy Mother of God!" he cried, looking for his deliverers. And then he saw them.

From beyond the ridgeline just ahead, a formation of fifty or more sorcerers was coming up behind him.

They had to be the sorcerers placed to guard the Crystal Mountains to the northeast. He knew that they were ordered to stay there no matter what happened, but at the moment he didn't care about orders. They had saved him!

Swinging back around, he flew slowly, trying to regain his wind and also his nerve. He felt weak all over, as though every joint in his body had turned to rubber. He felt his heart racing like a trip-hammer, his mouth dry as cotton.

He was alive!

The formation which had been coming towards him now started to drop as one, all converging on a single point. José looked down and saw that they were racing towards the hoard of crystals.

Why would Sarnak have left so many of the precious gems out like that? He started to drop to take a closer look. His suspicions aroused, he looked again, and it was as though his power cut through the light to see light and power that could not be seen by ordinary eyes. And then he knew, seeing as through smoked glass, that the power emanating from one of the gems was different, darker, redder!

He looked again at his saviors and still they were flying downward.

"It's a trap," José screamed. "A trap!" His communications crystal, which could send the information, had been destroyed hours earlier from a near miss, so he couldn't talk to them directly.

"It's a trap," and he tucked into a dive, heading straight for the sorcerers, hoping to reach them before they landed on the pile where their shielding would touch off the great red stone concealed beneath.

Stunned and screaming, he found himself weaving as half a dozen bolts came up from the approaching party. They did not recognize him! Mind racing, José realized that they had seen him flying with the others and thought he was on the other side in spite of his uniform, and now there was no way to tell them differently in time.

"It's a trap," and at that moment he knew there was only one way to stop them, for if he tried to close and warn them away they would blast him from the sky.

Pointing straight down, he dove for the cache, trying to get close enough for an accurate shot. He glanced at the other sorcerers, hoping that they were far enough away, and fired a blast at the crystals.

The world before him disappeared in a blinding storm of light. As if picked up by the heart of a wave, he tumbled end over end.

In the last instant of life, he felt the remaining bombs he carried in the satchel crash against his chest, the glass containing the small red crystal breaking with the impact.

"God in heaven," Mark whispered, looking off towards the advancing column of sorcerers. As if from one hand all of them fired at the same time. Mark traced its path and saw what appeared to be three sorcerers in the distance disappear in a flash, while their companion turned and arced away.

"They're ours!" Mark cried. They must be the guardians of the Crystal Mountain. How or why they had been released, he didn't care, but come they had.

"All right!" Mark cried. "Up to Valdez and let's finish these bastards."

With a shout of triumph they started into their climb. The sorcerers who had been coming down on them but moments before, now paused at the sight of the enemy closing in the distance, and those now coming up from below. As one they broke, heading back towards their companions still engaged against Valdez.

Across that field of strife there came a feeling that the battle was now hanging in the balance. Both sides could claim victories and defeats in the day's action, for though Mark's attack had broken the flanking action, Sarnak's main army was holding its own against Shigeru's determined counterattack. Overhead the price for supporting Mark's sweep had been the near decimation of Valdez's forces, so that only an embattled handful were left, the rest having fallen to their death or spiraled back within the city, crippled and exhausted.

And in that instant it seemed as if the sun itself had come down from the heavens to tear open the earth with its light.

A column of fire, dwarfing any explosion seen so far that day, erupted on the hillside above the city. Upward it climbed, into the heavens, and the battle came to a stop as all watched transfixed. Overhead the battle simply disintegrated as the shock wave washed over and scattered those in the air.

"Turn with it!" Mark cried.

The flyers wheeled and were engulfed in a hurricane blast that did not subside until they were more than a hundred yards back inside the city wall, flying raggedly at rooftop level.

The blast was past them, but still the pillar of fire roared heavenward.

"What the fuck was that?" Walker asked, awestruck.

"I don't know," Ikawa shouted. "It looks like it took out our reinforcements."

"Let's get some altitude back." Mark's voice was shaky. "I think we lost our help. We better get upstairs, they're going to need us."

Suddenly from around the side of the ascending column, there appeared the flight of sorcerers that had seemed to be annihilated by the blast moments before.

"They must have been too far away from it," Mark screamed in triumph. "All right, let's go!"

But on the rest of the field, most still had either not seen the reinforcements to start with or were now waiting to see whose side they really were on.

The unidentified formation came on, skimming low. Suddenly a ripple of fire lashed out from the advancing sorcerers, striking into the shattered remnants of Sarnak's formation. With that single blast they pulled straight up, bearing for the scattered air battle overhead.

In that instant all who could see gave voice, half in triumph, the others in fear.

And as if the attack had been planned and rehearsed for months, there came another rippling sheet of blasts from beyond the western bank. From out of a low streambed a mile beyond the city, another fifty sorcerers appeared, skimming the ground, slashing into Sarnak's forces on the other side.

"It's Storm and Macha," Mark cried. "The battle is ours! Let's close and get this finished."

With a shout of triumph the Americans and Japanese soared heavenward, and their enemies fled before them.

Chapter 22

"It's finished here," Sarnak said quietly, still standing while all around him had been knocked down by the blast which had nearly crushed the tunnel above them.

Standing by the entrance, he watched grimly as the enemy sorcerers shot past not a hundred yards away and raced on towards the heart of the battle.

Moments before they slashed into the rear of his army, he saw the other formation emerging from the shallow riverbed on the western side.

Angry now with himself for having posted only a handful of sentries over there, he watched as the sorcerers from the southern army deployed before going in on their strike.

"Damn them," he mumbled, more to himself than to those around him. At least neither group had yet seen the tunnel entrances.

The plan had failed here, but there was still Tor. There was always the just reward he could now claim—and was that not the ultimate goal, after all?

He turned and looked at Mokaoto. "Take your equipment, destroy what cannot be moved out immediately, and prepare to blow the tunnel entrance. We're pulling out right now."

"But what about your army back there, and the sorcerers still fighting?"

"They're finished. I can save only what I have with me here. We leave at once."

Turning, he strode back into the dark recesses of the tunnel, already dropping from his thoughts the tens of thousands who had served him and were now dying as a result. There will always be more armies, and with the treasures that Tor would bring, there would be more sorcerers, as well. They would come to him begging to share in his power.

"Mokaoto."

There was no answer.

"Mokaoto!"

The entrance to the tunnel was empty, his assistant gone.

"Fool." Turning, he disappeared into the darkness.

Tor stood at the head of his army, poised at the sealed mouth of the tunnel, waiting for the signal from Sarnak. As soon as they knew that all available forces had been committed to Allic's struggle, his time would come.

He surveyed his strike force. Four hundred of his best sorcerers stood in the ranks. He wanted no ground troops for this raid. The Crystal Mountains were only thirty miles away; a quick flight and an assault with overpowering force on the unsuspecting garrison, and the Heart would be his.

The message crystal flashed brightly as Ralnath passed the word from Sarnak.

With a wave Tor activated the trap door. As planned, tons of earth and stone fell away into a side pit dug underneath the mouth long ago.

Beams of sunlight entered the tunnel's gaping entrance, clouds of dust rising and twisting in the wind.

"Follow me," he commanded. As one the sorcerers flew through the dust into the sunlight.

There, waiting for them, stood a regiment of sorcerers and crystal cannons. And in front of them all stood a pillar of light.

Tor came to an abrupt halt, his forces deploying around him. His roar of frustration was almost deafening.

"Most impressive, Tor. I can't recall when I've been more frightened," the shifting figure of brightness mocked in a chilling voice.

"Damn you, Jartan. How did you know?"

"I've acquired a new sorcerer with some most unusual abilities, and he detected your tunnel some time ago. I did a little searching of my own and had more than enough time to prepare this little reception. I've even brought the Heart with me, though I doubt you would want to be introduced to it." Tor had already noticed the monstrous crystal mounted on the hillside, glowing with an unquenchable fire, and aimed at him. Fear tempered his rage and he began to calculate his chances.

"I offer life to those deluded followers of yours, Tor. All who drop their crystals and surrender will live. The others die!"

Tor could sense the wavering in his ranks. He looked over his shoulder with a threatening glance. Those behind him stood rigid, caught between the wrath of their master and his opponent.

"Tor, I have waited three thousand years to meet you on the field of battle. You are mine."

Tor turned and launched himself at Jartan. Coming in low he aimed and fired a blast backed by thousands of years of hatred. The pillar turned to flame. With a coarse shout Tor fired again and again, closing the distance between them.

Behind him his chief lieutenant raised his arm to join the fray. Instantly a beam from the Heart annihilated him and those closest to him. All the others remained frozen with their shields off and their arms kept carefully pointed at the ground. They knew what was about to happen and had no desire to sacrifice themselves needlessly.

Tor continued to fire at Jartan, who appeared to stagger. Closing to twenty feet, Tor marshaled all his remaining strength and fired another blast, raising the color of Jartan's shield to white hot.

And Jartan smiled, revealing at last his hidden reserves. He raised his arms and instantly the field surrounding him spread to envelop Tor. The moment the superheated field touched Tor's shields they flared and vanished, searing Tor in the process.

The light inside was blinding, and Tor could barely make out the glowing figure that faced him. He felt, rather than saw, the careful blasts which shattered all of his crystals. A new shield formed around him, a shield of containment, that froze him into immobility.

The god Jartan stood before him in all his power: a figure of light and strength which stared at him with glowing eyes.

"As it was in the beginning when the gods came from Chaos, we can return to the universe of our birth."

Beneath Tor's feet the ground turned black and began to

swirl. Horrified, Tor could see the blackness grow and churn, flashes of barely controlled energy lapping at the edges of the shield. It seemed to devour his legs, spreading up within the shield. As it reached his groin he screamed, a scream of such terror and despair that all the others in the valley, Jartan's and Tor's troops alike, shuddered when they heard it.

A bolt slashed from Jartan's hand to strike Tor in the chest and draw the Essence out of his body. He tried to scream again but could not catch his breath.

Tor felt lightheaded as the last of his power left him forever. He was like a husk drained of its vitality until nothing was left but dust and bitter memories.

"Now join your father in hell!" Jartan roared.

The light that surrounded them pulsed and shimmered down.

Jartan stood alone. As a breeze shifted across the valley, the dust at his foot swirled and disappeared with the wind.

"Captain!"

Saito came swinging up to Ikawa's side and pointed across the battlefield. In the melee of the past minutes their formation had finally come apart as the battle disintegrated into individual duels.

Ikawa had managed to keep Saito and Welsh with him as they weaved back and forth, dodging blasts and hunting down any enemies who had yet to surrender.

Saito eagerly pointed towards the retreating enemy line.

For a moment Ikawa thought he was dreaming, or seeing a ghost.

"Mokaoto!"

His former animosity for his lieutenant was forgotten, so stunned was he to see a comrade whom he had thought dead. How he had suddenly appeared in the midst of this carnage, Ikawa did not even consider.

"Mokaoto." Slowing in his flight, he swung over and headed straight towards the lieutenant who, strangely, was still dressed in the uniform of Imperial Japan.

Saito swung in beside his commander crying out for joy. But Welsh, as if sensing something wrong, pulled up higher and hovered above the other two.

Mokaoto came up towards them, his features set in a mirthless grin.

"Mokaoto," Ikawa cried, slowing to hover in midair, his

shield shimmering down, "never did I dream to see you again."

"Of course not, you traitor to your people," Mokaoto said softly, drawing in closer.

"What?" Ikawa said, confused by this greeting.

"You embrace the enemy that destroys our homeland," Mokaoto cried. "You are not samurai. But I still am!"

He raised his hand, and Ikawa tried to raise his shield in defense. The blast snapped out at close range, catching Ikawa on the shoulder.

With a cry Ikawa fell backwards. A second blast snapped at Saito who raised his defensive crystal and struggled to absorb the blow.

"You bastard!"

From the side opposite Mokaoto's shield hand, Welsh dropped, firing a direct blast. Mokaoto spun, firing wide.

Welsh ducked and fired again. Mokaoto shifted, trying to drop beneath his opponent, but Welsh was ahead of him and shot again. This firebolt cut into Mokaoto.

But Welsh was exhausted, still weak from his earlier injuries, and he had expended all the power he had.

Mokaoto, numbed from Welsh's blows, tried to line up for another shot and then saw several of the Americans winging in to give aid. To stay would mean his death.

With a scream of rage he fired blindly, and turning, dove away.

Mark and Walker dove towards the fight.

"It's that Mokaoto bastard," Walker cried, and he set out in pursuit while Mark cut down to help Saito.

Mokaoto dove into the billowing smoke that now obscured most of the field of battle. Walker, cursing, chased him and they disappeared from view.

Circling downward, Mark came to land beside Saito.

"How bad is it?" he asked.

Saito looked up at him, eyes wide with fear.

Reaching down, Mark helped him to pull open Ikawa's scorched tunic.

Ikawa's right shoulder was burned, the flesh blackened from neck to upper arm.

"I never did trust him," Ikawa said weakly. "I was just so glad, though, to see him."

"I wish I had him," Mark said, choking back his fury.

"You know at the moment I wish you had," he said, trying to force a smile. "You'd have shot first."

"You're damn right."

Ikawa grimaced with pain.

Mark looked at him, panic-stricken. *Don't die,* he wanted to scream. *Don't die and leave me now.*

A shadow passed over him and he looked up to see Welsh landing beside them, while several others were coming in from the distance.

"You saved my life, my friend," Ikawa said, looking up at Welsh.

"I should have hit sooner. I knew that bastard was up to no good."

"You did well enough," Saito replied, looking to him and then to Mark. "He saved my captain's life. I owe him—I owe all of you whatever I have."

"You would have done the same."

Mark looked around and saw Walker and the rest of the offworlders settling to land, forming a defensive perimeter around their fallen commander.

Looking back towards the city, Mark saw where Shigeru and Nobuaki stood by what appeared to be a small wagon.

"Come on," Mark said, "let's pick up those two ground fighters and get Ikawa back into the city. The battle's finished for us; the reinforcements can take care of the mopping up."

"There goes one," Welsh suddenly cried, pointing up towards a low flying demon coming out of the city behind them.

"Let him go," Mark shouted. "They're finished."

But Welsh, the anger of battle still in his soul, soared upward in pursuit, cutting back in towards the city to head the demon off.

"Not one," Nobuaki cursed, "not one did I hit. It was always you."

Shigeru chuckled good-naturedly, leaning against the side of the smashed wagon where they had found to their shock Sarnak's one remaining heavy crystal, which must have survived the air strikes and been dragged out of the city in the retreat.

In their mad attack the two had overrun the wagon before the enemy could even fire the weapon. They had then used it against the packed formations of Sarnak's troops and demons until the battle had finally swept past them, leaving the two with the crystal in its wake.

"I cannot help it," Shigeru said, "I cannot fly as well as the others. But when my feet are on the ground, then I can fight."

His companion spat out a curse and slumped down beside the crystal, watching as thousands of the enemy swarmed up the distant hill or plunged into the river. But he could not shoot, for soldiers from the city were mingled among their foes.

A shadow passed over him and he looked up.

"A demon!" Nobuaki cried, and leaping to his feet he swung the crystal around, ready to take aim.

"Look out, he's mine!"

Welsh shot past not a dozen feet overhead. A single jet of flame shot from his hand, catching the demon, sending him tumbling to the ground.

Welsh pulled up and looked back at Nobuaki. Then, laughing, he waved and went into a victory roll.

Nobuaki had been cheated yet again, and now the American was laughing at him! Suddenly all the hatred, all the pent-up rage that had been building for months was before him, a target to focus on.

A bolt shot from the heavy crystal.

Crying in horror, Shigeru leaped to his feet and knocked Nobuaki away from the crystal.

Shigeru raced across the field, praying that it was not so, that it was a bad dream. He slowed, came to a stop, and then fell to his knees, crying in anguish over Welsh's shattered body.

"Oh god," Mark whispered, wishing that he had not seen what had just occurred.

Together they had all gathered around Ikawa and were preparing to lift him into the air when Walker, who was circling above them, had cried out.

Within seconds they were all aloft, Saito and Smithie helping to lift Ikawa.

They landed by Welsh's body and Shigeru stood to face them, tears streaming down his face. Without another word he turned from the group and strode back to the heavy crystal where Nobuaki was coming to his feet.

With one hand Shigeru dragged him back before the others.

Mark looked around the group and his heart froze. Minutes before he had seen them gather as one around Ikawa. Now they stood apart, the Americans to one side of the body, eyeing with suspicion the Japanese who stood crestfallen on the other side.

"You slant bastards," Younger growled.

"Shut up," Mark said quietly.

"Never trust them, that's what I've always said. So now Welsh is dead. You're not fit to command these men, you never were."

Mark was silent.

"And I say he is," Kraut shouted, coming up to stand behind Mark.

Mark realized that it was now an open challenge that could no longer be avoided. There was no rank to pull here; it would have to be up to the men.

"Younger, I always knew you had your head so far up your ass that there was a ring mark around your neck," Walker snarled, coming to stand with Mark.

Smithie looked at Younger, then spat on the ground by his feet and came over to Mark.

"Giorgini," Younger snapped, but all could sense the growing fear in his voice.

Giorgini looked at Mark and those who stood by him. For a moment Mark could see him wavering, and Younger turned to stare at him.

With head lowered, Giorgini went to stand behind Younger.

Mark breathed an inner sigh of relief. He now knew beyond all doubt that he commanded the men behind him through respect, and not by titles from Allic, or a rank given back in another world that seemed like a half-forgotten dream.

"I've had it with this chickenshit outfit," Younger shouted, his voice nearly breaking. "We're leaving."

"You've made a pledge to serve Allic," Mark said quietly.

"Fuck that. The hell with him and his damned princedom," Younger cried.

There was a low growl from the Japanese, and even from the men behind Mark.

"You've condemned yourselves by your own words," Mark replied evenly. "I'll spare you now only because we once served together. You can leave, but you must leave your crystals here."

"Without crystals we're sitting ducks out there," Giorgini cried.

"They're no good to you anyhow, once you've broken oath," Mark said. "While you wear Allic's crystals he will always be able to track you down."

Younger looked down at the bracelets on either wrist and Mark suddenly realized that Younger had completely forgotten that one fine point to the contract.

Younger looked back up at him with hate-filled eyes. He wavered for a moment, then tore the crystals from his wrists and waist.

He turned to face Giorgini, who still hesitated. With a curse Younger tore Giorgini's crystals away.

Without another word the two lifted into the air, wobbling. They could still use the Essence, but without crystals their control was far less precise. They turned north, heading away from the fighting. As they left, Mark overheard Younger telling Giorgini about one Redfa, a merchant. Had this confrontation been planned?

For the moment Mark had forgotten what had triggered it. Then the cold memory came rushing back.

Nobuaki stood before him, his eyes wide with shock.

Mark and the Americans were silent. Nobuaki turned to look back at his companions, but they dropped their heads with shame and moved away.

As they stood in silence, Valdez came skimming across the field, Storm at his side, with Goldberg flying behind them. All three were shouting triumphantly, but as they approached the circle of men they fell silent.

"I am without honor," Nobuaki whispered. "I gave my pledge to Prince Allic and I have broken it. Though I still hate all of you." For a moment defiance glared in his eyes.

He looked back again to his old comrades, hoping beyond hope that they would rally to him. But all he saw now was shame and anger.

"I have no one now, my honor has been stripped away," Nobuaki said. "All I have left to me is the path of seppuku."

The Americans looked at each other, wide-eyed. Mark looked at Ikawa, who lay on the ground, alive now only because of the man Nobuaki had slain. The pain and rage in Ikawa's eyes told him that there was nothing to be said.

"Shigeru, will you be my second?" Nobuaki asked.

With a grunt of assertion the warrior stepped forward, picking up a sword from the ground.

Nobuaki stood silent for a moment, looking to the sky. He went to his knees by Welsh's body and drew a dagger from his waist.

Mark turned away. He wanted to stop this in spite of his rage over Welsh, but he knew that only when the blood of the two had mingled would it be complete.

He heard a grunt of pain as Nobuaki drove the dagger into his body. A second later there was the whistling hiss of the sword and the sound of a body falling to rest atop Welsh.

The party stood transfixed, and then one by one they turned and started to walk away.

Mark felt a hand slip into his. It was Storm.

Mark wanted to speak, but too much had happened. He knew that he would heal, that soon they would again love, and that his life in this world would go on. But at that moment he was numb beyond all caring.

Sensing his thoughts she squeezed his hand lightly, and flew off with Valdez to direct the mopping up of the battle.

At last Mark turned back, averting his eyes from the two bodies. Ikawa was still on the ground, Saito standing beside him, ready to help him back to the city.

As Mark approached them he glanced at the rest of the men who were heading back to the city on foot. They were not separate but mingled together, Smithie by Shigeru's side, talking to him, his hand on the giant's shoulder as if to comfort him. Kraut was with several others, and somehow they had found an intact bottle on that field and were passing it back and forth. Goldberg walked to one side, weeping for his lost friend, a Japanese soldier on either side of him, offering words of comfort.

Mark knelt by Ikawa's side. The two were silent for a moment. At last he looked over at the two bodies and then back again to the others.

"We've become one at last," Mark said softly.

Ikawa reached out and grasped his hand, and Mark pulled him to his feet.

"Yes, my friend," he said softly. "And most importantly, again we have survived."

Epilogue

"Down there, do you see him?" Mark asked, pointing towards a sorcerer flying low several miles ahead.

Ikawa nodded, and spoke into his communications crystal.

"Checks out," Ikawa replied several seconds later. "One of Macha's people carrying a message, that's all."

Mark knew that chances were good the other sorcerer was friendly. This region had been swept and reswept a hundred times, but there was still that edge of wariness towards anything that might be a threat.

Resuming their course, the two flyers dropped into the river valley that cut through the heart of Sarnak's old realm, repeating yet again their standard patrol sweep that took them from the old frontier, up the valley to the inner fortress line, and then back out again.

Everything below them was now occupied territory, there hadn't been a hostile sighting of any kind in nearly a month, but caution was still in order. Mark found it hard to believe that peace had returned.

After the defeat of his army and subsequent flight, Sarnak's fortresses and battlements fell easily to the combined forces of Allic and Macha. Even Patrice took advantage of the situation and sent her army into the fray.

Allic still had not completely recovered from his wounds,

but had left his healers only ten days after the battle of Landra was over. With half his face bandaged he directed the conquest of Sarnak's realm.

To Mark's amazement it was taken as a matter of fact that Allic's eye would one day heal completely and regain its sight, but for now Allic sported an eye patch which gave him a rather piratical look. For Pina the prognosis was not so good. Limbs, even eyes, that were damaged could be healed in time. But something that was completely destroyed was gone forever. Still, he had the one good arm, and could fight almost as well as he did before, hanging his defensive crystal around his neck. By the closing stages of the campaign he was up and again playing his part.

Sarnak's land had been conquered and subdivided between Allic and Macha as partial payment for their losses. Macha had taken the western third of the land that bordered his realm and Allic took the rest.

It took a little convincing to persuade Patrice to be happy with just the booty gained in the initial assault and to retire to her old borders. In a way Allic had been disappointed, as he was half hoping for an excuse to pick a fight with Patrice and overthrow her too, knowing that Macha would be more than happy to help him. Having her as a neighbor meant problems eventually, but Patrice acted as if she knew what Allic and Macha were thinking and was extremely careful to be cooperative and accommodating.

No one knew what had happened to Sarnak; he seemed to have vanished from the face of Haven.

Kochanski was still in Asmara with Jartan, and Mark had talked with him several times via crystal. He seemed to be hard at work doing some kind of research but would not elaborate, saying that Jartan preferred to keep it a secret for the time being. Mark knew that of them all, Kochanski was the happiest, although upon further reflection Mark had to admit that he had never been happier either. It was just that Kochanski had managed to avoid the depression and exhaustion that followed the nightmare of extended conflict.

Ikawa noticed something in the early morning light, and gesturing to Mark, they began a shallow dive. Seconds later they were flying over one of Allic's other sorcerers who was assisting a large group of Sarnak's ex-soldiers as they tore down a guardhouse and retaining wall. They exchanged cheerful waves, although Mark noticed the POWs looking on sullenly.

"Have you noticed that the people still don't like us?" he commented as they regained altitude, continuing their patrol.

"Hardly the oppressed and ravaged land one would expect when dealing with Sarnak," Ikawa agreed. "I would be proud to call this land my own: river valleys, terraced mountains, and a loyal populace. It seems a well-ordered place. Somehow it doesn't quite match with the monster who slaughtered thousands, and even betrayed his own son."

"Damned if I know," Mark replied. "There's still one hell of a lot we don't understand about Haven. But all things considered, we haven't done badly. We've got our powers, there's Leti and Storm, and Allic's promise that we'll soon have border marches of our own. For the moment I'll not complain."

Ikawa grinned and matched Mark's victory roll with one of his own.

The sun was halfway up the morning sky as they came into the courtyard of Dirk's refurnished fortress. Allic had made it his center of operations for the conquest and assimilation of Sarnak's realm.

Saito happened to be on duty when they landed. "Anything happen on patrol worth reporting?"

"Not a thing," Ikawa replied. "Valdez and his team are still going through Sarnak's castle room by room, and Pina has finally finished exploring the complex of tunnels. We've brought back a map of the entire maze."

Mark shook his head. "I don't know what the hell Allic's going to do with those tunnels. What good are they to him?"

"You can ask him yourself," Saito replied. "He flew in from Landra last night. Seems the rebuilding is coming along ahead of schedule. He's got those captured sorcerers and demons busting their asses night and day."

Ikawa was silent. Mark remembered Ikawa's theory that Allic's rare trips back to Landra were the result of his enormous guilt over the devastation of his city.

Mark gave Saito a friendly poke in the stomach.

"Looks like you're getting a little fat and lazy to me, Saito. What say we drag him along with us tomorrow, Ikawa?"

Laughing, they left the old sergeant and headed into the central keep. Turning into Allic's audience chamber, Mark was nearly swept off his feet by the impetuous rush of Storm.

Laughing, Mark returned her hug. "When did you get in?"

"Just a short time ago," she replied, smiling at Ikawa over Mark's shoulder.

Ikawa bowed and started to turn away when from around the corner came Leti, followed by Allic and his jester, Varma.

Losing the battle of self-control, a grin of delight lit Ikawa's features. He rushed forward into Leti's embrace.

"Some of Allic's men have set up a buffet for us," Leti said, and then looked over towards Mark and Storm. "Come on, you two, get a little food first, you'll need your strength."

Allic exchanged a mischievous smile with Varma as Mark and Ikawa talked with their companions.

"Didn't my schedule call for a month-long patrol for Mark and Ikawa once they got back?" Allic said evenly, looking to Varma.

Mark and Ikawa looked up, flustered.

"Don't even start," Leti retorted, fixing Allic with a chilling stare.

Storm was even more graphic.

Allic laughed and motioned them away. "Go ahead with breakfast, I'll join you in a moment."

Still chuckling, Allic turned to Varma as the others left the room.

"Such insolence, my lord," Varma joked. "How dare they take such liberties with you?"

"Why don't you go and explain the breach of etiquette to them. I'm sure my sisters will be quick to comply with your command."

Varma looked back at Allic as if he were mad.

"Are you going to tell them?" Varma asked, changing the subject.

Allic was silent, studying his diminutive friend and advisor.

"The bitter mixed with the sweet." Allic watched the two couples walk up the corridor together. "Would they really be happy if they knew Jartan might have found a way for them to get home? Let them enjoy this respite for a while. There will be time enough to tell them later."

He paused for a moment. "Strictly speaking, they still owe me over two years service. But I owe them for saving my realm and my life. I plan to give them border marches and titles as reward, but I'm still not sure about releasing them before they've tasted all there is of Haven."

Varma was silent, a sad smile crossing his face, and then he walked over to the sideboard where he pulled out a flask and two goblets.

"Little early in the day for that, isn't it?" Allic asked. "You should watch out for your health, my friend."

"After what we've been through the last several months, dying from a morning drink is the last of my worries," Varma said, laughing.

Their guffaws echoed up the corridor so that the two couples turned and looked back at the demigod and his jester, arm in arm raising their goblets in salute.

The couples stopped for a moment, as if debating whether they should return, but the debate only lasted a few seconds. With a cheery wave they turned and disappeared from view.

"It looks like it's going to be a stormy day, my lord," Varma said ruefully.

"Better pour out another drink, my friend," Allic said, a whimsical smile lighting his features. "I think we're going to need it."

Appendix

The Pantheon of Haven

DANAR: Not the strongest god, but the purest of heart and spirit, and the natural leader. He chose his land on the eastern continent, and was killed in the Great War.

ALEENA: A healer, a source of support to others. She was closest to Danar, and chose her land to be next to his. They held court together in their palace by the great sea that bordered both their realms. Since Danar's death she has lived in seclusion, founding the cults which believe that Danar might someday return.

CHOSEN: Ruled his region of the southern continent with an iron hand, giving his subjects a maze of sometimes contradictory laws, dietary restrictions, and unusual social customs.

REENA: The most distant of the eight, she rarely chose to communicate with her brethren. Her land is a large island on the opposite hemisphere of Haven.

BORC: The friendliest of the gods. He journeyed often to his siblings' courts to socialize. His people were great mariners, as Borc was the god who most loved the seas. His murder by Horat started the Great War.

MINAR: A god of quick temper but great heart. He created the Oracle of Derr on the edge of his realm to continue the exploration of the universe. Later, he retrieved the bones of those slain in the Great War and made temples to them within the grounds of oracle. His land borders Jartan's to the south.

JARTAN: The most powerful god. Of all his siblings, he loved Borc and Minar the most and chose to make his realm between them. He was also the most cunning of the gods, and the first to see the danger behind Horat's madness.

HORAT: His awesome fighting power and ferocity, backed by the others' strength, enabled the pantheon to defeat the Old Gods. His people were as violent as he, and their worship and sacrifices drove his pride and ego to know no bounds, and eventually drove him mad.

WILLIAM R. FORSTCHEN received his B.A. in education at Rider College and taught for several years before retiring to write full-time. He is the author of the *Ice Prophet* trilogy, *Into the Sea of Stars*, *The Alexandrian Ring*, and *The Assassin Gambit*. THE CRYSTAL WARRIORS is his first fantasy novel.

Recently Mr. Forstchen moved from Oakland, Maine, to the gulf coast of Florida, where he lives with his wife and their dog and cat. He enjoys the wildlife of his new home—particularly the fire ants in his backyard, which he likes to napalm. His other hobbies include sailing, Hobie Cat racing, skiing, and the study of military history.

GREG MORRISON has made his home in Pennsylvania since 1961 and lives with his wife Patti in the Harrisburg area. He attended Penn State then joined the army as a deep-space telemetry analyst, serving in Ethiopia and Turkey. Currently he is co-owner of an executive recruiting firm specializing in the fields of data processing, engineering, and finance. His collaboration on THE CRYSTAL WARRIORS is his first fiction sale.

BIO OF A SPACE TYRANT
Piers Anthony

"Brilliant...a thoroughly original thinker and storyteller with a unique ability to posit really *alien* alien life, humanize it, and make it come out alive on the page." *The Los Angeles Times*

A COLOSSAL NEW FIVE VOLUME SPACE THRILLER—
BIO OF A SPACE TYRANT
The Epic Adventures and Galactic Conquests of Hope Hubris

VOLUME I: REFUGEE   84194-0/$3.50 US/$4.50 Can
Hubris and his family embark upon an ill-fated voyage through space, searching for sanctuary, after pirates blast them from their home on Callisto.

VOLUME II: MERCENARY   87221-8/$3.50 US/$4.50 Can
Hubris joins the Navy of Jupiter and commands a squadron loyal to the death and sworn to war against the pirate warlords of the Jupiter Ecliptic.

VOLUME III: POLITICIAN   89685-0/$3.50 US/$4.50 Can
Fueled by his own fury, Hubris rose to triumph obliterating his enemies and blazing a path of glory across the face of Jupiter. Military legend...people's champion...promising political candidate...he now awoke to find himself the prisoner of a nightmare that knew no past.

THE BEST-SELLING EPIC CONTINUES—
VOLUME IV: EXECUTIVE
89834-9/$3.50 US/$4.50 Can
Destined to become the most hated and feared man of an era, Hope would assume an alternate identify to fulfill his dreams ...and plunge headlong into madness.

VOLUME V: STATESMAN
89835-7/$3.50 US/$4.95 Can
the climactic conclusion of Hubris' epic adventures:

AVON Paperbacks

Buy these books at your local bookstore or use this coupon for ordering:

Avon Books, Dept BP, Box 767, Rte 2, Dresden, TN 38225

Please send me the book(s) I have checked above. I am enclosing $_____
(please add $1.00 to cover postage and handling for each book ordered to a maximum of three dollars). Send check or money order—no cash or C.O.D.'s please. Prices and numbers are subject to change without notice. Please allow six to eight weeks for delivery.

Name _____

Address _____

City _____ State/Zip _____

ANTHONY 12/86